# THE TESTAMENT OF MARCELLUS

# THE TESTAMENT OF MARCELLUS

MARIUS GABRIEL

# BOOK I

# JERUSALEM

# CHAPTER ONE

# DINNER WITH PILATE

We approached Jerusalem from the north and so came upon the execution ground outside the city, a piece of raised land between two roads, situated where everyone could see it. Stark against the sky were three crucifixes, though only one bore a human form. I stopped my horse and told my attendants to wait.

Men become lawyers for all sorts of reasons, some to make money, others because it's a convenient entrée to politics, yet others because human nature intrigues them. I am one of those comparatively rare persons who enters the law because he is interested in the Law itself – the Law that should be just, practicable, logical and serve the widest interest of the greatest number. Which was why, although I detest circuses and all such spectacles, I dismounted and walked up the hill.

I had to cover my face with my traveling cape. The place stank of death. The hill was stony and flat topped. Two soldiers were playing at dice near the crucified man. They had one of the mastiffs with them. Seeing me, the dog launched itself towards me, baying. I stopped and had time to feel fear before a sharp whistle from the soldiers pulled the dog up. I continued, accompanied by the gaunt animal, which rumbled constantly in its throat, sniffing my heels. An assortment of ravens, magpies and other crows were squabbling among the stones. At the edge of the field a group of women huddled, shapeless under their drab garments. Otherwise, the place was deserted.

The soldiers stopped their game and stood to attention. They saluted as I reached them. "Stand at ease. I'd like to see the crucifixion."

As they took me to the foot of the cross, the women at the edge of the field began screaming, unearthly wails which made my hair stand on end. They had risen to their feet. I saw wild faces in the shadow of their head coverings.

"They think his time has come," one of the soldiers said. Like most of the legionaries in the region, he was from some eastern province and spoke more Greek than Latin. He looked up at the crucified man. "Not yet, worse luck for him."

I followed his gaze. The cross was not very high, a stout, blackened post with a crosspiece fitted into the top. The man was naked, his scrawny and rather hairy body caked with blood from a severe scourging. Crucifixion varies widely according to the whims of the local official and his soldiers. Many crucifixions in Rome at that time were done with ropes, which tied the criminal to the cross, leaving him to die of hunger and exposure. Pilate used nails. This man had been fixed to the wood with iron spikes through each wrist and another through his ankles. His knees were drawn up and pushed to one side. His buttocks rested on a ledge but the perch was too small; he kept sliding down so that the blade of his pelvis seemed to thrust out of his pale skin. The tenuous muscles of his legs shuddered with the effort of pushing himself upward, using the spike in his ankle bones as leverage.

I asked about this agonized restlessness. The soldier tapped his legs with the lance. "When they sag like that, the throat closes. They can't breathe. Though they want to die, their legs keep them alive. It's always the legs that lead a man into trouble, running to the brothel, running to the tavern, running into battle. Now he's trying to run away from Hell."

"You're a philosopher," I said. "What is this wretch's name?"

"Bar-David."

I looked for the placard which is affixed over criminals, stating their crime, but there was none. "And his crime?"

The philosophical soldier was swarthy, with a hard bitten Levantine face set on a muscular neck. His jaws were open in a permanent, toothless smile. "His crime, sir? Being facetious."

"I thought he must be a rebel."

"A facetious rebel, then. This is the consequence of a highly developed sense of humour. His friends will all end up the same way."

The tortured man's breaths sucked raggedly in his throat. The screaming of his womenfolk, or perhaps the sound of our voices, seemed to have roused him. His head quivered. He twisted his neck and looked at us for a moment before turning his face away. The tendons of his neck convulsed. "Water," he whispered.

"He's been asleep and dreaming," the philosophical soldier said. "You wouldn't think a man could sleep on the cross, would you, sir? But they do, now and then." He raised his voice. "No water. I'm being kind to you."

"How long will he last?" I asked.

"He's a tough one. He'll probably live to see his friends crucified in front of him tomorrow. The governor likes to set them up facing each other, so they can contemplate the workings of Fate." He jerked his thumb at the wailing women. "They think they'll get the body, but he'll rot here till he falls to pieces. Governor's orders."

The harsh crying of crows filled the silence. From this hilltop the crucified man could see the road and watch all the traffic entering and leaving the Holy City, if he had not been nailed in his own box of agony.

I thanked the soldiers and walked away, glad to have somewhere else to go. The magnitude of the man's suffering had dwarfed me. The soldiers went back to their dice. The women – his mother, his wife, his sisters – slowly fell silent and sank back to the earth like spirits retiring to their graves.

There was a roadblock at the northern gate, manned by half a century of soldiers, who were checking the travellers one by one. It was mid-afternoon, the hottest part of the day, and most had been on the road since dawn. Some of the weary attempted to sit or lie by the side of the road while they waited but the soldiers marched on either side, beating the strays back into line with rods and lances. Their faces were unsmiling and they wore full armour despite the heat. They had mounted three artillery pieces to cover the road, large crossbows which could kill a man in armour at four hundred paces. One of my attendants approached the soldiers, explaining who I was. They took my documents to the commanding officer.

I had travelled with a group of Galileans for most of the day. I say I had travelled with them but in fact they had done their best to keep a distance between themselves and me, covering their faces each time I drew close and huddling around the man on the donkey, who appeared to be their leader. They stood silent now, an uneasy group of rough-looking men. Their leader had lowered his chin on his chest and seemed to be meditating or praying. The donkey lifted its tail and dropped dung on the road. I wondered if he knew that to Romans it was an evil omen for an animal to defecate on its way to a shrine.

I edged my horse towards him. Some of his people at once attempted to stop me. "He does not heal Gentiles." The speaker was a pugnacious-looking man whose eyes seemed to have no whites. One saw many such eyes in Judaea. Dust made the eyes red with blood, then brown, then so dark that the pupils appeared to merge with the whites.

I was curious. "Is your master a physician? Why does he travel like a thief, with his face hidden?"

"The sick flock to him and block our way," he replied sullenly.

"He must be a good doctor, then."

"He is more than a doctor," another man said. They were a strange mixture of pride and defensiveness.

"Let me speak to him."

But for the Roman soldiers I think they would have resisted me. I pushed past them so I could approach him. His eyes were still closed and I was able to study him. On the road I had thought him a young man, but now that I was beside him, he seemed closer to middle-age than to youth. That was perhaps because his face was battered, bearing the marks of ancient violence. His nose had been broken, thrust to one side. One cheekbone was sunken, taking away the symmetry of his features. As he slept, or brooded, that face seemed to me like a broken house from which the tenants had fled, or a stony field where nothing grew.

But he spoke to me, without opening his eyes. "You come too late."

I was surprised. "Do you know me?"

"You have been following me."

"Today, yes."

"Today and tomorrow."

"I think you are mistaken."

He raised his head and opened his lids at last. His eyes were very dark, but they made his ruined face come to life. "Who is this who travels with you?"

"You mean my servant."

"I mean the woman beside you, whose face is veiled."

For a moment I felt my flesh creep. I was disconcerted. "There is no-one beside me!"

"If you say so."

"What is it that you can see beside me?" I pressed. A spirit?"

"Perhaps it is only your shadow."

"You did not mean that. What did you mean?"

"You carry the law with you. It is your crown. It casts a shadow."

I was astonished by his words, since I had thought them – or something like them – a short while previously. "It seems to me you are inspired."

"You have ears to hear."

"Your people guard you very closely."

"Not closely enough."

"They treat you as their king."

"We have an emperor in Rome," he replied. "We have Pilate in Jerusalem and Herod in Galilee. We do not lack kings."

"I see the way they look at you," I said, and indeed, his followers never took their eyes off him. "You are surely a great man in your own country."

5

His smile was unexpectedly sweet. "Do I seem to you a great man?" he asked.

"I think you must be."

"Then listen to me, Marcellus: judge as you would wish to be judged. That is the beginning of the law and the end of the law and the entire law."

Again, he had played that trick on me, confounding me. He was not educated in the Roman sense but he had a brilliance of insight that could almost be called supernatural. To acknowledge that one understood him was to enter a world where everything was changed. Perhaps he simply heard things and construed them cleverly. Perhaps it was greater than that.

"How is it you know my name?"

"You have told it to me."

"Have I?" As I tried to recall whether I had indeed told him my name, the soldiers came to fetch me. I wanted to converse with him more, but he closed his eyes again and seemed to sleep. "I'll remember what you said today," I said. He did not respond. I turned to the pugnacious man before I left. "What is his name?"

"He is Jesus of Nazareth."

I noted the name. The officers were very courteous and offered to send a guard with me to the Praetorium but I declined with thanks. I put in a word for some of my companions of the road and also asked them not to molest Jesus and his followers. I waited to ensure that my requests were complied with and then entered Jerusalem.

He and his group followed me. Just inside the gate, a multitude was waiting to greet him. If he was travelling incognito, these people, at least, had known he would arrive. I heard them shout praises and saw that they strewed his path with palm-leaves. It was another ill omen. To the Roman mind, the palm is the victor's trophy and to Rome there can be only one victor. I was confirmed in my thought that he had not long to live.

Pilate turned out to be a thoroughly unappealing man who made no effort to disguise his resentment at my arrival. His wife, by contrast, was a charming woman. It has often been my experience that the most unenviable husbands find the most enviable wives. So it proved in this case. Pilate was short, dark and surly while his wife, Procula, was one of those golden women who are in perpetual midsummer. He made some efforts to be amusing at dinner but soon lapsed into ill humour, something I was to find was a pattern with him.

The governor's residence adjoined Herod's palace and was rather grand. It had every convenience including hot and cold running water and indoor privies. The apartments were large, painted with frescoes of the Labours of Hercules in which Hercules, whether tearing apart the jaws of the Nemean Lion or cleaning the Augean Stables, wore the same wild eyed look. There were particularly handsome mosaic floors. There was an atmosphere – charming in its way – of remoteness about the place, of foreign artisans copying the Roman taste. On entering the dining room, however, I was startled to see that the table was lit by two large, golden oil lamps, each with seven branches. These were sacred objects and could only have come from one place. There were also golden goblets set with gems, dazzling things of Asiatic manufacture. The spoons and forks were silver, each piece decorated with twining Tritons. I was astounded that Pilate was bold enough to exhibit this plunder, making a positive display of his rapacity.

The meal itself was good. There was even a fish course: Pilate kept lampreys in a pond to supply his table. He devoured them with relish though they are not my favourite dish – their skeletons are spiny and their flesh gelatinous. He somewhat resembled his eels, both in having a mouth full of sharp teeth and in the way he was angrily sucking at his province. He complained bitterly, once his few pleasantries had been exhausted, about the intractability of the Jews and their skill at avoiding taxes.

"Like trying to squeeze blood out of a stone. Rome asks me why the revenue is so small. You'll be able to tell them, eh? They'll believe you if they don't believe me."

He bared his lamprey's teeth. The letters from my uncle had left him little option but to make the best of my visit. In fact, he seemed to be entertaining some hope that I might be persuaded into furthering his cause in Rome.

"The question is not one of revenue," I replied. "It's the constant tumult in Judaea which the Senate views with concern. The Empire is at a difficult point."

He snorted. "You appear to be in the emperor's pocket. You could ask him why, if he's determined never to return to Rome, he executed the one man who kept the Empire together."

One did not usually discuss the political situation in Rome openly at that time. Tiberius had allowed Sejanus to govern in his place while he holidayed in Capri year after year; but Sejanus's growing power had eventually threatened the position of an emperor who had not appeared in the capital in a decade. The bloody purge had shocked everyone but still Tiberius did not return, striking from afar like Jupiter hidden in a cloud. "Sejanus overstepped certain limits," I said.

"Well, he's dead now." Pilate spoke with the bitterness of one who had been a protégé of Sejanus. "And the purge continues. The best and ablest men in Rome lie rotting in the Tiber for our enemies to laugh at. In the meantime, Spain is left without a governor. So is Syria. Our outer provinces are being ravaged by barbarians." He raised an eyebrow at me. "Or is it now treason to say these things?"

"They're matters of common knowledge."

"Tell the Senators not to be concerned about Judaea. I keep my foot on the neck of the Jews."

"Yet there are insurrections almost constantly."

"I quell them."

"They should not begin in the first place. Strength is a good thing, but it should be tempered with justice."

"Ah. I see." He laughed shortly. "Who sends me this advice? Curled and perfumed old men in Rome who have forgotten what it's like to draw a sword?"

Ignoring the offensive reference to my uncle, I went on, "And firmness should be tempered with wisdom."

"You're very free with these words, Marcellus – justice, wisdom and the rest. It's deeds which matter in this world, not ideas."

"No decent deed can be born without a noble idea for its mother."

He lost patience and struck the table. "These people hate us. You understand? They hate Rome, they hate our gods, they're waiting only for a chance to overthrow us and cut our throats. Turn your back on them and they'll thrust a dagger between your shoulder blades. Offer them kindness, they'll return it with treachery. There's not one of them, man, woman or child, who has not poison in his heart. Go among them and tell them your noble theories of kindness and justice, see with what gratitude they'll respond!"

"We mustn't weary our guest with grumbling." Procula spoke to him in a light tone but was clearly anxious to curb his rising temper.

"Hold your tongue," he snapped. There were only three of us at the table; Pilate and Procula were childless. He hadn't shaved in several days, which added to his saturnine appearance. She, by contrast, had prepared herself for the occasion with care. Her gown was white and her hair reminded me of rows of ripe wheat. She was then about twenty five years old, having married Pilate at fifteen. She was so beautiful that I cannot look back on that occasion without an ache of yearning. To watch her do the simplest thing was a pleasure to the senses. Her true name was Claudia; the locals called her Procula, attempting to render "Procuratora," meaning the wife of the Procurator. It had become a nickname used by all. Unlike Pilate, she was popular with the Jews and I had already come across stories of her kindness.

"How was the voyage, Marcellus?" she asked me, seeming not to notice her husband's glare.

"Very rough."

"That tells me nothing." Her eyes were the colour of wild honey. "Can't you make it into an Odyssey for me?"

"How?"

"Well, you could say, 'Furious Poseidon pursued us from Rome to Naples and penned us up in the bay there for a week. We thought

9

he had subsided into the deep, but he was waiting for us again as soon as we left port. He towered over us, his roiling beard darkening the sun, his trident discharging three-forked lightning.' Isn't that much better?"

I couldn't help laughing at her mock Homeric declamation. "Much better," I agreed, "even if it sacrifices truth to art somewhat."

"Let us leave truth behind tonight. Continue."

"As a matter of fact, furious Poseidon broke our mast. They had to cut down a tree on some nameless rock to replace it. There was no seasoned wood there. I feared it might start sprouting leaves and bear fruit. The final stretch, from Cyprus to Caesarea Maritima, was the worst of all. The first thing I did when we finally got ashore was make sacrifices in the Julian temple."

"Well, God be thanked that you were delivered safely."

Procula poured wine for us with her own hands. Pilate saw that my goblet was brimming. He picked it up without asking my leave and tossed half the contents onto the floor. "That's a whore's trick."

Her cheeks coloured at the insult but she continued to smile. "I have a whore's plan," she said. "I want to make him drunk, so he spills his secrets along with the wine."

I was embarrassed at the exchange. "The harbour at Caesarea is one of the wonders of the world. A marvel of engineering."

"It's the seat of the Procurators of Judaea," she said dryly. "Even Poseidon shrinks back from that shore."

"My host was an old friend and colleague, Glabulus We had a pleasant reunion."

"Oh, we know Glabulus well," she said. "Don't we, husband?"

Pilate shrugged, knowing that Glabulus would have had little cause to say anything good of him. "He's a fine fellow," he said sardonically.

"I also met some of the prominent Jews there. There's a large Jewish district in Rome now, with shops and synagogues. They're well established again after the expulsion. I've been able to make progress in Hebrew thanks to a certain Martha. She gave me introductions to her friends and family in Caesarea."

"Who I suppose complained about their oppressor?" Pilate asked, looking down his nose at me.

"We had an interesting discussion."

"I miss Caesarea," she said. "Life is gay there. There's no society in Jerusalem."

"There's no shortage of society here," Pilate retorted.

"Merchants, whose language is the denarius? Soldiers, who exhibit their scars and explain how they got them to anyone who will listen? Your staff, who talk of nothing but taxes? They're all such pudding heads."

"You are too proud."

"You're the first to complain about what bores they are." She smiled at me. She was luminous. I was aware of being newly shaved and presentable, of having the gloss of Rome on me, of being a welcome diversion for a lonely woman thrown by her husband's position amid a distant and incomprehensible race.

The main course was taken away and it was the moment to make the offering to the household gods. There was an elaborate lararium set into the wall, painted with images of Pilate and Procula on either side of the alcove. I watched her as she took the wine and the saffron cake to the altar. Her movements were graceful. She was a woman to whom it was easy to lose one's heart.

After we had said the customary prayers, Pilate swirled the wine in his goblet. He had been drinking heavily. By now his lean cheeks were flushed, his lips swollen. "What other criticisms do you have to deliver to me?" he asked.

"Indeed, I'm not here to criticize."

"But you are critical," he retorted. "In every lift of your eyebrow and curl of your lips, you are critical. You're like the impersonation of Criticism in a play. You have the art of the sneer, the deprecating smile, the airy dismissal. Say your piece. You may as well get it over with now."

I smiled. "Is that the impression I give? Forgive me if I do. I'm merely interested in the state of the Empire."

"Great Hercules! 'The state of the Empire!' Other men are interested in advancement or wealth, but Marcellus is interested in the state of the Empire." He drained his goblet. "And pray tell me, how does the Empire fare?"

"The Empire is changing."

"In what way?"

"Some of our clients are coming to view Rome as a curse. We build a circus or two, but there are so many who can't pay our taxes and whose lands are confiscated by the collectors."

"That's the law."

"Yet it's painful that the wealthy acquire huge farms from these little tragedies and build, as I have seen with my own eyes, palaces which outdo Rome."

"You speak like Cicero," he said. "I could close my eyes and be in the Senate."

"I don't mean to preach."

He showed his teeth. "Oh, but you do. You think yourself so clever. Parading your book learning. Descending from Rome like a god in a play to teach me how to govern Judaea."

Procula leaned forward. "I don't think he meant that, husband."

He turned on her. "Enough." He said it with such a savage tone that she shrank back from him.

"You've misunderstood," I said, trying to sound pleasant.

"I understand perfectly. You're the Senator's handsome young nephew, the pride of Roman manhood, sent here to chastise me." He struck himself on the chest. "Me! Well, you can tell Vitellius that if he wants to replace me, he'd better send someone even bloodier than I am. Because this rabble will eat us alive." He flung his arm at the window as though the roar of a mob could be heard outside. In fact there was only the chirring of insects. It was late and the city was asleep.

I rose to my feet. "I've trespassed on your hospitality. Forgive me if I offended you."

"I haven't finished."

"But I have. The day has been long and I must sleep. Thank you for a wonderful banquet. Good night."

Procula rose from her couch. He bawled after her, "Procula!" but she shook her head at him and followed me out.

In the loggia, away from the guards, she took my arm. "Don't be offended."

"I'm not offended."

"He drank too much."

"The wine was good."

"He creates many problems for himself, Marcellus. Try to understand him."

"He'll be angry with you. Go back to him."

She released my arm. "But it's true, isn't it? Vitellius has sent you to make a report on him?"

"I have no official function, or he would have been told."

"You're close to your uncle, aren't you?"

"He has two sons. I was their tutor."

"That means that you have his confidence."

"I hope so."

"And when you return to Rome, he'll ask you to give him your impressions."

"Only as nephew to uncle. Not in any other capacity." I was aware that she wanted to bring something back to her husband. It was best to be blunt. "Your husband's enemies say that he's too violent."

"And he's of the wrong party."

"Pilate isn't suspected of treachery, Procula. He's too far from Rome to be involved in that. The problem lies here in Judaea." I hesitated. "Your table is magnificent. Those candelabra –"

"I've begged him to return them. He laughs at me. Don't think he's stupid. He's a clever man. But he's very obstinate."

"I can see that."

"The Jews are not an easy people to govern. Sometimes I think he was sent to be their torment and they were sent to be his. Forgive me for detaining you. You must be very tired. I'm sure you're long-ing for your bed."

"Thank you for tonight. I didn't expect to find such delightful companionship in –" I hesitated.

"In Pilate's wife? What did you expect to find? A harpy, I'm sure." She raised her face to mine and kissed me. It was a charming gesture from an antique time. I don't suppose anyone remembers such customs now, but at that moment it was a warm compliment and I was affected.

She was almost as tall as I, but where I felt myself to be solid, she shimmered like a flame in the darkness. Our lips touched chastely. The moon was in her eyes and her skin smelled of aloes. Then Pilate began bawling her name from the dining room. She gathered her gown and went back to him, leaving me to find my way upstairs.

When I reached my room, I had the immediate impression that someone else had been in it for some time, and had departed only moments earlier. One senses these things. Perhaps that was why Procula had detained me in the moonlight with a kiss, to give their spy a chance to make his escape.

I had locked my documents in my wooden trunk. The key was with me, but it's not difficult to pick such locks. When I opened the box, it seemed to me that the contents were disturbed.

Despite my weariness it was hard to find sleep. The sense of loss which always arrived at the end of each day rushed in with especial force. It had been Procula, I knew, who had stirred my emotions. After the death of those we love, we go through months and years which seem unreal. For a long time I talked to Livia, argued with her, wept for her, desired her though she was no longer here. I would become angry with her, beg her to answer me. As the traces of her existence faded away, the smell of her skin vanishing from the clothes which still hung in the cupboards, her possessions gathering dust, so my own identity seemed to dwindle to nothing. Vitellius was impatient with me. At that time I was trying to rediscover my own meaning, for him and for myself.

At length I slept but woke again after a short while, as one does after a long journey, with pounding heart, unable to tell where I was. I sat up in bed, groping for the cup of water. There was the muffled sound of some disturbance in the house. I opened the door of my bedroom to listen. It came from Pilate's quarters, which occupied the whole floor below my bedroom.

I went silently to the top of the stairs to listen. I could hear his rhythmic grunting and the sound of thudding and now and then her moans. It was impossible to tell if the sounds were of copulation or a beating or both. There were guards outside their door so I remained where I was, listening.

After a while there was the sound of furniture falling and I heard him shouting at her, accusations or insults, I could not make out. One can tell a man is drunk even when one can't hear the words he speaks. He laughed. Then she cried out so sharply that I almost started downstairs, despite the guards.

I heard water running into a bath and heard (as I thought) the sounds of her getting into it. Perhaps what I thought was the sound of her weeping was only the whimper of Pilate's mastiffs. I listened to the night for a long time. Then I went back to my bed to seek sleep again.

# Chapter Two

# Breakfast In The Praetorium

My awakening the next morning was pleasant. A maid brought me a glass of pomegranate juice, tart and spicy, and took away my dirty clothes. A young orderly came to provide me with a hot bath and a shave. "The Governor invites you to join him for breakfast at the third hour," he told me.

"Thank you."

A man was being flogged down on the parade ground. I didn't care to watch the spectacle myself, but the orderly relayed the details of the man's punishment to me as he shaved me.

"The Governor flogs them in the morning, then nails them up. He'll be feeding the ravens with his eyes for lunch."

"Thank you for the information," I said dryly.

"Don't let's lose our appetite over him, sir. They'll break his legs in a day or two." He was a red haired, enterprising plebeian youth named Rufus. He offered to acquire for me anything which the governor's hospitality failed to provide. "I know some nice, clean girls. Just say the word."

"I'll bear that in mind."

"Or boys, whatever comes natural. There, I think they've killed him," he reported, glancing out of the window. And indeed the echo of the blows had continued for a long while after the screams died away. I acquiesced to a facial massage, which he assured me would take ten years off me. I don't think it did, but I felt braced, all the same.

I decided to take a stroll before my breakfast with Pilate. The air was cool and the streets still relatively empty. It was a pleasure to stretch one's legs.

Jerusalem was a fair city at that time. The temple was the dominant feature. It could be seen from miles away, a glowing, white marble complex of fortress-like structures with a somewhat closed aspect to those with Classical sensibilities, but certainly among the greatest edifices in the Empire. It was built on a flat outcrop of rock, the Temple Mount. That which was sacred was confined to the quite modest central building. Around it was a square about the size of the Mars Field which was open to the heavens. Enclosed with high walls and elaborate colonnades, this sacred precinct was a kind of city in itself, filled with a thriving market which served the needs of the worshippers.

The Praetorium, which was not far away, was a forbidding hulk, a barracks enclosed in a compound which it shared with Herod's palace. It hadn't been built with any sensitivity to Judaean sensibilities and stood as an implacable reminder of Roman power. I thought it a pity that it hadn't been located more diplomatically. It could have been placed in the Roman quarter of the city, where there was a small circus and a theatre.

The old city had its own beauty, ancient and complex, a garment of a thousand patches. The local stone is honey coloured, the roof tiles are baked of a somewhat pale clay. Olives and other grey leaved trees are common. The colours are bleached, faded, worn. The air was pungent with the smell of burned meat, a smell which ever afterward I came to associate with Jerusalem.

I strolled through the upper city to find myself in streets of considerable grandeur. Here the priestly families had their palaces, towering fortresses guarded by uniformed servants who glared but dared not challenge me as I passed. The facades, at least, seemed to me not unlike the houses of the very rich in Rome, decorated with stucco and stone designs of flowers and fruits. Behind high walls were gardens, where I could hear the voices of women and of children playing.

Now and then I would see faces appear at the balconies and peer down at me. At one particularly elegant white palace a woman of striking loveliness appeared at an upper window, flanked by two young girls, all wearing elaborate braids. They looked down at me with expressions of haughty displeasure and then slammed the shutters closed.

As I penetrated further into this enclave of wealth and privilege, I became aware of the disturbance I was creating. Voices called from house to house warning of my approach. A small crowd of young men started to follow me. Eventually I was confronted by two of the chief priests themselves, who emerged from one of the mansions, splendidly robed and accompanied by several servants. The scent of perfume rolled from them.

"Are you lost, my lord?" one asked me disdainfully in Greek.

"I'm taking a stroll."

"May we be so bold as to enquire your name?" the other said.

I told them my name. "I'm a guest of the governor." They glanced at one another. The servants were well armed with clubs and sticks, but interfering with a Roman was not a safe course of action, even in their own purlieus. They were angry at my presence but uncertain as to how to deal with me. "It seems that I'm disturbing you," I said.

The older of the two men arranged his beard on his breast carefully. He wore a robe embroidered with designs of pomegranates in beautifully coloured thread. "This street is for the chief priests and their families alone. It would be best for all concerned if you went no further."

I smiled. "Very well. Forgive the intrusion." I turned and went back the way I had come. The liveried servants followed me all the way down the street, walking at a discreet distance behind me. I had been shown my place most emphatically, but I was amused, rather than angered. The followers didn't leave me until I was completely out of the Upper City. I went back to the Praetorium for my appointment with Pilate.

Pilate's courtyard was a pleasant quadrangle planted with apricot and almond trees, having the lamprey pool in the centre. The voracious animals swirled and churned under the dark water from time to time. Pilate was seated at a campaign table, piled with scrolls and letters, listening to the morning report from his aide-de-camp. An old legionary was in attendance and a secretary was seated beside Pilate with a wax tablet in his lap. Pilate himself wore a military tunic and a leather breastplate. He greeted me with a better show of courtesy than he had shown last night, inviting me to help myself from the tray of fruits and breads which stood on the table. "Try the honey. They say it's special. If you don't mind, I'll finish hearing the report while you breakfast."

"Of course."

"Continue," he commanded, when I had seated myself.

"Yes, my Lord." The aide-de-camp was one of those knotty men whose age is hard to determine. He had written his notes on a strip of papyrus from which he read, glancing up at Pilate from time to time. It was a dreary list of allegations, arrests and reported crimes, most of a very minor nature, to which Pilate listened somnolently. He was still unshaven and seemed pale, perhaps from last night's wine. By day he was even less prepossessing, the sunlight showing him to be more lined than I had thought, with bags under his half-closed eyes and a long, crooked nose. He raised his hand suddenly to stop the aide-de-camp. "What was that last item?"

"A man complains that his fig tree has been cut down, Excellency, near the Bethany gate."

"You hear, Marcellus?" he said, turning to me. "A fig tree! What do you make of that?"

I concealed my amusement. "Cutting down a fig tree is not a major act of rebellion."

"You think not? I would call it an act of the most destructive malice. Whoever would cut down a fig tree would cut his grandmother's throat."

"You're very partial to figs, it seems," I said.

He snapped his fingers at the ADC. "What are the details?"

The ADC motioned his head to the old soldier, who spoke stolidly. "A party of Galileans entered the city yesterday, sir. Their leader cursed a fig tree because he found no fruit on it. One of his followers cut it down as soon as he had passed."

"Mark that." Pilate rapped the table with his knuckles. "A Galilean. He cursed a fig tree for not having fruit – in April! On this whim they cut it down. What else will they cut down if their leader curses it? Will they kill Herod so that this peasant can eat figs on his throne? Whose was the fig tree?"

"It is one of the chief priests who makes the complaint, Excellency."

Pilate grunted. "That's no surprise. These Galileans come to Jerusalem superstitiously, truculently, against their will. They hate the temple and they hate the priests but most of all, they hate Rome." He pointed a finger at the ADC. "I want to hear more of this. Bring me the man who cut down the tree." He dismissed the soldiers.

"What argument is there between the Galileans and the temple priests?" I asked him.

He shrugged. "They're factions. There's no sense in their quarrels." He waved the letter from Vitellius. "Your uncle has written to me commanding me to show you whatever you want to see."

"I think he intended it as a simple request."

"A simple request from a great man is nothing less than an order," he replied dryly. "I have half an hour to spare. How can I oblige you?"

"If it's not an imposition, I'd like to ask a few questions. Just to satisfy my curiosity."

"Ask what you want."

"I heard a man being flogged this morning."

"A rebel."

"Did he cut down a tree?"

"A tree has been cut down for him, at any rate," Pilate said.

"He'll be crucified?"

"He's on his way as we speak."

"Was there a trial?"

"No."

"I hear there are others waiting in the cells. Will they also be crucified without trial?"

"What need is there of trials?" he said impatiently.

"Where a man's life is concerned, there should be more than a single voice to condemn him."

"Mine is the only voice that counts. I won't tolerate defiance."

"It's a particularly cruel punishment."

"Nailing men to a cross has more effect than reading out proclamations."

He was evidently so proud of his ruthlessness that there was little point in proceeding further down that line. "I understand that you bring the army to Jerusalem each year for the Passover?"

"A strong hand is needed. One spark in the city and the whole of Judaea will go up in flames."

"And that was why you marched into the city with images of Tiberius and set them up on the Temple Mount?"

"Are we to be ashamed of our emperor?"

"Tiberius gave you no command to bring his image into Jerusalem. You knew that doing so would be against the emperor's express wish that you should not offend the religious convictions of the Jews."

"Unless you speak for the emperor himself, let us leave his name out of this."

"But surely you knew that Jerusalem would be plunged into turmoil? Didn't the priests beg you to take down the standards so as not to destroy the peace which existed? You answered them with violence. This is contrary to your commission, which was to maintain peace and respect their holy places."

"I don't give a curse for their sensitivities. I am not here to pander to their whims."

"That is a puzzling remark. Jerusalem is the breath and being of the Jewish faith."

"At the Passover the Jews celebrate their release from the Egyptians, who kept them in bondage five hundred years. It takes little imagination to understand the symbolism. In their fevered minds, Rome can be overthrown, too. That's why I bring the standards into the city. That's why I flog and crucify. What else puzzles you?"

"There are complaints that you have seized the temple treasure."

"The garrison needed water. An aqueduct had to be built."

"But the money was consecrated to their god. And when the priests sent a delegation to plead with you, you waylaid them and beat them yet again. You have taught them to distrust you. If they cannot come to you with words, then they may come to you with force."

"Let them come." He leaned back in his campaign chair, his leather breastplate creaking, his small, dark eyes fixed on me. "You've had some military service, they tell me."

"A few years as a cavalry officer in Germany."

"Then you surely understand the necessity."

"Of killing priests? Was that the policy of a wise governor?"

"It's the policy of a governor with a legion of three thousand in a city of eighty thousand."

"Some would say the reverse. The Empire is held together not by garrisons but by consent. Invisible threads run from Rome to its farthest corners – "

He cut in impatiently. "I'm aware of the invisible threads that run from me to the Senate. Marcellus, every Jew has a pile of silver under his bed, but when he's asked to pay for public works, he pulls his beard in anguish and wails that he's destitute. If they won't pay taxes, then they must be relieved of their silver by force."

"But you had no right to expropriate the temple treasure for a military work."

"This is not Rome! Don't lawyer me."

"I must ask the questions that my uncle has given me."

"Your uncle always detested me, as do all your family. Now that Sejanus has fallen, of course my name is on the list."

"I know of no such list."

He sneered. "Do you not? I think I could tell you, with accuracy, every name on it. Your uncle and his party are inventorying the Empire, choosing plums for themselves. Judaea is just such a plum, waiting to be picked and given to someone of the right party." He rose and walked to the pool. I followed him. There, he spoke more quietly. "You can get rid of me and put some weakling in my place, but if you do, there will be a real rebellion. These are not people who can distinguish between kindness and weakness. As for the few things I steal, they're no more than my due. The salary of a provincial governor is not very high." Our reflections swayed on the surface of the water, which was almost black and smelled of decay. The eels were flickering shadows that pursued each other, then vanished. I noticed that the larger animals had two or three smaller ones fixed to their sides. "I like fish," Pilate said. "It's one of the penances of coming to Jerusalem. By the time fish reach the city, they stink."

"You've solved the problem elegantly."

"You found the flesh succulent last night?"

"Very fine."

He threw a piece of cake in the pond. Several of the eels rose to compete ferociously for the titbit. "You've charmed my wife," he said, watching his pets.

"She's a very cultured woman."

"You mean she appreciates your eloquence," he said. "She has little company here. Your visit has lifted her out of a melancholy."

I thought of the sounds I had heard last night. "A melancholy?"

He threw another piece of cake to the eels. "She wants to show you the temple this morning. She needs distractions. If you'll indulge her you'll be doing her – and me – a kindness."

"I would welcome that."

"Then it's settled." His hard little eyes met mine for a moment. "I'm sure you find her more sympathetic than you do me. She seems to understand these people more than I."

He was a clever man. I had anticipated he would try to attach some spy to me so he could monitor my movements. Using his wife ensured I couldn't escape. However, the prospect of a morning with Procula was undeniably appealing. Pilate had won the first round and I was eager to get away from him. "Thank you for your time, Governor."

He dusted crumbs from his hands into the pond. "We'll arrange another dish of lampreys for supper, since you enjoy them so much."

"How kind."

"Something to look forward to," Pilate said with a thin smile.

As we rode in her carriage, I could smell the aloes on Procula's clothes and her hair. It was a Judaean custom for women to burn incense and perfume themselves in the smoke. Procula had evidently adopted it. It was alluring and very un-Roman. She wore open sandals which displayed her toes, each small nail polished like a seashell. They seemed to sum up everything that was desirable and unattainable about her. She had no bruises from whatever had happened in the night. However the fashion at that time was for thin garments which clung to the curves, showing only the hands, feet and face, and it was possible any injury was hidden by her dress.

"Did you pass a peaceful night?" she asked me.

"I was a little restless from the journey. I'm afraid I annoyed your husband last night. I should have been more tactful."

"It's not difficult to annoy Pontius. No special qualifications are needed."

"And I heard a disturbance in the night."

"Husbands and wives argue." She reached out and took in her fingers the little silver pendant I wore around my neck, with the face of a satyr, given to me as a wedding gift by my wife. She studied it carefully. "Did you never argue with your wife?"

"Not so violently."

"She was a granddaughter of Agrippa?"

"Yes."

She released the pendant and let it fall back against my throat. "A good marriage."

"It was a good marriage, but not because she was Agrippa's granddaughter."

"Good heavens," she said, "it was it a love match, then!"

"Why do you mock me?"

Procula had a face typical of central Italy. It's a smiling land and hers was a smiling face – at least at that time – with a full, soft mouth and wide cheekbones. Her eyelashes were so thick that she needed none of the antimony that women commonly use to give themselves that dark, languishing glance. Her colouring was that of the summer, of ripe fruit and golden wheat. Her voice was rather throaty; she had the accent of a country girl, slightly slurred, rather than the crisp diction of city women; but she spoke well and intelligently, though often with irony. "We Romans are apt to marry only after considering the practicalities. Family, finance and so forth. We must marry those we are told to marry – or divorce those we are told to divorce – and we do so soberly, obediently and without joy. It's quite refreshing to meet a man who married for love, rather than to advance his career. How long is it since she died?"

"Two years."

"So long a widower? Aren't there any wealthy spinsters left in Rome?"

"I'm not a fortune hunter."

"Then pretty ones, or clever ones, or aristocratic ones?"

"I don't believe in marrying for the sake of being married."

Her golden hair was tied up in elaborate braids. She patted them now and then, a nervous gesture which belied her air of confidence. "You would only marry for love?"

"I have no plans to marry for love or anything else."

"Poor Odysseus. No Penelope spinning and unpicking at home in Ithaca. And one hears that you nursed her with the utmost devotion to the end."

"You know a lot about me, it seems."

"You've come to spy on my husband. So of course I spy on you. I must study you and find out your weak points, the way a general will study an enemy fortress and find where he may shatter a wall or scale a tower."

"I hope I'm not your enemy."

Again, the patting of the braids with those slim fingers. "You have no choice but to be my enemy." I caught a sharp glance from beneath her eyelashes.

I shrugged. "I took a walk through the Upper City this morning. I didn't get very far before I was asked to leave." I told her what had happened.

"If you hadn't been a Roman, their servants would have beaten you. That quarter is where the Sadducees live. Your presence alone would have defiled them."

"I hope they have recovered by now. The houses were most beautiful."

"They're the wealthiest and most aristocratic people in the city. Don't go there again or they'll complain to my husband." She stopped speaking and drew the corner of her cloak over her mouth. I saw that we were passing the procession of the condemned man. Bleeding copiously, he was bowed under the weight of the baulk which had been loaded onto his shoulders. It was his final task on earth to drag this thing through the streets of the city to the execution ground, where he would be nailed to it. A cheerful party of soldiers followed him, one swinging a hammer and some iron spikes.

"Does it disturb you?" I asked.

"After ten years of marriage to Pontius, I'm used to crucifixions," she replied.

"It's a terrible spectacle," I said.

"It's a work of art in its own way," she replied. "You men take such pleasure in these things."

"I take none. A legionary said something odd to me. He said the men are being crucified for having a sense of humour. What did he mean?"

"You should ask my husband," she replied from behind the veil.

"Pilate told me the men were rebels."

She was silent for a moment. "My husband announced that he would confiscate a part of the temple gold again this year. A group of twelve young students mocked him. They paraded in front of the Praetorium with bowls, collecting small coins to alleviate the poverty of Pontius Pilate, to the amusement of the citizens. He arrested them all. He's been flogging and crucifying one or two of them every day."

I was disgusted. "That is tyranny."

"They knew the risk they ran. I presume they thought the joke too good to lose."

I was struck by her cool tone. "You're not shocked?"

"It matters little whether I'm shocked or not." She took the veil away from her face. "Are you ever visited by her spirit?"

"Whose?"

"Livia's."

"Why do you ask such a thing?"

"Every widow claims piously to have been visited by her husband's shade, urging her to remarry. If you were visited by your wife, she might say the same."

"I would give much to be visited by her. But wherever she is, she doesn't come to me."

"She's forgotten you. In the underworld we cross Lethe and we forget everything. Otherwise death would be as unbearable as life. You're an Etruscan, aren't you?"

"I am of Etruscan descent."

She laughed. "You mean that you're thoroughly Romanized. Why so mealy mouthed? Are you ashamed of coming from a race of sorcerers? Can't you call up her shade?"

"There are no Etruscans left. You made us Roman citizens, compelled us to speak the Roman tongue and worship Roman gods, swallowed us into the Roman identity. You burned our cities and slaughtered our nobles on the altar of the divine Julius Caesar. My gods are dead, Procula."

"I think mine are, too," she replied.

We had reached the temple precincts. We got out of the carriage. A soaring flight of snow white marble steps ascended to the entrance, high above us. I was awed.

"It's like climbing into heaven."

She gathered her gown in her hands, revealing strong, shapely calves, and set off swiftly up the stairs. Her slave, Hephaistion, hurried busily ahead of us to clear the way, his shaven head gleaming and his ears glowing in the sun like beacons. Crowds thronged these white steps coming up and down, chanting in Hebrew with exalted faces. One felt one's heart beat faster and one's breath come quickly.

The entrance was surmounted by a golden eagle and divided by two huge columns. Procula unveiled her face to the attendants at the gate and they admitted us without question. Then we were pushed into a deep portico where we were assailed by the noise of a market and the acrid smell of animal dung and smoke. The colonnades were filled with merchants selling cattle, sheep and hundreds of turtle doves for sacrifice.

The hubbub was in no way restrained by the sanctity of the place; men haggled and shouted with earnest energy, animals were dragged to and fro, bleating and kicking and pissing. We filed between the stalls, avoiding the worst of the excrement on the ground, which accumulated as quickly as it was swept up by the attendants.

It was a vivid scene, filled with colour and noise. Some were selling striped garments of many colours or religious objects both of cheap metals and of silver. From an adjoining court came the sound of women singing and I could see dancers moving between the columns. The market was so densely crowded in some places that we could hardly make our way forward. In one place the stalls belonged to moneychangers, sitting in front of piles of strange coins, singing out exchange rates and wrangling with their customers; Roman money was not allowed to be used to purchase animals for sacrifice, or to make donations, because it bears the image of Caesar.

From the portico, worshippers streamed across the plain towards the temple, leading sacrificial animals to be slaughtered. We followed the flood of pilgrims, somewhat battered by our journey through the stoa. All around was the sound of chanting and singing. Procula's slaves had bought her a white dove in a wicker cage.

As we approached the temple, we were met by an official, short and bearded, wearing a splendid robe. He greeted Procula with the effusive courtesies I had become accustomed to from Jews and took her turtledove. He spoke fair Greek.

"This is Simeon," she told me. "I've arranged for him to show us the inner courtyards."

"I thought it was forbidden for Gentiles to enter."

"He'll give us robes to wear Nobody will pay us attention." She whispered to me. "A little money clears the way."

"I see."

"Don't look so sanctimonious. You claim to be a student of religion. I'm offering to show you a secret."

I turned to the official. "I was nearly beaten by the servants of the Sadducees this morning. What is the penalty for trespassers?"

"You'll be dragged out and stoned. Not Pilate nor anyone else will be able to save you. But you're safe with me, my lord."

I glanced at Procula. Her face was calm. "Are you afraid?" she asked me.

"I'm afraid for you."

"I'm not afraid for myself, so you may relieve yourself of that anxiety. Come."

Behind a massive pillar we put on the robes he gave us. Then we entered the inner courtyard behind Simeon, leaving the slaves behind us. The place was filled with the smoke of burning flesh. Greasy and acrid, it stung the eyes when the winds blew down. In the centre of the court towered the altar, the fiery heart of the Jewish faith, elevated to the sky on huge stone blocks and approached by a long ramp. The blaze of heat from the constantly burning sacrifices was ferocious.

Those who prepared the sacrifices worked with dazzling skill, wielding the ritual knives so swiftly that the blades appeared to be made of light. The slaughter of an animal, large or small, the cutting out and inspection of the requisite joints and organs, took no more than a few moments. Others arranged the quivering flesh in the appointed manner for the flames while the remainder was carted away.

To carry off the blood of so much butchery, channels had been cut in the floor, with running water flowing through them. Around the courtyard, as Simeon showed us, were basins, mounted on wheels so they could be filled and emptied from some sacred well. These were used to wash the meat clean. The largest of all, an immense bronze vessel mounted on the figures of twelve oxen, was deep enough for a man to be immersed in it. The floor was slippery with blood and the air was filled with the spray of it and the smell of it.

"I will take your dove, my lady." He left us for a moment and took Procula's sacrifice to the butchers. The bird was quickly prepared for the flames.

Such a gigantic offering was unknown in Rome; it was like one of those mighty sacrifices that Homer tells us of in the Iliad, when hundreds of cattle and rams were burned on the beaches of Troy to appease the Olympians. My impression was of something more ancient than Rome, steeped in the barbaric colours of gold, smoke and blood.

Beyond the altar was the temple proper, its entrance flanked by the two bronze columns that Simeon called Boaz and Jachin. At the top of each was a brazier from which smoke poured into the heavens.

Since the Emperor Augustus, we Romans had been fascinated by the god of the Jews. Our own beliefs ran deep yet we wanted to add the Jewish god to our pantheon and we were first offended, then awed to learn that Yahweh would share a temple with no other god. That added to the exclusivity of the religion. The Jews had made many converts in Rome by this time; Judaism was popular among the upper classes (as Christianity was later to become among the lower) and even now, scattered and humbled as they are, the Jews continue to proselytize. It's said that their number is increasing, despite the catastrophic war.

Now I found myself in the temple of this single divinity, invisible and unrepresentable, who required of them so many sacrifices without allowing a single statue in his name. His name could not even be written or spoken. It was more than a local cult; it was an absolute, a reduction of the truth into a single word, a terminus. He was a jealous god and a hungry one, his nostrils spread wide to inhale this outpouring of sacred smoke.

In the midst of these thoughts, I saw a face turned to look at us angrily, then another, then several. A shout arose. A group of priests wearing tall hats strode towards us, their robes billowing. They had the same bearing as the men who had stopped me in the Upper City that morning, carrying the unmistakable trappings and haughtiness of power. In one flash I foresaw a dreadful catastrophe, Procula and myself stoned, my noble mission to Jerusalem ending in disgrace and riot. I pulled her away, trying to hide behind a pillar. The hubbub was rising.

Simeon reached us, pale and trembling. "Have they discovered us?" I asked.

"I don't know. You must go quickly. I beg of you, don't mention my name."

"Wait!"

But he grasped Procula by the wrist and vanished with her into the crowd of officials, which was now becoming tumultuous. I made my way after them as best I could, anxious not to be separated from them in the crush.

There was shouting in the square but it seemed we were not the cause of it. We went as quickly as we could back to the stoa, to find it in a state of riot. Animals were running loose, including a flock of white pigeons which had been released and which fluttered aimlessly in the colonnades, their wings feeble from imprisonment. We glimpsed tables overturned, merchants scrambling to recover their money and other valuables from the dirt. So fierce was the riot that its ripples were spreading outward through the whole vast organization of crowded courts. The temple guards were marshalling with shields and staves. Hephaistion appeared, bleating in near hysteria. He seized Procula and began pulling her away from the mob. We allowed ourselves to be carried away through the surging crowds. The doves found their wings at last and scattered through the pillars into the sky like silver coins thrown from a generous hand over the heads of the crowd.

The midday meal in the Praetorium was a lavish feast of roast kid, quail, pigeons and all kinds of spring vegetables, piled on a mountain of barley, with Pilate at the head of the table.

Procula sat at the other end of the table and had placed me beside her. She conversed with everyone in her carefree way, telling them of our "adventure," as she called it, at the temple. There were a dozen or more guests at the table today, all dressed in fine clothes. Most were Pilate's officials, a few with their wives, heavily decked with gold jewellery; Jerusalem was a remunerative outpost of the Empire. Introductions were made, but I caught none of their names. These were the "pudding heads" Procula had spoken of. Through the meal, they cast sidelong glances at me but didn't address a word to me, as though their master had forbidden it.

"We didn't find out what had happened," Procula said, "but I wager that my husband already knows."

Pilate raised his head from his plate and glanced down the table at me. "It was your friend, of the fig tree."

"The man who cut it down?"

"The man who cursed it. One Yeshua, or Jesus, of Nazareth. A prophet and a magician. He's the author of your disturbance at the temple." His dark eyes were mocking. He enjoyed showing how swift his intelligence services were. "He's paving his way to the cross more quickly than I anticipated."

I am skilled at controlling my expression, and did not show that I was familiar with the man or his name. "What was the source of the quarrel?"

"He got into an argument with the bankers and overturned their tables."

"Perhaps he was dissatisfied with the rate," someone said. There was laughter.

"Did I not say to you, Marcellus, that a man who would curse a fig tree would be capable of anything?" Pilate seemed in good humour for a man who would crucify youths for making a joke. He rose from his couch, goblet in hand. He was wearing the purple edged toga of a magistrate and a wreath of ivy around his brows. He cut a strange figure with his unshaven jaws and saturnine face. "My friends," he began, "today is the first day of the Megalesia, the festival in which we celebrate the divine mother of our gods, Cybele."

We all murmured the pious formula, "Mother of gods, saviour, hear our prayers." I had forgotten the day, but of course this was the occasion of the banquet and the fine clothes.

"Today in Rome," Pilate went on, "good citizens will be feasting and rejoicing in the name of The Great Mother, as do we. She is here with us today." He raised his goblet. On his signal, the slaves carried a large object to the side of the table. We all turned to look at it. There were gasps of wonder.

The figure of the goddess sat on a silver throne, her palms turned up on her lap. She was life size. Her face, hands and feet were made of wax, fitted into sockets in a wooden torso, skilfully painted to look warm and alive. Her expression was serene but watchful. She wore her tall, castellated crown, the waves of her hair tied back. At her pale feet lay the sacred offering of flowers, fruits, herbs and bread. We applauded; the thing was really breath-taking. Pilate was pleased with the effect he had created. At his signal, the Great Mother was covered with a light veil embroidered with silver. She continued to watch us through the diaphanous fabric.

"In her honour we are performing the plays of our Roman dramatists in the theatre each night this week. I'm sure you will all attend." Again we murmured formulas. Pilate remained on his feet, looking at us all with his small eyes, which seemed to miss no detail. "Here, at the edge of the Empire, we celebrate our gods and our glorious history. We do not forget. Our ancestors founded a city on the banks of the Tiber, planted wheat and forged iron from the hills. With that alone, we have become masters of the world." He looked at me. "What does our Etruscan guest say?"

"We perhaps forget that it was Etruscans who founded the city," I replied from the other end of the table, "Etruscans who planted the first wheat and forged the first swords."

He laughed. "It's Romans who wield the swords, Marcellus. That's what people remember. The metal entering their flesh. They never forget that. Other empires have risen and fallen but ours will endure. And why? Because we are willing to strike. We're willing to inflict whatever injury is necessary to ensure obedience. When we lose the courage to strike, then indeed our empire will begin to wane." He sat down again, drinking deeply. The guests applauded loudly. I clapped politely. The speech had been aimed at me but I had no reply to make. It was a holy occasion.

When everyone had left the table, I looked at magna mater under her silvery veil. From childhood I have had the privilege of seeing the gods nod, that tiny inclination of the chin which they give to their favoured ones. In my mind I beseeched Cybele to give me a sign, but today the wax mask did not move.

# CHAPTER THREE

# THE INFORMANT

Pilate summoned me during the afternoon hours. I had been writing some letters, which I locked in my trunk before I left my room, though I had few illusions as to the security of that receptacle. The ADC with the knotty face led me to the cells, through narrow stone corridors and down precipitous stairs, to a stone flagged room where Pilate was seated at a desk, on which was laid his sword. Standing before him, with his back turned to me, was a Jew, whose linen tunic was illuminated by the light from the embrasure of a narrow window.

"I thought you would like to see this fellow, Marcellus," Pilate greeted me. "He is the one who cut down the priest's fig tree."

"Jesus of Nazareth?" I asked.

The man turned to me. It was not Jesus. His face was pleasant though his eyes conveyed an impression of heat. They were black, the whites smoky. The glow of the sunlight on his linen garment illuminated his face from beneath, making his beard glitter on his angular cheekbones. He was somewhat freckled. He smiled slightly when he heard the name. "I am Judas of Kerioth," he replied in a quiet voice. He spoke the Greek of a relatively well educated man.

"He is the treasurer and accountant of the Galilean party," Pilate said, leaning back in his chair. "A man experienced in the uses of money and understanding its value well. Aren't you?"

"Yes."

"A frugal man, a cautious man, more accustomed to closing the fist than opening the palm. And yet, this curious mathematician has hacked down the priest's fig tree, a most prodigal act, scattering September's figs in April. Can such a deed be explained?"

"Can it be explained?" I asked the man.

"I did it as a warning," he replied.

"A warning of what, and to whom?" I asked.

"A warning of September, to April."

"I don't understand you."

"The tree which is cut down now will bear no fruit in autumn." The man hadn't changed his quiet smile. He was examining my face and dress without any fear. Some Jews, I had noticed, had this fearless way of gazing at one; it wasn't that they were unaware of the authority that every Roman had over them – it was simply that they were unafraid. They had a kind of inner conviction of superiority, rather like those who handle large and fierce dogs, or keep the lions in the circus maximus. The possibility of being bitten was there, it was just ignored. "What right had he to curse a tree?" he went on in his soft voice. "The man grows too great. He thinks that the earth itself will obey his whims. After I cut down the tree, the disciples were all shouting, behold! A miracle! A miracle!" He laughed silently.

"You're speaking of your master," I said. "Is he seeking power?"

"Power comes to him, whether he seeks it or not," the man replied. "The ignorant flock to him, wherever he goes, to be healed of their sores, to see miracles and hear wonders."

"And does he provide wonders?"

The man moved out of the light. In the cool darkness of the cell, the colour seemed to drain out of him. "I believed he did, once."

"Did you see him produce miracles?"

"Wherever he goes, people are healed. The blind see and the deaf hear. But he is impatient with the sick. He wants the world to hear his message."

"Which is?"

"The kingdom of God is at hand." He said it with a bitter inflection, as though echoing the diction of his master.

"How long have you known him?"

He made a gesture with one hand, though whether he meant by this a long time or a short one, I couldn't gather. Perhaps he simply declined to answer.

"In short," Pilate said jovially, "the mathematician Judas is offering to be our informant."

Judas turned his gaze on Pilate. "My lord, I am loyal to Rome and faithful to my God."

"I didn't say that you were a traitor," Pilate pointed out, "but an informant. The difference is obvious. You're willing to furnish us with information? Evidence? Reports?"

The man inclined his curly head. "Yes."

"Why are you doing this?" I asked.

"To keep away ruin," he said. "I am a prophet, too. I see where the man is leading us."

"You mean that he's a rebel?" I pressed.

"He himself does not know where his footsteps are taking him. He has walked across half Palestine, with his eyes fixed on heaven, and the crowd which follows him grows more numerous and louder and more turbulent each day."

"It seems you have little love for him."

"I loved him more than myself," he replied.

"Once?"

"Yes, once."

"And why was it that your love turned to hate?" I asked.

He was losing his air of amused civility. The anger that had been banked up in his smoky eyes was beginning to show in his face. "Why?" he retorted. "It was not at a particular hour or on a particular day. Something passed away, something else took its place."

"You have no love left for this man?"

"Why do you press him?" Pilate asked laconically. "His motives are his own business."

"I'm merely curious," I said, and indeed, he interested me. His self-confidence hid something much more volatile. Lawyers learn to expose the inward workings of men with their questions, but Pilate was right. There was no sense in finding out what he really was. The discovery of his own self might change his intentions completely. For the time being, he was convinced of his moral superiority and of the rectitude of his actions. "Let it be."

"From now on," Pilate said, "come directly to me. Don't give your true name, announce yourself as Mercury. Let nobody see you enter the Praetorium or leave."

The man nodded. "I know who Mercury is."

"Good. Go on winged feet, Judas." Pilate dismissed him with a gesture. He gave us each a lingering glance, as though wishing to remember our faces, and then departed. We listened to the sound of his footsteps fading up the stone stairs.

"An interesting fellow," Pilate said, "didn't you think? He doesn't ask for money. Yet that is a man who has spent his life counting, reckoning, calculating the value of everything. They made him their treasurer. They repose so much trust in his honesty with money that they neglect to see that he detests them in his heart." He laughed. "He'll be reckoning up their ledgers to the last halfpenny while his master is being nailed to the cross."

"Will it come to that?"

"'The kingdom of God is at hand.' You heard him. It's the usual thing. But that accountant," he said with satisfaction, "is an interesting case. I knew it meant something, the moment I heard of the fig tree." He rose and buckled on his sword. "You think me a crude sort of man, Marcellus. A brute. You'll see how subtle I can be." He tapped his long, crooked nose and winked at me.

"I'm impressed," I acknowledged. And I was. I hadn't expected such insights in the man.

At the evening meal, Pilate was in jovial mood, at least to begin with. There was a guest, a Roman merchant named Petronius. This individual, dull as he was, had amassed a large fortune in Judaea through the export of precious woods, which were now very fashionable in Roman houses. He was a balding, jowly man, who talked in a soft, incessant drone. I think he was being exhibited to me as an example of the wealth and cultivation of Pilate's friends. Certainly, he seemed to know everyone who mattered in Rome and exhibited a skilled memory by repeating long speeches which they were supposed to have made. He even recited to me an address which my own uncle had given to the Senate on the occasion of Tiberius' birthday.

"Your uncle is a great man," he concluded, "a man of vision and unswerving loyalty to Rome and its emperor."

"I will pass on your kind words," I said.

"In that case," he said, "I'll add a few more." He launched into further, carefully modulated encomiums. He was an accomplished sycophant. Fortunately, Procula had contrived it so that he was couched next to Pilate at one side of the table, while she reclined beside me at the other. In this way, although he attempted to engage my attention several times more, I was allowed to concentrate on Procula.

I thought her extraordinarily beautiful that evening; more than that, she was gay and bright, warming me with the sort of female companionship I had missed so much since Livia's death. It was not at that time the fashion for Roman women to talk much at table but I had been raised in an Etruscan family where women were expected to be cultured and witty. Nowadays in Rome, of course, women talk without restraint at any meal, though what they say is often neither witty nor decent. It was also not the custom for women to recline at meals, as Procula did, which gave me an opportunity to admire the slender grace of her limbs.

We laughed a lot on our side of that table and more than once I caught Pilate's eyes on us. Perhaps we were foolish to have enjoyed ourselves quite so obviously. We thought – or pretended to think – that there was no harm in it. She and I were close to one another in age, I being the elder by some five years. Pilate appeared then to be around forty. We were like spirited children playing in the presence of dour adults. Pilate's good mood darkened steadily and eventually Petronius, too, composed his features into a disapproving pout and fell silent.

"Let us share the joke, Procula," he said grimly, as she burst out laughing at something I had said.

"Marcellus was just being silly," she replied, her eyes sparkling at me.

"Let us hear how silly Marcellus was being," he said, turning his eyes on me.

"It was nothing," I said, smiling.

"My wife is easily amused these days," Pilate said. "She grasps at empty trifles and lets her duties slip."

"Perhaps it is the spring," the merchant ventured. "Women are affected by the spring in unusual ways. Now, for example, my late aunt –"

Unluckily, Procula caught my eye at this point and giggled. Petronius, offended, fell silent at once and said no more about how the spring had affected his late aunt. Pilate's brow grew very black. He bawled to the slaves to bring the next course. Then he turned to his wife. "You forget yourself, madam. You forget the ditch from which I raised you. How dare you insult my friend? Before the night is out, I will make you remember who I am and who you are."

I saw the colour drain from her cheeks and grew angry in my turn. "You will not beat her again so long as I am in the house," I said.

"I'll have you put in chains," he snarled at me.

"That would not be wise," I replied. Then I held my peace, knowing I was probably doing more harm than good.

The savage look faded slowly from Pilate's face. "Sejanus is gone, Petronius," he said, his eyes holding mine, "cornered like a lion by the hunters. And now the foxes come out of their holes to bark at the moon."

"I am sorry that I offended you, Petronius," Procula said quietly, with downcast eyes. "It has been some time since I've found any-thing to laugh at in this house."

As an apology, it was calculated to anger her husband even fur-ther. He glanced at her from under his brows. The merchant waved his hand. "No need for apologies, my dear Procula. The whole affair is forgotten already."

The slaves entered with the next course, a dish of pastries, each one elaborately shaped and decorated as a sign of the Zodiac. The crab and the scorpion were especially marvellous. I expressed my admiration, though by then none of us had any appetite for food.

Petronius leaned his double chin in the palm of his hand and looked at me. "Tiberius is a rotten tree who must fall one day. Who do you think will succeed him as emperor?"

"They say it will be Caligula."

"That wild boy? But he is nothing to Tiberius."

"On the contrary. Tiberius dotes on him. He has adopted Caligula as a grandson. More to the point, Caligula enjoys the support of the Army."

"Caligula is unstable. He would bring the Empire into ruin. Some are saying that the next emperor may be your uncle. He's the last great man left in Rome. And he's the only one Tiberius still trusts. He's the emperor's closest friend. They say that Tiberius may make a will appointing your uncle as his successor." He arched his top lip, as though blowing me a kiss. "And then your position would be enviable – you would be the emperor's favoured nephew."

"Rumours abound when an emperor grows old," I replied. "But my uncle has never sought such high office. It's not in his nature." Petronius replied with a knowing, silky smile. Many were predicting, as Petronius did, that Vitellius would be emperor one day. In the event, he did come to govern Rome for a period while Claudius was away in Britain; but it was the younger of his two sons, my ex-pupil Aulus, who finally became emperor. It was a brief and gluttonous reign. His head ended up on a pole, that of his elder brother in a noose. "Even if it were to be offered to him," I said, "I believe he would refuse."

"What would he accept, then?" Petronius asked. "Below the office of emperor, there are many great posts in the Empire."

I shrugged. "I can't possibly comment, Petronius."

"Of course," he murmured.

Knowing that I was principally to blame for the ugly turn the evening had taken, I made an effort to cultivate Petronius after that, listening attentively to his dreary accounts of the great ones he knew and of their opinions of everything under the sun – the man seemed to have none of his own – but Pilate remained sullen, drinking steadily from his jewel-encrusted goblet. Procula was quiet, now, keeping her eyes down. We lay together on the couch, head to head. I could smell her hair. Under the scent of aloes, her body had a distinctive smell which I haven't encountered in any other woman. I believe I would know it in the dark, among a thousand women.

Once again I was roused from my bed that night by the sound of a disturbance from Pilate's quarters. I had anticipated it. Once again I stood at the top of the stairs, listening to the grunts and cries, trying to decipher whether they represented a beating or a rape.

Or perhaps it was the sound of a mating enjoyable for both parties. The thought struck me like a leaden shot from a sling. I stood there, my skin burning, straining to decipher the muffled sounds in the darkness.

Sexual intercourse is the most beautiful of all our interactions, yet it's seldom edifying to watch or listen to. As children we assume it's a violent assault, accompanied by cries of pain. Even as adults, we may find it difficult to tell if the experience is a pleasure or an affront; and sometimes for the performers themselves it may be impossible to distinguish suffering from delight. In her final illness, Livia had wanted to make love, though her body was wasting. She wanted to say farewell to me in the flesh, as in the spirit. I recall how we both wept as we did those things that had once given us such joy. At the end she had cried out in a long wail which I could never forget. A month later she had been dead.

Since then, two years had passed without my feeling more than a flicker of interest in any woman. And now, Procula. Why Pilate's wife, one might ask? I have no answer. I have known many men conceive a sudden passion for a married woman, or a Vestal Virgin, or some other lady of difficult access. I've seen them approach madness to obtain one night with the object of their desires. I've defended some of these men in court – and in one case, a woman. We say such people have been struck by the dart of Eros.

Towards Procula I did not feel that kind of mad lust, even though my feelings for her had arrived so suddenly and so fully formed as I stood there at midnight, in a strange house in a remote province of the Empire. I wanted to snatch this golden siren off Pilate's rocks before they sank and carry her with me for the rest of my life.

I was served breakfast in my own room the next morning. After my bath and shave, Procula's slave, Hephaistion, appeared, rubbing his hands and bobbing. "My mistress is indisposed today," he told me. "She begs you to excuse her and offers you my humble services as a guide to the city in her place.

I was disappointed. "I prefer to walk alone, in that case."

"It isn't safe." He smirked. "If I don't go with you, the Governor will send a detachment of soldiers to escort you."

"I see."

"Today there's a spectacle of some interest, my lord. Herod Antipas will enter the city with his retinue. We can observe near the gate, if you choose."

There was little choice but to accept the arrangement gracefully, though it did not suit me. I have a dislike of slaves who have taken, or been given, grandiloquent names; they're invariably meddlesome busybodies. This Hephaistion was clearly intended to dog my footsteps, making it impossible for me to speak to anyone privately.

As I left the palace, with Hephaistion chattering beside me, I came across some dozen Jews prostrated near the doorway, wailing and covering their heads with dust. I stopped. "What is this?"

"The families of two of the rebels who will be crucified," the slave replied. "They are begging for an audience with Pilate so they can plead for clemency, or at least to have the bodies for burial."

"Will he see them?"

He seemed amused by the idea. "I think not, my lord."

As I passed, the wretched people called out to me, beating their breasts and faces. I was forced to turn away. There was nothing I could do. The guards made no effort to dislodge the supplicants from their post at the bottom of the steps. Pilate perhaps regarded the display as evidence that his rule was effective.

Herod Antipas came to Jerusalem every year for the Passover. Though he and his father had built the Temple, and he maintained the palace nearby, he was effectively a guest of the Roman governor, since he was king in Galilee but not in Judaea.

He was preceded by a procession of musicians blaring on huge brass wind instruments and pounding drums of all sizes. His guard followed, magnificently attired in leopard skins and carrying spears and shields which glittered in the sun. There were about seventy of these, not enough to rival Pilate's legion in the slightest, but enough to provide a gaudy show. Despite their Oriental appearance, these men were Gaulish and German mercenaries, huge barbarians who butchered and raped and burned wherever Herod's will was disobeyed.

The King himself presented a suitably exotic spectacle when he clattered through the gate in a chariot made of gilded wood and pulled by four richly caparisoned horses. He was a tall man, grasping the reins in one hand, with the other on his hip. He wore a deep purple toga with broad golden hems and a tall purple drum of a hat, something like the headgear of the temple priests. Long, curling locks flowed from his temples. His hair was a rich black, though he was over fifty. He was dark skinned, with somewhat bulging black eyes and a hooked nose. He raised his hand to the crowd which had come out to greet him, his teeth flashing in a smile.

Hephaistion sneered. "The crowd cheers him because of the legionaries. Otherwise they would have greeted him with rotten vegetables."

"He seems popular enough," I remarked.

"He has brought his new wife," Hephaistion said in my ear, "but she travels separately, in a covered carriage. He dare not show her in public, since she left her first husband to marry Herod Antipas. Her presence would cause a riot. He has tried to force his marriage on the Jews. There were those who spoke against it, but he killed them. One was John, called the Baptist, a Galilean prophet who called Herodias an adulteress. In her fury, she made Herod execute John, but that gave the people more cause to hate him."

"These Galileans are turbulent, it seems."

"They're a strong-willed race. Herod tries to please them and the Romans at the same time. Both distrust him. He builds synagogues for the Jews and temples for the Romans, as his father, Herod the Great did. But Herod the Great was a powerful and cruel man. This Herod Antipas is neither fish nor fowl."

Herod's tall purple hat disappeared in the direction of the palace. The last of his retinue tramped through the gate and the crowd started to disperse, apart from those collecting the fresh dung of Herod's horses. It had been a colourful spectacle, as the slave had promised. We spent the rest of the morning strolling through the city. Jerusalem was now crowded to capacity for Passover, which was due in a few days. Every hostelry was full, the streets thronged, the Roman soldiers visibly tense. The houses were being cleaned from top to bottom; everywhere doors were standing open while brooms swept dust into the streets.

We Romans, too, were in festival mood. The performances at the theatre, well-worn comedies of Plautus and Terence, promised to be something of an ordeal, though I could see they were welcomed by the expatriate Roman population of the city and the number of wealthy Jews who attended. Having seen them all from my youth, performed by the best comedians of Rome, I was perhaps rather spoiled; but, the local Romans were extremely proud of their level of culture and I was careful to be complimentary.

That evening, we travelled to the theatre from the palace in a carriage. Procula kept the lower part of her face veiled, her eyes decorously lowered, the very model of a Roman wife. The theatre itself was small but gracefully proportioned, apparently a gift from Herod Antipas to the Roman citizens of the city. Like the stadium, where Greek games were held with naked athletes, it was part of the monarch's vision of a Hellenized, Romanized Palestine where the circumcised and the uncircumcised would gambol together under the amiable eyes of their reconciled gods.

We arrived halfway through the first act and were seated in an ornate booth close to the actors, as was Pilate's privilege, but he made no effort to lower his voice in deference to the performers. It was early evening, and becoming cold. Braziers had been lit, both to illuminate the stage and to keep the spectators warm. I had rather hoped to meet Herod Antipas, but he had wisely stayed away from the performance. Pilate leaned back in his chair to look at me. "Where did my wife take you today?"

"This is the first time I've seen her all day," I replied, smiling.

Pilate's face darkened at once. He looked quickly at his wife. "What does he mean? Have you insulted our guest?"

"No."

"Have you been with him today?"

"No. I sent Hephaistion."

"I gave you instructions to accompany Marcellus wherever he wished to go," he said. "Why is that you cannot be obedient to the simplest request? Why is it that you take such pleasure in defying me?"

"I take no pleasure in defying you," she said quietly.

He slammed his palm onto the arm of his throne, a gesture he often made when angered. "By Hercules, I say you do. What is your explanation?"

His voice had carried and the actors on the stage, a couple of elderly Roman hams and some mumbling locals, faltered for a moment.

"My explanation is that I did not wish our guest to see me like this," she replied, drawing aside the veil from her face. I saw that the corner of her mouth was bruised, her lips swollen. He had struck her across the face. She covered herself again. I turned to Pilate, bitterly angry, but he wouldn't let me speak. He rose and stamped off the stage. Again, the actors faltered, thinking they had offended in their wretched performance.

"I'm truly sorry," I said when he had gone. "I've caused trouble for you."

"The fault was my own."

"We should not have laughed together at the table last night."

She raised her eyes to mine. "I am not a good wife, Marcellus."

"Whatever you have done, he should not strike you."

"Should he not? I think you believe the world is a courtroom. But the strong do as they please and the weak have to bear it. There's no punishment for wrong and no reward for right. We're all left to get along as we best can."

"But men have made laws. I believe in justice. I've built my life on it. It's everything to me. Do you love him?"

Her eyelids drooped, her thick lashes fanning her cheeks. "He's my husband."

"A husband who ill-treats you in private and insults you in public. There's no disgrace in leaving such a man."

She opened her eyes quickly. "Leaving him? What do you mean?"

"Divorcing him."

She laughed a little in shock. "Where do you think I could go, Marcellus? What do you expect me to do with myself?"

"You could remarry."

"Is that your answer?"

"You're young, intelligent and beautiful. Nothing I've seen makes me believe that you love your husband. For my part, I'll do whatever I can to help you."

"What do you mean?" Her eyes were wide with alarm. "You are frightening me! What power do you have to separate us?"

"None. But the Senate knows that Pilate is guilty of cruelty, corruption and maladministration from the reports which reach it. He'll be recalled to Rome."

She let go of her veil, showing me again her poor, bruised mouth. She was pale. "Has his guilt already been decided? Condemned without a trial, in his absence? You might have spared us this elaborate charade in that case."

"He'll be recalled to answer for his behaviour. But I don't think that he will escape punishment. You must consider your own future." I waited for her reply but she made none. "These things are hard to say, but I must say them. The emperor will condemn him to exile. You may possibly be exempted."

She seemed to have lost her breath. "And if I don't choose to be exempted?"

"Then you must go with him, wherever he's sent. The emperor may take no account of your personal worth, in any case. There may be no reprieve for you. Your best hope is to separate yourself from him now, before the axe falls."

"You lied to me, Marcellus. You told me that you were not here in an official capacity."

"I'm here to observe and to report. I told you that. Whether official or not makes no difference." She was silent, staring blindly at the play. "He's not worthy of such a sacrifice," I said. "You don't have to be destroyed with him. There's no moral obligation for that, no justice in it. I beg you to consider what your position would be in some wretched hole in Gaul or Spain, penniless, forced to earn your living in some menial task, unprotected against barbarians, cut off from all comfort and all respect."

"Comfort and respect have been strangers to me for some years," she replied wearily.

"Then consider how much worse your husband would treat you under such changed circumstances. He would vent all his bitterness on your spirit and your person. Your life would be hideous."

"You are cruel," she said.

"It would be crueller not to say these things."

"Falling in love with someone who dislikes you," quavered the stage Parmeno in execrable Latin, "is a double folly. You waste your own time and you annoy her."

Their performance was, if anything, even worse, since they were now watching us anxiously from the corners of their eyes as they blundered around the stage. Terence's witty dialogue needs to be spoken quickly, his nimble Greeks should be all fire; this was dismal.

"Think about what I've said, Procula. We will talk more tomorrow, if you choose." Procula made no sign she had heard me.

Pilate returned to the booth at length, bringing with him the smell of wine. He had removed the crown he wore in public; it had left an angry red ring around his balding brows. He said nothing further to either of us, but slumped with his chin on his chest. We sat like straw dummies until the last, ineluctable line had been inescapably mangled. The audience applauded and threw coins. The comedy was over and we went back to the Praetorium. We were due to eat a light supper, but Procula excused herself, looking exhausted and pale, and went straight to bed. It was my intention to do the same, but Pilate detained me.

"The Galilean spy is here," he said, "Judas. Let us see what he has to say." I could hardly bear to look at him. That he had struck his wife in the face had removed any trace of pity that was left in my heart. But I went down to the cells with him nevertheless. Our footsteps echoed in the stone stair wells. "I see by your expression that you think I am a bad husband," he said, his tone almost jovial. He seemed to have recovered his temper. "Did you never have cause to discipline your wife?"

"Never," I said shortly.

He laughed. "I wish you could have seen your face when she pulled her veil aside. Ha! Ha! You were stricken to the heart. You don't think she planned that effect carefully?"

"She doesn't seem to me to be that sort of woman."

He grunted. "There's only one sort of woman, Marcellus. You've taken a fancy to my wife, it seems. And she, of course, to you." I made no reply. "Well," he said calmly, "that's natural, I suppose. You're younger than I and she's a handsome woman. But you can't venture to judge a marriage from what you see on the outside. Ours is a happy one. The lack of children is a sorrow, of course, but it isn't too late to hope. You've found us at a low point. I told you that she had fallen into a melancholy?"

"I remember."

"She lost a child. Her first pregnancy in all the years of our marriage." He made a gesture, as if throwing something away.

"Over and done with, as far as I'm concerned. I don't harbour any reproach against her. But for women it's different. They brood on such things. And she bled a lot. She's still weak. Overall, I think it does her good to have you stroking her hand and whispering in her ear."

"I have not touched her hand," I said, very stiffly, "nor have I whispered in her ear."

He rubbed his bristly mouth. "Well, well, whatever you say. Here is our singular accountant."

We entered the cell. Judas was seated on the bench, wrapped up in his cape, for it was a cold evening. He looked up at us and once again I was struck by the sense of half-concealed passion in his gaze. I certainly wouldn't have trusted him with money or anything else, though he was well formed, and his face handsome enough. There was something about the man that struck me as arrogant and cold.

"I have been waiting here for an hour," he greeted us sharply. "It is dangerous. The disciples will ask where I have been so late."

I expected Pilate to snarl at the man's impertinence, but he spoke placatingly. "My apologies. We were unavoidably detained. It's a cold night. Do you want food or wine?"

"I may not eat or drink with you," he retorted.

"Ah. I forget these things."

"You must receive my report and then I must go." He had a strong sense of his own importance, of the dignity with which he deserved to be treated, and he clearly felt that both had been infringed.

Pilate made an accommodating gesture. "Of course. Tell us what your master has been up to."

Judas was still not mollified. He was leaning forward as though ready to get up and hurry away. "I am among the inner circle," he said, looking from me to Pilate. "One of the twelve! And of those, none understand him as well as I or have served him so faithfully. You would never find another so close to him willing to help you."

"We value you highly. Please continue. What has he been doing?"

Judas shrugged. "He's made his point."

"What point was that?"

"He calculates everything, even when it seems most spontaneous. He wanted a confrontation with the Sadducees. He achieved his result. He shocked the whole city. He established himself, among the ignorant, especially, as a teacher of piety, a new Isaiah or Jeremiah. He's the wonder of the hour. Or so he thinks. He's been preaching in the temple each day."

Pilate raised his eyebrows. "And the priests tolerate him there?"

"They have little choice. Crowds flock to him. He heals the sick and interprets the Scriptures. He sits in the Royal Portico beside the sages. The Sadducees are too wary of the common people to attack him, but they don't intended to yield to an upstart from Galilee, either. His life is in the balance."

"You make him sound as cynical as –" I was about to say as yourself but changed my phrase. "As a common mountebank."

"He is not common," Judas replied, turning his dark and bitter gaze on me. "No, he is not that."

"So you still love him, in some sense?" I asked curiously. Pilate frowned at me to tell me to be silent, but I wanted to penetrate a little into this strange man's mind. "I ask because I wonder what you anticipate will befall your master. You're speaking, after all, of his death."

"He must die," he said sharply. "It does not depend on me. Nor do I bear the blame. He sought his own death. What matters is to give him the best death possible."

"Crucifixion isn't a very good death," I said.

"It's the Roman death. If the Sadducees accuse him, he will be stoned, which is the Jewish death. Herod is seeking him in Galilee – if he's taken by Herod's men, he'll be cut in pieces, which is the Gentile death. Are those good deaths? One of them must be his. By the best death, I mean the death that destroys only him, and not all those connected with him."

Pilate cut in laconically. "Does he assert that he's the Messiah?"

Judas turned back to Pilate, his expression changing subtly. "He doesn't say it in public. But there are glances, whispered conversations, secret meetings."

"Among the twelve?"

"Yes."

"So you think he has said it to some of them?"

"Perhaps."

"But not to you," Pilate said with a dry smile. "Perhaps you're not so intimate with him as you thought?"

"Or perhaps he knows that you're betraying him?" I suggested.

The man's sallow cheeks grew pale, the marks of the sun standing out lividly on his skin. His eyes, by contrast, seemed to darken. "I would have trusted him with my life!"

It seemed a strange remark. "He evidently doesn't trust you with his," Pilate retorted. "If he declares himself the Messiah, I can crucify him at once."

"I still don't understand what the word means," I said. "Who is the Messiah?"

"The Messiah is God's anointed," Judas replied, "who will shatter unrighteous rulers! With a rod of iron he shall break in pieces all their substance, he shall destroy the godless nations with the word of his mouth, and he shall gather together a holy people, he shall have the heathen nations to serve him under his yoke, and he shall be a righteous king, taught by God."

"This is your Scripture?"

"It's the promise of Solomon," he replied.

"And you Jews await this saviour?"

"Daily, hourly," he said with a mirthless smile.

"Then why do you betray this Jesus?"

"Because he is not the Messiah," he exclaimed. "The Messiah will be known by every Jew. He will arrive with a host of warriors, clothed in glory. This is no more than a man! I have seen him bleed!"

"You will see him bleed again," Pilate promised. "But to arrest him on no charge is asking for a riot. You must bring me evidence. Make him say it to you and be prepared to swear to it. Or make him say it where he can be overheard. Then you may be sure that I will be swift."

"It's not so easy," Judas said sullenly, "He lets it be understood without declaring it. You understand? People whisper it without him needing to say anything. He's no fool. He's been in many tight places before. To snare him is not a simple matter."

"But you're a clever man," Pilate said insinuatingly. "Your mind is far better than his. He's a demagogue, but you are an intellectual." The shameless flattery seemed to soothe the man's pains at once. His face smoothed itself out and regained its healthy colour. He nodded his agreement. "The Jews celebrate Passover soon," Pilate went on. "If you want me to crucify your Jesus, you'd better act quickly. The chief priests don't approve of executions over Passover. Do they?"

"It would defile the feast," he replied. "They would stone the soldiers."

"Then let's nail him up in good time, eh? By the time the pilgrims all go home, full of mutton and wine, his name will be forgotten. Otherwise he'll spend the Passover glorifying himself and we will have a rebellion on our hands. The line of crucifixes will stretch to the sea, I assure you."

Judas pulled his cape around himself. "I will see what I can do."

"I place implicit confidence in you, Judas." Pilate leaned forward and spoke into the man's ear. I could just overhear his words. "I know you are not doing this for a reward, but there will be one, nevertheless. And a richer reward than you may think. Rome shows her gratitude in gold." The man nodded indifferently. The promise of gold meant less to him than the jealousies that tormented him. After he had departed, Pilate jerked his thumb at the doorway. "There goes an unhappy fellow. He's like one of those husbands who are unfaithful to their wives because they dread being cuckolded."

"I'm curious to meet his master."

"You'll find him of little interest, I should imagine. But I'll try to satisfy your curiosity if it's in my power."

"Thank you."

As we went back up to our quarters, he referred again to his wife, assuring me that their childlessness hadn't been due to any failure on his own part. "I do my duty whether she's in the humour or not," he declared. "I'll do it tonight and I will continue to do it. She has lost one child but another may come. You have no children either?"

"My wife had many problems with her womb. She was already sick when I married her, I believe. There were occasions when we believed she was pregnant and then all would end in a haemorrhage."

He grunted. "If Procula doesn't conceive again, I will adopt one of my nephews."

"I wish you well, either way."

We parted at the top of the stairs. I went to my bed with my mind full of unwelcome thoughts.

# CHAPTER FOUR

# MAGNA MATER

It had been arranged that the next day, Procula was to take me to the burial ground, which I was interested to see. It would also give me a chance to pursue the conversation I had opened with her the night before.

The cemetery sprawled in a valley at the foot of the Mount of Olives. It was very large, containing family tombs that were hundreds of years old. Although there were impressive monuments to be seen, the dead had chiefly been laid to rest in innumerable caves, either natural or excavated, which dotted the rocky mountainside. Boulders were used to seal these crypts. The bodies of the dead, so Procula informed me, were not cremated as we Romans generally do, but were wrapped in linen with spices and allowed to decay in the crypts until only the bones were left. These were then laid in smallish stone sarcophagi for their long rest.

The place was empty but for a few distant figures and a young gardener hoeing weeds from between the stones. Cypresses and wild olives grew at the edges of the cemetery. The wind was blowing her dress against her body as we picked our way among the rocks, revealing and concealing as the fancy took the air. She was in a strange mood – remote and melancholy – and it was a strange place. It had a silent, wild, abandoned atmosphere. I commented on this.

"For the Sadducees," she replied, "to even come near a corpse is defilement. The handling of bodies for burial is governed by many ritual laws. Usually, only the closest relatives do it. And the burial must be completed before sunset on the day of the death, if possible. After that, visiting the grave is rare." She paused. A jackal, perhaps rummaging for bones, had been disturbed by our presence and slunk away through the rocks. She watched it disappear. "When my father trapped a fox, he would nail the animal alive to the door of the barn. They would scream for hours. I would run away with my hands covering my ears. I couldn't understand how such a gentle man could do such a terrible thing. He said it would keep the other foxes away. Now even to see a fox brings the memory back."

I forbore to point that her husband now did the same to men. We sat together on a stone wall sheltered from the wind, the spring sunlight warm on our skin. Hephaistion and the two attendants remained discreetly on the other side of the cemetery.

"Do you think the soul feels pain after death?" she asked me. "People talk of Hell and eternal punishments, Sisyphus and Tantalus and all the rest. Isn't there enough suffering in life without anticipating it in death?"

"You think about death too much."

"We're sitting in a graveyard, are we not?" Three Jewish women were picking their way across the rocky hillside, their heads bowed and veiled. They appeared so humble that even the guards were not interested in them; they were like brown leaves blown by the wind.

"I wanted to continue our conversation of last night," I said.

Procula grimaced. "Ah, yes. When I woke this morning, I thought it had been a nightmare. But here we are."

"Have you mentioned anything that I said to you to Pilate?"

"No. He was drunk last night, in any case."

"You must contemplate your course of action, Procula."

"Action?" she repeated. "I am a Roman woman, Marcellus. We don't act. We're acted upon. We obey, that's our lot in life. You fought against the Germans. They say that the barbarian women take up axes and clubs and go into battle alongside their men. Did you ever see such a thing?"

"Yes. I never want to see it again."

Procula pulled the wind-twists of hair out of her eyes. "Sometimes I think I would like to be such a woman," she said, "wearing the skins of wild beasts and splitting my enemies' skulls. But I'm not. I was married at fifteen. Before that I obeyed my father, now I obey my husband."

"He doesn't think so."

"He's enraged by the slightest disobedience. He's been angry with me for years. But the truth is that in large things, I do whatever he asks me." Her voice dropped. "Except love him. I never learned to do that. But in all else, I think I've lost the power to act on my own."

"How did you come to marry Pilate?"

She shrugged. "My parents thought it was a good match. I was said to be beautiful as a girl. They hoped to find me a husband above my station. Pilate was introduced by friends of friends. He seemed old to me and not very handsome but he was an equestrian knight. I think he liked my hair best of all. He asked me constantly if it was dyed. And I suppose I seemed gentle and affectionate. He wasn't deceived about the hair, but he was deceived about the other things."

She had found a small plant growing among the stones of the wall and was stroking its leaves absently with her fingertips. Her fingers were, like her feet, well made and well proportioned. She wore a golden wedding ring in a design of clasped hands. The bones of her cheeks were rounded, the skin covered with a fine down which caught the light. Her mouth had a slightly bitter downward turn this morning, the bruise Pilate had given her already fading. The skin of her lips was covered with tiny, soft creases. One compares fine skin to satin or silk, but of course there's nothing made by hands that is as fine as the skin of a beautiful woman; only the petals of orchids or roses can compare, and they're not one-tenth so beautiful, and do not glow with life and make one's heart ache with their vulnerability.

"Procula, you said yourself that we Romans marry for practical reasons. For women, marriage is a vocation. You're not a barbarian, bare breasted and swinging an axe. But you may have certain expectations from your marriage, and if these are not fulfilled, you may divorce without difficulty or shame. These days it's rare for a woman to remain married to an unsatisfactory husband. Unless she wishes to be celebrated for her blind devotion."

"You mean, I must find myself another husband?" she said. "That should be easy, considering I am – how did you describe me? Young, intelligent and beautiful."

"You're all those things and more."

"Must I sell myself once again to some wealthy old man? Or perhaps I will find a poor young one to share my widow's pension?"

"If I thought you would accept me," I said quietly, "I would ask you to marry me now."

She turned to me in astonishment. "What are you saying, Marcellus?"

My heart was in my throat, almost stopping my words. "I am saying that I want you to be my wife."

Her lips were parted for a moment without making a sound. Her eyes searched mine as though looking for some sort of crude joke. "For such a sententious and predictable man, you have a habit of taking my breath away. Where does this come from? A few days ago you were telling me you had no intention to marry again."

"I had no such intention – a few days ago."

She shook her head. "Then some god has played a joke on you by making you infatuated with the first woman you set eyes on when you woke up!"

"I think you're indeed the first woman I saw since Livia's death," I said. "I mean truly saw, with the eyes of my heart. The first woman I looked at."

I was restraining myself from touching her, but she drew back with a little gasping laugh. "You're mad. I wouldn't accept you under such circumstances."

I hid the pain her words had given me. "Circumstances change."

"More wise utterances! I'm amazed, Marcellus."

"What amazes you so?"

"More things than I can put tongue to! Just for one – are you really so much better a man than he is?"

"I'm regarded as one of the foremost lawyers in Rome. My specialty is ethics. All Rome respects my judgments on moral principles."

She drew her hand through the space between us. "And this is ethical?"

"I'm not talking of a clandestine affair. I want you to divorce Pilate and marry me."

"While you destroy him!"

"The Senate will destroy him, not I. In a few years I myself will be a Senator. To have you at my side would be the greatest pride of my life."

"You've known me for a week. Less!"

"I need only look into your face to know everything I need to know. I don't expect you to feel as I do, Procula. I was living in autumn. The first moment I met you, I thought, this woman is my midsummer. I hope one day it can be the same for you."

"Midsummer lasts a month. Is this because we laughed together once or twice?"

"You know that it is not," I said quietly. "You know why it is." She dropped her eyes, the first sign she had given that she recognized some feeling in herself. "Please don't think I'm shallow, or that I'm not speaking from my heart."

She looked up again and searched my face intently. Her pupils were usually large; when they contracted, they revealed that the heart of her eyes was golden, like her hair. "Tell me the truth – why were you sent here?"

"To see for myself."

"To see what? My husband's misdeeds?"

"And the problems of the position."

She gave a little breathless laugh. "Up to now I thought you were a fool. But I suddenly realize how clever you are, Marcellus. It's you who will replace my husband, is it not?"

I hesitated. "Vitellius will be given the governorship of Syria. The prefecture of Judaea will be mine if I wish it."

She was paler than ever. "At least you're honest."

"I haven't decided whether I'll take it or not."

"You'll take it. You'll profit from the destruction of Pilate. Do you want his wife as well as his authority?"

"My legal practice is successful," I said. "I make far more money in the courts than I would as governor of Judaea. I would accept the post only if I thought I could thereby serve Rome – and the people."

"How noble you are! Should I tell my husband this? And that you have been offering to marry me behind his back?"

"You may tell him what you please. I care nothing for him. He thinks he can outface or suborn Vitellius. He's mistaken. For you I feel a terrible anxiety. Banishment is harsh fate. You would fall from the summit of the civilized world into a life of danger and poverty. You would die far from your country and your people."

"How good you are with your threats." She touched her bruised mouth with trembling fingers. "I've underestimated you. My husband is brutal, but at least he's of the human family. I'm beginning to think that you are a creature made of stone or ice."

I felt the force of her reproach. I took her hands in mine. They quivered with little, unsteady movements. Her palms were damp with sweat. "I'm neither stone nor ice," I said quietly. "I control my emotions because I've been schooled to do so, and I plan my life because an unplanned life is in the power of others. But everything that I am is yours if you'll take it."

"And I will be the wife of the emperor's favoured nephew? I'm glad, at least, that you don't try to tell me you love me."

"I know that we will soon love one another, even if we don't do so now."

"You're a strange man."

"I am a very simple one. If you recognize that and leave your preconceptions behind, we may find happiness. I've looked for you all my life and now that I've found you, I will not let you go."

I was serious in everything I had said to her. I wanted her with a deep conviction that she was the love of my life. It may seem strange that this knowledge came almost before love itself had a chance to grow. Perhaps I seem cold and Roman and lawyerly, deciding with my head who my heart would fasten on; but in truth I had as little choice as a man falling from a tower. I knew that I would love her for the rest of my life; and perhaps all love is in some way like this, foredestined, unavoidable, lit with a brilliant, cold light.

Perhaps if I had said this to her that day, she would have understood me more. If I had unpacked my heart for her and made the explanations that, in hindsight, I could have made, she would have seen that my feelings were true.

But perhaps not. A woman's heart is not like a man's. It moves more slowly, but more surely. A woman's love takes time to grow; a man's may appear in an instant. A woman's love is constant forever. A man's love is like those lights we see at twilight, flickering brightly and then waning as the wind blows it away.

We were interrupted at that point. The three old women had approached. They had made their slow way towards us through the graves and were waiting patiently to be noticed, huddled against the wind.

"What is it?" I asked.

One of the old women came forward. She kept her head bowed, but we heard her cracked voice. "Gentile lord, there is one who begs you to hear her."

"Who wants me to hear her?"

She handed me an ostracon of clay pottery. Scratched on it in an uneducated hand were the words *mariam mater iesui*. I have the piece of terracotta on my desk now as I write. She did not scratch the words, of course – she asked someone more learned to do it for her – but it brings her back to me at once, this small, worn piece of clay, scratched with the words, "Mary, the mother of Jesus."

"Where is she?" I asked.

The woman raised her head slightly. Above her veil I could see that her brow was lined and her eyes rheumy. "She's lodging in the house of Eleazar, who keeps the inn by the Fish Gate. She begs you to see her. She asks this in the name of God's mercy."

I could see Procula's attendants hurrying over to us, Hephaistion bounding over the stones like a rabbit. I made up my mind and spoke quickly. "Tell her I will come tonight," I said. I found a coin and gave it to the woman, who took it in both withered hands. She bowed and shuffled back to her companions without looking at us or speaking again. They resumed their slow progress around the cemetery, hesitating here and there as though seeking a grave whose location they could no longer remember. The young gardener watched them, leaning on his hoe.

"Why have they come to you?" Procula asked.

"I don't know. But please say nothing of this to Pilate."

"I am not in the habit of hiding things from my husband," she replied.

"Hide this. Perhaps you can save one fox from being nailed to the barn door," I replied, speaking low, for Hephaistion had arrived.

He rubbed his hands together unctuously and asked, "What did the old women want, my Lady?"

He was so plainly Pilate's spying creature that my hands itched to beat him. Procula looked into my eyes and answered calmly. "They're always begging. I gave them some money."

"Not too much, I hope, my Lady?" the man smirked.

"Not too much. Let us go," she said, "I'm getting cold."

He bobbed his shaven head and led the way out of the graveyard. The wind was rising. The sky was turbulent, the clouds beginning to be torn. As we walked, she gathered her hair in her hands, tying the ribbons which the wind had worked loose. I thanked her for her discretion. "Tell me," she said quietly, so the attendants couldn't hear, "had you planned to speak to me in this way today?"

"Perhaps I hadn't planned to go so far," I said wryly. "I am aware that I may have spoken inopportunely."

"Really! That must be very rare. You're worse than Cicero. Worse than Parmeno in that dreary play. You never say anything which isn't formal or rhetorical. How can one know where your emotions lie, Marcellus?"

"I'll try not to make speeches to you. I would like to say what's in my heart but that's not always a good idea."

"I'm sure your clients are grateful for your eloquence. But I'm equally sure you didn't woo your Livia with courtroom speeches."

She was so beautiful, walking in the wind, knotting her tresses behind her head. Her eyes were tawny and clear. "I think that you know very little about women."

"You're right. I am an inept wooer."

"Even Pilate knows more about women than you. He's bestial, but he doesn't moralize. Sometimes a blow is more bearable than words. Sometimes to be taken by force is preferable to being asked – when one cannot refuse."

"Is that what women want? Brutality?"

"I am speaking for myself. Pilate knows more about me, let me put it that way. He gives me a place and I fill it. You treat me like a fragile vase that may break. And that fills me with terror that I will break."

"Doesn't my company give you any pleasure?"

"My life isn't concerned with pleasure. I'm not free to do anything that I want to do. Do you understand me? Where there's no choice and no volition, it's better to be given orders than to have to pretend."

"You make me very sorry for you."

"Perhaps that is the emotion you have mistaken for love," she replied dryly.

The evening meal was served early so that we could attend the performance at the theatre. "The program is Plautus's *Amphitryon*," Pilate announced, wiping his fingers clean. "It should be a pleasant evening, eh, Marcellus?"

"It's a play I've never particularly liked." I didn't add that to see it mangled by Jerusalem's players was an even less appealing prospect.

"Why not?"

"It deals with the cuckolding of a mortal by a god. When Amphitryon learns that Jupiter has been sleeping with his wife, he professes to be honoured. It seems unconvincing."

"Unconvincing?" He looked at me with hard little eyes. "You think he would be happier to be cuckolded by a man?"

"I don't think he should be happy to be cuckolded by anyone."

"By the cuckolding, he becomes the stepfather of Hercules. There's honour in that, I think. A man may love his wife, but to share her with a god is no disgrace." He turned to his wife. "What is your opinion, Procula?"

"The play is a comedy," she replied quietly. "In comedies we laugh at the things that make us weep in real life."

Pilate grunted. "I see that a visit to the graveyard has done wonders for both of you. Well, Procula and I will be attending the performance. You're welcome to abstain if you choose."

"Perhaps I might be allowed to visit your library?" I suggested. "I've been told there are rare works in it."

"If you prefer dusty old scrolls to the theatre, I can't stop you."

"Thank you."

"You'll be spared the theatre again tomorrow night, Marcellus. We dine with Herod Antipas at the palace."

"A signal honour," I said.

"It remains to be seen which performance you prefer," Pilate said, "second rate actors or a second rate King."

The seated figure of the Great Mother watched us silently through her veil. Fresh offerings were placed in front of her three times a day, the smell of the lilies growing stronger all the time. As the daylight faced, the appearance of the wax lost its artificiality and she became frightening.

I retired from the table and asked the slaves for a light to read by. They brought a candelabrum with five tapers. The blaze of light it provided was superfluous; the library was a disappointment, little more than a cupboard containing a jumble of parchments and scrolls in a variety of languages, some of them unintelligible to me, many so gnawed by mice that they were falling to pieces. The most appetizing items in it were some random chapters of Polybius, with which I had to content myself. I took them up to my room.

The scrolls had been transcribed by someone whose Greek was imperfect and there were many errors. I thought back to the pages of Greek I had made my nephews construe and took a blade and a reed pen and set to the task of making corrections to a scroll nobody would ever read in a library that was never visited, hoping to calm my wayward mind.

I worked this way for perhaps an hour when I heard Pilate and Procula leave the palace to go to the theatre. I put on a cloak, for the evening was cold and I wished in any case to hide my face. I spoke to Rufus, the young orderly. "I'm going for a stroll. I don't need attendants." I went out into the night.

Jerusalem was a silent city at night, for all its daytime bustle. Occasionally one caught the sound of voices or music from behind the locked doors, but the streets were empty, only a few patrolling centurions appearing in the larger streets. I was able to evade these and reached the Fish Gate without – as far as I could tell – being followed.. Finding the house of Eleazar was difficult; half the houses in the city served as hostelries at Passover and every second doorway bore the sign that it had guests. Luckily, a young boy was looking out for me. He whistled when he saw me, and opened a doorway, letting a slash of yellow light fall on the cobbles. I went inside.

The house was dark and quiet, a warren of low, vaulted passageways through which the boy flitted, a shadow among the shadows. I followed him to a dim kitchen where an elderly man was raking the ashes from an oven. The occasional glow of the coals provided almost the only light. He didn't look at me as he worked. The boy invited me with gestures to sit at an old table behind the oven. I took off my cape. The red brick walls were still warm from the day's baking. In the summer it must have been unbearably hot, but at this time of year when nights were still cold, the warmth was welcome.

The room clearly served as the eating place for many families, whose simple wood and terracotta utensils were stacked in rows, awaiting their owner's hands. From what I had learned about Jews, I knew that considerable care had to be taken in kitchens not to infringe their strict dietary laws; certain foods must not come into contact with each other, blood should never be consumed, and so forth. These obsessions were a source of amusement to Romans – we eat like pigs – but they served to keep the Jews separate from all other peoples. Somewhere in the house I could hear the sound of a dulcimer being played, soft and plangent notes.

I waited for no more than a few moments before she came rustling into the room. She was a small figure, wrapped up in rusty black clothing, her hair covered with a fringed widow's shawl. She brought a faint smell of cardamom and cloves into the little room. She carried a small clay lamp which was guttering as the oil ran low. I thought that she did not look well. "Forgive me for presuming, my lord," she said, putting the lamp down and smoothing her dress with trembling hands.

"It's no presumption. How much did you pay the women to bring me your message?"

"One denarius, lord."

I took a denarius from my purse and held it out to her. She put her hands behind her, like a child. "I will not take it."

"Please take it. I know the value of a denarius."

Reluctantly, she took the coin and put it away. "Will you have wine?"

"Yes, thank you." She poured me a cup from a clay jug and took the chair opposite me. The lamp made a small pool of wavering yellow light. She searched my face with her eyes while I, in turn, studied her. The lines in her face went deep. Her lips, that had once been soft as Procula's, were papery. But her deep set eyes were rich with feeling. "What did you want to ask me?"

"They say that you spoke to my son on the road."

"Did your son tell you that?"

"My son does not speak to me."

"And yet you're the mother of the Messiah?"

I had spoken lightly. "I do not say that he's the Messiah," she retorted swiftly. She broke off and touched her lips with her fingers as though to seal them against unwise utterances. "Do you think I wouldn't know if he were the Messiah?"

"I was joking, forgive me."

"It is no joke. The mothers of those boys have lain in front of Pilate's house for five days and five nights. Their sons are nailed to Pilate's crosses."

"If you've called me to ask me to intercede for your son, I must tell you that I cannot do so. I have no authority."

"But they say that you are an advocate."

"That's true."

"And that you were sent by Rome to cut Pilate's claws."

"Pilate's claws will be cut, but not by me."

Her eyes showed that she did not know whether she could trust me or not. "Is the wine good?" she asked.

It was somewhat sweet, as wines are apt to be in that part of the world, where the sun is so hot. "It's very good."

"I brought it from Galilee," she said. "It grows in the stones. If you drink slowly, you will taste every bucket of water that I poured on the roots. I am little but I am diligent."

"I can see that."

"I know how to make things grow. With time and patience. With tears and love. I have four sons and two daughters, lord. It is hard to see a vine cut down."

"Please believe me. I have no power over Pilate."

"You can save my son! Order him to go away from the city. Have him exiled to some faraway land where at least he would be safe!"

"I'm afraid that it is too late for that. Your son himself said that to me. It was the first thing he said to me: he said, 'You come too late for me.' And I felt that he was prophesying. Can't you get him to return home with you?"

"He has no home. Herod is hunting him in Galilee. Here in Judaea, his life is in Pilate's hands. He has nowhere to lay his head. Wherever he goes, he's recognized."

"Does your son preach rebellion against Rome?"

"Ah, my lord, he isn't so simple. If it were only that, there would be a place for him in the world. He preaches obedience to Rome."

"But that's good."

"No, because the Zealots hate him for that."

"He's not of their party?"

"He wants no war with Rome, as they do. The Zealots took him for forty days. They carried him up to the hills, trying to persuade him to join them. They tempted him with the power he might have as their Messiah." She was clasping and unclasping her work-hardened hands, the calloused skin rustling. "But they misunderstood him, my lord. He teaches men to love their enemies and forgive wrongs. He forbids deeds of violence and anger. They were angry with him in the end. They threatened to kill him. They kill everybody who wants peace."

"Then your son is a friend to Rome."

"Tell Pilate that!"

"His enemies say he declares himself to be the Messiah, who will shatter Rome with a rod of iron and give freedom to the Jews."

"He is surrounded by traitors."

"I hope he knows that."

"I have never heard him say such a thing. It is the Sadducees who accuse him of that. They hate him. They say he offends God."

"Why?"

"The educated don't take instruction from the unlearned. The rich don't listen to the poor."

"And for this, they want to kill him?"

"Our God is becoming a rich man's god. There's no room in his house for whoever has no sacrifice."

"Your god loves sacrifices, just as our gods do," I replied. "It follows that the gods love the rich, who give them silver and gold, more than the poor, who give only words."

"You are jesting again."

"Why are the rich rich and the poor, poor?"

"And the poor shall not be heard by God?" she said with a flash of anger.

"Pilate says all Jews are rich."

"You don't know how poor the poor are in our country, lord. They're too poor even for the angels to notice. My son gathers them in. They gave him no place in the synagogue because they said he was ignorant. The Sadducees have their temple and the Pharisees have their synagogues, but he has the fields and the mountains and the sea. They wait days for him to come, sleeping in the open. He tells them that God loves them because they are poor and that they must love one another as God loves them."

"That is a great crime," I said gently.

We could hear muffled noises from the other side of the wall, where the old man was raking out the oven. "Forgive the noise he makes," she said. "Tomorrow the bread must be unleavened. He's making sure the oven is untainted."

I thought for a while. There was almost certainly a wide gulf between her account of her son, told in the plain speech of a country woman, but with insight and intelligence, and the real life that he lived. She would naturally see his teaching as harmless. Perhaps she was too innocent to perceive the danger in what he taught, or unable to see how the principles on which she had raised him – for it was clear that she was a woman of strong character – could be seen as subversive. It was something of a puzzle to me that I had come at all. Curiosity is an easy explanation to give – but it wasn't that alone. Listening to Pilate and Judas of Kerioth planning his death, I had conceived a sort of sympathy for Jesus of Nazareth. I had still not grasped what was so truly revolutionary in his teaching but there was a certain pleasure in going behind Pilate's back. "How is it that you're estranged from your son?"

"It is a different generation. He says the old do not listen to the young. He tells his disciples to abandon their mothers and leave their fathers unburied. After he was baptized by John he never came back home again. He doesn't stop traveling. He found other people to take care of his needs, few as they are. They have a little money and they pay his accounts, hoping for a place in heaven." She made a bitter face. "They took my son from me. But they will not save him."

"Would he listen to his brothers?"

"James is closest to him and is also holy. He's afraid to show himself because if Jesus is arrested, he'll be taken too. Jesus will not be guided by the others. They grew up on the bread that Jesus earned for them, but he went hungry and knew fire and blood instead of food and drink."

"How was that?"

"He was born into troubles, my lord. When he was a little child, the old king Herod died. The people rejoiced and raised up their heads because a great evil had been lifted. They burned Herod's citadel. My son stood in the street pointing at the black cloud that hung over us, day and night. The young king sent his soldiers. So many were crucified. The blood of his kinsmen fell on my son's face. I wiped it away with the hem of my dress, but long before John baptized him with water, he was baptized in blood. We worked for seven years under the sword to rebuild Herod's citadel. Jesus grew up a slave, or little better. He dreamed and spoke to spirits. He learned to feed others with his words in a world where there was no bread."

"Words are a dangerous sort of bread."

"To poor Jews, words are better than bread," she said.

"You Jews are indeed fascinated with words," I said. "You pile up mountains of them. Certainly more words than bread. Perhaps that's why you're so troublesome."

"There are famous men in our land who speak a hundred words to my son's one, but they are less holy than my son."

"Then he has a gift?"

She shot me a sharp glance from her dark eyes. "He has a great gift." Her tone was a mixture of pride and grief. "He can heal the sick. He casts out devils." She hesitated. "They say the wife of Pilate loves you."

"That is not so."

She was alarmed by my tone. "I don't mean in the way of sin, but that she looks on you with favour. Her husband is a beast but she's almost a Jew."

"I don't think that Pilate listens to anyone, not even his wife. But I will talk to her." The little lamp was starting to gutter. "I will do what I can."

"Thank you, thank you." She clasped her hands and rested her chin on her knuckles. "Do you have a mother, my lord?"

"I had one," I replied gently. "I seem to see her now."

"A little woman? With a face like this? And eyes like this?" There were suddenly tears spilling down her brown cheeks. "Do you remember her?"

"Please don't cry," I said, very affected by her tears.

"You're right. A mother's tears are worth nothing in this world. Forgive me. It's a hard thing to lose a son." She wiped her eyes, too weary or too full of grief to speak.

There was little more to say. I helped her to her feet. She was as light as a feather, and again I had the impression that she was not well. I kissed her on the cheek, remembering my own mother, long ago. The boy led me out into the street again.

I reached the palace at the same moment that Pilate and Procula were returning from the theatre. He, as often on these occasions, was drunk, having poured wine down his throat all through the performance. I heard him on the stairs loudly reviling the actors.

"I'll have them all scourged," he bawled. "I'll have them crucified."

I encountered them on the landing. He was staggering, clutching his wife for support. At his other side was one of his bodyguards. He peered at me. "You're right. The play is nonsensical. You escaped a night of torment."

"I'm glad to hear it."

"You're not such a bad fellow. You have more hair than I, at any rate. Do you see how bald I am becoming?"

"Let me help you to bed."

I took the place of Procula, who followed behind, carrying the governor's crown, which had fallen from his head as he groped in his hair. Pilate's fingers dug into my shoulder. He was crooning some old song, his eyes closed.

At Procula's command we laid him on a leather couch in his bedroom. The soldier saluted and left us. She gave me the crown, with a wry expression. I laid it on a chair. She unfastened his shoes and belt. He began to struggle, seeing where he was. "No! In my bed! With my wife!"

"You're better here," she said.

"There's only one thing left that you can do to please me," he said, his voice slurred. "You won't do it willingly, so I'll take it." He lunged at her. I restrained him. He turned on me with a face of fury and groped for his dagger. "By Hercules, you dare to come between me and my wife?"

"Don't be a fool." I took the weapon from his fumbling hands and cast it aside. "You need to sleep."

We pushed him back onto the couch. He glared at me, his eyes not able to focus. He was fumbling at my throat. "You'll learn," he said thickly. "You will learn."

I held him down on the couch. With a groan, he let his head fall back. His eyes closed. His hand slid away from my throat.

"He'll sleep now," she said. I glanced around the room. The marital bed was large and ornate. It had been bought, I thought, in happier times. The smell of aloes, which was Procula's scent, was everywhere. He was already starting to snore. His face was sunken, his mouth open. He looked old.

"Can we speak privately a moment?" I asked.

"Come outside." She led me onto the terrace which adjoined their bedchamber. The night was cold but the sky burned with stars. By contrast, Jerusalem was in darkness, only a few fires visible. I told her that I had spoken to the mother of Jesus that night.

"What did she want?" she asked.

"To plead for her son's life."

She shuddered, pulling her cloak around herself. "Poor creature. What did you say?"

"I will appeal to Herod Antipas."

"What mercy can be expected from him?"

"He's only half a Jew at best. He knows the common people don't accept him as their King. There was a universal outcry when he executed John the Baptist, and John was a hermit who lived in the wilderness. Jesus is here in Jerusalem – and the common people listen to him. Herod will ingratiate himself with them if he protects Jesus."

"This is not Rome. The common people have no power here. And Herod is with the Sadducees, not with the poor."

"We have an audience with Herod tomorrow. I can try."

"It's a forlorn hope."

"Otherwise there's none. She spoke of you, Procula. She said that you were known for your kindness. She described you as 'almost a Jew.'"

She made no reply for a moment. At last she said, "I became pregnant after nine years of waiting. Then I lost the child. A son. I didn't want to live any more. I didn't know why the gods should treat me so pitilessly. I had always been devout. I made the requisite sacrifices and I prayed with my heart. Nobody could explain it to me. I took poison to escape myself and my husband."

"Oh, Procula!"

"I was no better at procuring death than at creating life," she said. "I survived myself. But after the death of my child it seemed to me that our gods were nothing but figures of wood and stone with painted smiles. You would get more help praying to a living whore than to a stone Venus."

"We all feel these fears from time to time."

"There is one god. That's all I know. Or there is none. But those whom our poets describe, with their spites and fears and jealousies – they're not gods. They're puppets which we pull with our own strings. I'm not a Jew. I'll never be. Judaism is a religion of community, it's celebrated together. I'm alone. And It's too late for me to learn all the observances. Nor do I care for them. If you like, I've invented my own god and I worship him in the name of Yahweh."

"And Pilate hates you for this apostasy?"

"Pilate loves me. If he hated me, it would be far easier."

I stared at her form in the darkness. "You're the loneliest person I know. Except myself."

"Does that bring us together?"

"My room is up there, above yours. To hear him abuse you wrenches at my heart. If I have to listen to it one more time, I will come down and kill him."

"Pray do not make me a widow," she said dryly. "It's bad enough being his wife. Is this part of your courtship? You are truly an inept suitor. Last time we were in a graveyard. This time my husband is snoring a few yards away." She leaned on the balustrade. "Yet, I suppose your very ineptness is a guarantee of sincerity. How did you woo Livia?"

"I didn't woo her. I just asked her to marry me. In that case, there was the advantage that she didn't already have a husband."

"And she accepted with alacrity?"

"I have been in love only twice, Procula. The first woman whom I loved is dead. You are the other. I have no skill with courtship. It would demean us both if I were to start flattering you and dispensing honeyed gifts. I've never behaved in that way."

"That much is obvious. Well, Odysseus, you have courage. To come into the Cyclops' cave and blind him and also try to run away with his wife takes some spirit."

"I'm not Odysseus. I am not Marcellus, either. Marcellus is the name Rome gave me. I was born in Perugia, which Augustus burned to the ground, quenching the fire with the blood of its citizens. In my family we remembered many whom the Romans slaughtered. We spoke Etruscan and worshipped the ancient gods, not those borrowed from Greece and given Latin names. My father's brothers were haruspices who could read the lightning and understand what the thunder said. I saw them buried in great tombs under the hills, whose walls were painted with the monsters of the underworld. I learned the true history of my people and the true nature of Rome. Now they're all gone under the hills. I've lived my life in a kind of twilight. I told you that my gods are dead. I don't even say their names any longer. Only a handful can speak my language now, fewer still can read it. My wife is dead and took with her any hope of a posterity. I can live in the past or I can go forward into the future. With your hand in mine, I will go anywhere you choose."

"What is your real name?"

"Velthur."

"What does it mean?"

"It's a name given to a child one hopes will be a warrior. Procula, I am not going to rehearse the arguments I've already made. I will say only that I love you – and that I will cherish you all my life if you will come to me."

She made no reply. Perhaps I could have tried to take her in my arms and kiss her then; I wasn't a skilled enough seducer to attempt such a manoeuvre with her husband snoring on the couch. I left her there on the terrace and went back to my own room.

Judas of Kerioth came to Pilate early the next morning, just after dawn. I was awake when Rufus the orderly brought me Pilate's summons. I dressed and followed him to the cells, where Pilate was sitting with the informer. Neither seemed in a very good humour; Pilate was bleary from last night's wine and Judas appeared pinched – it was a blustery, chilly morning. Pilate told me curtly to sit. Judas was trembling slightly, perhaps because the cell was so cold, but his dark gaze was steady on my face.

"He says you spoke to the mother of Jesus last night," Pilate said without preamble. "Is it true?"

There was no point in lying. "Yes."

"Why?"

"She sent a message to me."

"What did she want?"

"To declare her son's innocence. And to plead for his life."

He turned, coughed and spat in a corner. "You have no authority in these matters!"

"That's what I told her."

"Did you give her my name?" Judas asked me.

"No. But she seemed to be aware that her son is surrounded by traitors."

The word appeared to infuriate Judas. He rose to his feet. "Who is the traitor?" he demanded fiercely. "Jesus is the one who betrays! It's left to me to repair the damage he's doing!"

"Be seated," Pilate said wearily. He looked unwell. "Did this woman say anything of material significance?"

"She denied that her son claimed to be the Messiah."

"She's not part of his inner circle," Judas said contemptuously, seating himself again. "What does she know? She counts for nothing. A stupid little peasant woman, full of her son's importance. His brothers and sisters are the same, puffing themselves up with his miracles. He cares nothing for them. The ones that matter to him are his cronies from the lakeshore – Peter, Andrew, James and the rest. They're his congregation. He speaks his heart to them, not to anyone else. His mother can have nothing to say of any value." In this speech, he repeated the word nothing with a biting emphasis each time. "He loves those who fawn on him, not those who speak the truth."

"You're in a bitter mood this morning," Pilate said dryly. "Have you had a squabble?"

"He maddens me," Judas muttered. "Last night a woman came to the house. She broke open the costliest of oils for him. He took it as his due. I asked him whether he had considered how that oil had been paid for. He rebuked us all because none of us had thought to spend a year's wages on a bottle of whore's perfume for him!"

"Did I not tell you that this is a frugal accountant?" Pilate said to me laconically. "If we don't crucify his Jesus for insurrection, we may yet crucify him for extravagance."

"It's a kind of madness that has overtaken him," Judas said, speaking half to himself. "He prophesies in riddles and talks as though he sees God before him. It's as though he wants to die. But he's shrewd. He sleeps each night in a different house so he can't be taken by surprise. Do you know how he chooses his lodging? He sends one of his disciples ahead and tells him, 'You will see a house with red flowers,' or 'You will find a young water seller with a jug, follow that person to his house and ask for lodging.' His disciples think it's magic, but it simply ensures that nobody knows where he will stop that night." He smiled at us with no humour, showing even white teeth against his beard. "The yokels who follow him are open mouthed. I think I am the only one among them who truly understands him."

"You're a clever fellow," Pilate agreed indifferently. "But he's a fox. Repeat the tale of the denarius."

"It happened a day or two ago. They constantly try to trap him into disclosing his real thoughts. They asked him directly whether it was lawful to pay taxes to Rome. To have said no would have been insurrection. To have said yes would have offended every Jew in the city. He asked for a denarius to be brought to him. When he had shown that the image on the coin was Caesar's, he declared that it was lawful to give to Caesar that which was Caesar's and to give to God that which was God's. It was a clever answer. But when they heard this, the Zealots were angry with Jesus. Caiaphas dared not act against Jesus while the Zealots were waiting for him to give them a sign. The Zealots look coldly upon the Sadducees for many reasons – because they acquiesce to Roman rule, because they acquiesce to Herod, because they foster inaction and prevent war, because they're rich. But now I believe that the Zealots have withdrawn their protection from him."

"Will the Sadducees act against him?"

"Only if they believe that Rome will protect them against the mob."

Pilate nodded slowly. "The mob, yes. Leave the mob to me. I think you must take your tales to the priests."

"I do not understand."

"I've done with this. Go to Caiaphas and his crew."

"You won't act?" Judas looked astounded.

"I will act in concert with them. Not alone. The man has given too little evidence of sedition. The Passover is upon us and you have not delivered what you said you would deliver. I am tired of you. They must bring a charge against him. I will execute it."

"It would be better if you arrested him!"

Pilate yawned. "On what charge? Allowing a prostitute to rub him with oil? There would be a riot."

Judas was rising to his feet again in agitation. "This will cause grave division among the Jews."

"The problem is a Jewish problem."

"You promised me –"

"I promised you nothing." Pilate's voice was growing harsh. "I won't cause an outrage on the eve of the Passover merely because of your spite."

"Pilate, you said –"

"You insolent bitch's bastard," Pilate growled, "how dare you call me by my name?" His face was stony. Judas, by contrast, had become pale, his lips trembling. "I say it once more – take your tales to the priests. If they don't act swiftly, I'll nail you up – and some of them – instead of Jesus." There was no question in my mind that Pilate meant what he threatened, no matter how tiredly he slumped in his chair. Judas must have had the same impression, for he said not another word, but hurried from the room with trembling lips. Pilate spat again, wiping his mouth. "The wine was sour last night. It gave me a vomit." He gestured at the door. "That fellow was amusing at first, but I grew sick of his snarling and snapping. And as for you – how dare you go to that woman behind my back?"

I wasn't so easily intimidated as Judas of Kerioth. "I wanted to hear what she had to say. According to her, the man is neither a rebel nor an agitator. She says he is a friend to Rome."

"I don't care what he is," he replied tiredly. "I no longer wish to hear his name or think about him. In fact, I don't care if I never see another Jew so long as I live. I wish I could crucify them all."

"You don't understand me, Pilate. This man is an ally."

"An ally? He is turning their temple upside down, and you call him an ally?"

"He tells them to be obedient to Rome."

"You are naïve. I am going back to my bed." He heaved himself to his feet but swayed so much that I took him by the arm and helped him up the stairs. "What were you whispering to my wife on the balcony last night?"

"I was advising her to leave you."

He grunted. "As a rat leaves a sinking ship, eh? She'll never leave me, Marcellus. You may be sure of that."

"Do you believe that she loves you so much?"

"Love!" He was limping heavily. "Love has nothing to do with it. You'll never understand her. Don't expend your energies in that direction, you're wasting your time. A man of your age should be filling his pockets with gold. Forget women. That sickly wife of yours is gone. Count yourself lucky. You might have spent the rest of your life nursing her. Why are you hurrying to put your head in the noose again?"

"I wasn't aware that I was."

"By Hercules, my foot pains me." He leaned on me more heavily. "You think Procula an angel. And me a brute. Despite my warning that marriages are not what they seem. Let me tell you something: there's only one man in the world who wouldn't get sick of seeing her face on his pillow each morning. I am that man. Even if you succeeded in carrying her away, you would be cursing your bargain inside a year." He grinned at me crookedly. "I haven't lied to you yet and I don't lie to you now. We deserve one another, Procula and I. Leave us be."

I shrugged but didn't answer. I thought he was probably still drunk from last night's excesses. His head hung on his chest and by the time I found a centurion to take him off my hands, he seemed asleep on his feet, his face pale and sweaty.

# CHAPTER FIVE

# A BANQUET WITH HEROD

Herod's part of the palace was no more than a few minutes' walk from Pilate's quarters. He received us in a state apartment. As he strode towards us, his arms spread out, I almost did not recognize him. The flowing locks I had seen in the chariot proved to have been a wig, now discarded. His own hair, which was grey, was cut short with a boyish fringe. It was immediately clear he had modelled his appearance on that of the Emperor Augustus, whom I remembered very well from my youth, even down to the white toga with the violet hems which Augustus affected. The gorgeous Herod Antipas for the public eye had been replaced by one with the appearance, at least, of a Roman patrician.

"My dear, dear friends!" He enfolded Pilate warmly, appearing not to notice that Pilate stiffened with distaste under the embrace, and kissed Procula on the cheeks several times. When introduced to me, he clasped both my hands in his, making me aware that he wore a number of very large gold rings. He exuded a powerful scent of roses. "I admire your uncle greatly, my dear boy," he said. His protuberant, dark and melancholy eyes glowed with warmth. "I hope you'll convey my greetings to him on your return. It's a pleasure to meet you. Welcome to Jerusalem!"

I thanked him and complimented him on the arrangement of the palace. The room was sumptuous, the arched roof supported with rows of painted columns and hung with huge lamps which blazed with tapers.

"It's my favourite among all the homes I have, though alas I am here so seldom. But you must meet my consort." He clapped his hands and called, "Come, my beloved!"

Herodias made an entrance that could hardly have been more impressive, appearing at a far door and walking slowly towards us through the length of the hall. Like her husband, she was dressed in white and violet, but her garments were queenly. I lack a tailor's science to explain them, but they were of silk, with flowers embroidered in gold and pearls, far more magnificent than Procula's plain stola. On her head she wore a tall hat like the one Herod had worn in the chariot. Her hair was dark red, perhaps dyed, tied around her head in serpentine coils. She was a breathtakingly beautiful woman, though it can't be said that her face had either much warmth or much vivacity. Her beauty was of the sort that seems like bronze. That Antipas adored her was as clear as day. He positively fawned on her as he made the introductions, caressing her slender brown arms with his beringed fingers.

Her greetings to Pilate and Procula were cool, but on me she bestowed a smile of calculated brilliance, her green eyes meeting mine boldly. "I've seen you in Rome," she said.

"I don't think so," I replied, "I should have remembered."

"Oh, you were pointed out to me," she said, keeping her hand in mine, "but you didn't regard me." Herod beamed over her shoulder at me, from all of which I deduced that they feared they were the subjects of my enquiry as much as Pilate was and were anxious to conciliate me from the start.

This was confirmed when Procula murmured to me, "We have never met her before. This is for your benefit."

"She's very beautiful," I replied.

"Let's take a turn in the garden before we eat," Herod said, "the evening is pleasant." He took Procula's arm and Herodias took mine and so we walked out into the garden in pairs, leaving Pilate to walk in solitude.

The air was temperate, the courtyards of the palace still warm from the day's sun. Several fountains had been set in motion, their rippling music very soothing on the ears. I could feel Herodias's fingernails exploring the muscle of my arm. It was small wonder that Herod had succumbed to her charms. She was his niece and his half-brother's divorced wife, which had outraged Jewish sensibilities. Worse, Herod's former father-in-law, the King of Nabataea, a proud Arab, had been furious when his rejected daughter had arrived back home. He was building up to a war. All in all, Herod's impulsive marriage had been a disaster to his kingdom. I wondered whether the pleasures of marriage had been worth his loss of prestige.

"We miss Italy so much," she said as we walked. "One tires of the desert and longs for civilization. Yet it's so necessary for us to be here. If only one could climb on the back of a phoenix and be whisked away whenever one desired."

"Rome is rather a sad place at present."

"But Capri is not," she said, kneading my arm.

"You've been there?" I said in surprise.

Her mouth curled into a smile that was half proud, half sly. "I have been. I assure you that the Romans would be very surprised to see how their emperor distracts himself."

The lurid tales of Tiberius's life in Capri were just starting to reach our ears at that time. I had been somewhat sceptical of the rumours. "How does he distract himself?"

"It would sully my lips to repeat what my eyes have seen," she said archly. "But believe me when I say that my eyes have never seen anything like it. Nobody's safe from him – neither old women nor young children. And what he can't perform he delights in watching."

"Really?"

"Were it not that I was a Queen, my virtue would scarcely have been safe. He offered me half a million sesterces to go to his bed. He told me if I would bring Salome, he would double the sum to one million sesterces. Imagine. And I refused," she added, as though amazed at her own virtue.

Herod laughed, pricking up his ears. "Are you talking of Tiberius? My dears, you must listen to this. She's been to Capri. He invites beautiful women there, but not, alas, ugly old men like me." We stood in a circle beside a fountain while the Queen held forth, her eyes bright.

"He's surrounded himself with every kind of depraved creature. He cavorts with any number of them at a time, inviting them to perform any act upon his person, however lewd. When his own appetites are exhausted, he commands others to continue their play and lies drinking wine, directing their activities and telling them what he wishes to see."

Pilate was staring at her. Procula's face was blank. But Herod, plainly excited by her words, laughed again. "Tell them about his paintings."

"Every theme from antiquity that's in any way salacious has been painted for him. He has them everywhere and he delights in pointing out the finer details in case you miss them. I daren't even tell you what was painted on the walls of the bedroom I was given. I could hardly sleep at night. And he has a library of the filthiest books, filled with illustrations, which he commands his creatures to enact for him."

Pilate was half incredulous. "Surely this was some festival, kind of Saturnalia?" he growled.

"It put the Saturnalia to shame," she retorted. "He has boys and girls got up as satyrs and shepherdesses who'll drag you into some bower and ravish you, whether you acquiesce or not. Every night there was a performance in which he himself played the main part – or tried to. He's an old man and often has some difficulty in rising to the occasion." She laughed heartily, showing fine, white teeth.

She was a clever woman, though gross in her thought and speech. She would have continued in more detail but Herod finally sensed that her conversation wasn't altogether to our taste. He cleared his throat. "Let's see what the cooks have prepared for us, my friends. It will be humble fare, I'm afraid, just a family meal, but at least it should be wholesome."

Such modest statements always presage dazzling display. On this occasion, the wholesome meal consisted of many dozens of savoury dishes brought in on gold and silver platters by an army of servants. More interesting than the food or the silverware was the arrival of a sixth person at the table, Herodias's daughter Salome. This was the child of her marriage to Boethus, Herod's brother. She was a slim, silent girl almost at marriageable age. She had her mother's glassy green eyes but if she was to inherit her mother's beauty, she hadn't done so yet. Her hair was abundant, reddish and frizzy and she had the face of a hungry vixen. She wore a plain white chiton and no jewellery. It was hard to see in her the dancing girl who had claimed the head of John the Baptist, except in her lithe body and a certain sinuous grace in movement. Herod, however, plainly doted on her, seating her beside him and feeding her constantly with choice tit-bits, so that she did not have to touch the food with her fingers. She said almost nothing through the meal and reclined with her head on her mother's shoulder when she was full.

The banqueting hall was decorated in blue, crimson and gold. It was heated by rows of tripods and was extremely warm, rather too much so for we Romans, but evidently comfortable for Herod and his family. Some of Herod's courtiers were present, too; dressed in magnificent robes, they ate at the far end of the table. They listened to everything, applauding and laughing at the appropriate moments like an appreciative audience.

A group of musicians played for us throughout the feast, producing music of some refinement from harps and lyres. At the centre of the table was a huge golden bowl supported by fawns, a magnificent thing which Herod claimed had been a gift from Cleopatra to his father.

The meal began with a mountain of ducks, geese, pigeons and herons served in a bewildering array of sauces. Herod, perhaps attempting to elevate the tone of the conversation, began talking of his own grandiose projects. Like his father, he was a great builder. He was inordinately proud of the reconstruction of the Great Temple, now approaching an end after many decades. He boasted of the tons of marble that had been quarried and of the immense pains that had been taken to ensure that every detail of the construction was irreproachably correct.

"My soul is that of an architect, dear friends. I'm never happier than when I see my dreams taking shape in stone and mortar. I wish to leave behind me wonders that will be remembered for a thousand years."

His great civil project was the building of a splendid new city, which he had named Tiberias in honour of the emperor, to be the capital of Galilee. It was being built near Emmaus on the shore of the lake, which he was planning to rename the Sea of Tiberias. It was to contain a glittering palace for himself, a stadium and a synagogue second only to the Great Temple. He had, however, hit a few snags.

"My workmen uncovered an ancient cemetery while they were digging the foundations. Nothing more than a few broken skulls. However, this renders the whole city ritually unclean to the tediously orthodox. They have spoken against it and I can't get a Jew in Galilee to settle there."

"What are you going to do?" Procula asked.

"I'm settling it with Gentiles to begin with. The Jews will eventually follow – even if I have to drive them there at the point of a sword. They truly are the most wearisome people on this earth." It was to be noted that he seldom spoke of the Jews as his people, or of himself as a Jew; and one of the dishes served up during the meal was a suckling pig, of which all three partook. It was hard to reconcile his velvety manner with his reputation as a bloody tyrant, but I suppose that he'd never had to cut a throat with his bare hands. His words were enough. Pilate, at least, had been a soldier.

For some time he and Pilate exchanged a series of complaints about the Jews and their maddening obstinacy, the only sign of any real concord between them. Pilate was plainly bored by the monarch and did not have the manners to disguise it. Since the subject of troublesome Jews had been raised, I entered the conversation to mention the name of John the Baptist.

Salome, who had been drowsing quietly, opened her pale eyes and said in a husky but passionate voice, "He was a horrible man."

Her mother, too, roused herself from glazed boredom. "He called me a whore," she said icily.

"Well, darling, he called you an adulteress," Herod said soothingly. "That isn't quite the same thing."

She and her daughter shot him angry green stares. "He was an insolent dog." The prophet's death had evidently not ended the enmity of Herodias and Salome, or the apparent grievance between them and Herod.

Herod spread his hands placatingly. "It's all over, my darlings. Dead and buried."

"Apart from the insult to the Queen," I ventured, "what was his crime?"

Herod smiled at me. "As our companion Pilate will tell you, these provinces are like dry grass. Sparks have to be stamped out at once. We're not speaking of level headed, phlegmatic Romans. We're speaking of religious fanatics who would have all our heads on poles if we gave them half the chance. The man John was gathering multitudes around him and setting himself up as a judge of all that was good and bad in Palestine. It only takes one unwise word from such a one to set the hills ablaze."

"But he hadn't preached rebellion?"

"He was a thorn in Herod's side," Herodias said succinctly. She had been drinking rather a lot, possibly to amuse herself during the conversation between her husband and Pilate. She looked at me with disfavour. "We plucked it out."

"John was a fool," Herod said. "He talked too much. He put on a hair shirt and set himself to wash away sins with dirty river water. He was putting the Almighty himself out of business. He was typical of a sort of troublemaker which abounds in Galilee. You must understand, my dear Marcellus, that the Jews are haters of civilization. Their ingratitude is truly astounding. Look what we have done for them! We've given them glorious cities, a temple to dazzle the eye of God, roads, harbours, mines, wealth beyond their imagining. My father and I between us have brought Judaea more glory than a thousand years of their goat herds and thieves. At last we begin to live in a country worthy of comparison with Greece, with Rome. But do they thank us?" He caressed Salome's wiry red hair. "No. They revile us. Everything we have done is as nothing compared to some tiny oversight in the rabid observance of their thousand and one laws. They plot against our throne constantly. They heap insults on our heads. Every act of kindness is repaid with a thousand treacheries. They called my father a sinner and a madman and they'll doubtless say the same of me when I'm gone. But for now, by the gods and the emperor who have entrusted me with it, I will keep my country peaceful."

I had heard much the same sort of speech daily from the lips of Pilate, but I tried to look duly impressed. "There appears to be another such prophet in your kingdom now."

"Aha. You refer to Jesus of Nazareth."

"I warn you, Herod," Pilate said laconically, "Marcellus has cultivated a soft spot for this Jesus."

Herod smiled at me with heavy lids. "A soft spot? For Jesus? Why?"

"He seems to be a holy man who threatens danger to nobody."

"Holy?" Herodias turned on me furiously. "Who is more holy, the king who builds temples or the beggar who curses him? Do you say that my husband is unholy?"

Herod waved away her anger with a flash of gold rings. "Marcellus did not mean that, my dear. This Jesus is a miracle worker. He raises from the dead and opens the eyes of the blind. Has he healed you of some disease, Marcellus? Leprosy, perhaps?" He chuckled.

"He has not healed me of anything."

"Nor will he. I've made detailed enquiries about Jesus of Nazareth. His name has been dinning in my ears for some years now. The man is completely uneducated but a clever trickster. His so called miracles are nothing but the effects of hysteria on the superstitious. He never heals in the same place twice. He hurries away with his pockets jingling. Why? Because if you were to return on the next day, you would see his cripples limping again, his blind still blundering and his lepers more unclean than ever." He threw his head back and laughed heartily. I saw that several of his teeth had been replaced with gold ones, workmanship that is only performed by our Etruscan dentists for the very rich. "He excites the mob with prayers and incantations, spits in their eyes and calls on all the devils of hell, tells them they're healed, and the credulous fools believe every word."

"That can't be so in every case," I said.

Herod shrugged. "Perhaps a few believe it so much that it seems true. More likely he travels with a troupe of well-rehearsed actors who act out marvellous cures to encourage the others. I know my Galileans, Procula. They're cunning, deceitful and guileful beyond your chaste imaginings. I've known them since boyhood. Jesus of Nazareth is only the latest in a long line of these abracadabra men."

Pilate was watching my face. "His mother came to Marcellus to plead for his life."

Herod's full lips curved downward. "How sad. But perhaps the good lady should have brought up a wiser son."

"Even if he's a trickster, what harm does he do?"

"Oh, incalculable harm. His followers call him the Messiah, sent by God to depose the wicked Herod Antipas and the tyrannical Pontius Pilate. He stirs up the most ferocious aggression against authority. We sense it in the air, do we not, Pilate?"

"Yes."

"Your Jesus may seem like a holy man, but I assure you that he sees himself as King. And the superstitious multitude is quite prepared to believe him. So long as they can overthrow government and evade their taxes, they would follow an ass."

"What will happen to him?" I asked.

"I must behead him, if he's lucky, or Pilate must crucify him if he's not. Since he's had the astonishing impudence to present himself here in Jerusalem, it seems he'll be unlucky."

"Is there no possibility of sparing his life?"

"None whatsoever, my dear Marcellus. To spare his life would be to sacrifice the lives of countless others and to see almost a hundred years of civilization torn down." He reached over and laid his hand on mine, his palm soft and warm. "Please. I understand your compassion and I commend you for it. But consider. Should we leave this man to grow greater and greater? How great will he grow? Should we allow him to attract an army of tens of thousands around himself? And by our inaction proclaim to the world that we're afraid of him? Or should we act now and by a simple piece of surgery remove all danger? Pilate tells me you've seen some warfare. I don't wish to see a war between Rome and the Jews. I'm sure you don't wish it, either."

I tried again. "The execution of John wasn't popular. Might protecting this Jesus not show them your merciful side and draw them back to you? Perhaps he could be exiled. Away from the Jews, he would soon lose his following and be forgotten."

"I have no merciful side and I don't care whether they're with me or against me," he said, smiling. "And exile is for lions, not for foxes. But you, Marcellus, you have touched me. Your concern for this man's life is most noble. I would like to mark your fine sentiments with this gift." He worked a gold seal ring from one of his fingers and pushed it onto the little finger of my left hand, the finger of Mercury. It was a heavy thing, set with a Gorgon's head carved from a carnelian. I stared at it blankly. "Now you'll remember this night forever," he said, smiling. There was a ripple of applause from his gorgeous courtiers.

Herodias leaned forward, her eyes bright with the wine she had drunk. "Who do you think can piss further, a man or a woman?"

"The answer is obvious," Pilate replied.

"Which?"

"A man, of course."

She smiled in triumph. "You're wrong. In Capri, Tiberius put it to the test. I saw it with my own eyes. He asked the man with the longest pipe to piss as far as he could. We measured where it fell on the mosaic. And then a Pompeian whore bent herself over and pissed a full pace further." She burst into laughter and clapped her hands. Salome smiled and nestled up against her mother again.

"Indeed," Pilate said dryly, "it seems women will soon rule the world."

"My dear Pilate, they already do," Herod said. "They have the equipment to rule us and we're only equipped to serve them." He joined his wife's laughter and rose. "Come, let us leave melancholy subjects behind and drink wine."

We left the dining hall to go into a much darker room, lit only at one end by flaring torches. We were seated on huge leather divans, Pilate and Procula at one side of the room, myself at the other. The scent of frankincense coiled through the air.

Herod spoke to his stepdaughter. "Salome, my little lamb, will you oblige Marcellus?"

The child went without argument to a small stage lit by the torches. The female orchestra had been replaced with a male one, two drums, a lyre and a flute. They struck up a fluttering, swift rhythm.

From a distance, Salome changed in some subtle yet powerful way. The childishness vanished from her movements and her face, so vulpine close by, took on the pale beauty of a young goddess. To my astonishment, she slipped the plain white chiton from her shoulders and stood naked before us. The music was a writhing, repetitive melody like those played by the desert nomads. She moved almost imperceptibly at first, then with more power and speed. Her arms uncurled like serpents which flickered and struck and coiled around her head. Her feet spun like leaves in autumn. Her body swayed like a flower nodding on a windblown stem. It was impossible to keep track of the images she made as she flowed like water through the courses of the music. She did not look at us, but rather at her own limbs as they rippled and floated. Herod watched her avidly, oblivious to anything else. Her mother, too, seemed to see nothing but her own daughter. They were holding hands. It was as though all that was between them was embodied for the time being in the twisting white flame of Salome's dance. Across the room, I could see Procula intent on the dance. Pilate, however, yawned and picked his teeth. Herod's ring was heavy on my finger, the carnelian face snarling at me, yet I couldn't take it off without causing deep offence.

Salome's dance was prolonged past the point of amusement. As it came to an end, the girl began to shudder like a prophetess in a trance, her spine arching and her knees parting. It was the only part of the dance which left nothing to the imagination, this pale virgin imitating the abandon of Helen in the arms of Paris.

We applauded at the end of the performance with a sense of relief. The girl put on her chiton with complete naturalness. She gathered an amphora from a small table and brought it to me.

"Drink to me," she said in her husky voice.

I held out my goblet. As she poured it, I caught the tang of her sweat. Her skin gleamed with perspiration. I raised the goblet. "May your daughter one day dance for you as you have danced for us here tonight."

Herod's courtiers applauded politely. I drank. The wine was flavoured with some heavy resin. My head began to swim as soon as I drained the goblet. Salome smiled at me and melted away into the darkness. Her place had been taken by three naked dancing girls, who began to perform for us with tambourines. Their bodies, fuller than the Princess's, gleamed and quivered to the insistent beats.

Herodias slid over on the divan to talk into my ear. "She danced for Tiberius at eight years of age," she said to me.

"She's a remarkable child."

"You say true." Her face, with its chiselled beauty, was so close to mine that I could feel her warm breath on my lips. "The emperor was besotted with her. She might have been Empress of Rome, if things had been a little different."

"Indeed."

"Tiberius was a great general, was he not?"

"The greatest, I believe, since Julius Caesar."

"Is it not strange that he should decline from Mars to Venus?" Her eyes glittered. "I wonder which is truly the greater god."

"We should find out which can piss the furthest." I was becoming very drunk or I wouldn't have said such a thing, but she laughed. I saw Procula's eyes on me from across the room. Herod was holding forth to her and Pilate, his plump hands describing towering palaces in the air. "You're very beautiful, Herodias."

"I inherit my beauty from my grandmother, Mariamne. Her husband, Herod the Great, had her killed but remained so in love with her beauty that he preserved her body in honey."

"You're a strange family."

"You may say so. My mother saw her mother's body in a bath of honey as a child. She said it was though she were preserved in amber. Drink." Herodias filled my goblet from the amphora.

"The wine is bitter," I complained.

"It's flavoured with spices. I'll drink with you. Look at the amphora. It's Greek, three centuries old."

I peered at the amphora in the dim light. It was painted with marvellous delicacy in black on a terracotta ground. I saw a man roped to the mast of a ship and three winged women perched on the rocks above him. "Odysseus and the Sirens," I said.

"He stopped his ears and had himself tied to the mast so he could enjoy their song and yet not be overpowered by it. Was that not hateful?"

"Odysseus was very shrewd."

"A plague on his shrewdness," she said. "He's the most despicable of all Homer's characters. He gave himself to nobody. When he slept with a woman, it was only to further his ambitions. He was always in disguise, hiding his true feelings, pretending to be something he was not. All he wanted was to return home to Ithaca to that equally cold wife of his – and he was no sooner home than he wanted to be off again. He was a deceiver."

She refilled our goblets. Though I was befuddled, I could see she was only pretending to drink. I felt my heart pounding. The music was loud, making my senses whirl. The naked bodies of the dancing girls seemed to blend and separate like oil on water. It was difficult to breathe. "You're a student of the classics."

"Yes. And why not? Homer was a woman, so they say. She painted two sides of the human character, the wily Odysseus who dissembles and survives and the furious Achilles who is himself and dies. How much better to be Achilles than Odysseus! To take the women you want and be done with them, to bathe in the blood of your enemies, to spit in the face of kings. To always be yourself! To die in battle, gloriously, not to slink away from all dangers, alive and yet never living. That is unworthy."

"I don't know if I agree with you," I said breathlessly.

"You must decide whether you're Achilles or Odysseus, my friend." Her lips brushed my ear. "You want that wife of Pilate's. I see it in your eyes. You want her honey, her silky flesh. How will you take her?"

"That's not so."

"Poor Marcellus, creeping through life, haunted by the shade of Livia Agrippina. Are you too afraid of her ghost to tumble Procula on her back? Or is it Pilate you fear? Power is not achieved by those who have tender feelings.

"Procula is not like that."

"You think she's better? I assure you, your Procula could piss as far as that Pompeian whore if she deigned to spread her legs."

I had a fierce thirst. She lifted the jug but I was afraid of what she had put in it and tried to push it away. She was insistent. I watched the dark wine flow into the goblet like blood. "She won't spread them for me."

"Have you asked her?"

"No."

"Ask her. You're the man of the hour. You hold those two in the palm of your hand."

"It would be a gross abuse ," I said thickly, "to take advantage of her in that way."

"Power is to be used," she said contemptuously. "Pilate is a hard nut. Wherever he falls he'll take root and survive. But she – she's a soft fruit. She'll split open and her juice will be wasted. You may as well drink it. She will be sweet." She looked into my face with brilliant green eyes. Her hand was on my thigh. "We must be friends, Marcellus. More is achieved with friendship than with enmity. You understand?" The wine had flowed into my loins and her fingertips found my arousal. I jerked away from her touch. She laughed at me. "My dear Marcellus, you're charmingly old fashioned. I like you very much. And Herod likes you, too. I can see that. Your little speech about Jesus of Nazareth was touching, but folly. Such a one as he can't be left to live. You must never again come to Herod asking him to spare the life of one he has condemned. Between rulers, this is not done. Let that be your first lesson."

I rubbed my aching temples. "I am not a ruler."

"You will be. That will come."

"feel unwell."

"It will pass and then you'll feel like a god." She glanced across the room. "Pilate is yawning. He doesn't care for anything but gold. Herod will leave cities, palaces and temples. That is greatness."

"I think I must get some air."

"I'll take you into the courtyard."

I tried to rise to my feet but my legs gave way. I felt myself falling, bringing down tables and ornaments. There was no shock as I hit the ground. I lay there stupidly, feeling a distant embarrassment. Arms pulled me upright but my legs wouldn't support me and I staggered. The couriers were all around me, holding me upright. Bearded, Levantine faces sneered at me.

I heard Pilate laugh sardonically. "It seems our honourable Marcellus has drunk more than he can hold."

"I don't know what's wrong with me," I muttered. "Excuse me."

"He's unwell," Procula said.

"He's drunk."

"Either way we must take him home."

"Nonsense." Herod's warm fingers massaged the back of my neck. "The night is young. He needs to lie down a little and let his blood settle. He will soon be himself again. Herodias will take care of him."

In a confusion of voices and music, I felt myself guided by other hands, steered out of the room. Faces drifted past me. In some other place, gasping for air, I lay back on a couch. The ceiling above me was painted with winged creatures. They seemed to whirl and flutter with the distant music.

A cool hand touched my brow. "I'm so thirsty," I whispered.

Something wet caressed my lips tantalizingly. One of the courtiers was holding a cup to my lips. I saw a bearded face with full red lips enhanced with rouge, smiling at me. I drank the bitter stuff. I heard the voice of Herodias. "You have taken your decision about Pilate already, I think? Is he to be arraigned?"

"That's for the emperor to decide."

"But he will consult you. And what have you decided?"

I thought I saw Pilate's face, hovering in the dark. "Hush! He's standing there!"

"You are dreaming. Will he be arraigned?"

Pilate's face had vanished. I lay back, confused and weary of the questions. "Yes, I believe so."

"And who will follow Pilate as Prefect of Judaea?"

"There are many good men in Rome. I can't say."

"You, perhaps?"

"It's not impossible." The drug had loosened my tongue and I regretted the words too late.

Her face hovered over me. "Do you wish it? Yes, I see that you do. You must shed a few scruples in order to attain power.

I felt myself sinking deeper and deeper into the power of whatever it was she had given me to drink. "Too much blood is spilled." My tongue felt dead in my mouth. "Jesus is holy."

"What if he is? What does holiness achieve, Marcellus? Do you think the temple was built with holiness? It was built by sinners. Holiness is worth nothing. And in the end it spills more blood than wickedness. To govern well it's necessary to be brutal. I think you could be brutal if you wished to. You would soon learn." Her fingertips massaged my temples.

I was seeing two of everything now. My eyes wouldn't focus together. Each seemed to see a separate vision. I closed my eyes, feeling deathly sick. "What did you give me to drink?"

"Only wine," she cooed. I felt her mop my brow. "I've heard Tiberius speak of Caligula. He took a viper to his bosom, there. The boy is poisonous."

"I doubt he will live long."

They were among the last words I remember speaking. For some time thereafter I was aware of her asking me about Vitellius, Tiberius and the Senate; but her voice faded in and out of a roaring in my ears. She asked me questions but I couldn't answer – or if I did so, I've forgotten what I said. I think the power of speech had been extinguished in me.

And then I remember only fragments. I see Pilate looking at me with contempt and hear his voice saying that I am drunk. I try to deny it but my head lolls.

I see the moon, swimming in the sky with shoals of stars.

I am in my room in the Praetorium. Rufus, the young orderly, is sponging my face. "Are they still flogging that man?" I ask. I can hear the thrash of the flagellum. Perhaps it's the thrash of my own heart.

Procula holds my head as I vomit into the basin. There's nothing but bile in my stomach. "They gave you mandragora," she says. "There's a cure, but you must keep it down. Try not to vomit."

The drink is bitter, astringent. I swallow but vomit it up again immediately. This time the vomit is crimson, strung with clots. Procula cries out. "We will have to wait a while," the doctor says. "We will try again in a little while."

"By then it may be too late," she says.

"The vomiting will kill him. You see how much blood there is. Wait a while."

I walk in darkness, under the hills. I recognize the place; this is the tomb of my ancestors. They lie on their sarcophagi, each husband with his wife, feasting and drinking. They greet me by my boyhood name in the ancient language.

"Where have you been?" my uncle asks me.

"Into the future," I answer.

"And what did you see there?"

"The death of our gods."

"Gods must die as men do," they reply, raising their goblets to me merrily. "Join us!" Green and yellow monsters coil around the sarcophagi, their shapes changing constantly.

"The plan," I say, "is to mingle all the gods into one and then to crucify him. I have the nails here in my hand."

"Please, Marcellus," Procula whimpers, "you're hurting me."

The psychopomp is with me now. Her breasts are bare. She carries her torch to light the way through the darkness. At her waist is the key to the gates of the underworld. Her wings are furled. She's young and beautiful. She shows me the scroll on which the deeds of my life are written; half the page is empty. I am not ready to go. Terror seizes me. "I am not ready!"

"We must wait again," the doctor says. "Let him sleep."

When I awaken, Jesus is sitting by my bedside. I recognize him by his sunlit smile, that Jewish smile which breaks from bearded faces, filled with as much sorrow as happiness.

"I have come for the nails." He holds up a coin for me to see. It is not Yahweh money, but an accursed Roman coin, with the head of a man upon it. I look closely. The head is my own, my name is written underneath it. I take the coin and give him the iron nails. He rises and looks down at me. "I will leave cities, palaces, temples," he says. "That is greatness."

"Remember your mother," I whisper to him.

"Try once more," Procula says. "Hold it down, Marcellus. Please, I beg of you."

The bowl is at my lips again. I drink and try to obey her. My stomach heaves and kicks like a goat in a sack. I struggle to subdue the sharp hooves that want to tear me open. Procula's hand clamps over my mouth. "No!" She commands me fiercely. "Keep it down!"

My throat burns with the acid of the vomit. It spurts from my nose, pours into my lungs. Procula's fingers bite into my cheeks, my lips are crushed against my teeth. "Keep it down!" she screams at me. I am drowning, burning, I try to obey. The acid burns the lining of my nose and gullet. I feel that this is death. I grow weak. I cling to her. A thin trickle of air winds its way through my clogged nostrils, bubbling and spluttering. Perhaps it is a rebirth.

Darkness.

Even when I received my wound in Germany and lay with fever for a month I was not so sick as that. I passed two nights in extreme terror, as if a lion were in my room, though there was nothing there. The visions faded into dreams and slowly left me. But the terror remained. My life had changed forever. I had passed a certain line which I don't know how to define, except to say that when I passed it, certain things vanished from me while other things grew in their place. A certain arrogance or self-confidence, a sureness of my own strength and moral rectitude, were stripped from me. I became detached from my own concerns. At the same time I acquired a kind of compassion which I had only pretended before. I learned humility.

It took me many months to understand how I had changed and to accept that I was different. At the time, I knew only that I was close to death. My body was poisoned, my limbs so weak that I could barely lift my head to drink. My mind had received an injury, as an organ will, and it was scarred. The orderly, Rufus, tended to me. He'd seen action and he knew how to manage a sick man.

I slept most of the time. I woke once to find Pilate looking down at me. "I never eat pork in this country," he said laconically. "It's deadly. That's why the Jews avoid it."

"You were there."

"You are mistaken."

I wasn't sure whether he was a vision or not. At another time I heard Procula's voice speaking close to me.

"They gave you mandragora in the wine. They wanted to loosen your tongue but the dose was too strong. I think they mixed it with amanita to make the effect more potent. They alone know what they have done. They're in a state of considerable anxiety about you. They send messengers every hour to enquire about your health.

They fear that if you die, Tiberius will depose them. The drug is a root which is sometimes found in the fields here. The antidote is root of moly, which the doctor gave to you. I thought you were going to die, Marcellus."

I couldn't open my eyes. "That would have suited many people," I replied.

"It wouldn't have suited me. You're my only friend."

A day or so later, when I was feeling stronger, I tried to thank her for what she had done. "Without you, I would have died."

"I did very little."

"It was enough."

She smiled wearily. Before she could reply, Pilate entered my bedchamber.

"You are here, Procula. How is it that I can never find you when I need you?"

"Forgive me. I came to bring Marcellus his medicine."

He looked from his wife to me, his eyes stony. "Always with your heads together. I think it is best that you two become strangers to each other."

Procula's face paled. "What accusation are you making?"

"I am making no accusation. I say that you should not be together day and night. It takes little for tongues to begin wagging."

"It was you who insisted we be together all the time," she retorted. "I never wished it."

"You appear to wish it now," he said grimly. "He has taught you to oppose me. You walk with him in public and laugh at his jests. You sit close by him and look into his face as he talks, and allow him to look into your face. When he contradicts me, you agree with him, not with me. Now you sit by his bedside and stroke his face with your fingers. While I suffer, you go to bring him his medicine. I think you forget who your husband is."

"I don't forget who my husband is," she said quietly.

He appeared to be angered even further by her denial. "Have you made an alliance with him? Has he set his sights on my wife as well as my position?"

"This is unworthy of you, Pilate," I said.

"Since you came to Jerusalem, Marcellus, you've put yourself between me and many things of importance to me. I've had little rest since you arrived and little pleasure in my life. I long for your departure. Until then, oblige me by not coming between me and my wife." He took her by the arm, his fingers biting into her flesh, and pulled her away. She did not look back at me.

The invisible lion remained in my room. The fear that it produced stayed with me for years. Even now that I am an old man, it has not quite left me. Perhaps the fear was always inside me and the poison of Herodias simply released it from its cell so that it could roam unfettered through the chambers of my mind. I do not know.

# CHAPTER SIX

# JESUS

Procula woke me before dawn. I had slept poorly, my dreams vivid and painful. Her voice reached me through an echoing tunnel of other voices, some belonging to people who had been dead for decades.

"Marcellus, Jesus has been taken."

I struggled to reach wakefulness. "By whom?"

The room was lit only by the lamp she had brought. She held a cup of water to my lips and I drank. "There was a struggle last night on the Mount of Olives between the Galileans and the temple guards. Some men have been hurt. They took Jesus before the Sanhedrin last night. They have accused him of sedition and sent him to Pilate for judgment."

"Where is he?"

"He's here in the Praetorium, under arrest."

"I'm coming."

She helped me to sit up. "I'm sorry. I know you're not ready."

"Help me dress."

I had been naked; she helped me put on my clothes. I could do almost nothing for myself. I could hardly lift my arms. She had to buckle on my sword for me since it was too heavy for me to lift. "Has anyone been killed?" I asked.

"I don't know."

"Has Pilate seen him?"

"He's still asleep. He was drunk last night again. He won't wake until it's light."

I peered at the window. There was no sign of dawn in the night sky. "There's a calendar in that case. Please give it to me."

She obeyed me. "What are you doing?"

"I am looking to see if today is proscribed." I peered at the scroll. "It's not. A trial can be held today. They'll try to crucify him. I'll need help, Procula. Can you find Rufus?"

"I've already sent for him."

We made our way through the silent halls of the palace, encountering only yawning legionaries at that hour before the night watch was changed. My legs were so weak that I was forced to stop and rest every few paces. Procula did her best to support me.

They were holding Jesus in the charge office, a small room with a desk. The scribe who recorded the charges had not yet arrived; his place was vacant. Jesus sat on the floor at the feet of three legionaries, his bound hands resting on his knees. His chin was on his chest. He did not look up and I couldn't see his face but there were splashes of blood on his linen coat. Nobody was paying any attention to him. Two of the Sadducees were present, wearing the robes and headdresses of the temple council, keeping apart from the others.

"Can you detain Pilate as long as you can?" I asked Procula at the door. She nodded and left. They all turned to me as I came in.

"Are you the accusers?" I asked the councillors.

The younger of the two, a man with a full beard and flashing eyes, looked me up and down with contempt. "Who are you?" I had no ready answer. I hadn't shaved during my illness and I suppose I must have looked like a madman or a drunkard. Luckily, the man's companion whispered in his ear and he became more conciliatory. "We have brought a criminal to Pilate, my lord," he said.

"What do you accuse him of?"

"Insurrection against the Roman authority."

My legs were about to give way. I sat carefully on a bench. "Insurrection carries the death penalty." When they did not answer, I asked, "You're aware of that?"

"Yes," the younger councillor said.

I nodded. "What proof do you bring?"

"That is for Pilate."

"I am this man's legal counsel. You may show it to me."

The Sadducee hesitated. He was puzzled by me. "There's nothing to see. He's accused by the Sanhedrin. The High Priest will appear before Pilate to give evidence."

The wind was swirling through the hall, bringing scurrying eddies of dust and leaves. I looked out through the portico. There was now a sullen streak of grey in the sky. The weather had been tumultuous and a storm was threatened for today. "You arrested this man at night. The council met at night to try him. Now you bring him to Pilate before dawn. Why has everything been done in darkness?"

The older man spoke up. "Lord, this man is followed by a dangerous rabble. They wounded some of us last night. He should be dealt with before his followers are aware of it, or there will be a riot."

"By dealing with him, you mean crucifixion?"

"Yes," they both said at once.

Rufus had arrived. I motioned to him to help me rise. "I wish to speak to the prisoner alone. Bring him to the adjoining room."

"Do not speak to the man," the older councillor said, raising his hand in warning. "There is nothing to be gained by letting him open his mouth. He has the tongue of a serpent."

"I know that already. Bring him through." Supporting myself on Rufus's shoulder, I went to the next room. It was the courtroom used for trials, with a handsome mosaic floor, rows of benches and a throne for Pilate, elaborately carved and bearing the insignia of the Republic, SPQR. I sat in it to wait for Jesus to be brought to me.

A soldier pushed him in. He had been beaten. His face was cut and his clothes were blood-stained and torn. He appeared exhausted. Nevertheless he smiled at me wearily.

"Do you remember who I am?" I asked him.

"I can see that you already sit in the seat of judgment."

"It's not my seat."

"It will be yours."

"Well, the man it belongs to now to will seek your death today."

"He will be remembered for it."

"Please don't prophesy in court," I said. "I must find a way to save you. Your only hope lies in asserting your innocence clearly and unequivocally."

"They have already decided my guilt."

I looked at his escort. "Soldier, cut his bonds."

"I don't think that's a good idea, sir," the soldier said hesitantly. "He's in custody." Nevertheless at my command he produced a dagger and sawed through the cords. Jesus rubbed his swollen hands slowly, looking around the courtroom. He was smiling. I had seen that smile in my dreams, holding as much sorrow as happiness. He had a great deal of natural authority. His face wasn't easy to forget. It wasn't remarkable, as was the face of, say, Caligula or Nero. But their faces were remarkable for the wickedness in them. His face struck one as holding only goodness.

"Tell me what happened last night," I asked him.

"A mountain of words was built."

"Did you try to defend yourself?"

"Against what they accuse me of? No. Their accusations are true."

My heart plummeted. "You confessed?"

"I confessed to loving God and to teaching others to love him."

"The charge is one of sedition against Rome."

His eyes settled on me again. "Do you think that Rome is different from Jerusalem? That Herod is different from Tiberius, or that Caiaphas is different from Pilate? To preach against one is to preach against all."

"Then you're a rebel, as they say you are."

He nodded. "I am a rebel in all things. I rebel against myself. My flesh rebels against my spirit and my heart against my head."

"What you will be asked here today is whether you taught your followers to take up arms against authority. Did you?"

"I teach them that there is no authority but God."

I did not disguise my frustration. "With every step I take forward, you push me back two!"

"Then stand still."

I tried again. "Did you tell your followers that they should not pay taxes to Rome?"

"No."

"Thank God for a clear answer. Did you tell your followers that they should take up arms against Rome?"

"No."

"Then you did not preach sedition."

"I did."

I grew angry with him. "You seem unafraid of the cross. It may be nothing to you to die, but there are those who love you. You could choose to live, if it pleased you."

"I do not have that choice."

I tried to restrain my temper. "I spoke with your mother." He closed his eyes but made no response. "She wept for you and begged me to help you. I promised that I would try."

"Her tears have nothing to do with you or me."

"The Messiah is self-born, is that what you mean? He owes nothing to mother, father or brothers? When you're on the cross you may regret this arrogance!"

"I thank you for your kindness to my mother," he said, opening his eyes again, "but she's nothing to you or to me."

"I've spoken about you to Herod. He says that you're a common trickster and that you follow in the steps of John the Baptist."

His gaze lost its focus for a moment. He seemed to be looking into himself, into some profound memory. "John was great," he replied.

"I believe you. But perhaps to say so, when John has been executed for his greatness, is not politic at this moment. I can see you were ill-treated last night. Did they question you with torture?"

"They struck me and spat on me."

"Did they compel you to say anything against your will?"

"No. I spoke freely."

"May I recommend that you speak less freely today?"

He smiled slightly. "I will not unsay what I have said."

"Can you remember what you did say last night? They will bring your words as evidence against you today and I would like to be prepared."

"Last night?" he repeated. "Last night and the day before that and the days and nights before that I have said the same things. I have said them in the open, in the synagogue and under the sky. I am not here because of what I said last night or last week. I am not here for anything I have done. I am here for what I am."

"You say that you are the Messiah?"

"I am the word of God."

I stared at him. He was no wild eyed fanatic, proclaiming his own greatness. He spoke with humility but with unassailable conviction. He was right: I understood him very little at that time. Over the course of that day, and over the years since then, I have understood him a little more. The world has changed in these years and it has changed partly because of him.

It was to be a strange trial, full of interruptions. At the time of which I am writing, the law was poorly defined where non-Romans were concerned. We judged non Romans by a different set of laws, which we called *jus gentium*, the law of other people. We are learning to understand that the law of other people is the most important law of all, enshrining as it does the most fundamental of human principles, those which distinguish us from the beasts.

The palace was waking up. Shouted commands and the sound of marching boots echoed through the halls as the guard was changed.

"I will do what I can for you," I said to Jesus. "If you cannot assist me then at least try not to hinder me."

"I have done with helping and hindering. I have said what I have said. The rest belongs to God." The guard took him back to the charge office. By now my nausea was strong on me. I staggered outside into Pilate's garden and vomited the usual watery slime.

Procula came to help me. "Is there any hope?" she asked me.

I leaned against a tree, shuddering. "I've had more auspicious pre-trial meetings with clients. He seems to want to be crucified. Are any of his followers here?"

"There's a little group outside."

"Perhaps some of them will speak for him."

"Pilate is in a foul mood. He's cursing everyone and everything."

"Perfect." In this court, Pilate himself filled all the roles – he was prosecutor, praetor, magistrate and imperial administrator. The possibility of persuading him against a guilty verdict and a swift execution was vanishingly slight. The sky was very dark. Wind was shaking unripe fruit off the apricot trees. The eels, either asleep or chilled, were not stirring in the pond. My mind was empty. I couldn't think of a single strategy to defect Pilate. Rufus picked up some of the green fruit, gnawing it absently while he watched me.

"The Governor's used to having things his own way," he said, "if you know what I mean. He's not used to opposition."

"I'm aware of that."

"They'll have that Jew nailed up in no time like hundreds before him. What's so special about him?"

"I don't know." I put my head in my hands.

"I mean, what does one more or less matter?"

"A line has to be drawn somewhere."

Over my illness we had become friends of a sort. He regarded me as an amusing curiosity and I had come to rely on his earthy solidity. He spat out the sour shreds of fruit, grinning at me. "Hope you'll collect your fee in advance, is all I'm saying."

I sat thinking fragmented thoughts, almost asleep from time to time, aroused now and then by a spattering of rain. The scribe arrived and began smoothing out his wax tablets. Jesus and the others filed into the courtroom to await the trial. Pilate came half an hour later with a face like thunder and limping heavily. He was wearing the purple edged magistrate's robe. I met him outside the courtroom.

"Have you injured yourself?" I asked him.

"Gout," he said tersely. "A word with you, Marcellus."

We went to a corner. My weakness made me lean against one wall while his inflamed foot made him lean against the other. "I told you this day would come," he said without preamble. "I understand that you favour this fellow, but there's no hope for him. If you're unable to control your feelings, I advise you not to be present."

"I stood by and said nothing while I watched you crucify innocent boys," I replied. "Today I will be at least the semblance of a lawyer."

His hard little eyes bored into mine. "Don't cross me, Marcellus. You'll regret it."

"This man isn't guilty of the charge."

"Your stupidity is quite divine," he said bitterly. "You still understand nothing, no matter how many times you're told. Your Jesus has sought out his own fate. They tell me you've already spoken to him?"

"Yes."

"And has he asked you to defend him?"

"No," I admitted.

"Then go back to bed. I'll crucify this man whether you oppose me or not."

He limped off to speak to his staff. I made my way to the courtroom. The scene had changed dramatically. The chamber was a blaze of coloured silks. There were now at least thirty of the temple councillors present, all in their robes of office. I realized that something like half of the Sanhedrin had come. Only the very old had stayed away. Others were present, too, including some of Herod's attendants, also in court clothes. I recognized the man who had held the cup of mandragora to my lips. He smiled at me slyly before turning his back on me. They were talking in groups, some gesticulating and appearing agitated, others murmuring quietly amongst themselves.

Attendants were bringing in additional stools and benches to accommodate the crowd. I could hear the crash of armour outside. Looking through the portico, I saw the courtyard filling with soldiers, their lances gleaming in the stormy light. Pilate had summoned what appeared to be an entire cohort of some three hundred men. He was evidently taking the occasion seriously. The legionaries formed ranks under the bawling of their officers and stood stolidly in squares. The presence of the soldiers raised the tension considerably; a shudder seemed to run through the courtroom.

"There's a mob of Jesus' followers gathering outside," Rufus murmured in my ear. "We might see some fun and games before the day's out." I listened. I could hear the noise of a massing crowd from beyond the walls. I felt my stomach sink.

I glanced at Jesus. The accused man himself was ignored in all this hubbub. He sat quietly on a bench with his eyes closed. His wrists had been bound again. Nobody addressed him or even looked at him. He seemed unaware that he had turned Jerusalem upside down. I took my seat. He made no sign he noticed my presence.

There was a short trumpet blast and Pilate came in. We all rose. He hobbled to his throne and sat. He was attended by three lictors carrying rods and axes. His scribe settled down next to him with a wax tablet at the ready. Pilate gestured laconically at the court to be seated. There was a rustle of silks and a scraping of stools. There were now about one hundred persons in the courtroom and a group of several dozen in the adjoining office, crowded at the doorway.

"This hearing will be conducted in Greek so that all may understand," Pilate said in that language. "I, Pontius Pilate, Prefect of Judaea, will judge. Who accuses?"

One of the Sadducees, with a full, rich, red beard rose to his feet. "The High Priest Joseph Caiaphas accuses Jesus son of Joseph, also called Jesus of Nazareth, of sedition against the authority of Rome."

Pilate looked up irritably. As usual, he was unshaven, his cheeks pale beneath the stubble. He had put on his bronze crown. "Where is Caiaphas?"

"He's detained at the temple, Excellency. Today is an important feast for us. He will come later."

I rose. "There cannot be an accusation in absentia. If this man's accuser is not in court, he must be declared innocent and set free."

There was an uproar. The man with the red beard shouted above the noise, "I will send for Caiaphas immediately." Some men ran out of the courtroom.

Pilate held up his hand for silence. "The next person who raises his voice in this courtroom will be taken out and thrashed by the lictors in front of the cohort." In the stillness that followed, we could all hear the noise of Jesus' followers outside the walls. "Sit down, Marcellus. We will hear the circumstances of the case while we wait for Caiaphas. Proceed."

The red bearded man rose. "My name is Eleazar, son of Simon the Scribe. There are so many accusations against the man that it's hard to know where to begin, Excellency."

"Begin somewhere," Pilate advised dryly.

Eleazar cleared his throat. "Jesus of Nazareth, not being a priest, but calling himself a teacher and a prophet, came to the temple with violence. He and his followers produced a disturbance, overthrowing the tables of the merchants and accusing the priests of many crimes. He made himself a place in the temple portico and there preached sedition to all who would listen."

"What weapons did he carry?" I asked.

The man consulted with some of the others and turned back to me after a moment. "He had no weapon. But a man may be violent without weapons."

"That's true. But the temple is protected by an army of guards, yet Jesus was allowed to do as he pleased and say what he pleased until yesterday. Why was that?"

"He has many followers," an older man said. "We didn't want a riot in the temple."

"What did his seditious preaching consist in?"

"I would prefer that the High Priest answer the question himself," the man answered. The shouting of the crowd outside the walls was now growing louder, penetrating the courtroom. Eleazar gestured. "You hear them? This is the mob which follows him. This is why we arrested him in the night." They were beginning to chant his name with a single voice.

Pilate roused himself. "The court is adjourned until I restore order."

The courtroom broke up in some confusion. The lictors made a way for Pilate, thrusting people aside with their staffs. He turned and beckoned to me. I followed him into the corridor. We heard orders being shouted outside. The cohort crashed into movement, following their officers out through the gate to deal with the crowd. Procula had still not returned and I felt a flutter of panic in my belly.

"This is a squabble among Jews," I said to Pilate when we were in a quiet place. "It has nothing to do with Rome."

"I wish I could crucify them all," he said gloomily. Someone had brought him a cup of wine and some bread. He ate and drank greedily.

"That won't improve your gout," I said.

"It improves my temper." He gulped more wine, then offered me the cup. I hadn't drunk wine since the night with Herod, but I took the cup from him and drank, hoping it would take away some of my weakness. Sodden pieces of the bread he had dipped into it passed over my tongue and I had to fight down nausea. "What does this man mean to you?" he demanded, watching me drink. "Why do you waste your energy on him?"

"He's innocent."

"Innocence and guilt are legal concepts which have little relevance to the political world, Marcellus. I never concern myself with such things. To me, the execution of a man is necessary or unnecessary because of the result it produces on the province. In itself, it's nothing."

"To rule through fear is tyranny."

"The Republic is dead and gone. Tyranny is the order of the day. The sooner you understand that, the better for you." He took the cup back from me and drained it. "These priests have brought this man here for me to crucify. They all want him dead. If I let him live, they will be furious with me. More important, they will think me weak."

"What about those who support him?"

We could hear shouts and screams from outside as the soldiers dispersed the crowd. The sound of running feet and the baying of the mastiffs reached us. "So much for his supporters," Pilate replied. "They're a rabble. As soon as he's dead, they will evaporate. The priests, on the other hand, are here to stay. I summoned you because Herod is here. He doesn't want to appear before the multitude but he wishes to see you – and Jesus. I've asked him to wait in the dining room. Take Jesus to him."

"Very well."

"He's a windbag. Don't let him take too long, Marcellus. Let's not spend the entire day on this. It is not worth our time."

He turned on his heel and departed. The wine was making my stomach churn. I made my way through the crowd, feeling dizzy. When I told Jesus that Herod wished to see him, he merely nodded. Accompanied by Rufus and two guards, we went upstairs. The door of the dining room was opened by the courtier with the beard and the full red lips. He bowed mockingly as he ushered us in.

Herod was wigless and wearing a toga. I doubt whether anyone would have recognized him as the king. He was inspecting the statue of Cybele closely as we entered the chamber. Someone had lifted her veil so he could see better. He straightened. "Pagan religions have their charm," he said. "It's pleasant to be able to make statues of one's gods. This little example is rather well done. I have a weakness for magna mater." He turned to us. "My dear Marcellus! I am glad to see you out of danger." He would have embraced me but I evaded him by sitting down.

"Forgive me," I said. "My legs are rather weak."

"And to think my humble kitchen is to blame. I've had the cooks scourged, if that makes you feel any better. And this is the famous Jesus of Nazareth?" He turned to Jesus. He wore an air of indifference but his eyes gleamed. "I am glad to meet you at last. Your name is on everyone's lips."

Jesus made no reply. He watched Herod with languid eyes, as though at a play which bored him slightly.

"I'm sorry to drag you away from your important affairs," Herod went on, "but time is getting short and I fear that if we don't make one another's acquaintance soon, we may never do so. One has to seize the opportunity, as Horace says: *carpe diem quam minimum credula postero.* Seize today and have no trust in tomorrow. We have some similar sayings in our scriptures, have we not?"

When Jesus again made no reply, the bearded courtier struck him across the mouth. It was not a heavy blow, but pulled myself to my feet. "No one shall touch him again. Send your creatures away, Herod."

Herod made a gesture and his minions went to the other end of the room, where they stood whispering and sniggering. He walked around Jesus, inspecting him closely. "You say very little, for a prophet. I've met other prophets in the course of a long life and one simply couldn't stop them from talking. I knew your friend John, of course. Our acquaintance was brief but illuminating. He was less cautious than you, but more amusing, it has to be said. He described you as a clever young man. I've heard the same thing said by others. They report miracles of you, dazzling deeds of magic. You walk on the water, fly through the air, raise the dead from their tombs. It must be pleasant to have such powers. Would you favour your king with a little demonstration? Anything will do, however slight. You might, for example, cure the distressing squint of my fellow Matthias over there." Jesus did not respond. Herod turned to me. "He's your protégé, Marcellus. Why don't you ask him for some display of his powers?"

"I'm not as anxious as you to see them."

"Really? All my life I have longed to see a miracle. I've seen many strange things, but never a miracle. Will you not oblige me, Jesus son of Joseph?" Meeting with silence, he went on, "Let me make a pact with you, my young friend. If you can show me anything remarkable, anything at all, I'll go to Pilate now and tell him you're my subject and must be returned safely to Galilee. You'll be saved from the cross. What do you say?"

There was no reply. I said, "This is empty mockery, Herod."

"Is it? Pray, who is mocking whom? If you can't perform a miracle for me, then let us hear you prophesy. I am waiting." His courtiers chuckled in the silence. He turned to me with a shrug. "I told you, Marcellus. The wonderful being of fable, when examined in the light of day, turns out to be a quite unremarkable man who sweats and bleeds and stinks as other men do. What do you hope to gain by defending him?"

"I believe his power lies more in his thought and his principles than in any deeds he's committed. I don't believe he should be sacrificed to please the High Priest."

"Ah, yes. Caiaphas is not very happy with him. He's taken a place in the Royal Portico, where the sages sit. But what has he to do with the temple, except to offer a sacrifice and creep back to his village in Galilee?" He rounded on Jesus. "I have built cities and pagan temples for the Romans and the other Gentiles, but nothing so magnificent as this. They tell me you call the temple your father's house. You are wrong. The temple is my father's house. The temple was born in my father's mind. It was built by my father and by me. The priests laid the stones and fitted the wood with their own hands. A thousand slaves quarried the marble and brought the trees from Lebanon. Fifty years have passed in labour, my whole life. Does that seem nothing to you? Who are you to come, a dusty and ignorant carpenter from Galilee, and forbid this and forbid that? I tell you that a thousand years will pass, and you will be forgotten dust, and men will marvel at my temple."

"Did you build a temple," Jesus said quietly, "or did you build a marketplace?"

"You are insolent," Herod said, his cheeks flushing.

"You are insolent to say the temple is your toy." At last there was fire in his eyes. "The temple was born in the mind of David, a true king of the Jews and built by Solomon, his son, to serve all nations. It is the house of God. It belongs to him alone. Not to you, or to your father, or to the priests who laid the stones. What your father put on the Temple Mount is a marketplace where some may get rich from the piety of others, a slaughterhouse where innocent blood never ceases to flow, a portico of fools where empty words are traded for honour."

My heart sank as his voice rose, yet I stared at him like one fascinated. I can remember his face now as though it hangs before me in the air. His voice was that of an orator, not merely loud, but carrying, with a capacity to pierce space and reach the heart,

"Be moderate in your speech," I urged him quietly.

"He has asked me to prophesy, so I will prophesy. The temple will not stand, Herod. It will be pulled down, stone by stone, by those whom you now flatter and upon whom you now fawn. They have raised you and they will humble you, and all that you have raised will be humbled. And nothing will be left but bones."

Herod, too, was watching him intently. The flush had faded from his cheeks. I had expected him to be furious. When Jesus fell silent, however, he replied in a calm voice, "You have prophesied and I have heard." He looked him up and down. "He can't go to trial in this state. Matthias, give him your robe."

Looking aggrieved, but not daring to argue, one of the courtiers came forward. He took off his costly robe, which was embroidered with purple to show that he was one of the king's attendants. The soldiers pulled off the blood-stained garment which Jesus had been wearing and pulled the robe over his lean shoulders. Herod adjusted the fit of the garment with his own hands. "We won't see each other again," he said. He turned to me. "You may take him back."

We left the half-naked Matthias holding Jesus' stained robe at arm's length, the King sadly inspecting magna mater. As we walked down the stairs, I tried to advise Jesus against any repetition of such dire terms in the court, but it was very noisy and I doubt whether he was even listening to me. The High Priest had arrived at last and the court officials were reconvening the trial with trumpet blasts.

We entered the courtroom to find it more crowded than ever. Caiaphas had brought part of his personal bodyguard to swell the numbers of the temple contingent. He himself was an enormous man in his fifties, tall and very stout, made even more imposing by his blue robes and the towering pillar hat he wore. His grey beard rolled down his chest in ringlets. He had a deep, stentorian voice which he was using to good effect, berating some of his officials for some oversight; and when he saw Jesus enter the courtroom, he raised it even more.

"Behold, here is the accursed man," he boomed. He lifted his arms over his head. "And see, he wears the robes of a king! The desire of the righteous is only good, but the expectation of the wicked is wrath!"

Everyone turned to stare at Jesus in surprise. "Who has given him these clothes?" Eleazar demanded of me.

"Herod."

For a moment he looked astounded. "He has surely done it as a jest."

"He has done it as a jest," Caiaphas bellowed, "since this man says he is the Lord's anointed." There was an outburst of laughter as we took our places. They pointed at Jesus in mockery and slapped each other on the back. It was astonishing how he appeared indifferent to anything that was said to him, good or bad. He was able to exist within himself as though in the silence of a wilderness. Abandoned by his disciples and alone among enemies, he appeared calm and self-possessed. Of those who later squabbled to assume the mantle of his authority and fought to divide his power between them, none were present on that day to stand by him; yet he showed no fear.

Pilate entered and silence fell. He glanced at Jesus but made no comment on his clothing. "I see Caiaphas is present," he said shortly. "May we have the accusation?"

Caiaphas stepped forward, an imposing figure in his robes. "I am ready to swear an oath against this man."

Pilate brightened. "Excellent. In that case we can proceed to a judgment immediately."

"Wait." I rose to my feet. "In capital cases, the swearing of an oath alone will not prove guilt."

"Ask Jesus to swear an oath," Caiaphas said, pointing to Jesus. "Let him swear to his innocence, if he dares!"

"Neither you nor he should swear oaths," I said, aware that if he opened his mouth in this court, Jesus would almost certainly condemn himself immediately. "If you intend to bring a charge against this man, then let us hear it in detail."

"I bring a thousand charges against him," the High Priest boomed. "Do you question my word?"

"Do as he asks," Pilate said wearily, slumping back down in his throne. "Give the evidence so there can be no accusation that this trial was not fair."

"Let the defendant swear an oath attesting his innocence, Pilate," Caiaphas repeated belligerently. "If he cannot, then we know he is guilty without need of further procedure."

Pilate looked at him grimly. "Don't browbeat me, Caiaphas."

"This is a busy day for us," Caiaphas, said, leaning forward on the bench in front of him, which creaked under his weight. "Let us not waste the precious hours on this man."

"If you don't speak, it will be the worse for you," Pilate snapped.

They addressed one another on terms of familiarity, though not as friends. Caiaphas had been appointed High Priest by Valerius Gratus, Pilate's predecessor, some fifteen years earlier. He was as much a Roman appointment as was Herod, and in no position to argue publicly with Pilate. He seemed to swallow his pride almost visibly. He glanced at me. "What must I say?"

I hadn't taken to the man, who seemed to me a bully. "We're all here today because of you. There is the man you arrested and brought here. If you don't know what to say then I can't tell you."

"State the charge," Pilate growled.

Caiaphas reinflated himself. "This man, Jesus of Nazareth, preached sedition openly and in the temple. May he be destroyed utterly and his name be erased from memory!"

"If it appears that Jesus is guilty as charged, then the penalty will be crucifixion, otherwise he is absolved."

There was a mutter of voices. The trial had finally begun. Caiaphas and the chief priests would now be allowed to demonstrate the truth of the charge. Jesus would have a an opportunity to refute it. If he was unsuccessful, sentence would be passed and executed immediately. There appeared to be only one possible outcome.

It was now mid-morning and very blustery. Gusts of rain alternated with a leaden shaft or two of sunshine. It was cold in the courtroom despite the multitude of people there. The cohort had returned to the courtyard, though Rufus told me there was still a large crowd outside, now silent and well behaved.

Caiaphas was whispering with the other priests while we waited for him to proceed. Pilate appeared pale, moving restlessly in his throne, his hands grasping the lions' heads carved on the armrests. Jesus sat motionless with his eyes closed. At length the High Priest turned back to the court. He addressed Jesus directly.

"Did you not say you would destroy the temple?" he demanded. Several of the priests called out, affirming the accusation. Jesus made no response, not even opening his eyes. "He doesn't deny it," Caiaphas said triumphantly. "He has not a word to say for himself."

I was relieved that Jesus had chosen to remain silent. When he did choose to speak, he would probably outrage every soul in the room. I rose. "When did he say this?"

"He has said it more than once."

"That he would destroy the temple?"

"Yes," several of the priests called out.

"What was the exact form of his words?" I asked. "Can any of you remember?"

There was considerable argument. A portly, quiet looking man rose to his feet. "He said that he would destroy the temple made by hands and build another one not made by hands."

"Thank you. Did you understand this to be a literal statement of intent?"

"I understood it to be a parable."

"A parable?"

"Our rabbis explain things to us through the use of allegories and stories. This man, in particular, uses many such devices in his teaching. Many times it's apparent that his hearers don't understand him fully."

"Don't make me out to be a fool, Joseph," Caiaphas said loudly. "We all understand him perfectly! And it is not true that all rabbis teach in riddles. Only those who dare not speak their thoughts clearly do it."

"Or those who have thoughts that are difficult for the simple to understand," the portly man replied.

"You are saying that he was using metaphorical language?" I asked him, ignoring Caiaphas.

"So it seemed to me."

"And what do you think he meant by this statement?"

The portly man glanced at Jesus. "It's not easy to explain it in few words. I believe he was saying that worship in the spirit is more important than worship in the flesh."

"I don't understand you."

"Jesus is one who teaches that holiness is not achieved through ostentatious display, as in the sacrifice of costly animals or donations of silver and gold. He teaches us to pray in private, to forgive each other and to repent our sins. These things are invisible. They're forms of worship which cannot be seen, so they constitute a temple which is not built by hands."

Jesus had opened his eyes and was looking at the portly man calmly. "Thank you," I said. "You seem to have followed the teaching of Jesus with some attention."

"Only since he began to preach in the temple."

"What is your name?"

"I am Joseph of Arimathea. It's a small town a few miles from Jerusalem – where the prophet Samuel was born," he added with a touch of pride.

"And you're a member of the Sanhedrin?"

Caiaphas lumbered to his feet. "He was admitted because he's a rich man, not because he's a scholar or because Samuel was born in his town. He should not presume to contradict the findings of the council."

"Then how would you interpret this saying of Jesus?" I asked Caiaphas.

"It was a threat to overthrow the established order," he replied with satisfaction.

"He doesn't look to me like Samson," I replied.

There was laughter, some of it in surprise that a Roman should know something of their scriptures.

"He couldn't break one stone of the temple with his bare hands alone," Caiaphas retorted.

"Then you agree with Joseph of Arimathea that his language was metaphorical?"

Caiaphas glared at Joseph. "He was not speaking metaphorically. He was threatening a violent rebellion."

"Is it not possible that you misunderstood?"

"I'm not a fool. He had already committed violence in the temple when he threw over the tables of the money changers. His threat to destroy the whole temple was a natural consequence of such a beginning. As for what Joseph has said, Jesus attempted to persuade his followers that they should not offer sacrifices. The offering of sacrifice is the Law! To claim that it is not necessary, to claim to forgive the sins of others, all these things transgress the Law."

"Forgive me if I ask these questions. I am, as you see, a stranger in Jerusalem. I'm trying only to understand what isn't clear to me. Is it common for the Sanhedrin to hand a Jew over to the Gentiles for execution?"

His eyes narrowed. "It is not common."

"Why have you done so in this case? If he has transgressed the Law, why did you not stone him to death as was your right?"

He blinked as though he had stumbled against something. "The man is an enemy to all. He urged that the poor should not pay taxes to Rome."

"He did not," Joseph said quietly. "He said something quite different. He said the poor have access to the kingdom of God, even if they cannot offer silver and gold as the wealthy do."

An argument erupted among them, filling the courtroom with noise. The lictors pounded on the floor with their rods to no avail. The argument did not subside until Pilate heaved himself to his feet. "I am not here to listen to a theological debate," he said tersely. "I am going to relieve myself. I suggest you all do the same. When I return, there will be no more argument."

He limped out, pale faced, ignoring the pleas of the Sadducees that he remain. Jesus was led off by the guards. Caiaphas heaved a loud groan and looked at the sky. "It is growing late. There's so much to do. There will be no time for anything! Why are there so many delays?"

I went out. There was a rattle of thunder, more felt than heard, shaking the flagstones under my feet.

"May I speak with you a moment?"

I turned. It was Joseph of Arimathea, standing with his hands folded against his rounded belly. "What is it?" I asked.

He made a courteous bow. "Let us walk out of the wind and rain, if you please."

We walked down the portico together. He was a full head shorter than I and perhaps twenty years older. His beard was grey and cut square across his chest.

"You helped Jesus with your testimony," I said.

"Caiaphas is unfortunately a fool as well as a puppet of the Romans," he said. "I hope I give no offense."

"You give none."

"He's put there to bluster and make noise. He does it rather well. However the real power lies with Annas, the former High Priest, Caiaphas's father-in-law. It's Annas who has decided that it's better for Jesus to die. The Pharisees believe in the renunciation of material wealth and the sanctity of life. The Sadducees, as you observe, wear glorious robes and have no qualms about taking a human life."

"But he's not a revolutionary."

"It won't save him. This trial is not about sedition or theology. It's about something far more important – money."

We had stopped at the end of the portico. "What do you mean?" I asked.

Joseph examined his shoes, his hands clasped behind his back. His mild manner and rotund frame belied the acuity of his mind. "The temple has flourished like a great tree during our lifetimes. It has been made to drop a deal of fruit for many people." He looked up at me with small, wise eyes. "The money flows to the Sadducees and to Herod. Both claim the temple as their life's work, but it was paid for, and will always be paid for, by the labour and money of the poor. There's a third beneficiary of the flow of silver and gold – the governor. You know him well. Do you think that any of them will easily renounce such profits?"

"Can Jesus interfere with this?"

"You're not a Jew, so it's hard for you to understand how revolutionary the teaching of Jesus is. He's preaching a religion of the poor. A temple not built with hands. He's said that the first shall be last and the last shall be first. He tells us that the kingdom of God is imminent and that the only requirements for entry are prayer and faith. He teaches that repentance washes away sin. You understand? As things stand now, we're taught to believe the opposite – that wealth and sanctity are one and the same, that the sacrifice of a dove is less than the sacrifice of a ram, the sacrifice of a ram less than the sacrifice of a bullock. He's teaching that no blood needs to be shed at all for a man – or a woman – to enter the kingdom of God. No blood, no silver, no gold are needed. Only that which cannot be seen. He loves God. But he's turning us against ourselves and against each other."

I was silent. I could hear the mob in the street. They had started chanting his name, "Yeshua, Yeshua, Yeshua, Yeshua, Yeshua."

"He seems extraordinary to me," I said.

"And you haven't heard him preach," he replied gently. "He doesn't wash himself obsessively, he breaks the Sabbath on occasion, he's not over careful about fasting, or what he eats, or even with whom he eats. He'll sit as happily with a harlot as with a rabbi. In general he seems to believe that women are our equals in most things and spends far too much time with them. No man who comes into so much contact with women will be respected by the priests." He shrugged. "He's a Galilean and every Galilean is born with a document saying, 'This Galilean is a law unto himself.' But in nothing does he offend as much as in threatening to reduce their prestige and their income."

"And so for that he must die?"

"For that – and because he's gathering too many followers who may one day carry swords and shields. He himself can't control that.

And that, also, he knows. There's no way out for him, Marcellus. He's reached the end of his road."

We began to walk back down the portico. "What about the claim that he is a Messiah?"

"If he says he's a Messiah, he'll be expected to lead the Jews into the Final Age. If he denies that he's the Messiah, the ordinary people will be bitterly disappointed – many only listen to him because they believe he brings freedom. He can't be the Messiah and he can't not be the Messiah. There's no way out but silence." He sighed. "He's not the Messiah, of course. 'Messiah' is a political concept and he's not a political man. Between you and me, there isn't going to be any Messiah. We Jews want to be rid of the Romans without the trouble of fighting you. No offence."

"No offence."

"So we look to the skies for a Messiah. But the truth is we either have to fight or keep our mouths shut. As to the wisdom or unwisdom of killing him, I'm too simple a man to judge. Caiaphas is right. I should not contradict the decision of those more learned than I. But I agree with you – we should stone him ourselves, rather than give him over to the Gentiles to crucify. However, the priests are too afraid of that mob out there to give the order. So they have brought him to Pilate. I see that you have taken to Jesus."

"Yes."

"So have I. The first time I heard him speak, I thought he was great. Nothing has diminished him in my eyes. There are several of us on the council who feel this sympathy. But I warn you that he expects to die today and that there's nothing you can do to prevent it."

A wave of exhaustion passed through me. I felt Joseph steady me, stopping me from falling. "I'm sorry," I mumbled.

"So am I. His mother spoke to me yesterday and said that you were a decent man. His end has come upon him suddenly and far from his home. All his friends appear to have deserted him. I want you to know that I'll take care of the burial arrangements. He has no tomb, so I'll have him placed in my own. It's in my garden, quite nearby. I'll speak to Pilate, too. With him, a little gold eases the way. I'll arrange everything. Why are you crying?"

"I've achieved nothing."

"You've allowed him to have some dignity. And you've shortened the time of his suffering." He patted my shoulder. "I explain these things to you because you seem to understand a little – for a Gentile. No offence."

"No offence."

"I hear the trumpet sounding. Pilate will be in his chair soon. We had better go." He glanced up at the dark sky. "It rains a lot in your country, they tell me?"

"More than here."

"Here, rain is a blessing, especially in the spring. Jesus will be crucified in the rain, it seems."

We re-entered the courtroom. Jesus was in his place, between the two soldiers. He did not notice me and indeed, from that moment on, he neither looked at me nor spoke to me again. There was a sense of urgency in the courtroom now, a hustle of impatient activity.

When he saw me, Caiaphas strode over to me. He looked down at me, a giant of a man quivering with anxiety. "Marcellus, listen to me. You don't know what you're doing. This is the holiest of days. You're delaying everything for no purpose. I am begging you, let this go." He reached out his hand as though to lay it on my shoulder, but then obviously decided the contact would defile him. He contented himself with making a pleading gesture. "This isn't one of your Roman clients. This is a man who has to die. You're causing anguish to everyone. Stop. Stop. Stop."

Pilate's trumpet sounded. He came into the courtroom, now so lame that one of the lictors had to support him. His foot had been bandaged, no doubt by Procula. He sat with a grimace. Someone lifted his foot onto a small pillow, an action which made him grunt in pain.

Caiaphas turned to him. "Excellency, it's growing very late. It's midday. I'm becoming desperate. This has taken all morning and the Sabbath of Passover begins at sunset."

Pilate gestured to me briefly. "You see the problem. The eyes of Rome are upon us."

"If we don't finish this today, we will have to wait another week. The mob will grow bold while the man lies in custody. You won't be able to drive them away with a cohort – or three cohorts. Before you know it, Jerusalem will be ungovernable."

"Then stop complaining and proceed."

Caiaphas drew a deep breath and turned to Jesus. "Did you say that you were the Messiah?" There was a silence in the courtroom. Faced with the silence, Caiaphas groaned in frustration. "Do you say that you are the Messiah now?" he demanded. He repeated the question in Aramaic and then in Hebrew. "Interrogate the prisoner!" Caiaphas implored Pilate.

"Jesus of Nazareth," Pilate said, "do you deny that you are the Messiah?" I stared at Jesus. He sat with his eyes closed, his lips moving slightly as though praying. Everyone was gazing at him with suspended breath. Joseph of Arimathea had rejoined the councillors and was slowly stroking his beard. Pilate asked the soldier next to Jesus, "Is he speaking?"

The soldier put his ear close to Jesus, then shook his head. "No, sir. He is not speaking."

Pilate turned to me grimly. "Ask your client if he denies the charge."

I walked to Jesus. "They're asking you to deny that you are the Messiah," I said. "Will you not speak?" He made no sign that he had heard my words.

"The prisoner refuses to deny that he declares himself King of the Jews," Pilate said. "I find him guilty of the charge of sedition. The sentence is crucifixion. It will be executed immediately. The court is dismissed."

I was enveloped in a whirl of noise but seemed able to distinguish nothing. I sat as though turned to stone. They led Jesus outside. I do not remember that there was any triumph shown anywhere, only an anxiety to get everything done quickly.

Pilate paused by my chair. "You have nothing to reproach me with," he said to me.

I did not look at him. "I do not reproach you."

"I've instructed them to be merciful. Now I wash my hands of this." He went his way.

The death of Jesus was the most pitiful thing I have ever witnessed. You must forgive the poverty of my words to describe it. Yet Pilate had spoken truth; much mercy was shown. He was stripped and beaten before the cohort but the terrible flagellum was not used. The rod which struck his naked body was that used for minor offences and did not tear away his flesh. That was by Pilate's order. Afterwards, they clothed him again in the purple robe Herod had given him and he was taken to Golgotha.

Usually, those who are to be crucified are made to carry the horizontal beam of the cross to the place of execution. He did not have to bear that. By Pilate's order, one of the crowd was commanded to do it.

An extraordinary thing was the silence of the crowd. It was immense. The city was swollen with pilgrims at that time and it seemed that every one of them came out of his lodging to see Jesus walk to his death. I see their faces now: many weeping or covering their heads, some staring with wide eyes of despair, others simply watching a spectacle – but none laughing. In the courtyard there had been some mockery from the soldiers, Levantines from the Decapolis who laughed at every misfortune which befell a Jew, but from the crowd there was none. There was hardly a sound.

He, too, was largely silent. He spoke only a few times. Some women had offered him a drink to take away consciousness; he tasted it and then refused any more. As his limbs were being nailed to the cross, he prayed for forgiveness for his tormentors. Years later, his brother James was to do the same in his final torment.

As he was raised against the dark sky, a groan passed through the crowd. Thousands had come, covering the hills around the place of execution. They stood in silent multitudes, ordinary people with ordinary faces who had left their preparations for the Passover to see this. Of his disciples there was no trace. Nor did any of the Sadducees or councillors come, not even Joseph of Arimathea. I recall that there were others hanging on crosses at the time. It has been said that these men mocked and cursed him, but as I remember, they were in their final agonies and incapable of speech.

I did not go close to the cross but stood at the place where Bar-David had died. I had sent Rufus away and was alone. How can I express my feeling at that time? The death of a good man, an innocent man, is always terrible. It shocks one with grief. It contradicts the natural order. On this day it was as though more than one man were dying. It seemed as though far more than a single human life were passing away, as though an age of innocence had come to an end.

Herod's gorgeous robe went to the soldiers. Jesus was naked in his agony. Over his head a semi-literate hand had scrawled the crime of which he had been convicted. It contained only a single word, khristos, meaning Messiah in Greek. It was the word which had been used throughout the trial.

As Joseph of Arimathea had predicted, rain fell from time to time, occasionally blotting out the terrible spectacle.

He remained on the cross for about three hours. At one stage he called out in Aramaic, asking God why he had forsaken him. Otherwise he did not speak. Pilate's final mercy – which coincided with the religious imperative that he should be in his tomb before the Sabbath began – was to send a centurion to kill him with a spear thrust. On the battlefield in Germany I have seen many wounded enemies dispatched with such a thrust, up under the ribs and into the heart. He died with a loud cry some two hours before sunset.

Shortly after his death, as I sat on the ground weeping, a group of Galilean women came to me to ask for his body, the friends of Jesus about whom Mary had spoken. One of them was an elderly, authoritative woman, Mary of Magdala,. She was the only one not incoherent with grief. The others were like leaves blown in the wind. I told them that Joseph of Arimathea had made arrangements for the burial, which they seemed not to know.

The centurion who had dispatched Jesus returned with word from Pilate that the body could be taken down. This was another mercy, even if it had to be paid for (Joseph later told me he had given Pilate a heavy gold goblet as a bribe). I helped them with my own hands. The iron spikes had been nailed through collars of wood so that the body could not slide off them; these proved difficult to remove since the soldiers had by now all departed except a couple of guards. I asked one of them to bring tools, and with these we at last removed the nails. As his body was laid on the ground, the women began kissing his face and breast and crying out, the saddest of sights and sounds. We were all wading in his blood; it had poured from his heart onto the ground. Nevertheless he was less mangled than the other crucified men who had been dispatched at the same time and he appeared at peace.

Now at last Joseph appeared with his servants. He seemed to know none of the Galileans, nor they him, and in their grief they challenged him angrily. However, he clearly had the authority of Pilate, which they did not, and his men took the body despite the arguing and wailing of the women. There was between them already that rivalry and competition that was to mark the succession of Jesus for so many years. There were about a dozen women there at the end. Only women, no men. Jesus had given a special place to the women who followed him and at the end only they stayed with him.

Joseph's servants had brought a litter to carry Jesus. We followed the body to Joseph's garden and saw it wrapped in linen and spices and laid on a shelf in Joseph's well excavated tomb, which was cut out of the rock and had smoothly dressed walls, the burial place of a wealthy man. The servants rolled a stone across the entrance. It was now very dark. The setting of the sun couldn't be seen, but the Passover feast was about to begin.

I was the last one left at the tomb, as the only pagan who did not have a feast to celebrate. I felt abandoned by my gods. Rufus eventually found me there in the darkness and brought me back to the Praetorium. I couldn't face Pilate or Procula and I am sure they had no wish to see me. Rufus helped me wash Jesus' blood from my hands and I went to bed and slept.

# CHAPTER SEVEN

# "YOU THINK YOU KNOW ME"

I hardly stirred for two days, having exhausted my small store of strength at the trial. I didn't see Procula during this period, either because Pilate had forbidden her to visit my bedside or because she had decided it was wiser to stay away, I am not sure which. I was sheltering myself from wakefulness, too. The death of Jesus had grieved me deeply. I felt a sense of failure – not only failure to prevent his death, but also failure to understand him, to recognize the world he had inhabited. I wasn't eager to leave the shelter of my long slumbers.

At last, however, my strength began to return and I dragged myself out of bed on the first day of the week to face reality. Rufus, cheerful as always, helped me bathe and shave myself.

"It's been a quiet weekend," he informed me. "After all the fuss on Friday, the city calmed down. The Jews have all eaten their mutton and drunk their wine and in a few days they'll start going home to the provinces. We've lost weight, sir. We'll have to start fattening ourselves up again."

I looked at my naked body in the water; I had become bony and gaunt. The gloss of youth, which I had still carried, seemed to have been rubbed off me. I noticed odd details – the dry skin on the back of my hands, the grey hairs now to be seen in the mirror – and felt I had aged.

"Nothing to worry about," Rufus assured me. "I know how to feed a soldier up. I've got a nice fat rabbit for your lunch. My girls are cooking it for you. I don't trust the kitchens here."

I smiled at him. "How many girls have you got?"

"All you want. And that's another thing we could do with to bring us back onto form. A nice fat rabbit and a nice fat girl."

I didn't take him up on the girl, but I ate half the rabbit and felt better for it. As I ate, Rufus told me that Herod had already departed the city for Galilee with all his train. I asked him about Pilate.

"In a bad way with the gout. The skin of his foot is peeling off and he's screaming blue murder. Throwing things at the staff and cursing his lady."

I made no comment. After eating, I rested for a while on the terrace, where the spring sunshine was warm, and occupied myself with my old task of correcting the Polybius scrolls I had found in Pilate's library. It soothed my mind. I had now to contemplate my return to Rome. I had little further excuse to remain in Judaea and I had to deliver a report to Vitellius. I wondered how I would be able to explain to him adequately the importance of Jesus and whether it was perhaps best to remain silent on the topic, confining myself to Pilate's other transgressions. An accounting had to be made, but it had to be done in such a way that Vitellius could understand. I had also to decide whether I ever wished to return to this land as governor of this complex and troublesome people. As I felt then, it wasn't an appealing prospect.

When the shadows started to lengthen, Rufus told me there were visitors for me and asked if I wished to see them. I consented. The little party which made its way across the terrace towards me consisted of three of the women who had been at the crucifixion, led by Mary the Magdalene.

I greeted them and asked them to sit with me, but they preferred to remain standing. All had eyes swollen with weeping and such faces as one sees when the mothers and wives are allowed to gather their dead from the battlefield. Mary, as she had been at the execution ground, was in possession of herself despite her grief. She was around sixty, tall and straight, with the stern countenance that one sometimes sees on elderly Jewish women who resemble hawks, rather than doves. The others deferred to her in everything.

"We have heard how you tried to protect our Master," she said to me brusquely. "It was a vain attempt but we thank you nevertheless."

"Perhaps I only made things worse."

"Perhaps. It was better for Rome that he should die. But to us it is the end of all our hopes."

"His teaching will live on."

"But he's gone." She said it with a deep despair, yet she was a courageous woman and her lips did not tremble. She spoke good Greek, evidently having some learning. "I have lost many in my life. Husbands and children and more. But this is the worst."

"I am sorry. I, too, have lost."

She shook her head as if rejecting or denying my sympathy. "We have come to ask you for the body."

"It is in Joseph of Arimathea's tomb. You know that."

"Have you not taken it?"

"I don't understand you."

"We went at dawn to anoint him with spices but the stone has been rolled away and the tomb is empty."

"Was there nobody there?"

"Only the gardener. And he knew nothing."

The other two women were peering at me around her shoulders in a frightened way. "What have they done with him?" one asked.

"I don't know. Have you asked Joseph himself?"

"Joseph has already gone back to Arimathea," Mary said. "He would not have taken the body with him." She was watching me closely . "Is this a trick of Pilate's? Has he given an order for it to be removed?"

"That may be possible. But I've been in my bed for two days and know nothing of it."

"You remained at the tomb after we left."

There was an unmistakable note of accusation in her voice. "That's true," I replied, "but I did not interfere with the body. In any case I was too weak to have moved the stone alone."

"But your servant came."

"Yes, my servant came for me and led me home in the darkness. I went straight to my bed. You look at me as though you suspect me of something. Why should I take the body of Jesus?"

"To produce magic with it, perhaps," she said sternly.

I shook my head in disgust. "I am an ordinary Roman lawyer who does not dabble in necromancy."

"Then what is the explanation?"

"The most likely explanation is that Joseph commanded his servants to move the body to some other tomb. After all, that tomb was his own. He told us that. He did not promise that Jesus would rest there forever. He offered the place out of kindness, because there was no other."

"Then why did he not seal the tomb up again when he had done, to prevent animals or wanderers from entering it?"

"Perhaps to show you that he had taken the body. I don't know." I was growing irritable. "These are questions you should ask Joseph."

"We should not have allowed the body to be taken from us," she said, her face dark with a sudden wave of new grief. "It was all we had left. You and Joseph pushed us aside, though you were not his friends, as we were. Wherever Rome touches, she leaves woe behind. Woe to your enemies and woe to your friends."

She had raised her arm like a prophetess, her eyes glittering. I was beginning to wish I had not allowed them to come to me. I recalled the mother of Jesus' words, They took my son from me. The mother of Jesus, small and humble, would have been no match for such a one as this. "I repeat that I know nothing of this. I did my best to save Jesus from his fate but once sentence had been passed, there was nothing else I could do. I was not responsible for his death and I have not removed his body. There are many others you should talk to before approaching me."

"Who?" she demanded.

"The men of your group, for example. They were not in evidence at the crucifixion. They appear to have gone into hiding. Perhaps one of them has taken the body secretly, without telling anyone. The mother of Jesus is also in Jerusalem."

Mary at once frowned. She looked at me suspiciously. "We have not seen her."

"She's here. I saw her and so did Joseph of Arimathea. Perhaps he's delivered the body to her."

"What would she do with it?" she snapped. "She's as poor as a mouse. I have money. He should have given the body to me, not to her."

There was something disturbing about her egoism. "I must beg you to excuse me from further questioning," I said. "I respect your grief but this is not my affair. And I'm tired."

She examined me with her hawk's eye. "I see that you're not concerned to help," she said grimly. "Forgive me for having intruded on your rest."

"It was no intrusion," I replied, but she was already walking away. I watched them depart, Mary Magdalene's two companions having almost to trot to keep up with her strides.

When they had gone, Rufus brought me word that Pilate had heard I was out of bed and invited me to attend the evening meal at his table. I wasn't inclined for any more company that day, especially with Pilate in a foul mood, but at last I decided to go. The truth was that I was missing Procula and longed to set eyes on her again, despite all that had passed.

The meal was served early. It was hard not to compare this occasion to the first evening we had spent together. That night had begun in gaiety and ended in offense. Tonight was far more subdued. Procula did not recline on a couch but sat modestly in a chair; her hair was tied back in matronly style and she said little, sitting with her eyes downcast for much of the evening, the model Roman wife. I tried not to stare at her face, but looking at her seemed the only thing that took away the pain in my heart.

Pilate reclined with his bandaged foot resting on a pillow, eating and drinking with no moderation. At first his conversation was principally about his gout. He had suffered from several attacks, so he said, which always took the same form – an ache in the first joint of his big toe which swiftly became so unbearably acute that the slightest jar caused him agony, followed by a slow recession of the inflammation, accompanied by itching and peeling of the skin.

"My sister has written to me," he said, "saying that the physician Celsus now claims the disease is produced by deposits in the urine and is exacerbated by drinking wine and beer."

"That's what we Etruscans always believed."

"It's nonsense. My urine is as clear as crystal. Is it not, Procula?"

"Yes," she said dully.

"And the flow is good and strong. Not so?"

She was toying with her food, eating very little. There were shadows under her eyes. She nodded.

"You see? I've always cured my attacks by drinking copious amounts of wine. It's the only treatment."

Whatever caused him suffering was acceptable to me, so I agreed with his prescription. "The city is very quiet," I remarked, wishing to get away from the subject of his urine.

"Within a week the pilgrims will all have gone. Another Passover will have ended without rebellion. As soon as my foot improves I'll mobilize the army for our return to Caesarea. It's a rather tedious three day march. But I look forward to the sea air."

"And fresh fish."

"And fresh fish." He glanced at me. "And you, I presume, will begin preparing for your return to Rome."

"Yes."

"I advise you not to think of remaining in Jerusalem once the army has left. The city is far from safe when there is no military presence."

"I see no reason to delay my departure. I'll probably leave in the next few days." Procula made no sign that she had heard my words. She hadn't touched wine tonight, drinking only water. This talk of leaving had filled the atmosphere with a profound melancholy, at least for me.

"Good." He twirled the goblet in his fingers. "You've seen something of the problems that I face. And something of the measures I'm obliged to take in dealing with them. You arrived with a mind filled with preconceived opinions. I hope that you've revised some of your prejudices. I would be disappointed to learn that you took a poor opinion of me back to Vitellius."

"It's somewhat late now to be worrying about the impression you've made on me," I said dryly.

He reddened. "I haven't tried to make an enemy of you."

"Nor I of you."

"Then perhaps we can both hope for good results from your visit."

I merely nodded.

"You disappeared after the trial so you probably haven't yet heard that I freed some prisoners on the day he was crucified. I judged it politic. The man was popular and there was some public reaction to the sentence. Those young men you were so concerned about – the last of the rebels – I let them go. I think they have learned their lesson."

"I'm glad to hear it. You showed much clemency."

"He'll soon be forgotten. These sort of people appeal principally to those who love novelty. As soon as another nine-day wonder arrives, they are happy again. And by the way – your friend, Judas, is dead."

"By his own hand?"

"That's a shrewd guess." He drank. "But I neither know nor care."

Procula rose from her chair and went to make the offering to the Lares. The altar was recessed into the wall. On either side had been painted somewhat naive figures of the master and mistress of the house. Pilate was shown in his magistrate's toga and crown, looking more cheerful than he ever did in life, holding aloft a cup of wine. Procula was in white, with very yellow hair waving around her head, holding a cornucopia brimming with flowers and fruit. I watched her as she broke the saffron cake and poured the wine. She murmured prayers so quietly that I couldn't hear her voice.

Pilate, too, was watching her. "You were very thick with that fellow, Joseph of Arimathea. What was he whispering to you?"

"He was trying to explain the nature of Jesus' teaching."

"That's a matter of indifference to me. The gods of Rome are good enough for me. As you've probably guessed by now, my wife and I hold differing opinions on the subject of religion." She returned to the table. For a moment her clear brown eyes met mine, the briefest of glances. I felt my heart twist in my chest. "The Empire brings many strange things to Rome, among them strange gods. Mithras, Astarte and Jehovah now vie with Apollo and Jupiter. We will have all the gods of Asia in the end, and so many feast days that we will never do a day's work."

The wine had loosened his tongue and he rambled on in this inane fashion for a period while Procula and I sat in silence. As drowsiness overtook him, he drank more and talked less.

"I've had a visit from some of Jesus' disciples with a story that his body has been taken from the tomb," I said during one of the silences.

"As long as he hasn't rolled away the stone himself," Pilate said with a chuckle, "and isn't wandering around showing his wounds to everyone."

We were silent for a while longer after this sally. Procula finally folded her napkin. "With your permission, I'll go to bed."

"I'll join you soon," Pilate said, waving her away. "Don't sleep until I come." She retired without another word. It seemed that a lifetime had passed since she had kissed me at the foot of the stairs. For form's sake, I drank another cup of wine with her husband and listened to his boasts and brags. Then, myself sick and weary, I went to bed.

The next day I felt strong enough to want to stretch my legs. The rain had passed and the sun was hot again. I left the Praetorium and walked through the streets alone. After the bustle of the preparations for the Passover, the quietness of the city was strange. Doors were closed, shutters were fastened. Although work was forbidden only on the first and last days of the festival, there was little movement. The soldiers lounged in the sun and the citizens seemed to have no haste. Some of the silence may have had to do with the crucifixion of Jesus.

I directed my steps towards Joseph of Arimathea's garden to see the empty tomb for myself. The garden itself was a grove of olives, a picturesque spot. The brush had been knee high when we had carried Jesus' body there but, as Mary of Magdala had reported, a gardener had been at work, probably on Joseph's order. There was no sign of the gardener now, but the undergrowth had been cut down and was stacked in neat bundles to dry for the fire. The place presented an orderly but somewhat lonely appearance.

The tomb was open and empty. The stone which sealed it had been carefully cut and though its weight was immense, two men could move it to and fro. As I stood looking at the empty stone chamber, pondering, someone else approached. I turned and stared. The man was so familiar in face and outline that my heart leaped for a moment; but he was different. Where Jesus had been compact and quick in movement, this man was slow and rather gangling. His coloration was different, too; Jesus had been rather dark, where this man had pale skin.

He caught my stare with a small grimace of pain. "You think you know me but you don't. I am James, the brother of Jesus."

"You're very alike."

"So it has always been said, since our childhood. You are Marcellus?"

"Yes. I am sorry for your great loss."

He nodded slowly, his eyes with their swollen lids turning to look at the tomb. "He was everything to me."

"Your mother must be very ill."

"She has not eaten or spoken. I fear for her life. I've sent word to my sisters to come and bring her home. I must remain here in Jerusalem."

"Did you remove the body?" I asked him.

He shook his head with that slowness which was evidently customary with him. "I did not touch it. I have been hiding myself for fear that the Romans would take me, too."

"Then who has removed it?"

"I don't know."

"Mary of Magdala and the other women came to see me. They're also ignorant."

He spoke simply. "He had another life with them. From the time he was baptized, we saw little of him. We remained in Galilee and they took him from us. To him she was all sweetness," he added, apparently meaning Mary Magdalene, "but to us she was like an enemy."

"They were the only ones who remained with him at the end. His disciples vanished when he was arrested."

"They were afraid, as I was. Mary of Magdala is afraid of nothing."

"Have none of his disciples said anything?"

"I have seen little of them. They are prostrated with grief and still afraid of the Romans." He looked up at the hillside from which the tomb was cut, blinking at the bright light. "There is a hole in our lives. We should say prayers for him but I cannot find enough men." Tears rolled down his cheeks. "I could not be with him at his death. And now I cannot even see his body. They have taken everything from us."

I tried to give some crumbs of comfort. "He faced his death with extraordinary courage and dignity. As they drove the nails in, he prayed for their forgiveness. I can also tell you that his torment was lessened in many ways and that he died with relative quickness at the end."

He began to repeat his brother's name in Aramaic, as the crowd had done during the trial, "Yeshua, Yeshua, Yeshua, my brother." It was a litany of loss. He clasped his hands and began to pray silently, his body rocking back and forward at times. I watched him. Despite his physical resemblance to Jesus, he did not have that warmth with which his brother seemed to include everyone in the scope of his interest. He was less aware of others. But his holiness was evident from the first moment one saw him. Where one saw Jesus as a man first, and then as a holy man, with James it was the other way around. And James was more a Galilean than Jesus – he had not the charm and polish which would have made him more approachable.

I waited for a long time while he prayed. When he seemed to have finished at last, I said, "Please convey my respects to your mother. I will remain in Jerusalem for a few days longer and then I will travel back to Rome. Tell her that if there is anything I can do for her, she has only to ask."

"There is nothing."

"Nevertheless, tell her."

He wept and nodded without looking at me. He started to pray again and I left him there.

On that day I began to prepare for my departure. I sent a letter to Glabulus in Caesarea, telling him I would arrive within a week and asking him to find a passage for me on the first ship bound for Rome. I did not mention in it any of the happenings in Jerusalem; it would be better to commit nothing to writing. I also wrote to friends in Rome, including Martha, my teacher, telling them some of my adventures and announcing my plans to be home before the beginning of summer.

I had now been in Judaea for some weeks. I didn't wish to remain any longer. I was looking forward to getting back to my old life. But whether my old life still awaited me, I no longer knew. I had changed. And an existence which did not have Procula in it would be difficult to grow accustomed to.

Since Pilate had made the accusation that we were too close to one another, she had avoided me as much as possible. I took this to mean that she had considered her conscience and had decided that he was right. I hadn't repeated any words of love to her, though I am certain she knew my feelings were true.

Our acquaintance had been so brief. I had offered to take her back to Rome with me; that she had refused to entertain the idea was hardly surprising on such a brief acquaintance. She didn't share the certainty that I felt.

Her marriage to Pilate wasn't a happy one. In Rome, she could have been divorced simply and quickly without any shame. But the circumstances of her life here in Judaea were peculiar. To leave him would have required considerable courage, which I'm not sure she had. Moreover, she seemed to regard him with a mixture of fear and respect which, if it wasn't love, was sufficient to bind her to his side. There was a fragility about her which his personality supported. Without him, she could perhaps not have remained upright, as an ivy plant, beautiful and full of leaves as it is, can't stand without the tree on which it leans, even if the tree is rotten.

I did have one more opportunity to speak to Procula in private before I left Jerusalem. I did not seek it. It came at her behest; she sent one of her maids to summon me at the beginning of the next week, on a day when Pilate was away from the Praetorium preparing the army for the return to Caesarea. I saw her in her office, a small room where she attended to the household accounts and performed other such duties. I had never been in it before. It smelled of her and of aloes wood and some inexpert hand – hers, I suspected – had painted gay wreaths of flowers on the walls. As I entered, she rose from her writing table with shining eyes.

"Oh, Marcellus!" She greeted me with delight, holding out her hands. The reserve with which she had treated me for the past week had vanished; she seemed as gay as she had been the night I had arrived in Jerusalem and, if anything, more beautiful. Clasping my hands, she sat with me on a couch which stood against one wall. She looked into my face eagerly. "I'm so glad you've come. I have so much to discuss with you."

"I am listening," I replied.

"First, tell me – did you believe that Jesus was the Messiah?"

I was taken aback by the question. "He didn't wish to be a king, but to express the nature of God."

She laughed. "He was the Messiah. There's proof."

"What proof?"

"He has risen from the dead."

I was stunned for a moment. "Are you making a joke?"

"Oh, no. Nothing could be further from a joke than this. You told us yourself that his tomb was empty, the stone rolled away as if by some divine power."

"I didn't say there had been any divine power."

"He's been seen!"

I stared into her eyes that were sweet as honey. "Who has seen him?"

"Mary of Magdala. And others. They have seen him and some have spoken to him."

"Procula, I saw him die."

"The wounds are on his body. He shows them to people."

"Listen to me," I said patiently. "You don't understand. His wounds were not such as could be survived. The injuries to the wrists and feet were one thing; but I saw the centurion thrust the spear under his ribs. I have seen that done before. The blade passes through the lungs and the blood vessels and enters the heart. His life blood poured from him. He died and could not have recovered."

"It's you who don't understand." She was still laughing with the joy of her delusion. "He was dead. But he's been resurrected. He's returned from death. It's the greatest of all his miracles."

There was a bitter taste in my throat. "My dear one, you fill me with sorrow."

"Why? It's wonderful news."

"I hardly know what to say to you. Where is he to be found?"

"He comes and goes. He's appeared here in Jerusalem to Mary and some of the other women. He been seen by others, far from here, in the countryside. Some have seen him simultaneously in different places. This morning I was told that he's even been seen in Galilee, on the lakeshore!"

"Then his spirit is restless."

"It wasn't his spirit. It was the man in flesh and blood."

"A man of flesh and blood who can fly to Galilee and make himself appear to all sorts of people at the same time, in different places?"

"A man who can defeat death can do anything."

I pressed her hands. "Mary of Magdala is beside herself with sorrow and anger. Jesus cured her of a great madness and now she's mad once again with grief. What she sees and reports cannot be trusted. As for the others who loved him, they too are caught up in visions and dreams. It's not a miracle."

She drew a breath like a child about to impart a precious secret. "Marcellus, I've seen him too."

I stared at her. "Where?"

"Near where his body was laid."

"Did you speak to him?"

"I didn't dare. He was walking, lost in thought, under the olive trees. I remained where I was until he disappeared from sight. I thought my heart would burst, Marcellus."

I spoke gently. "You saw James, his brother. I've seen him there, too. I spoke with him some days ago. He's very like Jesus, but fairer skinned and not so tall."

For a moment, her smile faltered. I saw her gaze turn inward to her memories, trying to assess the truth of my words. Then she shook her head. "I saw Jesus."

"This is folly, Procula."

She withdrew her hands from mine. "Don't say that to me."

"I can't help saying it. It goes against all reason."

"Reason has nothing to do with what is holy. My husband killed this man and now he's alive again. This is a great treasure given by God."

"Others may have seen James, too, and mistaken him for his brother – especially if they didn't know Jesus well."

"Do you think people are so gullible? Even if I was mistaken, it doesn't matter. Others not so foolish as I have seen him."

I was about to argue further when I saw, in a painful moment of insight, how happy she was. This "great treasure" had filled a place in her heart that I had been unable to occupy. Even if I succeeded, with hard, logical words, in driving out the treasure, I would never be able to take its place. Inevitably, she would only come to hate me. This was what she had been waiting for through the loveless years of her marriage; not a living man but a dead one. She was right. It was something holy and I did not have the right to try and steal it from her. Nor was I able to join her, as she plainly wanted me to, in believing what I couldn't believe.

I took her hands again and kissed each one on the knuckles. "You've been given a great treasure. I'm happy for you."

"Oh, Marcellus, can you not have faith?"

I restrained myself from telling her again that I had seen Jesus die and had been bathed with his blood and had helped to bury him. "Faith, too, is a gift. I don't have it. It's a deep loss to me. It has made you even more beautiful. I will remember you always as you are this afternoon."

She began to cry. "I thought you would believe."

I couldn't bear to see her joy drain away. "Don't be unhappy. From the first moment I saw you, I wanted only to see you laugh. I'm sorry I succeeded so little. I have brought you much unhappiness."

"You've been a true friend to me."

"I don't think so."

"I know what you must do when you return to Rome. I can tell you that it has never made any difference to the way I've felt towards you. You have behaved with more honour than any man I've ever known."

"Well, that's something," I said wryly. "Dry your tears. You must have some left for the day I leave, or it will hardly be an occasion at all."

"The night before we dined with Herod you made me an offer, Marcellus. I apologize for the abruptness with which I stopped you from speaking. I want you to know that I'll treasure your sentiment for ever. But I can't accept what you offer me. It would dishonour us both."

I was silent for a while before replying. "I've told you my opinion and revealed to you my feelings. I won't pain you by repeating anything. I wish you happiness, Procula."

I managed to maintain my poise as I left her office but in truth I felt very sore inside. As I walked back to my room, I wondered

how Pontius Pilate would treat her "great treasure," and whether
he would be pleased to know that his executed prisoner was said to
be wandering around Judaea and showing his wounds to everyone,
as he had jestingly suggested. I foresaw that relations between them
wouldn't be improved by this fresh nine-day wonder and new addition to Procula's beliefs.

In the end I decided to leave some days before Pilate and the army
were ready. I did not see any advantage in traveling with them. He
allocated a small guard to me to protect me against the brigands
of Judaea and lent us some spare horses so we could make good
progress.

I need not have feared that Procula would have no tears remaining when I left. Pilate was his usual irritable self and at the last
moment entrusted me with a sheaf of correspondence to be delivered to his family in Rome. We bade each other farewell within the
Praetorium, displaying varying degrees of emotion. Rufus came to
shake my hand. I had already given him gold and told him that
if ever wanted another line of work he could find one with me.
Then I rode out of Jerusalem with the wind blowing in my face and
through the holes in my heart.

We reached Caesarea in two days, thanks to the ponies Pilate
had lent us. Glabulus had received my letter and was waiting for me
with the welcome news that he had secured me a place on a boat
that was leaving for Rome in two days. I had only to go down to the
port to pay the captain. She was a sharp-beaked Greek vessel with a
magical eye painted on each side of her prow. Her crew were mend-
ing her sails, which lifted in the breeze as though eager to fly. I liked
the look of her. I paid my passage and was set.

Glabulus and his charming wife were very good to me. To
Glabulus alone, my fellow lawyer and old friend, I recounted everything that had happened. I never told anyone else the full story,
though by the agency of Rumour, people in all quarters of the

globe somehow got to hear intimate details of my experiences, true and false.

We drank deeply that night and I had to be helped to bed by Glabulus' servants. Mindful of the rough passage I had endured from Rome, I took care the next day to make a sacrifice in the temple. It was another of Herod's gifts to the Gentiles, spanking new and ostentatious with gold and white marble. I recalled how Jesus had prophesied before Herod about the end of all his works.

That afternoon I wrote a long letter to Vitellius, to be carried by another ship. In the first part I recounted the most important features of Pontius Pilate's conduct and confirmed that he was causing outrage to his subjects, leading to a perilous situation. In the second, I outlined my recommendations for changes to be made to the system of government in Judaea, in particular a separation of the political and religious authorities and a greater flexibility in dealing with the question of Jerusalem. This letter was to ensure that, should I be lost at sea, my mission for Vitellius wouldn't be entirely uncompleted. The wind favoured us early the morning after, and we sailed for Rome.

# Book II

# Rome

# Chapter Eight

# Return To Rome

The voyage home was slow. We made good progress at first, stopping at Cyprus, Rhodes and Crete for supplies; but when we reached the sea of Greece, there seemed to be a thousand islands where the crew had business to transact or families to visit. Frustrating as it was, there was no remedy but to be patient as we zigzagged from rocky inlet to rocky inlet. I wasn't on a Roman vessel and the Greeks have their own way of doing things.

The prolonged tour, however, inculcated in me an appreciation for the beauty of those islands which, barren as they are, have a stark purity, washed by the sun. It was an opportunity to recover my strength. Like the rest of the crew, I worked or sat naked in the sun and was baked brown by its rays, growing a beard and learning the strange dialects spoken by the sailors until I was indistinguishable from them.

I did not encounter the Sirens, Scylla and Charybdis, or any of the other monsters of antiquity, but so long did the voyage take that it was high summer by the time the smoke of Ostia was finally visible on the horizon. I reached Rome in a ferocious heat wave and went straight to my townhouse, which at that time was located in the heart of the city and, like Ulysses, was unrecognized by all except a dog – Livia's little pet which I found very thin, although the slaves said they had cared for it. Perhaps it had pined in my absence.

Dionysius, my chief slave, had kept the house in good order. He was a trustworthy man who had been with me since before my marriage (having survived the purge of my servants which Livia undertook, as all new wives do). Though there was no Penelope at the loom, it was very pleasant to be back in my old surroundings. I bathed and then sat in my garden and read through the pile of correspondence which had accumulated in the months I had been away. The journey home had taken so long that some letters from Judaea had overtaken me on swifter vessels and were there before me. One was from Joseph of Arimathea. It had news of Jerusalem:

*The mother of Jesus is still here, with some of his brothers. The disciples are living communally in some poverty, financed by such of them as have a little property. They are argumentative, daily accusing the priests of having murdered their Master and often in open conflict with one another. They have many adventures of an undignified sort and are sometimes to be seen disputing in the street with their opponents.*

*They continue to insist that he was resurrected from the dead. I did not order his body to be removed from the tomb, and what became of it is a mystery to this day. They say that after leaving them with instructions, he arose into heaven with Elijah and Moses on either side. However their enemies accuse them of having stolen the body themselves in order to invent this tale.*

*All this makes them a laughing stock among those who might otherwise have listened eagerly to the teaching of such a saintly rabbi. Nevertheless, some Gentiles and some of the uneducated are drawn into their fold.*

*There is competition to choose a new leader. There are strong characters among the faithful but no deep intellects and a singular lack of learning. The man who succeeds Jesus most naturally is his younger brother, James, whom you know. He is a man of exceptional piety and although he does not have his brother's gift of preaching, his holiness is recognized by everyone.*

A second was from Glabulus, describing Pilate's arrival back in Caesarea, which was accompanied by fresh crucifixions and other atrocities. The third, and most important to me, was from Procula.

It was very short and conveyed only her hope that I had arrived safely, her thanks for unspecified kindnesses and conventional greetings, ending with the formula, "Be well, Marcellus, that I may also be well." It was, nevertheless, a treasure since it was entirely written in her own hand, which was large and innocent. There was no secret message to be found in it other than its own sincerity.

I sent Dionysius to make an appointment with Vitellius and he returned with kind greetings and instructions for me to come to Vitellius' house the next day. It was a meeting to which I greatly looked forward.

Lucius Vitellius was one of the most able men that Rome produced in that period. His origins were not so illustrious as to give his career the early launch it deserved, so that it flowered in relative old age. He was a southerner, born in the ancient Etruscan city of Luceria. He had been a steward to Augustus in his youth. Tiberius, too, had befriended him, but he did not attain his first consulship until his mid-forties.

Vitellius was very kind to me after my father's death, which occurred in my teens, taking me into his household. It was he who had taught me a love of the law and of government. I had been tutor to his two sons, which had given me an even closer tie to him. He received me in his library. He had a southerner's warm temperament and charm. "I can't tell you how glad I was to hear you were safely back in Rome," he said, grasping my shoulders. "Your ship was so slow that the letter you wrote me from Caesarea arrived weeks ago. I was sure you had been devoured by the descendants of Polyphemus."

"I am inedible, as you see."

He looked well, though his hair was greying and he was entering middle age. He gave an impression of massive solidity, with a large nose and small mouth, his eyelids prone to little warts. He called for wine. "We'll eat at midday, as usual. I can't promise you delicacies such as you'll have been fed in Palestine, but the cooks have been told to do their best. We have a quiet hour together. Sextilia is eager to see you but I've begged her to wait until lunch. Once she gets hold of you, there will be no more sensible talk."

We sat by the window. He ordered the scribe to take notes of our discussion. His having already received my letter was useful; it meant I could discuss the events I had witnessed without first outlining them. He listened imperturbably, resting his chin on his hand.

I explained my recommendations for restoring complete control over their religious affairs to the Jews. Any interference with the religion of the Jews, I said, was bound to result in disaster.

"In religion, they won't assimilate or be assimilated, Lucius. Yet there are enough good men among their priests and prophets to ensure that they will remain obedient to Rome in the political sphere – so long as we don't trample their beliefs. The killing of men such as Jesus of Nazareth has a disastrous effect, since they are lovers of peace and themselves beloved by the multitude. In the vacuum left by their deaths, bitterness and rebellion will inevitably grow."

I concluded by describing in some detail my evening with Herod and Herodias and its consequences to me. He was angry at what had been done to me, I could tell, but as always he kept his emotions under control.

When he had heard me out he asked a number of questions, then dictated some comments to the Syrian scribe. At the end, he was unstinting in his praise.

"You've done well," he said. "The emperor will be pleased with your thoroughness and the accuracy of your judgments. He's no longer in touch with the outside world as he once was. Reports such as this are vital for the running of the Empire." He glanced over the notes the scribe had made, then dismissed the man. When we were private, he continued, "Sextilia and I have bought a villa in Capri, to be close to the emperor. It's a beautiful island and it's not to be wondered at that the emperor doesn't wish to leave it. But I can tell you privately that he's become very reclusive. What Herodias related to you isn't altogether an exaggeration, though such orgies are by no means a daily occurrence, as she suggested."

"I see."

"They're rather an expression of the emperor's inner tensions, which are so strong that they seek release in violent purgation of feeling. He's been the victim of conspiracies and now sees them everywhere. His mind is deformed with suspicion and fear. The other side of the coin is this kind of wild outburst." His devotion to Tiberius had kept him alive through the terror that had followed Sejanus's fall but one could see behind his words what sort of monster the emperor had grown into. I did not envy him his villa in Capri or his closeness to Tiberius. For all the opportunities of advancement that it gave him, it was a dangerous friendship. He was aware of the danger. His solution was to seek power outside of Rome. He had long had his eyes on the governorship of Syria, one of our most important and wealthy provinces. It was currently without a governor, evidence of the emperor's indifference to affairs of state. Sending me to report on conditions in Judaea was an important first step in seeking the great prize. "I'm one of the few Tiberius still trusts," he went on. "I'll visit him in a few weeks, towards the end of the summer, when the weather has cooled. I have told him of my ambitions for Syria and he has indicated that he approves the idea."

"I'm very happy for you."

He nodded. "As for your own future, I would like nothing better than to have you in Jerusalem while I'm in Antioch. I trust you more than I trust any other man in Rome. If you have the inclination for the task, it's yours."

I bowed. "Thank you, Lucius."

"I know it's a difficult province. The Jews are a troublesome race and the possibility of a war is ever present. If you can make a success of yourself there, there's no limit to your ambitions." He paused so as to allow his words to sink in. "You've some time to make your decision. I'll be Consul in January of next year and that is a six month tenure. After that, things will be in motion. If you want to discuss this with me, to clarify your ideas, I'm always here."

"Thank you."

"I've had a letter from Pilate about you. I won't show it to you because it's offensive in parts and plainly an attempt to discredit you and whatever you say about him. One of his complaints is that you tried to alienate his wife's affections."

"He dangled his wife before me to try and distract me."

Vitellius smiled. "And you rose to the bait?"

"I was sad to see a decent woman in that situation. If he's exiled, she'll suffer terribly."

"He seems a poor sort of husband."

"The less said about that, the better," I replied. "The issue at hand is how he governs, not what sort of husband he is."

"I saw her, soon after the marriage. She was a farmer's daughter from Apulia, one of those blonde Greek types. A beauty in her teens, very sweet and gentle. That toad Pilate was lucky to have gobbled up such a butterfly. When he's been tossed off his lily pad, she'll be free for you. I would be happy to see you marry her."

"That will never be, Lucius."

"I'm a few years older than you, and I've learned never to say never. I have longed to see you express an interest in some woman other than your late wife. Even if this isn't an ideal romance, yet there's hope." He rose. "Come, my boy. Your aunt is eager to cover you with kisses." Arm-in-arm, we walked to the dining room.

Sextilia, Vitellius' wife, had been as kind to me as her husband. If anything, she loved me more. A lady of some asperity but fine intellect, she had acute political judgment and was skilled in the intrigues which continually took place around the emperor. Without her beside him, it's doubtful whether Vitellius would have travelled so far or so safely. She did indeed cover me with kisses, as Vitellius had predicted. The meal was the happiest of homecomings. Surrounded by those whom I loved and who loved me, I felt myself back in civilization and was able to laugh and relax for the first time in many weeks.

We discussed the future in optimistic terms. She was excited that the glittering prize of Syria was now a step closer and was eager for me to take Judaea so that "the golden East," as she put it, "would become a family concern." I didn't try to disguise my reservations. Rome was a big stage at that time; the world of Judaea was difficult and confined. I felt my life would be far more interesting if I remained in the capital.

"Every year, the Tiber is filled with the bodies of promising young men," she said to me. "The higher you advance, the closer your neck gets to the blade. Tiberius won't last forever and when he dies there will be even greater instability. Rome is too dangerous, Marcellus. But out there in the Empire – far away from the intrigues and the plots – there are opportunities for greatness impossible to find at home."

She was right, of course. The power of a provincial governor was unequalled by any post offered at home. Prejudices against living with barbarians kept many able men from entering the foreign service; and of course, in that period when Rome was so unstable, every second commander secretly imagined he could be the next emperor and did not want to leave the hive even while the fields of flowers nodded in the sun.

The afternoon stretched into a golden summer evening, one of those Roman evenings when the air is like wine. I didn't get home until late, feeling more content than I had done in years. A big copper moon had risen. It had been one of those occasions which one remembers for years because what was said bears such a strange relation to what happened later. A few words spoken on certain occasions have power to remain in one's mind for decades, shaping one's life for good or for bad.

In due course, my report was taken to the emperor, who later sent me a gracious message, thanking me for my work. Communications from Tiberius were rare and I was very flattered. As things turned out, however, Vitellius' ambitions moved somewhat more slowly than he had anticipated, in part because the emperor, caught between erotic manias and morbid suspicions, was difficult to move and dangerously unpredictable. Vitellius was Consul within a few months but two years were to pass before he was awarded Syria and I returned to Judaea.

During these two years I went back to my law practice and built it up again so that I soon had my hands full. They were years during which I established my reputation and earned high fees. Living frugally, as I did, I was able to put by enough to buy some properties and other investments which stood me in good stead for the rest of my life. And those two years also marked the beginning of a strange new relationship in my life, which began through the intervention of Livia's cousin, Felix, a man I hadn't seen since her death.

He arrived at my house at lunchtime a day or two later, unannounced. I was in my study and my slave Dionysius came hurrying to tell me of his arrival.

"Have you given him wine?" I asked.

"No. But he's calling for it." He cocked his head. "There he is now."

A hoarse voice could be heard from the garden. "Bring wine," I said. "Something—"

"Something cheap. Of course, master."

I made my way to the garden. The poet was sprawled on a couch set between two columns. He was fatter than ever and though he had put on a toga for the visit, it was greasy and unclean. His grey hair had grown so long that it fell over his face in matted locks.

"Felix. A pleasant surprise."

Felix raised his head. Despite the rolls of fat, his face was somehow sunken, black shadows under his eyes. His lips were grey. "There you are. The last Etruscan. I haven't set eyes on you since Livia's funeral. How are you?"

"Well. And you?"

"Less well. Ask them to bring wine, for pity's sake."

"It is coming."

Felix sighed with relief. "Good. We see too little of each other."

Dionysius brought the wine in a clay jug, with two cups. There were also some boiled eggs, walnuts, a slab of cheese and half a loaf of bread. I raised my cup to Felix. "Good health."

Felix attempted to echo the toast but his hand trembled so much that the wine slopped out of the cup. He put the cup back on the table and, without embarrassment, lowered his shaggy head and sucked his drink like an animal. I began to eat. When the trembling eased, he was able to lift the cup, pouring the wine into himself as though trying to extinguish some fire. "I ran out of booze last night," he said, wiping his mouth. "These days it doesn't take long before the Furies arrive. So you've been to the Levant?"

"Yes."

"And what are the Jews like? Do they have three eyes?"

"The general preference seems to be for two."

"How disappointing."

"And why do you say you're unwell?"

"I'm out of fashion." He reached for two walnuts, cracked them together in his palms, and picked through the fragments. His fingers were unsteady. "Flavius isn't interested in me anymore."

"I heard that he's no longer your patron."

Felix laughed, the phlegm rattling in his chest. His voice was hoarser than I remembered, coarser. "I'm destitute. All I have left is my genius."

"You've drunk everything else away," I said. "Flavius would still be your patron if you hadn't barged into his audience and insulted him so vilely."

He closed his eyes and waggled his fat fingers as though conducting distant music. "I was under the spell of the God."

"You shat at his feet."

"He was honoured. My shit is worth more than his gold."

"If you say so."

"I do say so. Would you like me to shit at your feet?" He opened his eyes to evil slits and peered at my shoes. "Shod as they are in fine Etruscan leather. My God. Don't you know what a tale those boots tell? Honest Romans don't wear shoes like that. They wear honest sandals with honest, horny toes sticking out. No wonder they all distrust you."

"I'll take your sartorial advice under consideration next time I am at the shoemaker's."

"Do. I know what I'm talking about." He drank off two more cups of wine. The jug was empty. He tilted it to show me the lees in the bottom. I nodded to Dionysius. The Greek slave slid forward with a fresh jug. Felix watched the dark red rivulet with greedy eyes. "Have you read my poems lately?"

"One or two."

"Did they make you cry?"

"I don't cry much these days. But I thought they were very good."

"'Very good,'" Felix repeated. "Just as well nobody can see the author, eh?"

"You certainly don't look healthy, Felix."

"'Very good,'" Felix repeated again, his voice suddenly rough with anger. "What do you know about poetry? Those Odes are masterpieces."

"I'm sorry. I'm not a great judge of poetry."

"You're not a great judge of anything." Felix swallowed noisily. "Not even of yourself."

I looked at him angrily. "I've been abused enough lately. Thank you."

Felix sank back in his creaking couch, waving his hand in some kind of apology. The alcohol had already softened his outlines, slurred his speech. His eyes were glazing. They drifted across the trophies which hung on the wall of the loggia, shields and spears from barbarous lands, my plain Roman sword wrapped in leather. Beneath them were the glowing frescoes of dancers I'd had painted for Livia. "The hero's rest. You live well."

"I live very plainly," I replied. "As you see." I poured him more wine. "What can I do for you? Some legal problem?"

"I need money." He saw my dubious expression. "I don't want charity. I have something to sell."

"What?"

"A slave."

"I already have slaves."

"This one is young. Female. She has blood in her veins."

"I don't need that kind of slave."

"This one can write."

"Livia's little dog can stand on his hind legs."

"She can write. She writes my poems."

"She's your secretary?"

"She's the author of my Odes. You don't think I can write that stuff anymore, do you? The Muse doesn't talk to me now. She can't stand my stinking breath. But the Muse talks to her."

I was genuinely surprised. "She writes your verses for you?"

"Yes. She's quite good. 'Witty and erotic,' to quote a critic."

I was amused. Felix was Livia's cousin and there had been a time when we'd been friends, before his descent into sodden self-pity. "She writes everything?"

"Almost everything. I correct now and then." He groped in his toga and produced a small scroll covered with scribbles. He tossed it to me. "Some of her things. You may enjoy them."

"I'll read them later." I nodded to Dionysius, who brought another jug of wine. I poured myself a cup and assigned the rest to Felix. "If you sell the slave who writes your poems, how will you live?"

"I don't intend to live." Felix belched, an action which apparently gave him considerable pain. He grimaced, rubbing his belly. "But I do want a dignified death. Dying poor isn't amusing. I want wine, drugs, doctors. I want a funeral and a memorial. You understand."

"I didn't realize things were that bad."

"I have attacks. I vomit blood. A lot of blood. The quack predicts the next attack will carry me off."

"I'm sorry, Felix."

"Don't be. I may not write poetry any longer, but I'm the author of my own destruction. The girl, now."

I sighed. "What use would she be to me?"

"At the very least, you could dictate your memoirs of Judaea to her."

"Is she Greek?"

"She was educated by Greeks. She doesn't know where she was born or what her race is. Who cares?" His face grew sly. "She's violet-crowned, pure, honey-smiling."

"That was Sappho."

"This is Sappho's soul reborn."

"Where did you buy her?"

"I won her at a game of dice."

"This is all some bizarre invention, Felix. If you need money I can lend you a little, for Livia's sake. She was fond of you."

The poet tapped his fleshy nose. "I'm not asking you to trust me. You're not a fool. I'm suggesting an arrangement."

"What kind of arrangement?"

"You hire the slave from me. Each week you have her, you pay me. Enough for wine, doctors, drugs. If you find what I've said is a lie, you give her back and stop paying. If I die, she's yours. Don't worry, I won't last long. I dream of a huge black dog almost every night. You know who that is."

I looked at Felix, a decaying hulk lying shipwrecked on the couch. I could see the shadow hanging over him. "You may live forever and ruin me," I said, trying to sound jocular.

"I may die tomorrow and you'll be the richer." He belched loudly again, rubbing his chest. "So you agree? Come and look at the girl. You won't regret it."

"I can't come today. I have work to do."

"Tomorrow, then."

"I'll try."

I asked Agata to pack a basket with food and wine for him and sent her son to carry it. "Terribly kind," Felix said at the door. "Come early tomorrow. I don't like to wait."

I watched him lurch down the street, followed by the diminutive figure of the boy lugging the heavy basket. Like all poets, Felix's speech was a farrago of lies and fantasies and one couldn't take what he said too seriously. But the idea that his poems were now being written for him by a slave – a female slave at that – was original, even for Felix.

Of course, Rome was now filled with curiosities of all kinds. As the Empire expanded, strange beasts and stranger humans were brought home from the edges of the world to amuse the masses. Lions and rhinoceroses graced the amphitheatres. It was quite possible to find slaves who had been kings or philosophers or mathematicians in countries which now bore a Roman name and were ruled by a Roman governor. So why not a woman who wrote hexameters? I was curious to see her, at least. It occurred to me that I hadn't asked her name. It didn't matter. She was probably a figment of Felix's drunken imagination. And in any case, if she existed, the name of a slave could be changed in a moment.

I unrolled the scroll Felix had given me. The handwriting wasn't Felix's. It was extraordinarily irregular. I presumed it was her hand. I read the first poem.

He doesn't even know he's reached heaven,
That fellow on the couch beside you.
He blinks at you, inclines his head to hear what you say;
He tastes the sweetness of your whisper and your laugh,
Casually breathes your breath, which has so uprooted my heart
That whenever I catch a glimpse of you, even for a moment,
My voice dies in my throat, my blood catches fire in my veins,
My eyes are sealed, my ears buzz,
Sweat pours down my flanks and I tremble from head to toe
And it seems to me there is only a blade of grass
Between me and death.

I laid the scroll aside, swept by memories of the women I had lost. Livia's little dog, a pathetic relic of a world that no longer existed except in memory, huddled against my legs. I touched the creature's bony flanks and it licked my hand perfunctorily, perhaps remembering gentler fingers that would caress no more.

I wrote some letters in the afternoon. One was to Joseph of Arimathea, thanking him for the news and sharing with him some of my thoughts about Jesus:

*As you know, my acquaintance with him was momentary. The impression he created on me is based principally on the few words we exchanged and the noble manner in which he died.*

*I was in the room when he was sentenced and at the foot of his cross when he died and yet somehow I failed to understand what had happened. I still do not understand it, even now. I heard him forgive the soldiers who drove nails through his bones. How can one understand such a thing?*

*Little as I comprehend, he has made me consider afresh what it means to be a Roman and what it means to have authority. My time in Judaea was short, but it has set my life in a different direction.*

I also included a guarded reference to my conversation with Vitellius and conveyed the hope that the situation in Judaea might be ameliorated one day. I sealed the letter with the ring Herod Antipas had given me, pressing the carnelian into the wax. It was the first time I had used it. The gorgon came out well, with her eyes glaring and her tongue protruding through her fangs. I used the ring to seal all my correspondence from then on.

The next letter was a formal note to Pilate, thanking him for his hospitality and wishing him good health. I wrote also to Glabulus, thanking him warmly and expressing the hope that I would see him soon in Rome, as he had promised. He was making a good living as the principal Roman lawyer in Caesarea and I wished him easy cases and fat fees until we saw one another again.

The final letter, to Procula, was the most difficult to frame. As things had stood between us when we had parted, there was little to say. I thanked her for her good wishes and assured her that I was safely back in Rome. I gave her a brief account of the long voyage home, its wanderings and its dreams. I concluded with the hope that she would keep me informed as to her doings now and then.

*I will always have the greatest interest in your life. I tried to tell you the feelings that I had for you while I was in Jerusalem, but I am a dry lawyer and not a poet. I know that I didn't express myself well. Perhaps I will never be able to express those feelings. They remain as something deeply precious in my heart.*

*I urge you once more to consider your situation. I will not refer to this again. I am sure your husband will see this letter, and I urge him, too, to consider you – and make some preparations for your future.*

*Life is filled with uncertainties. None of us may know what the morrow holds. A husband should prepare for his wife's future in his own absence, since his life, more precarious and perilous than hers, is always in jeopardy. But a woman also has a right to consider what she may do, on that morrow.*

It was one of the strangest letters I have written. I had tried once again to express my love but had used the hard, dry words, once again, of an advocate. There was nothing to be done. I was as I was. The gorgon sealed the paper with her protruding tongue and gnashing fangs.

From that moment, I tried to put Procula out of my mind. I had limited success in this endeavour, for she has been in my mind from that day to this. But I tried to steer my life, as I had said to Joseph of Arimathea, in a different direction.

I had taken Felix at his word and arrived at his house early the next day. A session of fruitless pounding on the locked door taught me my error. The poet lived in a noisome lane which trapped a multitude of disagreeable odours from the latrine buckets standing outside each door. Built by speculators and left to rot without maintenance, these structures burned down regularly, often roasting the families inside. Those which survived the Great Fire were pulled down by Nero to build grand boulevards.

Felix finally opened the door, bleary and stinking of last night's wine. "Oh. It's you."

"Yes, it's me."

"You'd better come in."

I followed him. The house was crowded with broken pieces of once-fine furniture, the air greasy with the smell of rats The poet gestured to a rickety chair but I preferred to stand. Felix hoisted his shift and pissed copiously, with frequent pauses and grunts, into a clay pot.

"You're a charming host," I said. "And what a lovely neighbourhood. I remember when you had a grand apartment with a view of the Tiber."

"This is my view of the Tiber now," he growled, showing me the brimming pot. He emptied it into the gutter outside his door.

"Where is the girl?" I asked.

He farted. "Sleeping."

"She sleeps more heavily than you do? Through the thunder of your farts and the cataracts of your piss?"

"You might have given us a chance to get ready."

"You told me to come early."

"I meant early in the evening. It doesn't matter. You may as well see her at her worst. Come."

He led me down a narrow, low corridor which twisted crazily left and right like a maze. The darkness was almost complete but I could make out the bulk of the poet ahead of me. I groped my way along, wondering what kind of fool's errand I was on.

I bumped into Felix's broad back in the darkness. He had stopped and was unbolting a door. It swung open. Dim grey light filtered through the darkness.

"There she is."

The room was tiny. A slit window, protected with iron bars, had been set above head height. A figure was lying on a straw paliasse on the floor, huddled under a blanket. Felix pulled the blanket away, revealing a naked female back. In the grainy light, I could see the raised weals on the white flesh. She made a small, wet sound with her mouth. I bent over her and caught the rank smell of cheap wine. "She's drunker than you are!"

"Impossible," Felix said with dignity. "More talented, perhaps. Drunker, never." He tried to rouse the woman, pulling her arm roughly so that she sprawled on her back. I saw a bleary face, limp breasts. I turned on my heel and groped my way back along the passage.

"Where are you going?" Felix called after me. "Help me with her!"

I was too angry to reply. Felix emerged backwards from the burrow, hauling the woman after him. She was still only half conscious. He dropped her on the floor with a thud and turned to face me. "Where did you disappear to?" he panted.

"Is this your poetess?"

"None other." He examined my expression. "Aha. You're disappointed. That's good."

"Unlike you, I don't have time to waste," I said grimly. "Goodbye, Felix."

"Wait." Felix grasped at the sleeve of my cloak. "I told you that you would see her at her worst. From here onward, everything else will be an improvement."

I jerked my cloak away. "Don't touch me."

Felix threw up his hands in a gesture of incomprehension. "But what's the matter, curse you?"

"You said she was young and beautiful!"

Felix lowered his hands. "Those are both relative terms, Marcellus. She's younger than you and more beautiful than me. Take a look at the poor little bitch. She's not as bad as she seems."

The woman had managed to pull herself onto a stool. She looked desperately ill, her face pinched, her eyes shut tight. She wore a shapeless grey garment which she was clutching tightly over her bosom.

"How do you afford enough wine to keep both of you so drunk?" I asked.

"She's a genius, Marcellus. Look what she wrote last night." He gestured at the wall. Scrawled in chalk on the blotched red plaster were a few lines.

With your smooth neck wreathed in violets
Sweet pink roses and purple crocus
And honey scented garlands of eglantine
We danced through the grove
To music unplayed, unheard.


The letters were badly formed and hardly legible. I shrugged. "It doesn't scan. And it's not finished."

"But what a start, eh? She needs whipping from time to time. But she's got the gift."

The girl suddenly leaned forward, snatched up Felix's pisspot and vomited into it, one hand clutching her dark hair to pull it away from the stream. Felix stepped back to avoid being spattered. "Behold. The Muse has left her."

"She's a drunken drab," I said in disgust.

Felix knocked the plaster with his knuckle. "She can't hold her liquor, I agree, but these are the vomits which matter."

I noticed that the plaster was covered with other straggling lines of verse, some faint and half erased. The walls of the room made up a battered and disintegrating book of verses.

"Sorry." The girl had finished vomiting and spoke in a whisper. Her eyes were downcast. Her face was triangular, with broad, somewhat Asiatic cheekbones and a small chin. Her mouth appeared bruised, perhaps by Felix. She seemed more Near Eastern than Hellenic, Lydian or Ionian, or perhaps Thracian. She was smaller than I had thought – the sack-like garment gave an impression of bulk, but her arms and legs were slender.

I was weary of the smells and sights of the house. "She's not a suitable ornament for my household. But thank you for the offer."

Felix's face crumpled. "Gods. Even if you don't like the poetry, take her to scrub your floors!"

I shook my head. "No. I don't want her."

"Why not?"

"For one thing, she's a drunkard, like you. For another, I don't believe she wrote a word of this poetry."

Felix stared at me for a moment, his mouth open. Then he lumbered over the girl. "A poem. Quick." He slapped her face.

"Don't abuse her."

Felix groped among the debris on a table. "Where's the whip? I'll beat hexameters out of her."

"Did he say I was young and beautiful?" The woman's voice was husky, almost inaudible.

"What?" Felix panted raggedly. "What did she say?"

She didn't look up as she spoke.

"Did he say I was young and beautiful?
Now you see that I am neither.
The burning coals which you lay on my skin
To punish me for my ugliness
Hurt less than the coldness of your face and voice.
But when you turn your smile on me
Sparks leap into my breast
And set my heart aflame."

Her Latin was fluent but she had a distinctive accent, aspirating some syllables almost like an Etruscan. Felix wheezed triumphantly. "Now, what do you say?" He staggered to a chair and sat down heavily, rubbing his chest, his eyes closing. "Oh, Gods. I'm dying."

I turned to the woman. There was something oddly unslavelike about her. She didn't have the common, dehumanized look. "Were you born a slave?" I asked.

She seemed to hunch her shoulders, her head down. "I was enslaved as a child."

"Where?"

"I don't remember."

"By whom?"

"Greeks."

"And your parents?"

"They died."

"What is your name?"

She raised her eyes to mine for a moment. Her eyes were large, liquid and black, holding me for a moment. "Daphne."

Felix hissed with laughter like a leaky bellows. "Daphne, pursued by Apollo. When he tried to rape her, she turned into a laurel. He found himself fucking a tree trunk. I'm not going to hide anything from you. If you try to warm her up that way, she disappears somehow. It's a trick she has. You find yourself screwing a log. Don't expect comfort from her. Her romantic inclinations are reserved for the Muses."

"I'm not of a romantic nature, Felix." I turned and walked up and down the room, thinking. Felix eyed me slyly.

"She's valuable," he said. "A slave who can read and write, who speaks Latin, Greek and who knows what Barbarian tongues. A slave who can toss off a poem in a moment. Worth a fortune. Worth fifty labourers."

I turned to him. "Then why don't you sell her on the open market?"

Felix gestured at the girl. "Look at her. They'd break her in pieces."

"What do you care?"

Felix's hoarse voice rose. "I don't want any more sins on my soul, Marcellus. Not where I'm going. Shall we talk terms?"

As I walked home I could hear the clonk clonk of her wooden clogs following behind me. It sounded as though she could barely lift their weight. I half-hoped to hear her break away and run for her life down some alleyway. I decided I wouldn't follow her if she did.

But when I reached home, she was still behind me, her head drooping, her hair hanging over her eyes, hugging her bundle of possessions. Her shoulders were heaving with the effort to catch her breath. She was probably dying, like Felix, lungs riddled with infection or belly rotten with cheap wine.

Dionysius opened the door. Like the well trained butler he was, he exhibited no surprise, his smooth face bland.

"I've bought a new slave. Her name's Daphne. She'll sleep in the little attic room until we decide where to put her."

"Yes, master."

"Tell Agata to make her something to eat."

But as the girl stepped over the threshold, she crumpled as though her ankles had been broken and fell to the floor. Dionysius helped me to raise her. She weighed little. Her head dangled limply. She was no more than half conscious.

"Master." Dionysius showed me a blood-stained thumb and index finger. "She's crawling with vermin."

"We'll wash her. Is there hot water?"

"Agata's boy can light the fires."

We took her to the bathroom. It had been installed at Livia's wish, and to her taste, with bronze spigots and a carved marble tub, simple but functional. It was the warmest room in the house and not often used in the summer; fires lit beneath the slabs of the floor heated both the water and the air. While the boy lit the wood, I and Dionysius undressed Daphne. She wore only a single undergarment, not fit to be kept.

"Burn it," I told the Greek. "Burn all her things. Fill the bath. And bring some soap."

"Yes, Master."

Naked, she was pale and undernourished-looking. The whipping Felix had administered was livid on her back, crusts of blood in places. Compared to the things I'd seen inflicted on slaves, the injuries were light, but I felt sorry for her.

She sat unresisting while I rubbed her skin with the soap that Livia had preferred to the strigil, a cake of pomade scented with violet oil which produced a foam able to carry away much dirt. She was extremely dirty. I was perhaps rougher than necessary and her flesh yielded under my palms, her bones frail. Her breasts were small and virginal.

"You've never borne a child?" I asked.

She shook her head without speaking.

I rinsed the soap from her body with a sea sponge. Between the weals, her skin was fine and delicate. "Why did Felix whip you?"

"He says the pain improves my verses."

"It certainly improved my arithmetic when I was a schoolboy. I didn't know it had the same effect on poets. I'm going to shave your head."

"No!"

"You have parasites."

"I will not allow you!"

I began to sharpen the razor. "I am not accustomed to arguing with slaves."

"You've already complained about my ugliness. I'll wash my hair with white ash if they will bring me a little. Please."

"Get in the bath."

She clambered into the hot water, gasping. The tub was large and she sank beneath the water, her eyes closing. A film of oil appeared slick on the surface of the water and the smell of summer violets rushed into my nostrils.

She surfaced and lay in the bath like one dead, her breathing almost imperceptible. Her body hair was black and fine, glistening wetly in her armpits and between her thighs. Livia had kept her body hairless, in the Roman fashion. I stared at this animal nakedness I had purchased.

"Why are you looking at me like that?" she asked, her eyes opening.

"The last woman I saw in this bath was my wife." I didn't know why I had said the words, and regretted them.

She seemed to read my thoughts. "You can say what you like to me. I am a ghost, like your wife."

"What?"

"All slaves are ghosts. If we were real people we would kill ourselves rather than go on living."

Her words struck me. "Many slaves are freed and rise to positions of considerable importance."

"And most die like dogs, still chained to the wall. Your other slaves are sleek and well fed. Don't you beat them and starve them to keep them on their toes?"

"I'm able to make myself obeyed."

"Yes, I'm sure you are." She put her hand over the dark triangle between her legs, as though aware of her nakedness for the first time. The boy entered, holding an armful of towels, wide-eyed and open-mouthed.

"Get her some clean, white ash," I commanded, taking the towels.

I walked to Livia's closet and after hesitating, opened the door. My wife's robes and tunics were laid out as on the day she had died. I had been unable to give them away. I stared at the clothes. Each garment had a memory, a song. There was nothing here that the slave could wear without transgressing the rigid dress code of the day. But she couldn't remain naked. Finally I selected a plain undergarment and a blue stola which had no memories for me.

I stared at the row of shoes. To give her a new pair seemed preposterous. Yet the pairs that Livia had worn were so intimate, still bearing the oval imprints of her toes. I picked a pair of plain sandals made of thin strips of leather. It was like dressing a doll, I thought.

I took the clothing and the towels back to the bathroom. The boy had brought her a bowl of ash from the fire. She crouched and urinated into the bowl quickly, then scrubbed her scalp with the resulting white foam, her small breasts quivering. "This will kill the lice," she said. "I've done it before."

"If I find any tomorrow, I'll shave your head and not ask permission."

"You will not find any."

I laid the clothes on the chair beside the bath. "You can wear these until I can get something more suitable."

She looked at the things with her liquid black eyes. "These are your wife's."

"Yes."

"She would prefer that I did not wear them because I am alive and I would prefer not to wear them because she's dead. But they'll do for the time being."

"You're very kind," I said. "You can wear them until Agata finds you something more appropriate.".

I left her to wash her hair in the bath and sat down at my desk to read through some papers.

When I saw her emerge in my late wife's clothes, the effect on me was strange. I stared at her blankly. Her hair and face were clean. Livia's clothes fitted her well; more than fitting her, they had taken away what I can only describe as a shattered look she'd had at Felix's, as though she had been put together from the fragments of other people. She walked differently, too, not stumbling in her clogs, but with some poise.

"I told you I was a ghost," she said to me. "Does it seem as though your wife has returned?"

"My wife was more than a gown and a pair of sandals," I replied.

"Then I must be different from her." She came to where I was sitting and stood in front of me. I caught the scent of violets from her skin. There were shadows under her eyes, something I was later to learn was part of her natural complexion. Although she was pale, her pallor seemed to overlay darkness. Her face was almost unlined. Her features were delicately cut; her nostrils, lips, eyes were as precisely delineated as though made not of flesh, but of marble.

"How old are you?" I asked her.

"I don't know," she said. *I don't remember* or *I don't know* were her stock answers to all personal questions.

"You seem to be very young. Perhaps no more than eighteen."

"It feels as though I have been alive for longer than eighteen years."

"Twenty or twenty two, then."

"Perhaps one of my previous owners may know."

172

"What has Felix told you about me?" I asked.

"He told me you would treat me better than he did."

"That wouldn't be difficult, it seems."

She shrugged. "I've had worse owners than Felix. He could have sold me into a brothel. He waited for weeks until you returned from your voyages so he could offer me to you."

"Nevertheless he kept you in a filthy state, beat you and made you drunk."

"He didn't have to make me drunk. I like being drunk."

"You will not be drunk here."

She looked at me speculatively. "You have a very commanding manner when you're not trying to seem pleasant. You Romans don't like to see your women drinking wine. I wonder why."

"How long were you with Felix?"

"I can't remember."

"He said he won you at dice."

"I believe that's true. My last owner was a profligate gambler. He would often stake me at dice."

"He didn't ask you for poetry?"

"Only Felix asked me for poetry."

"I doubt that I will ask you for any. You had better rest. We will decide whether you may be of some use to me."

And in this strange manner I acquired an addition to my household.

# CHAPTER NINE

# ROMAN WOMEN

From the start, she was not a particularly comfortable addition. Early the next morning, Dionysius came to tell me that she was still unwell.

"Where is she?" I asked.

"She is waiting in the kitchen. Agata is with her."

Sighing, I went to see for myself. Daphne was no longer wearing the blue gown I had given her yesterday, but a plain linen shift that Agata had found for her. She looked even more exhausted and sick than she had the day before. Her head was hanging. She did not look up at me.

"Has she eaten?" I asked Agata.

"She vomits everything, Master."

I lifted Daphne's chin. Her face was white, her eyes unfocused. I looked in her mouth and saw that her tongue was cracked and dry. "She needs water."

"She refuses to drink."

I took a bowl of water and led Daphne to my study. Sitting opposite her, I made her drink the water in small spoons. She retched several times, but slowly absorbed a cupful. "This is not from the wine," I said. "Where does this come from?"

"I'm sick," she whispered.

I touched her forehead. "You have no fever." I was aware of a strange smell from her skin. "Have you taken something?"

"No."

But some flicker in her expression made me suspicious. "You've taken something. You've poisoned yourself."

She grimaced wearily. "If I have, it was insufficient."

"What did you take?"

She seemed too tired to deny any longer. "Aconite."

I stared at her. It was not uncommon for slaves to attempt to take their own lives, which was why poisons and weapons were kept out of their hands. "You may yet die," I said dryly. "Aconite is very effective, even in small doses. You have pain in the heart?"

She nodded. "Worse than usual."

"Where did you get the poison?"

"I stole it from Felix."

"Why did Felix keep aconite?"

"He said it was his last refuge. He was very angry. He whipped me until he was tired."

I made a mental note to discuss this with the old monster. "He conveniently forgot to inform me that you might die on my hands."

She closed her eyes. "You could ask for your money back."

"What was the point of this, Daphne?"

"I didn't think I could face a new master."

"Were you so fond of the old one?"

"Felix told me to submit to you. I have been raped enough in my life."

"I have no intention of using you in that way," I snapped, growing angry with her. "Life is too precious to throw away, no matter how wretched it may seem."

"Is that what you think? Then you haven't lived long enough."

I threw the rest of the water in her face. She flinched, her eyes widening and becoming focused. "Don't be insolent," I said. "Do you think only you suffer?"

She wiped her face. "Let me die in peace, for God's sake. I hate all of you."

I left her before I could grow even angrier and sent Dionysius running to a physician who had served in the Army with me, Marcus Egidius. He came straight from his bed to my house with his bag of medical instruments. He took her pulse and studied her eyes and tongue. "It is aconite," he said. "I will need to examine her thoroughly. Hold her."

Weakened as she was, she fought like a wildcat. Agata had to hold her arms while Dionysius and I held her legs and we all received bites and scratches for our pains. Egidius inserted a speculum between her thighs and used the screw adjustment to dilate her. He squinted into her intimate parts while she spat curses at us.

"I thought so." With evident satisfaction, Egidius took his forceps and deftly withdrew a little damp bundle. "You see? They put it in their privates because they think that is more effective. But the absorption is actually slower. If she had swallowed this she would not have lived an hour. I hope you didn't pay too much for her."

I held onto her ankles grimly, for she was still struggling. "I fear I did."

Egidius prepared a syringe. "Having survived two days, she may yet live. Next time you want to buy a slave, call me in *before* you pay."

He rinsed her carefully with the syringe before retracting the speculum. She had grown exhausted by now and was trembling in all her limbs. She submitted to a draught of mandragora, which Egidius said was the only antidote. I was struck by the irony of it: what Herodias had poisoned me with was Daphne's cure.

While they dressed Daphne and took her upstairs, I gave Egidius the breakfast he had missed by hurrying to my house from his bed. "Do you think she really meant to do it?" I asked him.

"Who can say?" He looked up from his porridge. "You appear rather shaken."

I rubbed my face. "She takes me by surprise. I didn't know she was so wretched."

Egidius grunted. "Nobody can tell what is in a slave's mind."

"I look into hers and I see an abyss."

He grimaced. "Do you miss the Army?"

"Not much."

"I do. Life was simple. We were clean. We had honour." He spooned up the porridge. "There is little that is clean or honourable in Rome these days. I hate all these slaves everywhere. I hate what we do to them. And what they do to us. We degrade them in one way and they degrade us in another. I don't know which is worse. But the combined effect is a disaster. We're growing lazy and cruel. Our amusement is torture. We have become the most corrupt nation on earth."

"You need some honey on your porridge, I think."

"You may smile, Marcellus, but you know I am right."

"Yes. I know you are right. I have the same thoughts."

"Slavery is a sickness that is rotting our society." He jerked his thumb at the attic, where Daphne was being put to bed. "Why did you buy this creature, may I ask?"

"A favour for an old friend."

"She is trouble."

"I can see that."

"You think her handsome?"

I shrugged. "I don't consider her in those terms."

"Don't you? It's years since Livia died. You should take a wife."

"So they tell me. I don't see any I would wish to take."

Egidius smiled. "Call me again if she gets worse. And good luck with her." He gave me a tincture of opium to help her sleep. I thanked him, paid him, bade him farewell and went to see Daphne.

"So this is why Felix whipped you," I said, covering her with the blanket. "You deserved it. There are enough exits from this life without making another for ourselves."

"I wish I could find them."

"You would have found one swiftly if you had swallowed the aconite instead of putting it in your woman's parts."

"I did it so that if you took me, you would die, too."

Her reply silenced me for a while. I examined her face, wondering what sort of woman this was. "You may have destroyed your ability to bear a child," I said at last. "Have you thought of that?"

She croaked with laughter. "Do you imagine I want to bear a child, Marcellus?"

"Don't attempt to repeat this folly," I said. "Nobody will violate you here. Nobody will beat you. You will be expected to work. If you serve me well, you may earn your freedom one day. But I will not

MARIUS GABRIEL

keep you if you harm yourself or anyone else. I will sell you in the market. You may be sure of that."

Her eyes found mine. They were very dark, the opium having swollen the pupils. "How godlike you are to have in your hands the powers of freedom and imprisonment."

"And how foolish you are to keep such a blade in your mouth. You had better sheathe it. Felix may have appreciated your sarcasm but I do not."

"If I knew how to keep silent, I would."

"If I knew how to silence you, I would. For your sake and all our sakes."

She seemed very frail, lying in her cot, with her white face and her drugged eyes. Perhaps my reaction seems harsh, now. I was angry with her. I felt insulted by what she had done. But my heart was not devoid of pity. Her grasp on life seemed so tenuous. There was something in her that had touched me, even though I did not admire it or even understand it – some quality that haunted and perplexed me. I did not wish to see her extinguished. I believed that being gentle with her would be counterproductive. Perhaps I was wrong. I acted for the best. I stood over her as she drifted into sleep, then appointed Agata's boy to watch with her.

What Daphne's relationship with Felix had been was a closed book to me, although I later got some idea. She entered my service as an enigma. I owned her and yet one might as well claim to own a wild bird; it could be kept in a cage but never possessed as tamer things are.

Over the next days she remained in her bed. The poison left her body slowly. I administered the mandragora with care until she said the pains in her heart were gone. Her arrival had already cost me a lot of time and money and I was growing impatient to regulate the situation.

I made her get up and walk around the courtyard to recover her strength. "I have been looking at the manuscript that Felix gave me," I told her. "Your orthography is very confused. The letters are all of different sizes. Some letters are Greek, some Latin, all jumbled together. Many are reversed or upside down."

"I write as I feel. When I'm sad, I turn the letters upside down."

"That's absurd. Letters are things we all hold in common. You can't write them as it pleases you."

"Why not?"

"For the same reason that four can't equal six and black can't mean white."

"It means what it means to me."

"It has to mean something that we can all agree upon. Otherwise nothing can turn out as we expect."

"Do you really expect things to turn out as you expect they will?"

"Yes. I make plans. Sometimes the fates take a hand. But generally, the outcome is as I anticipate."

"How lucky you are to live in such a predictable world."

"We all live in the same world."

"And how lucky to have a mind so clear and orderly," she added.

"Are you mocking me?"

"Not in the slightest."

"I have warned you to keep your tongue in check. Not all of life is poetry, Daphne."

"I have some inkling of that." She had been leaning on me more and more heavily as we walked around the courtyard and now she stumbled. "Please, Marcellus. I need to sit."

"You cannot call me by my name," I said irritably. "You are a slave. You must call me 'Master.'"

"I will try to remember." She lowered herself into the chair and closed her eyes wearily. "How my legs ache."

I sat beside her. "Who taught you to write?" I asked her.

"I taught myself."

"How?"

"By copying what I found written on the walls of the pens where slaves are kept."

"And what is written there?"

"Names of people. Names of cities. Names of ships and legions and roads. Dates and places. Curses against Rome. Obscenities of all kinds. Letters from parents to lost children or between separated husbands and wives. Prayers. Spells. Incantations. Words of madness. Languages that nobody can read."

"No poems?"

"It's all poetry." Her dark eyes closed. I let her sleep.

In the hope that her arithmetic was better than her spelling, I gave her some simple calculations to do. The results were very erratic. She had an incomplete understanding of numbers. But I had to find her something to do. I gave her a slate and chalk, like a schoolgirl, and set her to copying letters and doing sums day after day, a task which bored her literally to tears on occasion. I could see that sometimes she could barely restrain herself from throwing the slate at me.

"Why must I do this?" she demanded passionately one day when I had given her the morning's exercises.

"Because there are very few men in the world who will keep you in order to write poetry, while there are many who will keep you to write neatly and do accounts."

"So you mean to sell me to someone else?"

"Persevere, Daphne."

Her eyes shimmered with tears of anger as she took up the slate again. Within two weeks, however, she had learned to write my letters and calculate my fees.

"This is an accomplishment I value as much as your hexameters," I told her, "given that I'm not a very poetic man."

"Such generous praise. You're playing Pygmalion with me," she replied dryly.

"Pygmalion carved Galatea because he was tired of real women. You call yourself Daphne, so of course you know Ovid?"

"I've read scraps."

"Scraps? No more?"

"No more."

"Would you like to read more?" I got the Metamorphoses from my library and gave it to her to read. "The story of Pygmalion and

Galatea is in Book X," I told her. She retired with it to her little room in the attic of the house, like a monkey climbing to the top of a tree with an especially delicious fruit. I was interested to see what she made of it.

I saw clients in the afternoon and went with them to the magistrate to resolve an issue of an inheritance. I celebrated with them in a tavern afterwards and returned home in the late afternoon, flushed with success and wine. Daphne was waiting for me with the copy of Ovid.

"Have you read these?" she demanded.

I smiled. "I read them as a schoolboy. We passed them around secretly amongst ourselves. They were considered highly immoral, not to say pornographic, and not suitable for boys."

"They are very erotic." She lay back on the couch, running her fingertips through her hair, a habit she had at the time, anxious to find any trace of parasites, since she still feared I would shave her head. But her hair was dark, glossy and clean, now. She had put on some weight since coming to my household. Her limbs were becoming rounded under the simple clothes she wore. Life may have been duller for her but it was certainly healthier. "What happened to Ovid?" she asked.

"Augustus banished him for praising adultery. At least, that was the charge. Augustus was rather stern about that sort of thing. When I was a boy, one whispered the name of Ovid as one might refer to some forbidden pleasure. He died in exile among the barbarians in a very pathetic state."

"That is the usual reward for poetry."

I smiled. "If you say so."

"Did you find the poems exciting?" she asked.

"They made me dream."

"Yes, they are all dreams, strange and brilliant dreams."

"I'm surprised Felix didn't give you Ovid to read."

"He had sold most of his books. He forbade me to open any of the ones that were left."

"Why?"

"He didn't want me to pick up the ideas of others."

"Perhaps he was right." The sun was setting and a shaft of golden light had touched the side of her face, revealing its soft curve and the fullness of her lower lip. We walked out into the garden. Livia had planted a cherry tree there some years ago and it was now bearing fruit. I picked some and gave one to her. She inspected them with a frown. "What are these?"

"Cherries."

"I've never seen this fruit before. Is it poisonous?"

"No. No escape for you here. But there's a stone. Be careful of your teeth."

"It looks poisonous," she said, not quite convinced. She tried one nevertheless. Her eyes closed as she absorbed the flesh. She didn't say anything. When she finally spat the stone into her hand, it was as smooth as bone. She inspected it.

"You can throw that away."

She closed her fingers around it. "I'll keep it."

"Why?"

"A memory."

"Was it good?"

"I won't forget."

"In Anatolia, the women colour their lips with cherry juice."

She bit one in half and rubbed the red stain on her own mouth. "Like this?"

"I suppose so." I had to turn aside.

"Why do you look away from me?"

"The red changes you."

"In what way?"

"In a way you would perhaps not like me to explain."

"Is it an erotic metamorphosis as in the poems of Ovid? I see by your face that it reminds you that I am a creature you possess, and which you can take to your bed at your pleasure."

I frowned. "I've told you, there is no danger of that."

"So long as I refrain from cherries?"

"I don't understand why you reproach me with this. Have I molested you?"

"Perhaps you're still afraid I have aconite in my woman's parts."

"I trust you have not!"

There was a gleam in her eyes. "I wish you could have seen your face that day. You looked as though you had sat on a scorpion."

"You are a scorpion."

"Then don't sit on me."

"You didn't need to use the aconite. I've never entered relations of this kind with slaves."

"Your feelings are noble," she said in her dry way. "But you have no wife. You're still young. For most men, the presence of submissive women in the household is an invitation. The majority of female slaves have to endure it. I expected you to use me in that way. Felix said that you would."

"He mistook me. A slave can never be said to consent to any master. She's under the gravest coercion. There can be no joy on either side from such a union. Is your life here with me no better than it was with Felix?"

She contemplated a cherry. "It's different."

"Better? Or worse?"

"He was dirty and rough. But with him, at least, I did not feel I was a ghost."

"Do I make you feel you are a ghost?"

"You're very scrupulous with me," she said obliquely.

"How did Felix make you feel alive?"

"He would shout at me and call me vile names. We would get drunk and dance. When he fell down I would dance over him and he would make up filthy stories about me. He would try to catch me so he could take me. We would fight. Then he would beat me."

"And you enjoyed that life?"

"You asked only how he made me feel less a ghost. You didn't ask if I enjoyed it."

"Your life here must be very quiet by comparison."

"You treat me well, Marcellus." She had never started to call me Master and by now I no longer expected her to. "Nobody has been as kind to me as you."

I had a painful recollection that Procula had once said much the same thing to me. "But I make you feel a ghost?"

"I told you – if I didn't feel like a ghost then I would kill myself."

"I want you to live."

She rubbed the red stain off her lips. "Then you must let me remain a ghost."

I didn't always understand what she meant by the strange things she said. Her life with me was a dull one, perhaps, but not an unpleasant one. In the mornings, while I was in court, she was free to do as she wanted. She would help Agata with household tasks if she felt like it, or simply read books from my library, her favourite pastime. I forbade her nothing and so she devoured poetry, histories, even dusty treatises on geometry and mathematics. In the afternoons I would dictate my work to her for a few hours. Sometimes in the early evening we would talk – many questions arose in her mind from the reading of books, since she was astonishingly ignorant about the world – until the evening meal. She ate with the other slaves while I would dine alone.

Felix, in the meanwhile, ceased any pretence that he was writing poetry. With the stipend I paid him he could afford both wine and doctors and so set about steadily drinking himself to death in the comfort of his hutch. I paid him occasional visits, but he seemed to need nobody and nothing but cheap wine. He never asked about Daphne.

Between some men and women there is a fellowship which allows them to talk of intimate things from the start. Perhaps it's a kind of mutual recognition. So it was between Daphne and me. Our conversations grew longer and became something I looked forward to. From discussing the poetry of Ovid or the calculations of Anaxagoras, we began to talk about ourselves. I told her about my origins and the kindness which Vitellius and Sextilia had shown me after my parents had died. She described what she could of her early life, trying to explain to me remembrances beyond words.

"I remember the sunlight on the sea in front of our house," she told me, "and the temple where we worshipped. I had two sisters who played with me. I remember my mother crying when my father died. I remember her blood on the floor when they killed her."

From what she told me, it seemed she had been enslaved by pirates, not by soldiers. She must have been about eight or nine. They had taken her and her sisters, Aglaia and Thalia, by boat to a large island, perhaps Sicily, and had sold them to slave merchants there. The sisters had been brought to Ostia and soon after that, separated. She had been passed from merchant to merchant and from owner to owner. She had worked in kitchens and laundries as a scullion, meeting some kindness and much indifference.

"The older women I worked with kept my hair cut very short, so I looked like a boy, to protect me against men. My breasts were always small and I was thin. But when my blood came, it was harder to hide. The women told me what to do if a man wanted me, so I was in some way prepared. They told me not to fight or I would be hurt even worse. They told me how to make it pass more quickly and easily." She had been very young when they had first raped her, a violation which had left deep wounds in her heart. She had learned how to become a tree, as she put it, so that the men could do what they wanted and then leave her alone. Only one man had been able to drive her to madness with especial cruelties; when she had resisted, he had chained and whipped her. She still bore some of the scars on her legs and buttocks. When the man's wife had found out, she administered cruelties of her own. She had spent a wretched year, her fourteenth, as I calculated, in this household before being sold to the gambler. "When he lost, he would beat me. When he won, he would rape me. It was always one or the other – he would never break even."

"I'm sorry, Daphne," I said.

"I should perhaps not tell you these things," she said, seeing my expression. "I don't want to disgust you."

"It isn't what is done to us that's disgusting, only what we do."

"I have done disgusting things, too."

"You had no choice."

"My life could have been far worse. Some slaves are crippled by their owners. Many of the men are castrated, like animals. When slaves are cheap, they're often worked or starved to death. Being a woman is in some ways easier."

"Did you ever see your sisters again?"

"I thought I saw my younger sister once, at a market where I was sold. I called to her, but it was only for a moment and then she was gone." Her eyes filled with tears, one of the rare occasions on which I saw her cry. "Some slaves are bought only once and spend a lifetime with the same owner. Others, like me, are bought and sold many times. It's very hard to find one's family. I don't even know what city that was and now it's years ago." She glanced at me. "Why do you ask these things?"

"I feel that we're becoming friends."

"Or as close to friends as two people can become," she said satirically, "when one owns the other."

"That should not preclude friendship."

"You are naïve."

"Why should friendship be precluded?"

"Because I am your possession. Because I am anxious to please you with every breath I take."

"I have not noticed that you are especially anxious to please me, even though I am your master."

"Nevertheless, I am especially anxious to please you." She gave me one of her rare, luminous smiles. "Even though you are my master."

Our friendship continued through such intimate and often sad discussions. To enable us to enjoy the pleasure we took in one another's company, we made changes in our routine, such as the evening meal, which we started to share. Our conversations had seldom ended by the time the supper was ready. We were loath to abandon them. Eating together is a warm ritual, which is why lovers do it with such joy. The owners of slaves are urged to avoid it, for the same reason. Against all wisdom, we fell into the habit of sitting at the table together. We would talk until late. This familiarity deepened our relationship considerably.

A further development came with the manumission of Dionysius. He had been with me for almost a decade and had been a faithful servant through good times and bad. He had passed the age of thirty, which meant that he could be freed and take Roman citizenship. I decided to free him and allocated him a sum of money with which to start a business buying and selling grain – he had an exceptional ability with figures. He later grew extremely wealthy, which I was glad to see. At the time of which I am writing, however, his manumission meant that my household grew smaller and more private. Agata and her boy alone were left. They slept in the rooms adjoining the kitchen. Daphne slept in the attic of my own house, just over my own bedroom. This produced a further subtle change in my relationship with Daphne, an increase in intimacy.

My high principles were easy to maintain when Daphne first came into my life, drab and beaten down as she was. There was, indeed, small merit in repressing my concupiscence, even when I saw her naked in the bath. She was a pathetic sight, ill and half starved. Later, when rest and decent food, as well as abstinence from wine, had begun to make her beautiful, it became a horse far more difficult to master.

Her impact on my life, indeed, was to be profound. It was through her that I embarked on what would be one of the principal themes of my life's legal work, the development of the law pertaining to slaves. It was by considering Daphne and listening to her words that my thoughts first turned in this direction. But I must not allow myself to be carried away in legal issues which can be of no interest to my reader. Let it be enough to say that, although I had never been particularly harsh to my slaves, it was Daphne who brought before me the true inhumanity of this form of commerce.

The succeeding weeks brought two letters from Jerusalem. They made an interesting contrast. One was from Joseph of Arimathea and the other from Procula.

That from Joseph was quite long, written in his usual, immaculate Greek. It was principally about Jesus. After a conventional greeting, he went on,

*Jesus of Nazareth appears to be one of those men who are thought more of after their deaths than during their lifetimes. For everyone who speaks of him, there is a different Jesus. To this one, he is a fiery rebel. To that, he is the voice of moderation. Here you will find him an ignorant peasant, there he is the voice of God.*

*I have always deplored those forces which divide Jew from Jew. I have felt more and more strongly that the amplification of the Temple by Herod has exerted an unbearable pressure on the Jews – pecuniary and spiritual. It has become as much a symbol of tyranny as the legions who march upon our soil.*

*And in conclusion, although many say that Jesus was a fool to come to that Temple, I feel that he came with his eyes open, expecting his death there. You could not save him because he did not wish to be saved.*

He went on to give some news from Caesarea about "your old friend, Pilate," recounting fresh misdeeds in that quarter which I had already encountered in Glabulus' letter. He cleverly managed to express the hope that he would see me again as governor of Judaea, without saying as much in words, and asked for any news I might give him of the Jews in Rome.

The letter from Procula was in her own hand and was shorter:

*My dear friend,*

*I think of you often and of the conversations we had. Here in Caesarea I am able to spend time with Glabulus and his wife. Your name passes across*

*our lips each time we meet, something which gives me relief since I am forbidden to speak it in my husband's presence.*

*He is much the same. The good news of which I told you before we parted continues to illuminate the darkness of my days. Without it, I would have little pleasure in my life.*

*You said that you would write to me but I think you have forgotten. I hope this will remind you. For my own part, I have little news to send that you would wish to hear. Be well, Marcellus, that I may also be well.*

There was so much unhappiness behind her simple words that I was moved. If I had been more impressionable, I might have construed this letter as a declaration of love. But I wasn't impressionable. I was now certain that when the time came for Pilate to go into exile, she would follow him there rather than face the rupture. I wrote back briefly:

*I have not forgotten you. Indeed, I am concerned about you constantly. But there seems little I can do to touch you or influence your life, so I refrain from tormenting you with advice.*

*Religion should be our consolation and not an empty show. I seldom visit the temples now and make few sacrifices these days. Perhaps I am indeed an atheist. Or perhaps I should say that I have become a humanist. I have the feeling so often that my gods have died, or are dying. That is a terrible thought. To discern their workings in our lives is sometimes very difficult. I am glad that you have found a faith which sustains you.*

It was a hard winter that year; ice formed on the Tiber, first at the margins of the river and then in gleaming swathes thick enough for the daring to walk on. Vitellius became Consul. Since he was a favourite of the emperor, the procession was unusually large and grand. It was a public display of his considerable influence and growing power. I was pleased for my uncle and old friend, who had worked hard for Rome and the emperor and was now entering the prime of his career.

I took Daphne to see the ceremonies, thinking it would be instructive. Her appearance drew some attention. Though she was modestly dressed, her face and carriage were so superior to those of other women in the street that people stared. She was entering the full flowering of her beauty. To walk beside her was to feel a flush of pride.

The courts closed for a week's vacation. I, in turn, gave Agata and the boy a week's holiday to visit her sister, who worked on a farm to the north of Rome. She took her son and so Daphne and I were left alone in the house. We spent the time peacefully, reading together by the fire or talking. We prepared our simple meals in the kitchen together. The house was silent, all the city seemed to be huddled around its fires, as we were. In the quiet, she opened a delicate topic.

"You've never remarried."

"No."

"Have you pledged yourself to remain wedded to your wife's ghost?"

"I have made no such vow."

"Then why are there no women in your life?"

"There are women, of course. You, for one."

"I am not a woman, Marcellus, I am a ghost, like your wife. I'm talking of the Portias and Flavias and Julias and Antonias they produce from moulds, all made of almond-paste, all sugary, pure and eligible. There's a wide choice in the market. Aren't you tempted?"

I smiled at her sarcasm. "Rome is not like Greece, Daphne. Well-brought-up Roman women don't engage in friendships with unmarried men. Still less have affairs. One can still be banished for adultery. If I were to call on one of those Portias or Julias, her father would demand to know the wedding-date. For a man with no wife and in no haste to remarry, the remaining options are few."

"You mean you go to the prostitutes?"

"You know the answer to that, Daphne."

"I don't know the answer to anything," she retorted.

"You know how unclean and unappealing the wolves of the Suburra are and what vile stews they inhabit. Can you think I would go there?"

"And the temple?"

"The temple prostitutes are little better. One runs the risk of finding oneself in the company of a madwoman. Or quite often, a madman with a painted face. In either case, necessitating a swift retreat and payment for nothing. Sex with a masked stranger is a sad business, in any case."

"Have you not felt anything for another woman?"

"That is another question."

"Then answer it for me."

I found myself telling her about Judaea, about my experiences there and my work for Vitellius. It was the first time I had spoken to her about the possibility of political advancement for myself. She listened to me in silence, watching me with her brooding, liquid eyes.

"So you will be a great man?" she asked when I had finished.

"If the fates choose it. Being a great man in the Empire is a tricky business. One can be given a triumph one year and be executed the next. When emperors die, so do many of their friends. Wherever there's an army, it wants to declare its leader emperor. It's better not to be between such great forces."

"And the wife of Pontius Pilate – what of her?"

"I fancied myself in love with her."

"But –?"

"But she was the wife of Pontius Pilate."

"You cannot have tried very hard," she said with some disdain. "As you recount it, Pilate is a brute and she is unhappy."

"Yes. However my position was such that to have pressed her would have been dishonourable."

Daphne made an impatient gesture. "You are too scrupulous. If Jason had cared about being honourable, Andromeda would have been eaten by the monster. You had power. You should have used it."

"It's strange to hear you, of all people, tell me that," I said gently.

"If I had power, do you think I would not use it? If you had truly loved her, you would not have let scruples stand in your way."

"Life is not so simple. It was not a fairy-tale. Besides," I added, "she didn't want me."

"Of course she wanted you. She wanted you to take her – not stand deliberating like Cicero about what was honourable or dishonourable!"

It may be wondered that I allowed a young slave to talk to me in this way; but we were no longer in the position of slave and master. We had gone past that long before. What we were, exactly, we did not know; but there was that intimacy between us that is found rarely in this life.

Inevitably, people began to talk. One's friends will often make assumptions about one's behaviour to which no stranger will stoop. People made insinuations and dropped hints, to which at first I was at first oblivious but which eventually became impossible to ignore.

The first such intimation came from Antiochus, a fabulously wealthy Phoenician merchant who had purchased himself Roman citizenship and a sprawling villa on the Palatine, overlooking the Forum. He invited me to examine his library. By now, like bathrooms and hot water, a library was an essential adjunct of a grand home, even if the scrolls were never read. Antiochus, at least, was liberal enough to allow favoured scholars access to his books.

The library was exquisitely-furnished, its windows facing east towards the sun, favouring early risers. There were desks and comfortable chairs presided over by a librarian, a meek Syrian slave who served cool water and made sure the scrolls went back in the right pigeonholes. The shelves, made of rare woods inlaid with ivory, covered the walls to the ceiling. The ten thousand scrolls, by contrast, were ancient for the most part. Some dated back centuries, rare works which were not to be found in any of the public libraries. I congratulated Antiochus on this wonderful collection.

"I plan to leave it to the citizens of Rome," he told me, "housed in a splendid public library which will be the cynosure of Roman

scholarship. White marble and red porphyry columns. Gold details."
He spoke with a slight lisp, stroking his curled and perfumed beard
with quick, nervous movements. "Not that I anticipate gratitude,"
he added with a touch of bitterness. "One should expect nothing
from Rome these days except vulgarity and loutishness."

"You speak with feeling," I said with a smile. "Has something
happened to annoy you?"

He shot me a glance from his sharp, intelligent eyes. "Does
nothing happen to annoy *you* in Rome, Marcellus?"

"Daily," I assured him.

"Come and see Cyrus," he said, hoisting his gold-hemmed
toga above his ankles to lead the way. I followed him. Cyrus was
Antiochus' protégé, a young Persian of great personal beauty
who had set himself up to be an actor. He had achieved some
success, playing comedies in the rich crimson robes of the hero.
In contrast to the magnificence of the rest of the villa, Cyrus's
room was small and dark, lit by a single oil lamp. The young
man himself was sitting at a desk crowded with *sigillaria*, small
clay statuettes of gods and heroes which are given as gifts on
December 25 for the Saturnalia, which was coming up. To judge
by the number of them, he had dozens of friends to present
them to. He turned to face me and in the low light I saw the split
lips, the swollen eye.

"How did this happen?" I asked quietly.

Cyrus peered into a little silver mirror and dabbed his mouth,
which was still oozing blood. "I was beaten by Severus's sons and
their friends after I danced at a party."

"Why?"

"For being a nancy-boy, of course. For dancing like a girl and –
other things which they kindly explained in great detail. At least
they didn't break my nose. I prize my Hellenistic profile."

I laid my hand on the young man's shoulder. "I'm sorry."

"Thank you." Cyrus patted my hand, then pushed it away.
"Don't worry about me. I'll be fine. Antiochus should not exhibit
me in this way."

"I am not exhibiting you. I want Marcellus to see what they did to you. What remedy do we have, Marcellus?" Antiochus asked.

"You mean, what legal remedy? You can take an action against Severus's sons for common assault and claim damages."

"You are willing to do this for us?"

"Of course. But I don't advise it. Severus is a General. He and his friends will turn the trial into a circus. It will attract an enormous amount of attention. They will bring a charge of indecency against you, Cyrus. I am sorry to say this, but a charge of indecency can mean confiscation of lands and wealth, exile, even death."

Antiochus winced. "After everything I have done for Rome? Look at my library!"

"From Alexander down to the present day, generals have all been book-burners, a curious instance of the sword being mightier than the pen. I am giving you good advice. Avoid legal action at all costs. Choose discretion."

"You mean, hide what we are?"

"I mean, avoid public displays."

"I don't intend to avoid anything." Despite the effeminacy of his manner, Cyrus had dignity and grace. "I can't change who I am, Marcellus."

"I know that."

Antiochus had tears in his eyes. "None of us can change who we are. The love between men is celebrated by every nation except Rome."

"But it is in Rome that you and Cyrus live."

"I don't intend to give up my acting career," Cyrus retorted, pouting as best he could with cut lips.

"Nor should you. You played Ennius so well last week."

Cyrus brightened. "You saw my performance?"

"And enjoyed it very much. Your voice is like honey, of course."

"I like Ennius." Cyrus began arranging the clay figures. I saw that his nails were long, stained pink with henna. "He strikes a chord with me."

"I would say you are among the greatest of his interpreters."

Cyrus seemed cheered. "You're flattering me. Still. Nice to know I made an impact. Something to brighten a thoroughly shitty day."

"Only, Cyrus – keep your performances for the stage. Don't dance at parties."

"I shan't be going to any parties looking like this, I assure you."

We left the boy to dab his swollen lips mournfully in the mirror. Antiochus seemed grateful for the little I had done. "Thank you for cheering him up. You are right. Your advice is good. In your position, of course, you have a special understanding."

"In my position?" I repeated.

He reached out and touched my hair. "You're going grey. And your hair's far too long. And you haven't shaved for a week. Other noblemen go to the barber every morning."

"I can't stand sitting with a hot towel round my head listening to the barbers gossip and their clients boast. It's like Hell."

He smiled. "Hell will be worse, believe me. But I agree with you about the barber shops, of course. However, you can't go around looking like that. My own fellow will do it for you. Come." He would take no refusal, so I sat obediently while his personal barber tended to me. He pared my bristles briskly with the razor and began trimming my hair with quick, well-practised strokes. "You should take your own advice," Antiochus told me. "You have to guard your reputation, just as Cyrus and I must do. It's bad enough you're an Etruscan, with those sly eyes and that quiet smile. If you are too public, they'll make you drink hemlock, like Socrates."

"I'm not irreligious."

"You're worse."

"I don't understand."

The barber finished cutting my hair and Antiochus admired the handiwork. "What a handsome man you are. Now you look like a real Roman again. Did the barber chatter too much?"

I examined himself in the polished mirror he held out. ""He was very silent."

Antiochus smirked. "That's because I had his tongue cut out."

I was not sure whether the remark was a joke or not. Antiochus gave me a little glass vial of the bergamot-oil which he used and I rubbed it on my shaved cheeks, relishing the sharp citrus scent.

I didn't pay too much attention to Antiochus's sly remarks about "my position." Like most Phoenicians, he was over-subtle. However, I soon received a clearer message from the wife of Gratus the merchant, Junia. One evening she invited me to her mansion to discuss a legal problem which she said was very pressing. Gratus was away on business and she had the reputation of a viper, so I wasn't altogether pleased to contemplate her as a possible client, but I went nonetheless. The mistress of the house welcomed me in the entrance hall, wrapped in a robe of white wool, her blonde hair piled artfully on top of her head.

"Darling." She kissed my cheek. "How lovely to see you again. Thank you for coming so soon. Come and say hello to Tertia."

Junia had named her last-born optimistically but there had never been a fourth or a fifth. Her sons were both serving in their father's business and she seldom saw any of her menfolk.

Tertia was discovered at the loom, of all things, industriously weaving a shawl. Her plump arms and neck were bared and shown to good advantage by the activity. She was a pretty young woman with her mother's statuesque figure. She lifted her smooth cheek to be kissed, lowering her eyelashes modestly.

"It's for my honoured grandfather," she murmured. "A gift for his birthday. Winter is here and I worry about him catching cold."

I complimented her on the fineness of the weaving, though I couldn't help noticing that the two or three lines she produced while I was there were very much inferior to the rest of the fabric and she seemed not very certain about the functioning of the apparatus.

"We must soon think about finding a husband for her," Junia said to me as she led me to the reception room. "She's almost sixteen."

"That should not be difficult," I said. "She's extremely pretty, her father is wealthy and if she regards weaving as an agreeable pastime, husbands will be beating a path to your door."

Junia gave me a chilly smile in answer to this sally. "The path is somewhat overgrown at the moment. Husbands seem to be a rare commodity."

The reception chamber was a grand hall with vivid frescos of dolphins leaping among scalloped waves. The vaulted ceiling was painted with the stars and planets against a deep blue sky. Booty from every quarter of the Empire adorned the room – a Greek marble nymph in one corner, a bronze Assyrian faun in another, exquisite painted ceramics of all kinds standing on plinths. The gleam of gold was everywhere. There was even a collection of Greek warriors' bronze helmets from antiquity. While I waited for her to explain the reason for this summons, she pointed out the floor. It was mosaic, delicately done to represent scattered roses made from tiny cubes of crimson, pink and gold glass. It had been newly laid, she told me, by Sicilian artisans at immense cost. Gratus' business was evidently doing well. The house was a gaudy palace.

A girl of about fourteen with amber skin and downcast eyes came in carrying a tray of wine and snacks.

"I hear you've bought a slave from Felix," Junia said. "He's your kinsman, isn't he?"

"Livia's first cousin."

"You like his poetry?"

"I'm not a very good judge."

"I think it's sickly. He used at least to be witty. Now he makes me queasy. He's taken to peering through keyholes."

"I don't understand you."

"It's unnatural for a man to understand women's feelings so well." She didn't elaborate. "Why did you want his slave?"

"I didn't want her at all. He needed money. I took her as a favour. She's just a girl."

"Is she? How kind of you. You should have had children of your own."

"The gods didn't bless us."

"The problem lay with Livia, not with you. You should remarry."

"It seems to me not so long since my wife died."

"It's been almost three years. You have plenty of money and an excellent career. You're still young. You should consider it your duty to marry some suitable young virgin. Livia wouldn't have wanted you to immolate yourself."

"I'm not immolating myself. I'm busy."

"So one hears," she said acidly.

"What does one hear?"

"That you're making a fool of yourself."

"In what way?"

The amber skinned girl was noiselessly pouring the wine. A few drops spilled from the jug, as they always do. Junia frowned. "This one is too clumsy," she said. She took a bronze implement from the table with a crown of sharp spikes.

"Don't," I said instinctively.

Junia drove the weapon deftly into the girl's side. The child doubled over with a whimper. "It doesn't do to be sentimental, Marcellus."

I said nothing. The slave slowly straightened, breathing carefully so as to make no sound. There was a red blotch on her tunic. Tears slid down her oval cheeks. Junia was watching my face, not the girl. "The world is harsh," she said. "We must find a meaning behind the jabs that life gives us. Otherwise nothing makes any sense at all."

I knew that the ugly little tableau had been enacted for my benefit, to send me a message. I was sorry that I should have been the occasion of suffering for the girl.

"Mend the tear," Junia commanded her. "Wash the stain. I don't wish to be reminded of your clumsiness the next time I see you."

"Yes, mistress," the girl whispered. She limped slowly away, holding her side.

"You're too soft hearted, Marcellus." Junia's eyes were bright and hard. "You positively winced when I prodded that creature."

"She seems so young."

"She's old enough. You're squeamish for a soldier. Did you wince like that in Jerusalem? They say you tried to prevent Pilate from executing rebels. Are your clients brigands these days?" I didn't answer. She laughed. "Of course, they all say you spoil your own slaves rotten. You don't like to shed a drop of their blood."

"I see no sense in injuring a horse I own. Why should I injure my slave?"

"Let me give you some advice about slaves. You can't treat that class gently. They'll take advantage of you. They'll turn the world upside down. And then where will you be?"

"I don't know. Where will I be?"

"On the bottom. With them on top. Is that what you want? In Rome, it seems it's Saturnalia all the year round nowadays, the slaves are masters and the masters are slaves. I won't stand for it. If a slave annoys you, scourge her. Let the blood flow. That's my advice."

"I'll try to remember."

"You can't be kind to them. There has to be order. Discipline. If your forefathers had understood discipline better, we Romans would still be living under your shadow."

"If we Etruscans had been disciplined we wouldn't have been Etruscans."

"Now you lead me into philosophical realms where my weak woman's brain is adrift," she replied. "I don't understand speculation. I'm old-fashioned. I understand the rod. Punishment and reward. Above all, duty. One sees so many men cavorting with their slaves these days, while decent Roman girls sit at home weaving. It's despicable to do such a thing, a betrayal of everything Rome stands for. You should be the first to understand that, Marcellus."

"Junia, I don't follow you."

"Let me just remind you that nobody will speak to a noble who marries a slave. That would be a fragrant thing to bring to a supper party, wouldn't it, a creature who had been covered by every man who felt like sticking it in her? You might as well marry a pot that men spit in. You'll be reduced to the company of freedmen, retired prostitutes and other such disgusting trash."

"Who says I intend marrying a slave?" I asked.

"While you were in Palestine you tried to seduce the wife of Pilate. Everyone is talking about it. You've freed that useful fellow Dionysius, have you not? And now you live alone with this bitch of Felix's as though she were your wife. You buy her beautiful clothes and feed her from your own table. I don't know what's happening to you, Marcellus. If you lack a wife, I can find you a suitable one less than a thousand miles from where we're sitting."

I tried to mollify her, not an easy task since I had no intention of being steered in the direction of the industrious Tertia. The acquisition of Junia as a mother-in-law wasn't a prospect any sane man would welcome.

The pressing legal problem turned out to be some minor matter that was cleared up by a few words of advice. I managed to extricate myself and walked home through city streets which were made fantastic by flaring torches and leaping shadows, thronged with pleasure seekers going out to drink or dine or to crowd the brothels and theatres. Junia was right in saying that Rome seemed to be in a permanent Saturnalia. One saw it especially at night. The orderly processions and the murmur of dignified men gave way to wild dances and alien music whirled on strange instruments. The air was rich with the reek of foreign food and exotic spices, of hashish and other intoxicating drugs. Faces loomed out of the dark as I walked, grotesque as carnival masks, then vanished again. One might be in Babylon or Tyre or some nameless tent city of the eastern deserts. We had invited all this foreignness into our capital and now we complained about it. I was disturbed by Junia's words and by the implication that all Rome was talking about me as one who was no longer loyal to Imperial principles. It wasn't a pleasant place to find oneself at a time when so many heads were insecure on their shoulders.

When I reached home, Daphne was still awake. She was sitting at my desk in the dim light of a single lamp, scratching with a reed pen on a piece of parchment. The room smelled of her violet oil and her hair. She peered at me. "Marcellus? What is the matter?"

"Why should anything be the matter?"

"I know your step so well. Usually you're eager to enter. Tonight you walk as though you were reluctant to enter your own home."

I sat on the other chair and looked at her face. She was smiling slightly. In the light of the oil flame, she was mysterious and beautiful "What keeps you working so late?" I asked.

"Foolish things that waste ink and parchment."

"What things?"

"Felix would whip me to write poems. You've never asked me for even one line. I wanted to give you a poem as a gift."

"Let me see."

"It's unfinished." Nevertheless she let me take the parchment. The lines were short:

If I had a pure white goat
I would wreathe lilies around his horns
And lead him to the altar
In the middle of the glade
And spill his innocent blood
With one sweet stroke of the knife.

The tether is torn
The altar is desecrated
And the glade ransacked
Of all its summer flowers
And all that I have left
Are these bruised violets.

I gave it back to her. "Is this for me?"

"For you."

"Thank you. I'm afraid I don't have a very good understanding of poetry."

"Poetry is the way we whisper things we're too afraid to say aloud, Marcellus."

"Has it never occurred to you to call me 'Master?'" I asked angrily.

She moved the lamp so she could see my face better. "If you command me to call you Master, I will do so. Is that your wish?"

"It would be more decorous."

She lowered her eyes. "Very well, Master."

"I think it would also be better if we no longer ate together, and if you only entered my study at my express wish."

She dried her reed pen. "You are unhappy tonight. Someone has taken away your joy. I hope you can find it again." She lit a second lamp for herself, bade me goodnight and went to her bed.

I sat listening to the silence of the house after she had gone. I thought of her, lying in bed, probably awake and in pain from the way I had spoken to her. Of course I understood her poem. The white goat was Daphne herself – or rather some part of her that had been taken and which she could no longer give to me, even though she wished to. The bruised violets were the words she offered me.

I was ashamed that I hadn't acknowledged the sadness of what she had written. I valued her worth as a human being highly. But Junia's sneers were still ringing in my ears, forcing me to contemplate the life that Daphne had lived, covered, as Junia put it, by any man who felt like sticking it in her. It wasn't her fault; it was the fault of the system which we had embraced. Nevertheless, she had been degraded and polluted, her glade ransacked, her altar desecrated. Even a spoiled little brat like Junia's daughter Tertia had that which Daphne could never have again – innocence.

I had taken her in a moment of folly and now I was responsible for her. I couldn't free her – she had no way of earning her income and was years away from thirty, the age at which she could become a Roman citizen. To sell her would be to betray any kindness I had shown her. Giving her back to Felix was out of the question.

I was on the edge of a catastrophe. *Sell her*, a voice whispered in my ear. *The problem doesn't lie with her, it lies with you. Only you may solve it. Harden your heart and sell her now, get rid of her before you commit some even grosser folly than you have already been guilty of.*

Ruefully, I thought of my imbecile attachment to Procula, the greatest folly of my life. And now this. How was it I showed so little judgment where women were concerned? Livia should never have died – though that was no excuse. Perhaps Junia was right, and it was time I began to pay attention to all the marriageable young Roman women that were being pushed my way. It was perhaps time to remarry, as Procula had once put it, soberly, obediently and without joy.

# Chapter Ten

# "How Your Voice Trembles"

Such were my thoughts. Whether they can be sympathized with or not, they reflected the troubled state of my mind. In the meantime, I went to the Jewish quarter to visit the friends I had made there, Martha and Simon.

Simon the merchant had been established in Rome for some thirty-five years and was now wealthy and respected, a Roman citizen with many friends in high places. It was his daughter, Martha, who had taught me some Hebrew, and who had also instructed me in some of the principles of the Jewish faith. She had been born in Rome and was as thoroughly Romanized as a Jewish woman could be, having, like her father, extensive friendships among the Gentiles.

She bore her affliction with bravery. She had been born with her spine twisted. She was as small as a child, though now at least thirty years of age. She had never married, not because she lacked suitors – there had been some over the years, attracted by her bright eyes, her warm disposition and her father's wealth – but because it was feared that to bear a child would be fatal to her. As a consequence she put her energies into her friendships, teaching and good works.

They received me warmly at their house, which was near the Portico of Octavia, a part of Rome where the Jews had congregated and had their shops and meeting places. Simon and Martha lived modestly, despite their wealth, having few things but those few of good quality. Their house was quiet and dark, with a front room where Martha taught and where they received visitors. I had brought some gifts for Martha from the land she had never seen (she was considered too frail to withstand the voyage) so the first part my visit was taken up with those things. We moved on to the present.

"There's a rise in hostility to Jews, Marcellus," Simon said. "Some Romans want us to be expelled again." Some years earlier there had been a notorious incident in which a group of Judaean swindlers, pretending to be holy men, had made a convert of a Gentile woman named Fulvia. They talked her into buying precious gifts for the temple in Jerusalem but they sold the goods instead. Her husband, who was well connected to the emperor, complained to Tiberius and as a result, all the Jews, amounting to many thousands, were expelled from Rome. It was an action which was supported by many Romans who benefited, directly or indirectly, from it. Some were able to purchase or steal properties and businesses at low prices; others were favoured by the cancellation of debts or the removal of business competitors. Many simply took pleasure in seeing disaster overtake the lives of the Jews. "There's an enquiry in progress. They say there will be severe repercussions."

"We're afraid that we may suffer," his daughter said, "because I have students and have made some converts, which they say is teaching atheism – and because my father has been successful in business." She had the face of a faun, with a long nose, glowing, round, dark eyes and a mouth which looked sadder the more it smiled. "We Jews have found that one accusation against a Jew will always be applied to the whole population."

"Who is conducting the enquiry?" I asked.

"The office of the Censor, Lucius Salvius Otho."

"I'll try to find out what I can," I promised. We moved on to discussing the crucifixion of Jesus. They agreed it had been an atrocious deed to crucify such a man, but they had heard separately from correspondents in Jerusalem about the episode and they had formed opinions of their own.

"This Jesus was a good man but a bad Jew," Simon said. "His teaching has appealed to a great following, it seems, especially to the poor and the humble. We hear from Jerusalem that his followers are doing their best to maintain that he was a Messiah. But most

Jews won't accept this. The Messiah will be a mighty king, and this was a simple carpenter from Galilee who was snuffed out with a snap of Pilate's fingers. In my opinion, the efforts to depict him as a Messiah are ill advised. They'll turn away many and will obscure the greatness of his teaching."

"They say that he arose from the dead and performed all kinds of miracles," Martha said. "Only the superstitious can believe such things. We Jews are not a superstitious people."

"They seem to have made some impression among the Gentiles," I said.

"That may be." Simon shrugged his plump shoulders comfortably. "Gentiles will believe anything. No offence."

"No offence," I said, smiling.

They treated me to a splendid dinner of fish, which came from the nearby river bank markets. Like many Jews in Rome, they lived on vegetables and fish, since it was so difficult to find other foods which were not ritually unclean to them. The fish was accompanied by fried artichokes, one of my favourite dishes, and some wonderful Falernian wine. We drank more than we should and were happy together. Martha complimented me on how my accent had improved. She asked me whether I wasn't yet ready to convert, having been in the temple in Jerusalem, though I think by now she had resigned herself to accepting that I was godless and a hopeless cause.

As I had promised them, the next day I went to speak to the Censor, Lucius Salvius Otho, about the enquiry he was conducting. He received me in his office in the Villa Publica, surrounded by men as foolish as himself, for he turned out to be a narrow-headed old man with a limited intellect and a strong prejudice against the Jews.

"Do you know," he said to me in outrage, "that they cut off their foreskins?'"

There were suppressed sniggers among the men in togas who sat around him. The scribe, whose task it was to record the Censor's thoughts on tablets of wax, looked bored and drew a tiny phallus in the wax with his stylus.

"I have heard that," I said.

"It's just disgusting," Otho said. "The prepuce is the most attractive part of the male body." This remark produced further sniggers. A flush spread across Otho's brow. He had been Consul some time past and his bust had gone up in the Forum. It was to be seen that the living Otho had taken to holding himself in the same pose as the marble one, with toga thrown over one shoulder and a sneer of disdain, a case of Life imitating Art. As the custodian of the public morals, however, his anger was perilous.

"About the case of Martha and Simon," I hinted.

The old man's thin fingers fidgeted with the hem of his toga. "I cannot promise anything," he said. "The woman converts decent Romans to her religion. As I understand it, this means renouncing all the Roman gods?"

"Yes."

"And what does their so-called god look like? Hmmm? Nobody knows. He is invisible. It's as clear a case of atheism as I ever saw. And she wants the men to mutilate their genitals. If that goes on, we as well as our gods will soon die out." I did my best to set right some of the misconceptions he was labouring under and to put in a good word for Martha and Simon. He heard me out and then pulled the toga over his shoulder in imitation of the bust. His mottled arm was stark against the white linen. "We have heard that you have made yourself a friend to this crafty, alien race, Marcellus," he replied sternly. "You're becoming known as a friend to many of Rome's enemies. You would be well-advised to remember where your loyalties lie." With no satisfactory answer, I was forced to leave.

One of his hangers-on followed me out and stopped me in the hypostyle, which was busy with men waiting for an audience with Otho. I recognized him as Cornelius, with whom I had served in Germany. He was short and powerful, his head covered with tight curls. He put a heavy hand on my shoulder in a gesture of false camaraderie. "I hear all sorts of peculiar things about you lately, brother. You had such a good reputation. Don't throw it away for the snipcocks and the other barbarians. We have to keep our foot on their necks or we'll end up in the gutter instead of them."

"Thank you for the advice."

He grinned. "I've seen that little slut you bought from Felix. She's a pretty piece. I'll buy her from you."

"She's not for sale."

"I'll pay well. Five hundred sesterces."

I pushed his hand off my shoulder. "She's not for sale."

"Then give her to me for one night. As an old comrade. Remember that day we charged the Teutons in the forest? Remember how your horse was killed under you and I kept those giants off you until you could get away?"

"I remember."

"Give me the girl for a night."

"I'm sorry."

His smile faded. "I'll pay, if you insist."

"I have a regard for the girl."

"And you've no regard for me? Is that what you're saying? Brother, to fuck a slave girl cleanses the stomach. Then pass her on to a comrade. To fuck the same slave girl every day is something else. You know what I mean?"

"You're married, Cornelius."

He grew very angry. "What does that have to do with anything? Women are women, Marcellus, and men are men."

"Very profound."

"You know what I mean. You Etruscans consider your women as equals. They're not. Women have their place. Their place is their place. Our place is our place."

"You're not an orator, Cornelius. Leave speeches to those more qualified."

"I'm qualified to speak with a sword, Etruscan." His hand was on the hilt of his dagger. "What I cannot say in words I may say in iron."

"Iron seems to be the language of the day," I said dryly.

Cornelius bent quickly and spat at my feet. People were staring at us now, edging away from the makings of a sword fight. It would be death, however, to draw a sword in this place. I pushed Cornelius aside and left the consul's forum.

"I will remember this," he called after me.

The result of this absurd morning was that I merely worsened my reputation as an ally of undesirables and was compelled to ask Vitellius to intercede with Otho, something I did not like doing. I advised Simon and Martha to leave Rome for a while. They went to their farm in the country and lived there quietly for a month or two until Otho's witch hunt was ended by Vitellius.

Two of my most important clients informed me they would dispense with my services after my visit to Otho. Others who had consulted me took their business to other lawyers. I later half-suspected that Cornelius's offer to buy or rent Daphne had been a deliberate provocation. Although it was customary at the time for desirable slaves to be passed around liberally among one's friends, it had come too pat after the bitter attack of Junia and my futile visit to the Censor's forum to be a coincidence. Perhaps he had been engaged to see if it were true what so many were saying about me. At the time, however, it brought into relief the difficulty of my feelings towards her, even though I had never touched her.

When I returned home from court the next day, I sent for her. She came to my study wearing one of my favourites among her dresses, a white linen tunic embroidered with violets. It was hardly a suitable garment for a slave and not even really legal, but violets were always her flower in my mind. She was also wearing a pair of sandals I had bought for her, the straps covered in gold leaf. She stood before me, her dark eyes fixed on mine. Her black hair had grown and now had to be held back in a net. As I stared at her I saw not a slave but a young priestess from the eastern seas. My heart ached.

"Why do you look at me like that?" she asked quietly. "What are you going to do with me?"

"You are a flame," I said, "and I am dry grass."

"This seems like poetry."

"Poetry is the way we whisper things we're too afraid to say aloud."

"Oh, Marcellus, I have no wish to do you harm."

"Nor I you."

Unbidden, she sat on the other chair. "Tell me what is in your mind."

"I've damaged my reputation with various sympathies I've expressed. I dared suggest that justice and humanity transcend Rome and the Romans. I've been told I'm disloyal. I've been a fool. In Judaea, I fell in love with another man's wife. Here, people say my relationship with you is indecent. I've decided that the best thing is for us to separate."

"You plan to sell me?"

"Yes."

Her face filled with pain. "You should have left me with Felix."

"You would be dead by now."

"That would be better than this."

"Don't talk like that," I said sharply.

She was silent for a long time, breathing carefully in a way that reminded me of the young girl Junia had wounded. "And you? What will you do?"

"I'll marry a Roman virgin."

"Which Roman virgin?"

"As you once told me, they produce them like almond-pastry, from a mould, all pure, sugary and eligible. There's a wide choice. Any Portia or Flavia or Julia or Antonia will do."

"Neither Portia nor Flavia, Julia or Antonia will tolerate my presence," she replied. "You're very wise to sell me."

"I know this hurts you."

"The morning you put me in your bath and washed my body with violet soap, I knew this day would come."

"I'll find a decent owner. Someone who will treat you as you deserve and who can appreciate your gifts. I'm thinking of a woman

I know. She's elderly and wealthy and has no husband or living children. She might be happy to have you as a companion. I'll speak to her."

"Thank you."

She swayed a little as she walked away. I was afraid she might faint. I, too, felt nauseous and weak after the brief interview. I was filled with an ache that I couldn't escape, as though I had swallowed a stone.

The woman I had spoken of was called Octavia, the widow of that Caius Sabinus who had been Consul a few years earlier. I had served with their son, who had remained in Germany. I had brought his armour back to them. Her dignity and self-control had impressed me. After the death of her husband, she had retired from Rome and now lived in a country house some five miles outside the city, in the company of dozens of dogs, cats and other animals, as well as a large library of poetry and literature. It was a beautiful ride, through misty farmland and woods now rifled by winter. Fresh air and the open scenery did something to settle my aching heart. It also pleased me that the road I took was an old Etruscan road, cut by my forefathers through the soft hills centuries before.

I found Octavia in the guise of a peasant woman, with her skirts tucked into leather boots and her patrician face reddened with exercise, throwing grain to her chickens, though she was wealthy enough to have thrown them gold if the fancy had taken her. She greeted me with pleasure and begged me to wait while she finished her tasks. The place was well kept in a woman's way, which is quite different from a man's. She seemed to have no workers around. Carrying a basket of eggs, we went into the house, which looked something like the villa Maecenas gave to Horace, I imagine, a mixture of rusticity and culture. Sitting in her library, I explained my mission while her dogs sniffed me and her cats clambered on me. She listened serenely, her roughened hands folded in her lap.

Retirement to the country had evidently brought her peace and a relaxation of the rigid standards of fashionable society.

When I had finished, I offered her some of Daphne's poems to read. "These will give you a better idea," I said.

"My eyes are so poor these days, my dear Marcellus," she said. "Won't you read them to me?"

I did so. While I read, she took out the pins which had fastened her silver hair and began to comb it out, her eyes hooded like a bird's. I read some four or five of the odes before falling into silence.

Octavia removed the last of the leaves and bits of chaff from her hair and tied it up again. "How your voice trembles when you read her words," she said to me. I made no reply. She looked at her hands. "Your slave girl is talented. Some of her lines are paraphrases of Sappho, but there's much that's original. She has a singular mind. I wonder where she came from?"

"I've often thought she must have come from some cultured household in Lydia or Thrace. She says that her parents were killed but she can't remember – or refuses to speak of – any other personal details. She seemed to know little about the world when she came to me, but she has a fine mind, as you say. She reads hungrily in my library now. She devours everything."

"Is she beautiful?"

"She could be a priestess or a queen. Would you like to see her?"

"No, I think not."

I was disappointed. "You don't think she would make a suitable companion for you?"

"She might. She could be useful around the farm and may even have some conversation worth breaking the silence for."

"Then will you not see her?"

She smiled slightly. "Do you remember when you brought my son's armour to me?"

"Yes, of course."

"You told me that he died calling for me."

"That's true."

"Perhaps you thought that would give me comfort. It has haunted me for years."

"I'm sorry."

"That he needed me and that I was not there for him is terrible to me. I wake in the night and hear his cries. It transcends everything. All those lies about it being sweet and proper to die for one's country, all the patriotic rubbish spouted by old men in the Senate eager to send boys to war, all the platitudes that are given to the mothers of dead heroes – all that is like the chirping of crickets beside my son's screams."

I was taken aback. "Octavia, I'm truly sorry."

"Do you know why I've come to live here? Because I can't stand Rome any more. I can't stand the hypocrisy and the cant. I hate the sight of slaves. I hate the whippings and the brandings and the crucifixions and the cruelty dressed up as noble deeds. It all sickens me." She gestured at the scroll I was still holding. "You want to bring this girl to me because you're too ashamed to admit that you love her. Because Rome has allocated her an identity below that of a human being. Do you think that burying her in the country with an old woman will solve the problem?"

"I was hoping that she could be useful to you and live here with you, safely away from the dangers of Rome."

"Does she love you?"

"I think so."

"The poem about the white goat was written for you."

"Yes."

"I should not throw away such love. Life is a lonely business, Marcellus. You described for me the battle in which my son was killed, where the armies hacked at each other in the darkness of a forest and no man knew whether the one he killed was an enemy or a brother. There's the illusion of a great company, but each one is alone. That's how most of us pass through life. When one encounters real love, it should not be thrown away."

"I can't marry her."

"Why not?"

"I would become an outcast."

"Then take her as your lover."

"She deserves more than that, Octavia."

"I think you're over-scrupulous. You can't reason everything out as though it were a case at law. You've found a chance of happiness. Why push it away? Is happiness so abundant in your life?"

"No."

"Seize it and let the consequences be what they may. That's the advice of an old woman who has lost much."

She wouldn't be swayed, though I tried hard to convince her – and in the end, even offered to pay Daphne's keep. She made me a meal of an omelette with mushrooms, which were now plentiful in the woods. She no longer ate meat of any kind, she told me, and prepared the food with her own hands.

The mist was thick as I rode back to town in the afternoon. I could see ice forming at the margins of the puddles. I hadn't succeeded in my plan, nor had Octavia's advice settled my mind, and I felt numbed by the long ride and the cold.

I reached home after dark, my clothing soaked through with the icy rain that had started to fall. Agata's boy had lit the hypocaust, which made the house warm and provided me with a steaming bath. I didn't see Daphne. I ate a light meal and retired to bed, hoping the day's exercise would give me a better night's sleep than I had been enjoying lately.

I didn't sleep long; I was awakened by the sound, mysterious and familiar and almost subliminal. I wrapped myself in my gown and went into the sitting room and opened the shutters. The snow was pouring from an opalescent sky, the first of the year.

I sat in the window to watch the spectacle and to think. It was deep in the night but the snow seemed to provide its own light, pervading the garden with a soft glow. Everything was already draped in white. The sound it made was silence thickened with beauty. Snow purifies everything. During the winter campaigns that we were forced to fight in Germany, I recall how it would rush down onto the battlefield, covering the blood-soaked earth and the unburied dead.

I heard a footstep. Daphne had come downstairs and appeared beside me. "It woke me, too," she said quietly. "I heard it falling on the roof." She sat beside me, bringing with her the scent of flowers and of her skin. Her dark hair was loose, hanging to her shoulders. "You were gone the whole day. I didn't know where you were."

"I went to see Octavia, the woman I told you about."

"Does she want me?"

"She called me a coward."

"Why?"

"For refusing to face the fact that I love you." Daphne made no reply but after a while, laid her hand on mine. "I have to face it now," I said. "I have loved you for a long time."

"I have so longed to hear those words," she whispered.

I turned my palm to face hers. Our fingers twined as if by their own accord. I kissed her then for the first time. Her mouth was warm and soft. In its depths lay sweetness that pierced me. I led her to my bed.

The last time I had seen her naked, she had been frail and ill, a waif blown into my life by a chance wind. I had hardly regarded her as a woman. How much had changed since then! I had changed, she had changed me. And she was transformed in herself, become luminous, beautiful. I kissed the curve of her belly and laid my cheek on the dark curls between her legs. "I'll never let you go."

Her fingers wove through my hair. "What I am, I give to you. I give it to you freely."

# CHAPTER ELEVEN

# THE SUMMONS

The love between a man and a woman is sacred thing, whether the world sanctions it or not. Those who condemn the illicit relationships of others can no more judge than one can judge the mysteries of another religion.

I don't think I even knew how happy I was. Happiness can sometimes be understood fully only when it's taken away. Nothing before in my life could have prepared me for such joy. She gave herself to me with all the treasures of her soul. She was my garden, replete with fruits and flowers and the surging growth of life. We were consecrated to one another.

She dazzled me. I would stare at her in awe sometimes, transported to other worlds by the lines of her face and body. I would study her as though she were a book, tracing the scents of her body and drinking them into me. Her mind was finer than my own, more spontaneous, richer in treasures. Her poet's soul that had captivated me. I learned to see the world through her eyes, not my own.

Though we were as discreet as we could be, the fact that I showed no interest in any of the Portias or Julias told its own tale. Besides, a man is different when he's in love; it can be seen in his every movement. As Junia had predicted, some more of my friends quietly dropped away. I stopped being invited to certain houses. Certain doors were closed to me, certain faces averted. A few even continued to give me fatherly advice to disengage myself "before it was too late."

I was unable to present her socially to Vitellius and Sextilia, or to any of my other friends. That did not really matter, not at that stage. My skill as a lawyer ensured that I always had work. I prospered, whether people murmured behind my back or not. There was little outward change in my life. But inwardly – inwardly everything was different.

I went to see Felix. We hadn't spoken for some time. I paid him his retainer regularly, but I was constantly uneasy that he would have some brainstorm and want Daphne back. He was quite capable of this sort of malicious vagary.

As usual, he didn't answer my knocking. There was only a solemn, bedraggled child, smashing the ice on the puddles with a wooden sword. I bribed him with a small coin to wake Felix.

The child clambered over the wall obediently. There was a hoarse roar of rage from within the house. Shortly afterwards, the child leaped back over the wall, snatched the coin from my fingers and bolted down the alley without looking back.

Shutters crashed open and Felix's shaggy head thrust out, his eyes swollen with sleep. "How dare you send that little demon in here?" he bellowed at me. "I'm a dying man!"

"I want to speak to you. Let me in. It's freezing."

Cursing, he unbolted the door. "Can't you ever come at a decent hour, Marcellus?"

"It's midday."

"Oh, gods. Midnight is early for me. Come in." We sat in his filthy front room. He looked much the same, no worse and no better. The income he derived from me at least paid for wine. He offered me some, and when I refused, poured himself a cup. "What's the matter?" he asked.

"It's about Daphne."

He grunted. "Yes, I thought I'd see you back here one of these days."

"I want to buy her."

"Ah." He grinned slyly. "She's become essential to your existence, eh?"

"I want to buy her outright. I'll pay five hundred sesterces."

"My dear Marcellus, I would squander your five hundred sesterces in a week. I've pissed away several fortunes already." He belched.

"The present arrangement suits me fine. A little bit of money every week, enough to pay my bills, and I'm happy. When I die, she'll be yours."

"You're taking rather a long time to die, Felix," I said dryly.

"How kind of you. I hear she's become beautiful. They say you dress her in fine clothes and parade her around Rome, covered in gold necklaces and bracelets. I take it from this that you've overcome her tendency to turn into a laurel tree?"

"I'll pay what you ask. But I want to own her."

Felix chuckled. "Do you remember how disdainful you were when you first saw her? You jumped back when she vomited all over your shoes and said she wasn't a fit ornament for your household. Now I wonder, which one of you is the slave?"

"Tell me what you want."

"Well, let's see. I might accept six thousand sesterces."

"Are you mad?"

"Six thousand – and on top of that, you'll continue paying the pension until I die."

"Six thousand sesterces is a fortune, Felix!"

"Yes, but you've improved her value, haven't you? I don't know as much about the law as you do, but I seem to remember that if a man rents a field to his neighbour, and the neighbour builds a house on the field, the house belongs to the original owner. You've turned her into a very valuable commodity." His eyes gleamed. "What if I were to tell you that others have been to see me, offering to buy her?"

"Who?"

"An old comrade of yours. Cornelius, he said his name was." I was silent and he smiled maliciously. "What if I said I wanted her back myself so I could give her a good whipping? Or sample the delights of her bed myself? After all, she's my property."

"Before I allow that, I'll cut your throat myself."

"Better to pay the money, Marcellus."

I sat in silence for a while. "Very well," I said at last.

"You've got the full amount?"

"I'll get it."

He threw back his head and laughed raggedly. "The look on your face is priceless. The great Marcellus, paying six thousand for a little laurel tree!"

I had brought writing materials with me and I drew up the contracts. He watched me, drinking and chuckling, and scrawled his name on both copies when they were done. "There, she's yours," he said, throwing down the pen. "I hope she's worth it."

"She's worth twenty times that."

"I believe you," he said. "Be grateful to me. When I'm dead, remember to make sacrifices to my thirsty shade."

And so she belonged to me. When I told Daphne how much I had paid, she was very angry. "What an old rogue! You should have let me go to him," she said. "I would have saved you all that expense."

"I'm superstitious. I didn't want to get you cheap."

"You will not have got me cheap, believe me."

We laughed like fools as we fell into bed. We formed a world in ourselves, we two. And then, late in the summer, Vitellius' call shattered the idyll.

Tiberius had surfaced from his nightmares long enough to nominate Vitellius governor of Syria, one of the highest posts in the Empire. I was appointed to his staff as envoy to Judaea, replacing Pilate – a considerable leap for so young a man with no Senatorial rank. Suddenly, my quiet life was transformed.

It was necessary to tie up all my cases, shut up my house and prepare for Antioch as swiftly as possible. Vitellius was anxious to make the voyage before the autumn storms could begin. I sent Agata and her boy to stay with relations. Arrangements had to be made for Daphne, so that she would be protected during my absence. I once again approached Octavia and this time she consented to take Daphne. I now also had to consider Daphne's legal position more seriously. It wasn't an easy situation. I made a will leaving Daphne her freedom and two-thirds of my estate, so that she would be a relatively wealthy woman and have independence. The other third would go to Octavia. Receiving her freedom in this way, Daphne would be entitled to Roman citizenship, without which she would remain very vulnerable, even if I freed her now. And there, in the quiet of the country, I was compelled to part with her.

Too many tragic events have been related here already for this episode to count for much in the scale of things. But we parted not knowing when, if ever, we would see one another again. Such partings are very sharp at the best of times. In our extraordinary circumstances, there was added uncertainty, added difficulty and added pain.

We walked together through the icy woods, the snow crunching under our winter boots. Daphne clung to me, too distraught to weep.

"I feel like Eurydice at the gates of the Underworld. I have just come back to life and now I am told I must die again – within sight of the sun and the open sky."

"I will return for you."

"You've been so kind." Our breath clouded at our lips. The cold had tightened her face, making her seem very young and vulnerable. "I feel your love in everything you've done for me. But I only want you, to be close to you. You are everything to me, Marcellus."

I felt helpless to comfort her. "You are everything to me. Write to me."

"I'll write to you in my heart's blood," she promised. We kissed under the pine trees' heavy branches and at last her tears fell.

We set sail from Ostia in pouring rain. Vitellius, however, was in high good spirits. He paced the deck, indifferent to the weather, as we cleared the mole and only consented to come below when Italy was dropping out of sight. In the cramped cabin which we were to share for the duration of the voyage, he slapped my shoulder.

"It's accomplished," he said. His short hair was dripping. "We sail into history, my boy."

I passed him a towel. "You'll sail into pneumonia if you don't dry yourself."

He towelled himself dry, happy as a boy. The cabin was so small that we constantly banged our heads or our elbows trying to manoeuvre against the rocking of the ship. "How good it is to leave Rome," he said with a sigh. "And how profound a relief to leave Tiberius behind. The emperor is growing very strange, Marcellus. I have passed so many sleepless nights in these last years that I think I've forgotten how to be at ease."

He was elated and eager to talk. However, the motion of the boat soon gave him seasickness, which lasted for the first week of the voyage, leaving him weak and exhausted. As the more seasoned sailor, I did what I could to make his misery easier. Anyone who has suffered this particular form of torment knows that it is impossible to apply oneself to anything until the nausea has passed. It wasn't until we left Sicily behind us that we were able to talk coherently about our joint future.

"The taste of victory is sweet, Marcellus. You have the fortune to enjoy it young. You're not yet thirty-three. I've wished this for you for a long time – since you came to me as an orphan. You have great abilities, but ability alone is seldom sufficient to advance a man." He pointed at the swelling sail. "This also is necessary. A following wind."

I smiled at his earnestness. "You've been like a father to me. That has been the following wind of my life."

"My boys have at times seemed less sons to me than you," he said sadly. "My own upbringing was harsh. Theirs has been too easy. I see in them a want of true feeling which disturbs me."

I made some light remark, but in truth, the boys were not worthy of such a father. As their tutor, I knew that. They respected neither him nor their mother. They were ambitious, self-indulgent and heartless. I believe that even then it could be seen that they would make a bad end. They were trusted by no-one – while it was a mark of their father's great character that he was a Senator, Consul three times, Governor of Syria, Censor of the Senate and the trusted friend of four emperors. He is also still remembered for having introduced delicious new varieties of figs to Rome, something of which he was very proud. He was too great a man not to know the true character of his sons. We sat in silence for a while before he spoke again:

"What have you done with your little friend?"

"I sent her into the country. She's with the mother of a comrade whom I buried in Germany. She'll be safe there."

"She's a beautiful girl. I would like to have known her, but things being what they are…"

"I understand."

"Of course, if you choose to marry her, that will be different. As your wife, she would be an honoured guest in my home, though I can't speak for any other." He paused. "That, however, would be a big step to take. You would suffer a loss of prestige and any children might face restrictions of various kinds."

"Yes."

"I could wish that you would choose mates other than slaves and other men's wives," he said in a tone that was half-affectionate, half-reproving. "There are other categories of women, you know. But I suppose the sincerity of your feelings does you credit." He sighed. "We won't see them for a long time. Roman women must have patience. Sextilia wanted to come, but the boys still need a firm hand. And it's important that she stays close to the emperor. She's our guarantee of safety." There was something in his face just then which gave me an inkling of how closely his life and that of Tiberius were entwined and how many sacrifices had been made to maintain his security.

In truth, I was missing Daphne terribly, and continued to miss her for the whole of my time in the east. She had become, as Felix said, essential to my existence. To be absent from her was a constant pain. I needed her in so many ways that wherever I turned, I was confronted by the lack of her. Nothing could take it away.

The voyage was a quick one, favoured by the lucky winds of which Vitellius had spoken. Vitellius and I exercised daily on deck, sometimes boxing with the crew or with each other to keep ourselves fit. It was during one of these sparring matches that I stumbled and had my nose broken by the burly Cyrenian first mate. The injury was luckily not severe, but the cartilage was torn from the bone. We had no ship's doctor and Vitellius set my nose with his own hands; it has been somewhat crooked since that day.

"Between the Cyrenian and I, we have rather marred your beauty," my uncle said apologetically. "Unluckily, no-one has made a bust of you yet, so nobody will believe you when you tell them how handsome you once were." I cared little for my beauty; however the twisted nose lent my face a certain sinister quality which has not come amiss in the life I have lived since then.

The tumultuous reception which was accorded Vitellius at Antioch revealed how widespread was the expectation of change in the land. The very spontaneity of the demonstrations were a guarantee of their sincerity. This was the first of many outpourings of popular feeling which were to greet us; for Vitellius represented all that was best about Rome – justice, order, peace and that Republican spirit that was always so welcomed by the ordinary people.

Our first days in Antioch were a prolonged triumph. The army greeted Vitellius with a huge parade, cheering his name until the heavens were deaf with it. My uncle was delighted with this reception. In the East it is impossible to keep any secret and it was known even before our arrival that I was to succeed Pontius Pilate in Judaea; accordingly, I was celebrated in my own right, especially by the Jews of the city. It didn't come naturally to me, I must confess. I often felt some embarrassment when confronted with cheering crowds or the adulation of officialdom. My uncle laughed at my diffidence.

"Enjoy it while it lasts, Marcellus. They'll soon enough be stoning you, take my word for it."

Antioch was more beautiful than I had anticipated, an immense city that was capital of our eastern Empire and a rival to Rome for grandeur. Augustus had made it a favourite and had built a temple to Jupiter Capitolinus on mount Silpius, the citadel. Wide avenues paved with granite and lined with marble columns radiated from this majestic structure. The city had grandiose monuments, soaring and elegantly arched aqueducts, an ample circus, temples, baths and a Forum to rival Rome's. Herod had contributed a beautiful stoa like that at Jerusalem. Later, when Jerusalem was destroyed by Titus, many of the exquisite carvings from the Temple were brought to Antioch in triumph and installed there, as though to emphasize the devastation suffered by the Jews.

This was indeed "the golden East" that Sextilia had spoken of, a pinnacle of power and wealth that was unique in the world at that time. I wrote to Daphne telling her of our safe arrival and trying to convey the impressions which I was receiving. I knew the letter would have to be read to Octavia so I curtailed the expressions of tenderness, which would otherwise have poured from me:

*The palace has been prepared for us and we are surfeited with every luxury that a man can taste, touch, smell, see and hear. I would describe it to you but that my words would sound strange in the austere silence of your rustic retreat. I feel somewhat as Alexander must have felt when he arrived in Babylon. Great wealth and great corruption are the goals of every citizen of Antioch. This is a city devoted to pleasure, luxury and beauty. In its soft and voluptuous lineaments can be seen what Rome will inevitably become one day.*

*What can I tell you? The light is golden and sheds a glow over domes and towers. Marble columns stand thick as trees in a forest. The women are splendid but alarming. They dress with no regard to modesty, rather welcoming the gaze of all who wish to feast their eyes on their naked breasts, which are adorned with gold and jewels of fantastic design. The men prize the arts of pleasure so highly that they have made a kind of religion of luxury.*

*My uncle has been received with joy and even I myself am singled out for honours by the Jews of the city, who are eager to see the back of Pontius Pilate. They have presented me with many costly gifts of gold and silver already. I have given all these back with assurances that my good will doesn't need to be bought. A prominent Pharisee, however, gave me a beautifully copied Septuagint, the Hebrew Bible translated into Greek. This last I have decided to keep.*

I passed on what gossip I thought would amuse her and Octavia and sent the letter with a gift of Syrian fabrics, perfumes and other feminine things. It was now the depth of winter and I didn't know how long it would take to reach Rome, or how long I would have to wait for a reply. I had no portrait of her. I had not even a memento to carry with me. I kept her face before me in my mind.

In the meantime, I was at once embroiled in another of Pilate's atrocities. A delegation of Samaritan senators had brought a case against him. Samaritans are a people with many things in common with the Jews, but not regarded as brothers by them. Their temple wasn't in Jerusalem but on the west bank of the River Jordan on Mount Gerizim. Though the temple had been destroyed more than a century earlier, the Samaritans still worshipped in its ruins. It was here that the outrage had taken place. Pilate had suspected a gathering of worshippers of insurrection and had sent cavalry and had attacked the unprepared Samaritans. He had put several hundred captives to the sword without trial.

It was characteristic of Pilate, and it provided a clear basis for his dismissal. "I'm sorry to ask you to leave the fleshpots of Antioch and the beautiful Jewish ladies who cast such languishing glances on you," Vitellius said. "You'll have to put away your lyre and pick up your sword. Conduct an enquiry and send witnesses to Rome with Pilate. Show no mercy, Marcellus. He's been there ten years and has never done one good deed in all that time." He drew up my orders, making me commander of all military forces in Judaea and giving me full powers as governor. I was to take the title Prefect.

I took a cohort with me, about five hundred men, which necessitated a route march of some three hundred miles along the Mediterranean coast, rather than the sea journey which would have been easier. Since Pilate's forces numbered only 2,500 at that time, I wanted to bring the Judaean army up to its usual strength of 3,000.

We set off at the beginning of the new year. The weather was cold but dry. I had not ridden so far since my days as a cavalry commander in Germany and my body responded eagerly to the exercise. I swiftly gained in strength and stamina. It was no displeasure to be in the company of soldiers again, either, to camp in the open and to share my life and fortunes with comrades. These were men of the Tenth Legion, Fretensis, whose symbols were the bull and the boar. It was a source of pride to once again see my name embossed on the breastplates of the men's armour, and to call them "mine."

I felt I was stronger and better defended within myself. Love softens a man; there's no doubt about it. As we rode through the cedar forests of Lebanon and contemplated the snowy bulk of Mount Hermon, I began to consider that my love for women had been a kind of enslavement that I should not have sunk so far into. During this long march, the anguish of being separated from Daphne was not so acute. Perhaps you will think me without feeling. Romantic love overwhelms men and women and yet it yields before great enterprises. To a woman, her husband is a god until her children come – and then her duty lies another way. She will never give him that absolute devotion again. To a man, his wife is his goddess until the trumpet of war sounds – and then it is as though she was only a beautiful dream. When he returns to her, there will always be a space between them. These are truths we all learn. That's why we pagans have the gods of love and war married to one another, but ever unfaithful to their vows.

Since we were not marching against an enemy, I ordered that the standards not be shown when we entered the territory of Judaea, to avoid offending the Jews by displaying the image of the emperor. In any case, they welcomed us with open arms. As fast as we travelled, the news of our mission travelled before us. We were greeted with jubilation along our route; the people were eager to feed us and provision us, the excitement growing as we drew closer to Jerusalem.

We reached Jerusalem in three weeks, making excellent progress over difficult terrain. Pilate had tented his army outside the city in a haze of campfire smoke and a stink of latrines. Of course they knew all about us. Armies are always disconcerted by a change of leadership which is not a promotion. They appeared dispirited and ill-disciplined as we arrived, the men not meeting our eyes and responding with surliness to our questions. Privately, I considered these men from the Decapolis unworthy to be Roman soldiers. It would be necessary to brace them and lift their morale. Incorporating my own men with them was a first step.

Before entering the city, I spent a final night under canvas. Pilate's commander came to receive me, a grizzled veteran named Quintus. I took him to my tent and showed him my orders from Vitellius but he hardly glanced at them before swearing the oath to me.

I gave him his orders. "Send a messenger to Pilate and tell him I'll see him before the Praetorium at the third hour tomorrow. You'll go with me."

"Yes, sir."

"You've let this camp become a pigsty. By sunset tomorrow I want it clean as a whistle. Empty the trenches and rake out the fire pits. Order the tents to be struck and reset in proper lines. Tell the men to clean their armour and equipment for an inspection. Warn that defaulters will be whipped before the whole army."

He stiffened. "Yes, sir."

"As you see, I've brought a cohort down from Antioch. See that they are fed and welcomed. Divide them in groups of eight among the other men."

I stood at sunset, looking up at the city with its temple gleaming red in the last rays of the day. I had travelled a long journey to return to this point. My feelings were mixed. Of triumph, there was little in my heart. Of melancholy, there was more. The task of replacing Pilate wasn't an enviable one. It would be necessary to regain the confidence of the Jews without giving rebellious elements any encouragement to attack. I was inheriting a dangerous situation and the likelihood of emerging with success or credit was greatly diminished. Nevertheless, I felt that I had qualities which fitted me for the task, in particular a strong sense of justice and an equable temper which are invaluable in managing the affairs of non-Romans.

I rode into Jerusalem in full armour the next morning, accompanied by two dozen men and my baggage. The city was strangely silent. The streets were lined with people, staring intently up at me as I rode by. Nobody spoke. Perhaps they were waiting to see if it were really true that Pilate's term was over after ten years, or perhaps they were trying to glean from my face what sort of governor I would be in his place. In any case, the atmosphere was eerie. The clattering of our horses' hoofs re-echoed from the stone walls. As I approached the Praetorium, something struck me. I looked down. It was a pink carnation, my favourite flower. I let it fall to the ground as though I hadn't noticed it, but it seemed a good omen.

# CHAPTER TWELVE

# "I HAD HOPED NEVER TO SET EYES ON YOU AGAIN"

Pilate was waiting in the square outside the courtroom where he had sentenced Jesus. He was seated at the campaign table at which I had interviewed him three years earlier, almost to the day, with his staff around him. As on that earlier occasion, today he was unshaven, wearing a leather breastplate. He looked heavier and somewhat balder. Otherwise, it appeared that little about him had changed. The cohort of men which he always kept within the city walls was lined up nearby, lances glittering in the early morning light.

I dismounted and walked up to him. He did not rise to greet me. I saluted. "Pontius Pilate, in the name of the Senate and the people of Rome, I relieve you of your command. Here are your orders from Lucius Vitellius, imperial legate and governor of Syria."

Quintus laid the orders in front of him. Pilate put his hand on the documents, though his eyes were fixed on mine. "This is an injustice." His voice was unsteady. "A gross injustice."

"Read the orders and acknowledge to me that you understand them."

I waited while he shuffled through the orders. Someone must have run outside with the news, because in the silence we could hear the cheering begin outside the Praetorium. The noise swelled and spread to other quarters of the city, up to the Temple Mount and the Mount of Olives. Pilate turned to his captain of the guard. "Have the crowd dispersed," he snapped.

"You have no authority any longer," I said.

His face darkened. "Then you give the order to disperse them."

"I see no need. Read the letters."

He did so, then tossed them aside. "I've read them." The governor's bronze crown was on the campaign table in front of him. He pushed it towards me. "I understand that this is yours, now."

I ignored it. "There are things we need to discuss privately." I turned to Quintus. "Dismiss the cohort to barracks. I want no soldiers on the streets of the city until I give the order."

I led Pilate into the courtroom. He walked slowly, limping as though the gout were still troubling him. Now that I looked at him closely, I could see that he had aged in these past two years, the lines deepening around his eyes, producing an impression of weariness which hadn't been there before. Though he was putting a stoical face on things, his hands were shaking. He had seen that Vitellius' orders effectively placed him in my custody.

"I had hoped never to set eyes on you again," he said bitterly.

"You'll remain here until after the Passover. I'll conduct an enquiry into the recent events on the west bank of the Jordan. When that's complete, I intend to send you to Tiberius for judgment."

"You'll undo ten years of unremitting work."

"I am hoping to undo ten years of bad government."

He laughed sharply. "You believe that this province can be happy and peaceful?"

"Yes."

"You're wrong. Jews are Jews. You may stroke them or strike them, they remain Jews. They'll always hate you." He pointed to the throne which Jesus had once called the seat of judgment. "You'll learn what it is like to sit in that chair. One day you'll hear a voice issue from your mouth and it will be Pilate's."

"I hope not."

"I suppose you've used your time in Rome to thoroughly poison the emperor against me?"

I lost my patience with him. "The gods gave you fortune, Pilate, and you misused it. Nobody else is to blame."

The joyful noise of the crowds in the streets came to our ears, a sound like the roar of the sea. "Enjoy it," he said dryly. "You'll hear them sing a different song soon enough."

"I'm astounded that you can't see that their rejoicing is an expression of how much they hate you, not how much they love me."

"They can't hate me more than I hate them. I presume you want to hang me up in a cage now, so they can pelt me with dung."

"I don't intend that you should undergo any more loss of prestige than is necessary. You'll remain in the Praetorium in your old quarters. I'll take the room I had last time. However, I expect you to be open with me in all that concerns the government of the province in general and Jerusalem in particular. If you attempt to keep secrets from me, or lie to me about what you have done, or prove obstructive, I'll show no mercy. Until you leave for Rome, you will not appear in public again and you will speak to nobody without my permission."

He grunted. "This Marcellus is preferable to the mealy-mouthed moralist."

"You have mistaken courtesy for weakness before. I recommend you don't do it again." They had brought wine and bread. He drank eagerly, his eyes closed, his hands shaking. I took no pleasure in his suffering nor did I want to prolong this encounter any longer than was necessary. "Please ensure that your personal staff attend the midday meal. I want to address them."

"You stole my wife from me and now you steal everything else."

I was disgusted at his words. "You're the author of your own fall," I replied. "As for your wife, she remains at your side."

"Her body is here. But you took from her that which made her alive, the light in her lamp."

"If that's gone, I do not have it, Pilate. She didn't give it to me."

"Then the wind of your wings must have extinguished it as you soared to greatness," he said with heavy irony.

"If I hear you misuse her," I said, "or offend her in any way, I'll throw you into your own dungeons and you'll go back to Rome in chains."

He made a weary gesture of assent. I left him there and went up to my room, followed by the soldiers carrying my baggage. I had come full circle. My old room was exactly as it had been three years earlier, even to the scent of aloes wood that had been burned in a small censer. The haunting, woody smell struck me to my heart. I indicated where I wanted my possessions placed and went to the window. The view across Jerusalem was hazy today, the cloud over the temple hanging motionless in the still air. The cheering of the crowd had spread across the city. I could see the streets filled with people. They would be expecting me to greet them at the rostrum. Someone had left the governor's crown on a table. I picked it up and put it on my brows. It was heavy and cold. I went down to greet the crowd.

I saw Procula again for the first time at the midday meal. I had thanked the citizens of Jerusalem for their greeting and had spent the morning setting up my headquarters in the Praetorium. I used the room Pilate had used, having anything personal taken out and retaining all the documents and records. Much to my pleasure, Rufus the orderly was still in the garrison. I at once appointed him my ADC. He was to prove invaluable in the months that followed, loyal, indefatigable and always ready for any emergency.

Procula entered the dining room beside Pilate. She was thinner and paler than before. She kept her eyes downcast and didn't look at me; nor did I offer her any special greeting, though this meeting had so much significance for me that my heart was thudding against my breastbone. When I looked at her more closely, I was shocked at the change in her. Her beauty now seemed somehow transparent, an image imprinted on something fragile, like glass or ice. Her hair, once glorious, had been tied back in black ribbons and there were angles in her face that were not there before. From midsummer she was passing into autumn.

Pilate's staff assembled at the table, all with glum faces, their eyes fixed anxiously on me. I told them to be seated, then made a brief address.

"I expect co-operation and obedience from all of you. Those of you who work well with me will continue in your posts. Those who do not will be sent back to Rome. I do not tolerate dishonesty in any form. I value loyalty and good service. Each of you will have an opportunity to speak to me over the next days. There will be changes. I expect you all to work with me to implement them successfully." I concluded by offering a grace to Jupiter Capitolinus.

The meal was eaten in silence. Procula sat near me. She didn't look at me. By the shadows under her eyes it seemed that she had been crying that morning. Pilate, by contrast, was red faced and seemed completely drunk. Despite appearing to concentrate intently on his food, he moved with painful slowness and let much of it fall onto the table or the floor. I've eaten happier meals than that one.

As they were all leaving the table, I stopped Procula and asked her to remain. She sat back down in her seat, very pale. Pilate peered over his shoulder at us, stumbling as someone helped him out.

"I won't detain you long," I said to her when we were alone. "This isn't a happy situation for either of us. We were once friends. I hope we can remain so. You're mistress of this household and I want you to continue to run it as you see fit. You don't need to consult me about anything. You'll keep your office, of course. Take what money you need from the bursar – I'll tell him not to question you."

She finally raised her eyes to mine. Their golden colour was as sweet as I had remembered. "You warned me this day would come," she said in a low voice. "I don't think I quite believed you."

"It is a pity you did not."

"Yes, a pity." She was unconsciously turning the wedding ring round and round on her finger. "You stopped writing to me. I think that you must have found someone else."

"Yes. I found someone else."

She looked down. "I'm happy for you. She's a very lucky woman."

"Whoever finds love in this world is lucky." I saw that she was crying. I hardened my heart. "There's one more thing: the golden candelabra that Pilate took from the temple treasury – have them brought to me. If there are any other ceremonial items of the same kind, please tell me where they are."

"There are some cups, and plates of gold. Also an ark of silver."

"Have them gathered together." She nodded without speaking. I rose to my feet. "I instructed your husband this morning not to abuse you in any way. If I become aware that he's disobeyed me, I'll imprison him. Please keep him mindful of that." She nodded again.

I left her there and went to my office. There were two scribes at my disposal, one Greek and the other Roman, and a team of messengers. This convenience enabled me to dictate a large number of letters in the afternoon, including one to Vitellius, telling him of my safe arrival and that I was now installed as governor.

I had no desire to see Pilate or Procula at the evening meal, so I ate alone at my desk and wrote by hand to Daphne:

*I have today put on the governor's crown and found it more uncomfortable even than I feared. I am compelled to be stern from the moment I open my eyes in the morning till I close them again at night. By the time you see me once more I will have forgotten how to smile. I hope you will teach me again. Pilate has spent the day drunk and I fear will keep himself in this state until he reaches Rome. As I write this, I can hear the smiths hammering in the armoury across the square – they are erasing Pilate's name from the medallions of the soldiers' armour and replacing it with my own. Three thousand times Marcellus will take all night. It sounds almost like the forging of links in a chain that will bind me for I know not how long. I send to you and Octavia my love and my wishes that you will be well and that the gods will smile on you.*

I sealed the letter and drank a cup of wine to help me sleep; and so ended my first day as Procurator of Judaea.

# Chapter Thirteen

# The Christians

The next days were filled with business. I interviewed various witnesses to the incident in Samaria, who gave so many conflicting reports that it was difficult to know exactly what had happened. However there was no shortage of accusers and it would be simply a matter of finding two or three who agreed on the sequence of events and the number killed.

I also attempted to find out from Pilate's own records how many official executions he had conducted during his tenure. It was a difficult task, since he kept only the most laconic accounts of such things and his punishment book was confused. The number appeared to run into many hundreds, at least. Of those killed in engagements or the suppression of "insurrections" there was no count. Once again, it would be a question of finding witnesses who would testify to the use of excessive force. I would interview Pilate himself later, but of course it was useless to expect him to condemn himself out of his own mouth.

My first visitor of any importance was Caiaphas. He came in response to my summons, magnificently robed, a towering figure with his beard freshly curled and his hands clasped over his belly. We greeted one another courteously and he congratulated me on my appointment, though with little enthusiasm. The memory of the trial of Jesus was still fresh in both our minds.

"I won't keep you long," I said. "I know how busy you are now that the Passover is approaching. I need to discuss various issues with you over the coming weeks, but they can wait. This is of immediate concern."

We went together to the Treasury, which was guarded by two legionaries. I unlocked the door. The display was spectacular. The two golden lamps stood among an array of plates and bowls for sacrifice, all of gold or silver. There were also crowns and shields and a magnificent ark whose inscription showed that it had been a gift from Philip, Herod's half-brother. How many thousands of sesterces it was all worth, I don't know, but I presume this was Pilate's notion of supplementing his pension when he retired.

Caiaphas literally staggered when he saw these holy things. He had to place a hand on the wall to support himself and began to pray.

"These items were apparently confiscated by my predecessor," I said.

"They are things he stole from us over ten years."

"I intend to restore them to the temple."

"You are a second Cyrus, my lord, giving back the sacred vessels which were stolen by Nebuchadnezzar and put in the house of his gods." He pronounced a sonorous blessing, for which I thanked him.

I had another visitor: in response to my summons, Joseph of Arimathea had come to the Praetorium. He was a very welcome sight to me and we clasped each other's hands warmly. That I had a good understanding of what was happening in Jerusalem was in no small part due to the correspondence we had maintained over the past three years. I valued his calm wisdom highly.

"I'm glad to see you here again," he said as we sat together. "It seems you have begun with an act of kindness."

"I hope there will be no disturbances over Passover."

"Amen to that. I expect there will be peace. I'm not the only one who hoped that this day would come." He had changed little, a rotund man with a prosperous appearance and a deceptively simple manner of speech. His beard was perhaps a little greyer. "I've brought you a small gift." He passed me a booklet, simply bound, its cheap papyrus pages covered with lines of Greek. "It's a collection of the sayings of Jesus of Nazareth. This is regarded by the

Nazarenes as an authority higher than the Torah. I had my scribe make you a copy. I thought you might find it interesting."

"Thank you. I accept this with pleasure."

"I've separated myself from their doings, unfortunately. Despite my admiration for the man, his followers have grown too quarrelsome for my taste. They live in somewhat squalid circumstances in a house here in the city and hold a synagogue of sorts in one of the rooms. They continue to declare Jesus the Messiah. I think they have given the word a new meaning of their own. James the brother of Jesus is the most distinguished of their sect but I think he has little to do with them. He lives separately from them, with his mother. The Sadducees don't like him but he worships at the temple every day, saying nothing to anyone but God."

"I should like to see them again."

"It's in your power to summon whomever you choose, Governor."

I smiled. "I asked you here in part to renew our friendship and in part because I would like your help. I want you to act as an emissary between me and the Sanhedrin."

He looked cautious. "Why do you entrust this embassy to me?"

"Because we're friends."

"And if I don't wish to act as go between?"

"Things being what they are," I replied gently, "you may consider this either a command phrased politely, or a request phrased pressingly."

Joseph looked at me thoughtfully. "Your uncle appears to have chosen with some acuity."

"I wish to do some good here, Joseph. I don't know how long I will remain in this post. I need capable men about me. You are one such. You're a member of the Sanhedrin but have an independent mind. You're wealthy enough not to be needed at every moment in your business. If I ask you for a little of your time, you won't suffer by it. Our mutual trust offers scope for us to repair some of the damage caused by a decade of Pontius Pilate."

"What do you intend to do with Pilate?"

"I'll send him to the emperor for judgment after the Passover. His latest slaughter of the Samaritan pilgrims will weigh heavily against him." We discussed the case of Pilate. At the end of half an hour I had persuaded him to become my ambassador to the Sadducees. I understood his reluctance; he didn't wish to be seen as a man in the pocket of the Romans. Nevertheless, there was much he could do to smooth communications between me and the princes of this city.

The festival of the Megalesia began the next day, with all the usual rigmarole. The figure of magna mater was brought out of her shrine and put at the table, together with fresh offerings. I offered prayers to her and to all the gods. The actors had arrived in the city earlier and had come to me with their program, which I approved, though I had no intention of attending more than the opening performance, which was to be one of the farces of Quintus Novius, a form of drama ideally suited to their minimal talents. To mark the day, I also requested that Pilate and Procula attend the evening meal and come to the play with me. Perhaps it seems heartless of me to oblige them to do this, but I was tired of eating alone and I wanted to see her face again.

Pilate was drunk before the meal even began. He overflowed with bitterness. "I see you've given them their gold back," he said, glowering at me. "They have been howling your name all day. I could wish for different music." She laid her hand on his arm to silence him, but he shook it off. "You desire their love. I assure you it's preferable to have their hate."

"I'm indifferent to their love or their hate. What concerns me is justice."

"You think I stole those things for personal gain," he retorted. "I held them as warranties for their good behaviour. Now you'll see how they despise you for your weakness."

"I can always take them back," I replied easily. "Let us offer a grace and eat."

In the event, I was the only one who ate. Pilate left his plate untouched and drank steadily, while Procula, once again in muted colours and with her hair tied back, sat in silence, toying with her food. I made no effort to stop him from drinking; the drunker he was, the better. He was evidently extremely angry at the loss of the gold. I was glad that his dismissal had come so suddenly that he'd had no time to melt down the "warranties" and hide them.

"I'm looking forward to meeting our friend Herod Antipas and his lovely wife again," I said. "I have received an embassy telling me they'll both arrive in the city before Passover. This year we will entertain them here at the Praetorium. I'm sure our kitchens are up to a plain Roman meal. Perhaps you'll see to it, Procula?"

Pilate glowered into his wine cup. Procula smiled wanly and nodded.

"Herod may not have such an appetite as last time," I went on. "I understand that his former father-in-law, King Aretas, is raising an army to invade Herod's territory. He is very offended that Herod dismissed his daughter and married the beautiful Herodias." I rambled on in this fashion without receiving much response from either of them.

I asked Procula to make the offering to the Lares. I watched her as she poured the wine and broke the cakes at the altar. My feelings were difficult to analyse. Our situation had changed so greatly. I had ascended, she had descended. I had come into authority, and moreover had the love of a woman whom I adored. She was now effectively my prisoner, as her husband was. I should have felt a sort of triumph. Indeed, had I been a different sort of man, I could have taken advantage of the situation in many ways. We all knew that. Yet it was painful to me to be her jailer. I felt the awakening of sorrowful old sensations, as our soldiers say they feel the ache in a limb amputated years before. I had, at least, the pleasure of watching her graceful movements. I tried to tell myself it was the pleasure one feels when watching a dancer, or some handsome animal, an admiration without emotional involvement.

When it was time to go to the theatre, Pilate was lurching on legs that seemed unable to support him. We had walked no more than a few paces out of the Praetorium before he fell. I sent him back to his room with one of the guard and went on to the theatre with Procula alone.

The performance was faintly amusing, knockabout street comedy made into a play of sorts by the addition of dialogue. I sat beside Procula in the governor's booth, idly watching the play, my attention on her.

"He's drinking very heavily," I said.

"It's his way."

"It must be hard on you."

"It's worse when he's sober. Then neither his life nor mine are bearable."

I glanced at her. Her face was pale in the darkness, her eyes fixed on the inane antics of the clowns on the stage. "I'm sorry to hear that. Is there no comfort for you?"

"There is consolation in faith."

"I plan to visit his mother and brother soon." I paused. "Perhaps you would come with me?"

"If you want me to."

"I'm not compelling you to come. Do you not wish to see James and Mary?"

"They keep themselves apart from other people, Marcellus. To go to their house will be a grave intrusion."

"I'll go once and no more. Don't you associate with the Nazarenes?" I asked her.

"Very often. But James and his mother are special."

"Why?"

"It's difficult for me to explain. Perhaps you'll understand more when you see them."

"I had a visit from Joseph of Arimathea. Coincidentally, he gave me a book of the sayings of Jesus. I've been reading them. They are truly extraordinary. If only one could understand them a little better. He's very cryptic at times. At other times, he sheds a brilliant light. I don't quite know what to make of his teaching."

"You can't read his words as though they were written by some Stoic philosopher."

"How should I read them?"

"Sometimes they have to be read with the heart, not the mind."

"My heart must be very hard."

"Your mind certainly is," she retorted.

The audience roared with laughter at the antics of the players. A man was pursuing a woman with a loaf of bread; the shadow cast on the screen behind them by the lamps made it seem as though he had an immense phallus. Without looking at me, she said, "Your face has changed."

"My nose was broken."

"It makes you look more forbidding. Perhaps you've become more forbidding."

"Authority is not good for making one cheerful."

"You still disguise your true thoughts in epigrams and rhetoric, Marcellus."

"It's my way of making life bearable. You smell of aloes."

"Do you like the smell?"

"I love it."

"So do I. It persists for days. Do you know what it's made of? Rotten wood. It comes from a beautiful tree in the jungles of India. When the tree is old and dying, it begins to make this wonderful smell."

"Frankincense and myrrh are made by cutting the bark of trees in Arabia. The Arabs call the drops that ooze out the tears of the tree. Perhaps trees feel pain as we do, and produce their own poetry, as we do."

"If that's true, you must make sure that your Daphne is always in pain. Then she will never stop producing poetry."

She had taken me by surprise. "I don't ask her for poetry."

She turned to me at last. The light of the braziers flickered in her eyes. "What is she like?"

I hesitated. "I'm not sure I can speak of her to you."

"Why not?" When I didn't answer, she went on, "I've heard that you bought her from your wife's cousin. They say she's very beautiful and writes Greek odes – and that you live with her as though she were your wife."

"None of that is untrue, I suppose."

"Why did you choose a slave?"

"I did not choose."

She turned away from me. "You're very cruel," she said in a low voice.

"Why is that cruel?"

She shook her head, her eyes on the stage. "Look. You've lived long enough to see yourself played in the theatre at Jerusalem." I followed her gaze. The players had suspended their farce. A divinity had descended from the top of the scene structure, clad all in silver and holding a thunderbolt, intended to represent Jupiter. With grand gestures, he was directing a procession of winged children who carried gilded wooden objects across the stage to the audience. Two seven-branched lamps were at the forefront.

The scene was in truth only marginally less farcical than the play but the entire audience rose to its feet with a roar of approval. They chanted my name until I was forced to appear from the booth and raise my hand to them. Only after a deal of noise were the actors permitted to continue.

"Why don't you smile at them?" Procula asked me.

"The whole thing is absurd."

"It was intended as a compliment. You note that they portrayed you as jovial Jupiter and not as angry Mars?"

"People will think I commanded it to be done."

She laughed quietly. "You're a strange man. You're vain enough to want to be thought modest."

"I don't want to be thought immodest. That's different."

"Marcellus, everyone will know it was a compliment from the people of the city to you. Did it not occur to you to make more political capital out of the gift?"

"In what way?"

"It was a magnificent gesture to restore the gold. Another man might have turned it into a public occasion and made speeches extolling his own virtue to the populace so that everyone saw how great he was."

"In the circumstance of restoring what you have stolen in the first place, it would be fatuous to proclaim your own virtue. Besides, I'm happy for Caiaphas to claim the credit. It will help keep the peace."

The audience, now in high good spirits, was laughing uproariously at everything the players did or said. "Will you marry your slave?" she asked.

"I can't think of such things, Procula. I may be away from Rome for many years."

"You'll return one day. She'll be waiting for you. Are you afraid of ostracism? Or are you afraid of meeting men who have taken her in some alleyway before you bought her?"

"Now it's you who are cruel. I offered myself to you, and I had heard your husband taking you with grunts of satisfaction."

"I wish you hadn't heard that."

"It made no difference to me."

"I hope that is a lie."

"Why should I lie? If I had heard you squealing with pleasure, I would perhaps not have spoken to you as I did. But I heard you crying."

"His lovemaking is not of a sort to make me squeal with pleasure, Marcellus. Sometimes you say terrible things."

"So do you."

"You were very quick to find another love."

"Almost a year had passed."

"Almost a year?" she echoed. "For a man, I suppose that's an eternity. You like my face and my body but as soon as they were out of your sight, you fell in love with someone else."

"That isn't fair. The refusals you gave me were decisive. You didn't want me. It would have been preposterous to spend my life longing for you."

"Indeed. The whole business is preposterous. I am the most preposterous thing of all. Forgive me. A woman may reject a wooer with all the vehemence in the world, but that doesn't mean she'll be happy to see him suited with another the next day."

We watched the remainder of the performance without further remarks. At the end of the show, we walked home, escorted by the guard. Jerusalem was normally an empty and silent city at night, since devout Jews didn't venture abroad in the hours of darkness, but tonight the streets were crowded with both Jews and Greeks who cheered us as we passed, calling my name. Once again, I was struck by a pink carnation. I stooped and picked it up this time. Throughout the course of my governorship, pink carnations were thrown to me – when they were pleased with me, that is. How they had chosen this flower for me I don't know, but it contented me very much to have them thrown at me. I gave this one to Procula.

We reached the Praetorium and went inside. When we were alone, she turned to me. She was holding the carnation. "I wonder if you know how strange it is to me to walk on the arm of a man who is cheered by the mob – and not loathed." I began to utter one of my usual epigrams when she put her hand over my mouth to silence me. Her palm was warm against my lips. Then she turned and ran from me up the stairs, her hair tumbling loose.

Months after I had parted from her in summer, a letter from Daphne finally reached me. From its date, she had written it in the first days of our separation and could have received none of my letters yet. It was the first letter I had ever had from her. It expressed the quality of her mind though it was hardly the tender message I had hoped for:

*I have tried to write a poem for you but there is nothing I dare not say to you anymore, so I choose prose. You freed me for the first time and forever. Nobody can make me freer than I am now. I know that you may never return to me. I know that you will be with one who is a more fitting wife for you than I. I do not wish to take any more from you. And she, too, needs to be freed.*

*Fortune is a wind which drives light vessels but not the great ships, which choose their own course. It is the dream of slaves. You have been the fortune of my life and my dream and I can wish for no other. I wish for nothing more than what I have now.*

I was perplexed and then angered by her words. They seemed so terse and cold. She had promised to write to me in her heart's blood! Later I began to see the love that lay behind them, but at the time I felt that I had waited a long time to receive nothing more than a few abstract phrases. I missed the warmth of her presence constantly. One word of tenderness would have meant more to me than these fine sentiments. Did she have so little faith in my love? I laid the letter aside with a sense of disappointment.

The city was once again starting to fill with pilgrims for the Passover. They streamed in from all parts of the province and the Diaspora, seeking lodgings in the districts around the temple. The atmosphere grew more volatile by the day and disturbances were a regular occurrence. They spread from one quarter of the city to another, flaring up and dying down like grass fires in the lightning season.

Since I made a practice of showing myself in the city, and did not remain enclosed in the Praetorium as Pilate had done, I witnessed some of these commotions at first hand. On one occasion I was thrown off my horse when he reared after being struck by a stone. I thought it had been meant for me, but when I picked myself up, bleeding somewhat from my hands and elbows, I found I was in a street full of rioting Jews.

My bodyguard formed swiftly around me and I drew my own sword, but they were not interested in us. Their venom was reserved for each other. One group was pursuing another with clubs and swords, which I had expressly forbidden citizens to carry in the city during the festival. They rushed past us, faces distorted with hatred or fear, howling slogans, many on both sides already injured.

It was difficult to tell one faction from another; neither side seemed to represent the official guard of the Sanhedrin. There was only a confused impression of enraged men, each one very like all the others, with a bearded face, billowing robes and thin, brown limbs in furious motion.

Then, with the swiftness with which these street battles can turn, the situation was reversed. The pursued came upon a part of the street where the pavement was loose. It was the work of a moment for them to wrench up sufficient ammunition to turn on their pursuers and unleash upon them a hail of granite cobblestones, which are a very good size and shape for killing a man.

The sky seemed to darken with missiles. The pursuers were routed, many staggering or falling with bloody gashes. They turned and fled. The pursued gave out a ragged scream of triumph and chased them back down the street towards us, hurling the cobbles with deadly accuracy. Not wishing to see my citizens slaughter one another under my very eyes, I commanded my men to come between the factions. It was as though they noticed us for the first time, so intent had they been on murdering each other. We formed a rather small group, being only twenty Romans among some hundreds of Jews, but there is a daunting aspect to locked Roman shields and levelled Roman lances, and the charge of the stone-throwers broke, allowing the others to make their escape, leaving behind a handful too badly hurt to run.

Even then, these wounded might have lost their lives, for the victorious cobble-throwers began stoning them. I went forward with only my sword to defend them.

"It's the Governor," a man shouted. "Hail, Marcellus!"

There were some cheers and some catcalls, as was the norm. I was in no mood for jokes. I struck one of them with the flat of my sword, making him stagger to his knees. "Do you think the streets of the city were made for you to commit murder with? Repair the paving, or I will scourge every last one of you!" They fell to work at once, replacing the cobblestones. Their spirits were high, since they had had the laurels. I pulled aside the man who had greeted me. "How do you justify this riot?"

He gestured at the wounded who had been left behind. "Christians, my lord!" he said, as one might say "Tigers." It was the first time I had heard the word.

"What is a Christian?" I asked.

"They're blasphemers! They claim that Jesus of Nazareth was the Christ!"

I was growing weary of hearing the name. "Why do you persecute them?"

"They persecute us!" he retorted. "They come to the temple shouting blasphemies and profanities. If they kept to their own place, and were silent, nobody would bother with them They are not even Jews. They are Gentiles and pagans from every land."

I inspected one of the Christians, who was groping along on his hands and knees, having had one of his eyes knocked out of his head. "Where do you come from, fellow?"

"Thessaly, my lord," the man groaned. "Oh God, I have lost my eye in Jerusalem, and I cannot find it again."

"It is still hanging on your cheek." I wiped the organ clean with my fingers and pressed it with some difficulty – they are much larger than they appear – back into the socket, an operation I have had to perform many times for my own soldiers. The wretched man clutched at his broken head. "The world has been split into two and one half does not match the other."

"It will mend itself with time. Go to a physician." He staggered away, aided by a kick from one of my guards.

I watched while they repaved the road, in no very good humour. The fall from my horse had been painful and I was aching. I was getting too old for such tumbles and I was beginning to see why Pilate had been so fond of nailing and scourging.

"They should be kept from the temple," the first man said. "You should post a guard to keep them out, Excellency!"

"I am not interested in your disputes," I snapped.

"But they claim to have your protection," he replied, adding slyly, "something we have just seen proof of."

"I don't care anymore for them than I do for you. I am happy to nail up a dozen from both sects, if you insist on impartiality."

Wisely, the man said no more, but went back to his work of repairing the road. It was almost exactly three years since the death of Jesus but the argument between his followers and the orthodox was continuing even more fiercely than when he was alive. On that occasion, by some miracle, there were no deaths, but a short time after this incident, I was asked to intercede after the killing of a young man by a mob.

His name was given as Stephen. He was a Hellenized Jew from one of the Ten Cities; his parents were not in Jerusalem and did not appear, but the Nazarenes sent an emissary to me at the Praetorium. Rufus brought me the man, telling me he was their chief.

"My ADC tells me you're the leader of the Nazarenes?" I asked him.

"Yes, Excellency. Perhaps you have forgotten me."

I studied him more closely. "I remember now." His eyes were strange, the whites stained brown so they seemed somehow blind. It was that which reminded me of the first time I had seen him, at the roadblock, where he had tried to prevent me from approaching Jesus. He was a strongly built man with a grim appearance but a gentle manner. His grizzled beard indicated he was no longer young and his face was battered. "I see your nose is in the same condition as mine."

"It was broken by a chance blow from an oar, Excellency."

"You're a sailor?"

"A fisherman."

"It is one of Pilate's complaints that there are no fish here, Peter."

"I fish for other things now."

"You speak good Greek."

"We Galileans are not as ignorant as some people believe."

"What is the matter here?"

"Forgive me, Excellency. The boy was innocent of any wrongdoing. They dragged him out of the city and stoned him. His body is yet unburied. We have brought it to you that you may see what they did. And we have one of the men responsible."

I went out with Peter into the courtyard where the body of the youth lay on a cart, wrapped in blood-stained linen and surrounded by a group of weeping men and women. They unwrapped the corpse for me. He was little more than fifteen or sixteen and a pitiful sight. As usual with a stoning, his body was broken and mangled in every part. The death blow had crushed his temple but his face, with open mouth and eyes, was undamaged. They pushed a man forward. He appeared frightened and dishevelled. "This is the man who urged the others to stone him!"

The man called out to me in good Latin, "Excellency! Excellency! I am a Roman citizen! Order them to release me!"

I held up my hand for silence. "Let him go. I want to speak to him." They obeyed. I beckoned the man to follow me and led him away from the others. I had given orders that the lamprey pool was to be drained. I hated the sight of it. The workmen had removed all the fish, some of them slimy monsters several years old, and had drained out the black water. I planned to fill it with papyrus and water lilies and perhaps a marble fountain. I walked along the wall, inspecting the work, followed by the prisoner. "What is your name?" I asked him.

"My name is Paul, Excellency."

"Where are you from?"

"I am from Tarsus."

"Where Antony fell in love with Cleopatra?"

He beamed ingratiatingly. "Exactly, Excellency!"

"And why are you here in Jerusalem?"

"To learn from the great rabbis."

"You're a Jew?"

"Yes."

"And why have you killed this innocent lamb on the eve of the Passover?"

His anxious look returned. "I took no part, Excellency," he said hastily. "I merely watched the men's clothes while they stoned him."

"To guard their clothes indicates approval for their deed." I turned to look at him. He was a short man with coarse, wiry hair receding from his forehead and a bushy, short cropped beard. He was very nervous, rubbing his hands together and peering up at me apprehensively. I didn't like his appearance but there was something interesting about him, as of a wily animal like a fox which seems timid but resourceful. "You encouraged them?"

He licked his lips. "Can I explain, Excellency?"

"Please do."

"The boy was a blasphemer. He was like one drunk on his own impiety. He raved like a madman. He said that his master, Jesus, was in heaven at the side of Moses. He said Jesus would return soon and tear down the Temple. He said he would build a new and greater one not made by hands."

"And so you were glad to see him stoned?"

"He might have yet escaped, Excellency, but when they asked him to answer the charges, he said the fathers had persecuted the prophets and the sons had murdered the Messiah. Caiaphas sentenced him and the Sanhedrin ordered the stoning."

The masons were scrubbing the stonework now. There was still a rank smell of eels in the tank. I commanded them to use quicklime to remove it and then walked on, followed by Paul. "I see that you're a devout individual."

He was growing bold enough to smirk at me again. "Yes, Excellency. I am a student of Gamaliel."

"If you've been taught by Gamaliel, then you should know the Commandments. Doesn't one of them prohibit killing?" I saw him compose his thoughts in preparation for a legalistic argument. "Before you reply," I said gently, "consider that I am within an inch of ordering the flesh to be scourged from your bones."

He paled and shrank back. "You cannot scourge a Roman citizen for the killing of a Jew!"

"Can I not? Shall we put it to the test?"

"No, Excellency! It is true that to kill is prohibited. Gamaliel teaches it. But if the priests say, "kill?" What then?"

"Is the word of your priests greater than the word of your God?"

"No, but—"

"I do not like *but*." I had considered whether to have him flogged, if only to ease my own feelings. Yet what point was there in arguing with these fanatics? We had walked back to the others by now. I beckoned to Peter. "He says it was ordered by Caiaphas."

Peter spread his large hands. "Caiaphas is our enemy. You, of all men, know that."

"But I can't intervene. It's a religious matter." I was determined to separate the Praetorium from sectarian conflicts of this type. "I am sorry for the death of this boy, but there's nothing I can do. I can't charge the Sanhedrin with any crime. And I will not quarrel with Caiaphas."

"But it is murder!"

"Consider that religion should be shaped for man, and not man for religion."

"That is contrary to our way of thinking."

"It was not contrary to your Jesus' way of thinking."

Peter looked at Paul grimly. "And this Cilician dog?"

"He is free to go. Don't impede him."

"My lord!"

"And from now on, restrain your associates from causing disturbances in the temple, Peter. Or believe me, I will begin crucifying and flogging, as my predecessor did."

"The temple is for everyone!"

"Not if the arguments therein conduce to the stoning of boys."

"Argument is the centre of our faith."

"You said you wanted a temple not built by hands," I said, losing my temper. "Build it! And stay out of theirs!"

Paul beat his hands together in triumph. "The Governor speaks, Peter. Hear him. Tell him not to allow his men to harm me, my lord."

Peter was furious. "He is accursed. His hands are stained with innocent blood."

Paul, having regained his courage with the swiftness of a fox emerging from a tight corner, straightened his garments and assumed an attitude of outraged innocence. "And your mouth is full of lies! You are damned and a blasphemer!"

I wearily commanded them to take the corpse and leave my presence. I was sick of their endless quarrels about religion and murders of one another. They departed, Peter and Paul still cursing one another.

Interestingly, this fellow Paul was later to become the most ardent Christian of all, and himself narrowly escaped being stoned by a mob for preaching heresy at the temple. It was typical of the volatility of the period that even fanatics could suddenly experience violent conversions, and risk martyrdom for those very beliefs they had been anathematizing a week earlier. He and Peter captained the two opposing camps of the Christians, the Jews and the Gentiles, and both quarrelled with James, so their disputations continued for years. They were, of course, in the process of fabricating a new religion, something which did not become clear until they had torn the old one to pieces. Nero executed them both as a public entertainment a few years ago. It was long overdue, I suppose. They had scuttled out of more nooses, traps and tight corners than most men see in their lifetimes. Be that as it may, one result of this episode was to help me take a decision. I summoned Joseph of Arimathea to the Praetorium.

"I've decided to dismiss Caiaphas as High Priest."

He tugged his beard, muttering in his own language. "Marcellus, you give with one hand and take away with the other."

"He was Pilate's man. He can't stay. The replacement should be a man who is acceptable to the Sanhedrin and who isn't connected with Pilate in any way. I want someone I can deal with on open terms."

"I won't question the wisdom of replacing Caiaphas. It's your decision. However I will remind you that the power among the priesthood lies with Annas, the father-in-law of Caiaphas. It's he who takes the decisions. It will lead to trouble if a High Priest is appointed who doesn't have Annas' approval."

"I understand that. I hoped you would convey my good wishes to Annas and tell him that it's impossible Caiaphas should continue as High Priest. Ask him to suggest three candidates most suited to replace him. I'll interview the three after the Passover and choose from among them."

"I'll convey your message to Annas. Does this derive from the stoning of the young Greek?"

"In part. But only in part. Caiaphas has held this post too long for any good he's done in it. He's as blood-stained a creature as Pilate. I'm tired of hearing that Jews have stoned Jews for some trifling disagreement of doctrine."

"Perhaps not always so trifling," Joseph murmured.

"The Sadducees are too proud. They think nothing of killing whoever stands in their way. They're obsessed with ritual and the common people mean nothing to them. You know that. One other thing, Joseph – can you tell me where James and his mother live? I do not wish to alarm them by summoning them to the Praetorium but I should like to see them again."

He told me where they lived and agreed to send a messenger of his own to announce my visit the next afternoon at sunset.

On this same day I received a letter from Rome. It was from my aunt, Sextilia. She was terse and to the point.

*I have not wished to speak to you on this subject before but can no longer hold my tongue. Your infatuation with your concubine is a grave danger to your prospects.*

*You have begun a brilliant career, thanks in no small part to the efforts of your uncle. For a young man in your position, the right wife is an inestimable advantage, the wrong one a disastrous encumbrance.*

*With a clean and modest Roman wife you may go into any society without fear that you will be embarrassed. Consider the alternative. Can you imagine yourself presenting such a consort as that to the emperor? Do not condemn yourself to a life of shame, Marcellus, for the sake of the passing pleasures of the flesh.*

There was more in the same vein. The conclusion was that although Procula was by no means a perfect choice, she was infinitely better than the "disastrous encumbrance" presented by Daphne. I was urged to take her as my own now.

I was irritated by the letter, though I understood it came from a real concern for my well-being. Very few of my friends had met Daphne and their assumptions about her were coloured by their own imaginings. To Sextilia, Daphne was a sensual courtesan who had ensnared me with sexual delights. No account was given to the idea of spiritual love between us. It was especially ironic that she had raised the idea of giving offence to Tiberius – that superannuated libertine – with a bride not "clean and modest." This was the second unwelcome letter I had received that week. I answered neither.

Procula came with me to the house of James the next afternoon. One of the inconveniences of being governor was the necessity of an armed escort wherever I went. It made discreet visits almost impossible. We went in the closed carriage, but James and his mother lived in a very steep street and we had to walk part of the way. It was a poor district of the old city where many of the houses were crumbling back into the rock from which they had been carved. Children scattered at the arrival of the soldiers and peered at us from around the corners with big eyes. The doorway to their house was made of immense slabs of stone and was very low, compelling us to stoop as we entered. The interior was cave-like, lit only by a single small window. They received us in the room where they evidently ate. We sat at a small wooden table.

James looked very much like his brother now. He appeared gaunt, his cheeks and eye sockets hollow. Mary seemed to have shrunk smaller than ever. She must now have been about fifty, but appeared older. Her hair, which had been grey when I had last seen her, was now all white. Her grief had somehow erased her; she seemed like a text that has been overwritten by other words. She greeted me with a moment of warmth and then sat motionless and spoke little. Procula, too, was still and silent.

I asked them first how they managed for money.

"Peter and the others send rations to us," James replied. "They are very just."

"But you are now an important man. You should not suffer such poverty."

"We need nothing more. My mother and I eat no animal food now, only vegetables. We fast many days each month. Most of our time is spent in prayer."

"I wish others of your sect led such a blameless life. Why are they so violent, James? I have seen them running in the street with drawn swords. Wasn't it enough that your brother was crucified? What is this new fashion for killing one another?"

"The son of Adam killed his brother. It is not a new fashion. It is a very old fashion."

"Religion should moderate that fashion, not adorn it with new and more horrible patterns." He made no reply to that, though he seemed to agree. "Peter brought a case before me recently, that of the boy who was stoned at the order of Caiaphas."

"I was at the temple that day. The boy was full of the spirit. He prophesied from the inspiration that was in him."

"And what happened then?"

"The old do not like to hear the voices of the young."

"And the rich do not like to hear the voices of the poor," I said, looking at Mary. I saw that she was wiping tears from her eyes. "I have come here to ask if you will use your influence with the Nazarenes to calm them. I don't want to resort to the methods of my predecessor."

"There is no difference between you and Pilate." He said it without bitterness, as a statement of fact.

"I hope there is a difference."

"Men do not kill because they are Romans or Jews," he said. "They kill because they are men."

"I understand that, as a philosophical point of view," I replied. "In more practical terms, I believe that the Christians should act with more restraint."

"God cannot be restrained."

"But men may be restrained," said, trying to remain patient. "In particular, the Christians should restrain themselves from rebuking other Jews for the death of Jesus."

He had a way of considering any question carefully before answering; he didn't have that mercurial swiftness of Jesus. "I do not rebuke them. I pray daily for their forgiveness."

"That in itself will madden many people," I pointed out. "It would be better still to remain silent."

"Stephen was silenced," James said, "but the stones that were stained with his blood continue to prophesy. If the stones are broken, the trees will speak. If the trees are cut down, the wind will speak."

"I am addressing you as a friend, James, but also as the Governor of Judaea."

"You are welcome in my house."

"And what does that mean? That I must hold my tongue because I am not a Jew?" I saw timid faces peering at us from the interior darkness of the house – James' wife and children, I presumed. They gave an impression of being melancholy and hungry. I judged that I had made my point and he had made his. "The last time we met was at the empty tomb."

"I remember the day."

"I left you there, praying. Since then many claim to have seen Jesus alive again. Even in Rome, I heard of it. They say you are one of those to whom he showed himself."

He was silent for a long time, rocking slowly to and fro as he had done at the tomb of Jesus. Mary said nothing, looking at her hands, her eyes veiled. At length, he answered in a soft voice. "I never saw him dead. I have only seen him alive."

"Alive – after the crucifixion?"

"Many people have seen many things. One cannot judge what another says he has seen. My brother was closer to God than I. I did not see him die and I never saw him dead. But I see him and hear his voice every day."

"Within yourself?"

"Within or without, it is the same. He did not hide himself."

I found him frustrating. He did not intend to open his mind to a Roman and a Gentile, that was clear. "Your brother died young because he did not hide himself."

"My brother died young but taught much. I have the rest of my life to consider his teachings."

"He is better off out of this wicked world."

"It is a wicked world, you are right. Those who consider themselves the best in it are often the worst, and those who believe themselves to be the worst are often the best."

"You Jews love to rank men above and below each other. We Romans tend to think all men are fundamentally the same. I note that there are many Gentiles in your sect."

"God calls who he will."

"Yes, but this is one of the complaints of the orthodox, James – that you admit Gentiles and make them half-Jews and bring them to the temple."

Mary lifted her eyes to me for a moment. "My son ate with harlots and tax collectors and he was not defiled."

I could see that they were waiting only for my departure. I placed a present of money on the sideboard, for the sake of those hungry faces in the dark. "If there's anything I can do, tell Joseph of Arimathea. He will bring the message to me."

Before we left, Procula kneeled at the feet of James and asked for his blessing. He laid his hands on her head and blessed her as she requested. Still on her knees, she took the hands of Mary and kissed them. Mary stroked her hair and murmured to her. I watched, feeling myself to be excluded from a mystery which they shared.

In the carriage, I said to her, "You see them often?"

"I attend the meetings which they hold."

"You mean religious services?"

"Yes – but they are not of the Roman sort. Something different."

"I would like to attend with you."

She lifted her eyes to mine. "Would you? I'll take you – if you promise to come as Marcellus, and not as the Governor of Judaea."

"I promise," I said with a smile. "You note that James doesn't say he saw Jesus come back to life. And he clearly distrusts those who said they did."

"He distrusts those who lie about it in order to be thought important. You're so ready to take away miracles, Marcellus. What do you offer in return?"

"I'm like Herod. I've seen many strange things in my life, but never a miracle. By definition, a miracle cannot be taken away. Either it is, or it's not. So I offer nothing in return."

"I suppose you're an Etruscan and to you a miracle is lightning hitting a tree or the birth of a two-headed sheep."

I was amused. "And what is a miracle to you?"

"It's something which manifests the power of God. Sometimes you can't see it, even when you look directly at it. You have to be looking elsewhere for its meaning to become apparent, in the corner of your eye."

I smiled and shrugged. "I'll tell you if I encounter such a phenomenon in the corner of my eye. It doesn't seem to me that James and Mary have seen such a thing."

"Perhaps they simply didn't wish to discuss it with you."

"That I can understand."

"We should not have gone there."

"Why not?"

"To them, we smell unclean, of blood and profane things."

"You smell wonderful to me."

"Marcellus, can't you see how holy they are?"

"I was as kind to them as I could be."

She looked at me strangely. "You're kind, but you should have gone on your knees to them!"

"I am a pagan," I said. "And my own gods are dead. I'm too old to go on my knees to new gods now."

"I'm sad for you."

"I'm sad for myself." I lifted her hand to my lips and kissed it lightly. "I'm not a very spiritual person. I'm a Roman governor in a strange land, hoping not to have to crucify any of my subjects today. That's all."

She withdrew her hand. "You shouldn't touch me like that."

"Does it really matter how I touch you or do not touch you now? Are we not past all those things?"

"Don't speak so bitterly," she pleaded. "I would give anything not to have hurt you."

"Any hurt is long past," I retorted. "I simply would like us to be friends without all this show of reproachful words, lowered eyes, withdrawn hands, heavy sighs."

"You are always so cruel."

"I do not intend to be."

"It is cruel to remind me that I made a terrible mistake."

I glanced at her. "I believed you were content with your decision."

"How could I be content?" she cried out. "To be with him? And you with her? Knowing what is between us?"

"You talk as though you loved me."

"Ah, Marcellus, you like to hurt me. Of course, I deserve it."

"If you loved me," I said carefully, "then the time to have said so was before, not now."

"When you wooed me with such gentleness, such tact? When you confronted me with your lawyer's arguments? 'Leave your husband at once, or face the consequences!' Was that when I should have seen that I loved you?"

"I have little tact. You knew that. But I think you also knew that my feelings were true."

"I understood neither your feelings nor my own! Not then! It was too soon, too sudden. You were so cold. You talked of love as though it were some distasteful law that must be obeyed. Of course I fled from you."

"Yet you were unhappy with Pilate."

"Until you came, I didn't know that I was unhappy. It was you who taught me that I was unhappy, Marcellus."

"That wasn't my desire."

"It was your effect."

"And now?"

"And now I cannot flee you, nor have you, and so I lower my eyes and withdraw my hands."

I did not want to pursue that particular line any further. "Our own feelings apart, Procula, it is not too late to separate yourself from Pilate."

"And come to you?"

"That is no longer a possibility," I replied. "But you can save yourself."

"I do not wish to save myself in that way," she said wearily. "I would divorce him to be your wife. But not in order to escape justice."

I was struck by the despair in her voice and the irony of the situation. "Nevertheless, I will attempt to protect you."

"Please do not. I have mangled my life and I assure you, I do not value it very highly."

We remained silent for the rest of the journey back to the Praetorium. When I had said goodnight to her, I went to the little library with a candelabrum, and finally composed a letter of reply to Daphne:

*It has taken me some time to understand your letter. At first, I was angry that you wrote so briefly and (it seemed to me) coldly. I saw the surface, but not the depth of your love.*

*There is no one who is a more fitting wife for me than you.*

*I have these past days been with one who was once important to me. I suffered when she turned me away, yet I thank the gods for that suffering now, since it led me to you.*

*I love you. I live only to be reunited with you and to tie our souls together in such a knot as no man, woman or god can undo. I live to see your dear face and to hear your dear voice.*

*Greetings from Marcellus, who thanks you for your offer of freedom, but prefers to remain your slave.*

A few nights later, Procula took me to one of the rites she had spoken of. I don't know what I expected. I have experienced religions at many levels and there is nothing so variable in all of human behaviour.

She took me to a house in the suburbs, a poor quarter of the city where the streets were narrow and winding. We had to leave the carriage in a little square, as before. I also left behind, much to their dismay, my bodyguard. I had taken seriously Procula's injunction to come as Marcellus and not as the Governor.

Procula and I walked on alone. These dirty, dark alleys, with their crowded tenements, made a strange contrast to the grand quarter of the priests. I carried a lantern, whose fitful gleam seemed only to deepen the darkness all around us. We met few people, only coming across a baker's boy, carrying a basket of dough to the oven, and a forge, where the smith was still hammering out sparks in his arched doorway. Otherwise, the place was as still as the grave.

"Do you come here, all alone?" I asked her.

"Why shouldn't I?"

"If you were to meet some fanatic in one of these streets, your life would be worth nothing."

"As to that," she said, "my life is worth very little to me now. But I think I'm safe enough. Even the fanatics bear me no ill will, despite my husband. It's one of the small miracles I told you of."

Nevertheless, I saw that she constantly looked over her shoulder to see that we were not followed, and seemed to take a circuitous route through passages and lanes where it would be very easy to get lost. She knew her way well, her sandaled feet making hardly any sound on the cobbles. We reached a house with a narrow doorway, where she knocked three times. The door was opened at once and we went in.

The house was one of those rambling warrens that were typical of the old city, the home to a dozen families or more, riddled with low and narrow passages which descended and ascended and turned awkward corners, as much of a maze inside as the alleyways outside. The place was full of people, seen and unseen, a-glimmer with oil lamps and alive with the murmur of voices, seeming to hum with excitement. The smells of food and other human activities were rich in the warm air. I, who had expected an air of reverence, was somewhat bemused by this atmosphere of a family gathering.

Procula took my hand so that I did not get separated from her. Her fingers were warm and gripped mine tightly. I allowed her to pull me along, unquestioning. The room we at last entered was a large, low space of irregular shape, made (as I could see by the arches and beams) by knocking together several smaller chambers. It was full of people. I counted over a hundred when we arrived and many more came during the course of the evening. Most were packed on benches which had been lined across the room in rows, but there was also a high table at one end of the room where those of greater distinction were seated. A menorah was burning, giving a flickering light to their faces. I saw Peter, with his broken nose and grizzled beard, taking his place in the centre. Beside him was James, pale and introspective, who in turn was beside his mother. The others were a varied group of men with a provincial appearance, poor Galileans as I guessed.

"Those are the disciples," Procula murmured in my ear, "Jesus' closest friends. Sitting on the other side of Mary are two of his brothers, Judas and Joseph. They were at odds with him while he was alive, but now are the first to proclaim him the Messiah. The others are men who followed Jesus and sat at his feet when he was alive."

"Which of them has the most importance?"

"It's between Peter and James. James will say little tonight, you'll see. But everyone knows that his brother's spirit is strong in him. Peter is the strongest character, but he's a simple man, a true Galilean. The Greeks say he's too harsh."

Though I was wearing plain clothes that evening, Procula and I were recognized as Romans and people made place for us on a bench near the back of the room. I don't think anyone recognized me as governor of Judaea, so my presence caused no interest.

I looked around. By now the hall was very crowded. There were several women besides Procula, which was always a striking feature of this cult; the presence of Mary at the high table was in itself an unusual thing among Jews, who accord little place to women in their religious business. I recalled the words of Joseph of Arimathea that the priests wouldn't respect a man who had so much to do with women. But indeed, there were many Gentiles in the congregation, as I could see, Greeks from the Ten Cities and further afield. As Peter had said to me, he no longer spread his net for fish, but it extended very wide, nevertheless.

The ceremony itself, if that is the right word, was also conducted mainly in Greek. As Procula had predicted, Peter took the part of priest while James sat brooding or praying beside him. The main part of the ritual was a re-enactment of the last meal eaten with Jesus. It was commemorated in a symbolic way, with bread and wine, which were passed around, reciting words he had spoken: the bread was his flesh and the wine was his blood. Where in a pagan ceremony an animal would be sacrificed and the participants perhaps marked with its blood, here Jesus himself was the sacrifice.

Their love for him shone like a lamp from each face. He was the be-all and end-all of their little cult. James rose to his feet to recite a sermon which Jesus had preached. I had never, as Joseph of Arimathea pointed out, heard Jesus preach. To hear James do so, in his quiet voice, was perhaps a very faint echo; but it was an echo nonetheless.

"How rich are the poor! For theirs is the kingdom of heaven!

"How happy are they who grieve! For they will be comforted.

"How proud are the humble! For they are the heirs of the earth.

"How lucky are they who hunger and thirst for righteousness, for they shall receive their heart's desire!

"How blessed are those who show mercy! They shall receive mercy.

"How blessed are the pure of heart! They will see God.

"How blessed are the peacemakers! They will be called the children of God."

These verses, with their antitheses, had a considerable impact. As one listened, one had the sense of the world being turned upside-down – that the powerless acquired power, that the mighty melted away. It was, in the truest sense, revolutionary. It was easy to see why the Zealots had at first mistaken Jesus for one of themselves. When he spoke, James' presence acquired a volume that it did not have in other circumstances. His face was illuminated, the face of an man transfigured. There was no sense that he was reciting a dogma or an incantation. It came from him like fresh water from a rock.

For their part, the participants were caught up in his words like swallows in the wind, crying out and lifting their arms. I thought of magna mater and her wax hands, of the hollow silences in our temples. I recalled my uncles poring over the livers of sheep, searching there for some divine revelation.

As a Roman, I was accustomed to solemnity during religious worship – the sonorous prayers of priests, the murmured responses of the congregation. Here I recognized something distinctly eastern, an impulse to ecstasy such as one sees in those Dionysian cults of Asia. Perhaps the wine had something to do with it, but I think it was a custom the Greeks among them had brought, for they began to rise to their feet and call out the name of Jesus, imploring him to return with ecstatic faces and gestures. Their swaying became dancing, their cries dissolved into inarticulate moans, or wordless babbling. It was a communal rapture. There was a moment during the ceremony when – perhaps it was the effect of the stale air, or the dim light on the faces, or the considerable heat of the room – it seemed that each person was bound together in one shimmering mass, and no one could be separated from those around him. I

THE TESTAMENT OF MARCELLUS

had felt such a sense of unity as this before, during battle, when desperation made a single creature out of a group of men, driving us onward to win or die. The borders between one personality and the next were obliterated. There was only one will and one purpose. Such experiences are very powerful, and unite individuals indissolubly. I have no doubt that this shared ecstasy was an important element in the appeal of this cult to the lower orders.

The presence of women, too, made it unique. We Romans prefer to separate the sexes in religion, as everyone knows. Women have their mysteries, men have theirs. The mingling of the sexes in one mystery added a new constituent, intoxicating and erotic. Women cast off their veils and showed their faces. Men and women, strangers to one another, could dance together, sing together – yes, and embrace and kiss. I found it arousing and I am sure many others did, too.

It was an impressive ritual, intended to disturb the mind, perhaps even to unseat it. I have never enjoyed losing myself, in wine, religion or any of the other drugs. Procula, like the rest, gave herself up to the dance. Like the others, she was exalted. She had glimpsed Jesus only once, hours before his death, yet it was clear in her movements and her expression that she accepted him as her god.

It was very strange to me to watch her, her eyes lifted, her face transfigured, as though in the act of love. She no longer seemed part of my world. She had become part of something I did not share or understand. As on the day she had told me that Jesus had risen from the dead, I felt a gulf between us. There was a part of her that I couldn't understand or even approach. Much as I admired the man, I couldn't accept him as a god. That she could was something which divided me from her profoundly. I do not even say that I clung to the old pagan gods I had grown up with; simply that I was unable to let go of who I was.

The ritual ended only when the participants became exhausted and began to collapse into one another's arms. With a declaration that Jesus (whom they now always called the Christ) had risen from the dead, as they too would also rise, and that he would return soon in glory, they parted from each other with many embraces and kisses. In all, it had lasted perhaps one hour, but in its quiet intensity it was unique.

The meeting turned into a communal meal. Everyone had brought food of some kind, which was now shared out. I could hear people discussing their faith, those who had known Jesus describing him to those who had never met him. Many people talked with Procula, eager for her words; compared with them, she was an educated woman and I could see how they respected her. I sat in silence, feeling myself apart from everyone else.

Among themselves, the disciples discussed church business with much intentness. I could see arguments being conducted, frowning faces and angry gestures. In the course of this discussion, James and his mother slipped away.

"What do you think?" Procula asked me. I could see by her swollen eyes that she had been greatly moved during the service.

"It is very interesting," I replied.

Her face fell. "Only that? Did you not feel anything other than interest?"

"What did you feel?"

"I felt that his spirit swept through the room on golden wings."

"Ah. I envy you, Procula."

"I'm bitterly disappointed," she said in a low voice. "I felt sure you would feel it. Perhaps it will come with time."

"Perhaps," I agreed. But I felt that the gulf between us would never be bridged in that way.

At last the evening was over. We left the house in small groups so as not to cause too much disturbance in the streets. As Procula and I walked back to the carriage, she asked, "Did you really feel nothing?"

"I felt a sense of kinship with those around us. But the feeling was human, not divine. Before they began to die, I have been in the presence of my own gods. The experience was quite different, I assure you. One felt terror, exaltation. Voices spoke in one's ears, the earth heaved, the air trembled. Perhaps you'll say those were the tricks of our priests, but I think it was another reality."

"I don't say that it was trickery, Marcellus. But your gods were gods of terror. Jesus is a god of love."

"I think terror is more prevalent than love in this world of ours," I said gently.

"Yes!" she replied swiftly. "That's true. But there's another world beyond this one! A perfect world, where we must strive to reach!"

"This is not Jesus," I said smiling, "but Plato. You worship with Hebrews but talk like a Greek."

"It's strange to me that you made such efforts to save him and yet you now deny him."

"Deny? I acknowledge him as a great man, Procula, but what else do you want from me?"

"I want you to open your eyes and see."

"See what? That this dead man came back to life and is a god? I can't see that. I never will."

"Then you'll never see who I am," she replied. And there we left the subject.

I declared at the outset that this was to be the chronicle of my life, yet now I wonder if, instead, it isn't the chronicle of Procula's life – or Pilate's, or Daphne's. All those lives were also my life. We were sewn to one another like the pieces of a garment. I can't be separated from them, or they from me. Nor can the whole life be shown, with its daily alterations; all the chronicler can hope to do is show a few details, to leave the reader with an impression of what was – or what might have been, for there is also the question of memory.

I am writing this now at a considerable distance in time. Over thirty years have passed since that evening in Jerusalem. And Jerusalem is no more. That breathless room is gone, with all the lives that were in it, burned to ash.

I try to recreate the truth, even if the details don't quite match, the way our antiquaries will mend a Greek vase, trying to preserve the frieze of figures painted by the hand of Sophilos or Kleitias, obliged to fill in what time has destroyed. There are blanks and empty spaces, the frieze winds in and out of nothingness. So also do we ourselves come and go, I think.

And there were fewer people in the world, then. Things were simpler. We all knew each other. Our mathematicians tell us that the population of the earth is increasing. I can see it in the great crowds that fill every space, now. That intimacy, that closeness between one and another, is leaving humanity. The human face is no longer easily recognizable.

I continued to read the words of Jesus in the little book Joseph had given me. I have lost the book now, alas, but much of what he said has become a part of me and I carry it with me in all the business I conduct. That, at least, I learned to see.

# CHAPTER FOURTEEN

# PASSOVER

Whether because of my warnings, or through some mutual settlement of differences, the violence between the Christians and the orthodox died down for a while. There were no more killings or riots over Passover. It was quiet. Herod and Herodias arrived in the city with somewhat less fanfare than the last time. They slipped into Jerusalem in a covered carriage so that nobody even knew they had come. They were attended by a much reduced bodyguard. Within a short while of his arrival, Herod's messenger came to me with a request for a private audience. I knew very well what he intended to ask. I sent a reply that I was engaged and instead invited them both to dinner the next evening.

As I had requested, Procula saw to the arrangements. I specified a very plain menu which conformed as much as possible to the Jewish dietary codes. It was no banquet, although Procula made the table beautiful with flowers and fruit.

The meal was an interesting occasion. Salome did not appear, since she (already a widow) was being prepared for her second marriage, to Philip, another of her great-uncles. Herod and his beautiful wife arrived in magnificent clothes, laden with heavy jewellery. They had brought princely gifts, too; a silver box containing rare incense for Procula and a silver bowl for Pilate. For me there was gold – a goblet shaped as a woman's head, exquisitely beaten. As an added tribute, the face of the goblet was unmistakably Procula's portrait. I thanked them graciously.

"A mere nothing, my dear Marcellus," Herod said. "I see that you're wearing the ring I presented to you. I am very touched. Very touched, indeed."

"I use it to seal all my correspondence. It brings back rich memories." They had arrived with a retinue of courtiers and retainers, including the insolent man who had struck Jesus. I sent them all away, explaining to Herod that I did not have food for them all. "Just a plain Roman meal such as the great Augustus loved to eat."

"Ah, the divine Augustus!" Herod said. Though he was offended at the dismissal of his creatures, he had to swallow it. They trouped out, escorted by my bodyguard. For my part, I had invited Rufus to the banquet and I presented him to Herod.

"This is Rufus, my ADC. It was he who nursed me when I was so ill after dining with you three years ago."

Herodias raised her hands in horror. "What a memory you have! You must promise me to forget all about that, Marcellus." She was as lovely as ever, though her husband appeared to have aged. He was now approaching sixty and he had a bloated appearance, his cheeks red and shiny. She had skin like alabaster. She wore an elaborate coiffure with golden ornaments, setting off her crimson hair. She showed her perfect teeth in a smile. "It is not really fair to bring it up at all."

"Oh, the memory is a happy one, I assure you. In fact, I plan to turn it into a tradition. Tonight we intend to poison you with something traditionally Roman – you will have to guess whether it is hemlock or wolfsbane. Next year we will come to you for mandragora or toadstools." There was an appalled silence. I spread my hands. "I am joking, of course. If anything on the menu tonight disagrees with you, it will be mere coincidence. Let me know if anything tastes odd to you."

"That is not very funny, Marcellus," Herodias said.

"Forgive me. To be poisoned is certainly not amusing. Tell me, because I have long wondered – did our dear friend Pilate connive with you in administering the drugs to me, so that my tongue would be loosened? You need not answer. You would hardly have dared do such a thing without Pilate's collusion. I recall seeing him in the room while you interrogated me."

They were all staring at me. "The wine was strong," Herod said lamely. "You were not accustomed."

"It was strong, indeed. Let us eat."

"You note," Herod said, recovering his poise, "that after the death of that fellow whom you wished Pilate to spare, we have enjoyed three years of peace? And my temple, which he prophesied would be in ruins, still stands? It never does to show mercy to these so-called charismatics. They're merely rebels in another guise."

"His followers are still in the city."

Herodias laughed. "A foolish rabble who will drift away. Without the man Jesus, they're nothing."

"We will see."

Herod leaned forward, wiping his hands. "My dear Marcellus, I don't want to kill these lunatics. It's they who insist on throwing themselves on the point of my sword. You'll find the same thing yourself. I hope that you'll have absorbed the lesson when you are put to the test."

"I stay out of their quarrels, Herod."

Pilate, as usual, ate little, preferring to drink in silence. He spilled his wine on himself and on the floor as before. Procula attempted to help him eat decently but he thrust her away. Perhaps it was unkind to exhibit him to his former ally in this way, like an ill-tempered bear chained to a post, but I wanted Herod to absorb the object lesson. To his credit, Herod refrained from bringing up the subject that was uppermost in his mind until two courses had been served. Then he turned to me. "We're faced with a crisis, Marcellus. My presence at home can be ill spared, but I made a special trip so as to be able to speak to you. The Nabateans are building up to a war. Aretas is massing his troops on my borders. He claims much of Perea as his own. It's nonsense, of course, but this is an extremely dangerous situation."

"Dangerous for you," I said.

"And for you!"

"Why? As I understand it, Aretas is quarrelling with you, not with me. You are the king of Galilee and Perea. You have a large army. This is your affair. King Aretas is your father-in-law, is he not?"

"The father of my first wife," Herod said sullenly.

"And this quarrel originates in the offense you gave him by divorcing his daughter, does it not? Perhaps you should have remembered that it's bad policy to cross an Arabian king."

"This is not a joke, Marcellus," Herod snapped, offended.

"I do not take it as a joke. I've received reports of troop movements on both sides. But I cannot spare a single man to defend you. You already have an army paid by Rome, do you not? You raise heavy taxes for your own treasury. This is a local conflict such as Rome expects you to resolve."

"You'll soon see how local it is when Aretas's army is camped within a day's march of Jericho!"

"Aretas will not attack Judaea," I replied. "He has his eyes on Eastern Perea. That is your province, Herod."

"Herod is a loyal ally of Rome," Herodias said sharply. "As was his father and his father before him. Do you mean to say you will abandon him now?"

"The quarrel was of Herod's making," I said, turning to her. "It has nothing to do with Rome. You wish to be celebrated as a second Helen of Troy, perhaps, but you may believe me that I do not intend to shed one drop of Roman blood in defense of your honour."

She seemed astounded. "But you have an army at your disposal!"

"I have one cohort of the Tenth Legion and a few cohorts of Pilate's men from the Decapolis. How many men, Rufus?"

"Three thousand, two hundred and ten," he replied, "though generally, Pilate's men are in poor condition."

"There you are. Barely a legion in all. And these men are committed to the defense of Judaea."

"With half a legion you could rout Aretas," Herod exclaimed.

"You have considerably more than half a legion."

"Aretas has cavalry!"

"I have faced cavalry on foot, Herod. There are means of defeating them."

"You could ask Vitellius," Pilate growled from his end of the table. "He has three legions at his disposal."

"Ask him by all means," I said, "though I can tell you that he's determined not to be drawn into local disputes." I knew that Vitellius, in fact, wouldn't lift a finger to defend Herod. He had told me so himself.

"Tough luck, Herod," Pilate said in a slurred voice. Unexpectedly, he began to chuckle maliciously. "It seems our Marcellus is reluctant to draw his sword."

"We old soldiers are always reluctant to draw our swords, especially in other people's pissing contests."

"This will be remembered," Herodias hissed at me. "We will appeal to the emperor."

"Well, I know you have a special relationship with him. I hope you succeed in arousing his sympathy."

"By the time Tiberius responds, it will be too late," Herod said in anguish. "The invasion is imminent. You must do something, Marcellus."

"You have wasted your time coming here. You would have been better employed drawing up your battle lines in Perea."

Herodias rose to her feet. Her lips were as thin as a snake's and her face was white. "I will not remain at this table. Come, Herod."

"Please, my dear," he said with a dismal smile, "be seated."

"Are you still hoping to get something from him?" she snapped at him. "Don't be a fool. Can't you see he will do nothing? Look at him! He's laughing at us!"

Herodias gathered her robes and stalked away from the table. Herod had little option but to follow his queen. "She is indisposed," he said awkwardly to me. He was still smiling wanly, but his eyes flashed with hatred. "Do please excuse her. We will talk of this another time, Marcellus."

"I will not talk of it again," I replied. "I've given you my answer."

He made a little bow and hurried after Herodias, while Pilate continued to chuckle hoarsely to himself at their discomfiture. Herod and Herodias had been married for five years by then and already his kingdom was falling apart. Perhaps it was a family trait, for his elder brother, Archelaus, had already done exactly the same thing before Herod, marrying his brother's divorced wife to the fury of the Jews and to the detriment of his career. Archelaus had been deposed by the Roman emperor and sent into exile. One would have thought that Herod would have learned his lesson from this example.

When Herod and his queen had withdrawn, I dismissed Rufus. Just the three of us were left. Pilate stretched out on his couch and held his goblet to the slaves for more wine. "I can't remember when I've enjoyed a meal more," he said. "I always hated those two."

"I owed them an old debt. Would you make the offering, Procula?"

Procula rose to make the offering to the Lares. We both watched her at the altar. "Who would have suspected that the kindly Marcellus could be so unforgiving?" Pilate said, swirling the wine in his goblet. "I suppose it's my turn next. You owe me an old debt too, as you see it. You've never forgiven me for crucifying that pious conjuror."

"There's nothing personal between us, Pilate."

He indicated Procula's slender figure at the altar. "That is personal." I made no reply and he smiled. The wine had blackened his teeth. "Bear in mind that as you punish me, so you also punish her. If she goes into exile with me, you'll suffer the torments of the damned, year after year, thinking of her wretchedness. Consider that."

"I do consider it. There's nothing I can do."

"You don't grieve for her?"

"That is another matter."

"Don't you want her?"

She turned from the altar to her husband. "Pontius, don't do this."

"But I will do it. You advised her to jump ship when you were last here, did you not, Marcellus?"

"I warned her that this would happen and advised her to prepare for it."

"By that, you mean you demanded she climb from my bed into yours?"

I made a weary gesture. "If that's how you like to see it. There is still some hope. If you're banished, she may be exempted. In that situation, most men would leave their wives behind."

"Not I. If I am banished, I'll take her with me."

"If Tiberius spares her, she can refuse to go."

"Procula? She won't refuse, you may believe me."

I glanced at Procula's pale face. "That is her decision."

She sat back down at the table. "You discuss me as though I were not here."

He gave her a crooked smile. "You're welcome to join the discussion, Procula. Tell him – if you're offered exemption from the banishment, will you take it?"

She spoke quietly, with lowered eyes. "I have already told him. My duty is with my husband."

Pilate gulped wine. "You hear her, Marcellus. She'll come with me. Her notion of responsibility won't allow her to desert me."

"It's not your responsibility to suffer for his crimes," I said to Procula.

She lifted her eyes to mine. "They're my crimes, too. I've been at his side for twelve years. The blood he shed stained me. The gold he took enriched me. I took what he offered me with both hands. I lived the life that he gave me."

Pilate rested his jaw on his fist to watch us. "You love her, Marcellus. It's to be seen in every line of your face. If you can send the woman you love into exile, then you're a stronger man than I think you are." He was drunk, but articulate. "I know all about your little Greek slave, of course. She can be nothing compared to Procula. A moth beside a butterfly. The moon compared to the sun. And if you are really amused by her, you can keep her on the side, of course. Procula will make a long face, but she'll probably tolerate it."

"What are you saying?" I asked him.

Procula spoke. "He's offering to give me to you in exchange for his freedom."

"Are you a party to this offer?" I asked her.

She looked away. "No."

"But you're willing to be traded for his escape?"

"Don't look so shocked," Pilate said dryly. "It's easily accomplished. You'll tell your uncle that I am not such a bad fellow, after all. He dotes on you. He'll accept the arrangement happily, if only to prevent you from ruining your life with the slave. I'll be sent back to Rome to be given some new post, with no blame attached. I'll divorce Procula and she'll remain here with you. We will all live happily ever after."

"Do you really think I'll consent to this proposition?"

"I told you once that guilt and innocence are meaningless to me. Perhaps you remember that little speech I made you? I've sent many men to the cross but I made the decision in each case for the good of the province, not to punish the guilty or to spare the innocent. I don't now believe myself to be guilty or you to be innocent. I believe only in what is logical. This is a logical arrangement."

"Indeed, it's very cool."

"No," he said, "it's not cool. I love her in a way you cannot imagine. But I have a life to live and a career to pursue, and that means much to me. She loves you. From the day you left Jerusalem to this, she hasn't smiled. She'll come to you if by doing so she saves me. But if you exile me, she stays at my side." Procula was silent. Pilate lifted himself to his feet with an effort. He stood, swaying, looking at us blearily. "She's my ransom. I leave you to discuss it together." He signalled to the slaves to help him out. With an arm around each of their shoulders, he left the room.

"Don't speak," she said in a low voice, when he had gone. "I know how he disgusts you. You need not say anything."

"We're not living in the days of the Republic any longer. Women have choices these days."

"I seem to have none."

"What is it that binds you to him?"

"He is the husband that I have, Marcellus. I don't want any other." She drank deeply from the wine goblet. I had not seen her have such an appetite for wine. "Or, since it seems to be a night for speaking from the heart, let me rather say that I love a man who no longer loves me. If he would have me, there would be a place for me in the world. But I missed my chance. When he offered, I refused. Now that I have learned to love him, he is in love with another woman."

I winced. This was indeed speaking from the heart. "Time has played tricks on us."

"It's always the same trick. A woman is like an iron brazier, a man like the wood inside it. She heats up while he burns. By the time her love is glowing red, his love is turning to ash, and he is ready for the next adventure."

"I did not think of it as an adventure."

She drained the goblet and continued as though I had not spoken. "So, since the man that I love is not available to me, I prefer to remain with the one I have." She laughed shortly. "And Pilate has his qualities. He's cruel and a bully, but he sets the boundaries of my world. He knows what I am. I don't have to pretend with him."

"Do you have to pretend with me?"

"I pretend with everyone. I can only get through each day by placing my feet exactly in the footsteps of yesterday, and knowing that tomorrow I will place my feet exactly in the footsteps of today."

"I don't understand you."

"I am not real, Marcellus." She looked at me with those golden eyes of hers. "You think you see me, but you don't. Every day of my life I've been afraid that someone will point at me and shout, 'She's a fraud! Look, she's not there!'"

I was taken aback. She seemed to be drunk, yet I remembered Daphne saying something not dissimilar to me, once. "You must have more hope for the future, Procula."

"My hopes ended when I lost my child, Marcellus. Do you love her?"

"Yes."

"And what do you feel for me? Is it pity?"

"Partly that."

She grimaced. "Give her children. That is my advice. If I'd had children, I would have been different. I would have something to be myself for."

"I don't understand this uncertainty, Procula. You have qualities that any woman would envy and any man desire."

"Ah yes. I am young, intelligent and beautiful, as you once told me."

"You are all that and more."

She drained the goblet again. "A model of Roman womanhood. Ornamental, dutiful, virtuous." She struck herself on the belly. "Look at these sturdy hips. Made to bear sons for Rome. And these breasts, made to suckle heroes. Well, I will go to my husband now, and see if he can father another child on me. Perhaps I can manage not to lose this one."

It was painful to see her in this state. "Don't drink anymore," I begged, for she was pouring wine again, "it's not doing you any good."

"On the contrary, it does me a great deal of good. It helps me pretend that it is you who lies on top of me, so I can lift my heels around my ears and welcome what I cannot bear."

"Procula!"

"Don't worry. I will tell him that you refuse his offer. He will not make it again." She finished the wine and came to me, her face flushed, her eyes full of tears. "Will you kiss me good night, Marcellus?"

I took her in my arms. Her breath was hot and reeked of wine. She kissed me as a lover, her mouth open, her tongue seeking mine.

The breasts and hips of which she had spoken were pressed against me. I felt my head swim as I was drawn into her need, her grief, her madness.

She drew back and looked into my face as though wishing to remember the moment for ever. Then she left me.

Passover came and went. The city emptied. Annas sent three priests to me from whom to choose a successor to Caiaphas. I interviewed them all and picked Jonathan, one of Annas's sons, who seemed the wisest choice. He was installed with pomp and Caiaphas retired after an unusually long period in office. Life became quiet.

I should be lying if I said I didn't consider Pilate's offer. I had loved Procula. I had loved her because she was beautiful, without knowing anything about her, without knowing anything about what went on inside her. That's the way many men love women, even the cleverest of us. It is not given to all of us to touch one another's souls. And since so many women are so accustomed to dissemble, and live lives whose interiors are never shown, it is easy for them to keep us at arm's length if they so choose.

That night in the dining room was perhaps the first occasion that I caught a glimpse of what she suffered. I was young then, and I thought the condition was particular to her. Of course, it was not. Women nowadays have much more control over their lives; at that time, women were almost powerless in Rome. They had only the lives that men endowed them with, and many suffered from depressions and feelings of incapacity, as Procula did. Suicides were common among women, as were hysterical complaints and outbursts of frenzy. We attributed them to all kinds of things, but now that I am older, I think that they killed themselves – or became ghosts, as Daphne put it – out of sheer frustration. Things have improved somewhat.

To love a woman for her beauty is a very shallow kind of love. I had not understood how shallow until I learned to love Daphne for the beauty of her character, her courage and her intellect. It may be seen that I had much to learn, yet.

I held them in Jerusalem as long as I could because I knew that the day of parting would be a hard one and because she filled my eyes. But it was a period of sorrow, like waiting for a death.

It was now the beginning of summer. I had chosen to remain in Jerusalem until the hot weather began, rather than go back to the coast at the end of Passover. The papyrus I had planted in Pilate's lamprey pond grew tall and lustrous. The water lilies bloomed blue and white on the surface. The palm trees of Jerusalem were bearing fruit. The rock pigeons sang, their chant melting into the heat. The atmosphere of the city had softened – and it remained that way. Whatever else I may have done wrong, I can truly say that Judaea was peaceful under my command, from first to last. I was compelled to crucify no-one and mount no military operations, quell no insurrections and persecute no-one for unpaid taxes.

Weeks passed unnoticed. The necessity of sending Pilate to Rome was pointed out to me in two letters. The first was from Vitellius. His letters came from Antioch every six weeks and were filled with good advice. This one addressed the issue of Pilate.

*Strike while the iron is hot, Marcellus. I warned you to show no mercy to Pilate. If you have completed your investigation into the affair in Samaria then send him to Tiberius now. The emperor grows old. About the woman, I say nothing. It is your affair. But he must be dealt with. He is a cunning man and if he is not got out of the way, he may prove dangerous to you. Do not delay. Do not allow him to remain there, watching what you do and planning what he may say to the emperor about you.*

*Other than this, I am delighted with the progress you continue to make. You have brought peace to your province. Your friend Herod has not dared approach me for assistance against his erstwhile father-in-law, but a conflict in Perea cannot be postponed much longer. If Herod is swept away, his provinces will naturally fall to you, and you will find yourself the governor of Galilee as well as Judaea.*

The second letter exerted a different, though just as powerful pressure on me. It was from Daphne.

*Your exquisite gifts of silk and perfume have made me so happy. Octavia cares little for these things, but I am fond of them.*

*I adore you Marcellus and long for you each moment. The seasons pass and I recall how we stood under the pine trees, whose boughs were so heavy with snow. You promised Eurydice that you would return for her. She awaits daily, looking from her window at the pines, which grow a little taller every year. She wants you and she wants your children and she wants the life that is ours together.*

I will not bore my reader with all that she said. Anyone who has loved and been loved knows what lovers say. The letter was completely different from the last I had received from her and its effect was to make my heart soar out of the melancholy into which it had settled. Together, the two letters made it easier for me to emerge from inertia into which I had settled as regards Pilate.

I summoned him to my office. He had grown lethargic of late. Never having been particularly fastidious in his dress, his inactivity and incessant drinking had made him slovenly, his clothes stained with wine and his jowls habitually unshaven. Like me, I suppose he had fallen into a depression. I had drawn up his orders to depart for Rome and answer to Tiberius for ten years of cruelty. I presented them to him. He stared at the parchment stupidly for a moment and then flushed a deep red.

"You refuse my offer?"

"You offered what was not yours to offer, Pilate. There was nothing to accept or refuse."

He sat heavily in the chair opposite my desk. "It need never have come to this."

"I told you that it would come to this."

His face changed. "I will fight. And if I lose, I'll make her suffer till her last breath."

I did not comment on this threat. I would no longer be drawn into his games. "You'll travel to Caesarea under escort. You'll return to Rome on the mail ship. It will have stowage for all your possessions. I am sending a delegation of Samaritans and Judaeans with you who will lay the charges against you before Tiberius."

"You'll come to curse this day."

"I curse it already. There's nothing more to say. Please prepare for your voyage."

The governor's residence was filled with their property, accumulated over years. Watching it being emptied, day by day, the furniture dismantled and the ornaments put in crates, the linen rolled up and the cutlery and crockery wrapped in bags, filled me with sorrow. The rooms took on a stark look, filled with nothing but the dazzling summer light. Even the furniture in my own room had belonged to them. I did not prevent them from taking anything. They had many rich and beautiful things. I hoped that some, at least, would be left to comfort her wherever they made their new life.

I never got a chance to speak to Procula alone again before they departed Jerusalem. In fact, we avoided one another, knowing there would be too much pain in any moments we might have together. The dining table and the couches and chairs from that room were all packed, so we ate separately and did not have even that in common.

The night before they left, I lay in my bare room on a mattress on the floor, listening to the owls. I couldn't sleep. I felt as though one of my limbs had been amputated, leaving me out of balance, a crippled thing that could move only in circles.

I wasn't present to see them leave. I made sure I was away from the city before dawn, on the road to Arimathea to visit Joseph. But I remember one look she cast me in the days before her departure, her eyes dark and piercing. It stayed with me forever, that look. It was our only farewell.

When they had gone, I walked from room to room alone. The air already smelled different. I had not known it, but the whole house smelled of her, of her skin, of her hair. That pervasive, almost imperceptible scent had gone, leaving me bereft.

I ordered the house to be repainted. Some of the frescoes were not to my taste and I had them redone. Some walls I simply had painted in red or ochre, preferring the emptiness to any design made by hands.

The painters called me to the dining room and showed me the altar, asking me what I wanted done with the figures of Pilate and Procula that had been painted on either side of the alcove. I stared at the images, Pilate holding aloft his cup of wine, Procula in white, holding a cornucopia from which flowers and fruit tumbled to the earth. In my mind I saw her break the saffron cake and pour the wine. I heard her voice whisper the prayers.

I had only once kissed her as a lover.

I ordered the men to paint out the images. They began with Pilate, broad wet strokes of the brush licking up his legs, obliterating his body, covering his face until only the wine cup was left. Then that, too was gone.

She went the same way, the white distemper covering her slender body, then the yellow abundance of her hair and the innocently smiling face. Then there was nothing but the smell of the paint.

After their departure, time lay heavy on my hands. The decision that I had taken had seemed ineluctable at the time. After the event, I was tormented by doubts. I loved Daphne, yet losing Procula had torn something out of my heart. Had I not sentenced her to a cruel fate, when I could have saved her – and saved her, moreover, for myself? To be mine, as I had once so passionately wished?

I even contemplated Pilate's unscrupulous proposition – that I could keep both women, one as a wife, the other as a mistress. It shamed me that such a thought even entered my head; but such thoughts will come into the wisest head when the heart is heavy. Fate had indeed been unkind.

I did not ride after them and recall them. However, I fell into the blackest of moods. Nothing seemed able to fill the void left by Procula. Letters from Rome were very infrequent; Daphne had been silent for months. There was no company, no conversation to be had in Jerusalem. Procula had been right when she'd described the gubernatorial staff as pudding-heads; I never knew such a dreary set of people. I was very lonely. I had set out to keep Jerusalem quiet, but a quiet city is a dull one, and there were times when I should have welcomed a riot or an insurrection to enliven my days.

It was hot. The sun lay upon Jerusalem like an iron weight. I took to spending a great deal of time alone. I dismissed my bodyguard and rode up and down the city, sometimes neglecting even to carry my sword or wear my armour. As Rufus angrily told me, I would have been an easy target for any assassin. An arrow, or even a cobblestone, would have put an end to my uncertainties forever.

In fact, the citizens seemed to take little notice of me. They had noticed Pilate, for his brutality. Since I harmed few and stole nothing, I was merely another Gentile among them, to be ignored, tolerated at best. Few of the ordinary people would speak to me. The men I questioned shrugged, pretending not to understand me. As for the women, all over the age of five had their faces veiled and one saw no more than a piercing glance from dark eyes before they were gone like cats.

I suppose I was a kind of King Log to them, a benevolent ruler whom they could afford to ignore, since I hurt no one. They did not know how lucky they were. Rome would in time send them one King Stork after another, spearing their flesh with sharp beaks and driving them mad – so mad, in fact, that Jerusalem would catch fire and burn in the end to ash. But for now, there was peace.

The autumn had come, with some relief from the great heat. The sky took on a blue colour again after the blazing white of midsummer. At last, one could breathe. And at last, the rains came, sudden squalls that beat down on the old stones for an hour or two, then blew away into the wilderness. It was during one such sudden cloudburst that I came upon James again.

I had been surprised by the rain with no cape, not even my helmet. I wore only my tunic and sandals and a leather jerkin. I dismounted and led my horse hurriedly to the refuge of a lonely grove of olives. I was already soaked by the time I got under the trees. I tethered my horse and was inspecting my clothes when I noticed that James had also taken shelter there.

"You were caught, too?" I said with a laugh.

"The rain came suddenly."

"It did. I'm sorry I didn't see you, standing there. It's become so dark." I peered up through the branches. The clouds were heavy and black and the rain was pouring down. It had grown cold. I shivered. "I know you don't like my company. I will share this cover with you until the rain is over. It won't take long. These storms are usually short."

"I am happy to have your company," he replied. "You need not feel unwelcome."

"Even though I am a Gentile?"

"You are a decent man," he replied. "And besides, you have been kind to my mother."

"She reminds me of my own mother."

"All our mothers are alike."

"I think you are right." I hauled off my jerkin, which was chafing me. He took it from me and hung it on a branch while I pulled off my tunic and wrung it out. "We learn to love them when it is too late."

"We learn many things too late." He was looking at my naked torso. "You have scars, Marcellus."

"That is because sharp things have been stuck in my hide," I replied. "No doubt I'll get a few more before I'm done." I hung my tunic beside my jerkin. "What brings you to this lonely spot?"

"I think you have forgotten the place," he said. There was something in his voice which made me glance at him, but it was so dark that I could not see his expression. "We met here once before," he said.

I looked around me, remembering. "Ah. This is Joseph's garden."

"Yes."

"The tomb is through the trees, over there."

"Yes."

"You're right. I had forgotten the place. I'm doubly sorry to disturb you. Your thoughts must be sad ones in this place."

"Your presence has relieved them."

A gust of wind blew the cold rain in on us. I hugged myself. "It rained on the day he was crucified."

"I remember."

"You were not there. I have never felt such despair as on that day. I was helpless. He wouldn't speak during his trial. Not a word. If he had consented to utter a denial, I think I could have saved his life, though everyone told me it was impossible."

"I think they were right."

My horse was shuddering and stamping as the rain spattered on his flanks. I soothed him. "And now they stone each other in the street over him. What do you think he would say, if he could see that?"

"He was no stranger to stones."

I grunted, wishing I was back in the palace, with a warm fire and a cup of wine. "Do you come here to pray?"

"And to wait."

I was irritated. "For him? He's not here. Nor will he come."

"You seem angry."

"I am angry. I am angry with him for not saving himself. I am angry with all of you for not saving him, and for surrounding him now with lies and illusions."

"Illusions?"

"Do you know what Herod said of him? That he was an ordinary man, who sweated and bled and stank as other men do. Yet look at you! Standing here in the rain, waiting for him to return from the dead. Well, you will wait a long time, James."

He did not move. He was a shadowy figure, listening to me in the dark of that storm, yet I felt that he was amused. "Are you hungry for miracles, Marcellus?"

"I've never seen one and I think I'm too old to see one now. A miracle is a toy. Children love them, but adults should not need them."

"You are right. Blessed are they who believe without miracles."

"Is that another of your brother's apothegms? I have a book of them. Yet I don't know what good they do me, or anyone else. Belief? What is there to believe in?" I struck the trunk of the olive tree beside me. "They say there is a goddess in this tree. Yet we cut it down and make a cross of it. There are gods and goddesses in every river, every cloud, every stone. For every babbling, credulous, mortal fool, there is a host of spirits and divinities. Yet not one of them can save a life or answer a prayer. You Christians dance and pray and fondle one another. Yet are you any better off than anyone else? More moral, more kind?"

"If you are trying to persuade me to become an atheist, you are wasting your breath."

"I persuade no one. It is others who try to persuade me."

"I have not tried."

"No, but your friend Procula has tried. You convinced her of your brother's divinity and like you, she awaits his resurrection with bated breath. But you know where she is now – on her way to exile and a lonely death. Who will save her?"

"I'm sorry," he said. "I know you love her."

"I am more inclined to respect your knife-wielding priests than your invisible church, not made by hands. Wherever God has hidden himself, he seems to have an appetite for blood. In fact, I believe he detests us, or he would not kill so many of us, and keep the rest alive, only to suffer."

The thunder rolled overhead. "There," he said. "Your Jupiter agrees with you."

"You are very sardonic."

"And you are in a bad mood because you are tired, cold and hungry. Don't curse God because of that. I have a little food. Will you share it with me?"

"I thought it was forbidden for you to eat with unclean persons such as I."

"I'll make an exception for you." He had a piece of flat bread, which he tore, giving me half.

"You Jews are very strange," I said.

"That is true."

"Your certainty is the strangest thing about you. Do you never have any doubts?"

"I myself have none. I can't speak for other Jews. We are not all as alike as chickpeas, you know. But I can tell you that we have a saying, 'One should learn to say, I do not know.' There is wisdom in that."

I ate the bread he had given me. "I have long since learned to say I do not know. But God has put me in a position where I am expected to have answers for others."

"He has done something rather similar to me."

"You are jovial today," I said. Indeed, James, who was usually so reserved and humourless, seemed to have acquired a warmth I had not noticed in him before.

"I am glad you find me so."

"Holiness seems so often to go with sternness."

"Didn't you once say that religion should be shaped for man, and not man for religion?"

"Yes. Perhaps you can explain to me why it is that religion so often seems to run counter to man's desires?"

I saw the shadow of his smile. "I would answer you that the hearts of men are dark, their desires cruel and bloody. But I don't think you would accept that. You believe that men are generally good, and that one man is as worthy as another. Or woman, for that matter."

"I think that all we want is for our children not to grow sick and die, to have enough money to buy our next loaf."

"Perhaps you're right."

"So what is your answer?"

"My answer is that religion teaches a man to say, 'I do not know.'"

"As easy as that?" I scoffed.

"It is no easy thing to say one does not know, Marcellus – to be humble, to trust in God, to renounce the things we cling to – even the life of one's child, or one's next loaf of bread. To forgive. To love. There is nothing easy about that."

"I'm disappointed. I thought that religion gave certainty."

"Certainty that there is no certainty." He offered me a skin of wine and watched while I drank. "Only God."

"The here and now is certain. It is hard to remember what we did yesterday, and impossible to know what we will do tomorrow. But the here and now is certain enough."

"And yet a man may be mistaken in everything," he said in a gentle voice. "Even what he sees, here and now."

I wiped my mouth and passed the wineskin back to him. "I am not generally wrong about what I see."

"I am glad to hear it."

"You mean that ironically. You think me arrogant."

"Perhaps that hide of yours has not been pierced enough."

"I am not anxious for any more piercings. I would simply like an answer."

"Have faith in God."

"And when God takes from me everything I hold most dear? What shall I do then?"

"Have faith in God."

"Even to the end? While God says nothing to me? What then?"

"Have faith in God."

I looked up. The storm was passing and the sky was growing light. "The rain has stopped. I must get back to the town. Will you come with me? The horse will carry us both."

"Thank you, I'll stay here awhile."

"Our conversation has been interesting," I said as I dressed. "Perhaps we can resume it some time?"

"That is up to you."

"Thank you for the bread and wine. Be well." I mounted my horse. As I rode away from the place I reconsidered the words we had spoken, as one does after a conversation. At the road, something struck me and I turned to look back at the man I had spoken to. He was already lost among the olive trees – James, or someone very like him.

A short while later, Tiberius died. An age was at an end.

The rumours said that Tiberius had been murdered, smothered in his bed in Capri by the Prefect of the Praetorian Guard. Nobody knew the truth. He was succeeded by Gaius Julius Caesar Germanicus, called by everyone Caligula.

I marshalled the army and made them swear the oath of loyalty to the new emperor. Then I summoned Jonathan, the High Priest who had succeeded Caiaphas, and gave him the news. I made the suggestion that some signal of joy would go far to winning the friendship of the young king in Rome. Jonathan was an intelligent man. He made a vast sacrifice of oxen and prayers were offered for the long life and good health of the new emperor. I was able to send Caligula a very satisfactory account of the services held in his honour. This was to have gratifying, if somewhat unexpected results later on.

Caligula recalled me to Rome. He wanted loyal people close to him, so he said, and so I entered the service of one of the strangest men I have ever known. The golden east fell into other hands. I had spent only a year as governor of Judaea but I was glad to come home. It had been the loneliest year of my life.

I handed over to Marullus, my replacement, and travelled to Antioch to say goodbye to Vitellius. Then I took the mail ship back to Rome, my heart filled with the prospect of seeing Daphne once again. I had not yet heard anything of the fate of Pilate and Procula.

# CHAPTER FIFTEEN

# LITTLE BOOTS

I arrived in Rome when the weather had grown cold, a lovely season in the Capital. My first action was to report to Caligula, which I did even before opening my house. I knew enough about him to know that an early audience was advisable. I left my baggage with Sextilia and went straight to the palace.

Caligula was then about twenty-five years old. He was a handsome young man, wiry and narrow faced, with the most extraordinary eyes, extremely pale in colour, staring brightly from deep eye sockets. What he lacked in natural intelligence, he made up for in fixations. He had an appearance of exaltation. He believed himself to be divine and convinced many others of the same thing for a while. His surname, "Little Boots," had been given him as a boy by affectionate soldiers who had been delighted by the miniature uniform with which he had been issued. For a while, at least, he had the support of the army.

He accepted my oath of loyalty and raised me from my knees. "I'm very interested in these Jews of yours, Marcellus. They were the first people of the Empire to offer sacrifices to me."

I was about to correct him and explain that the sacrifices had been for him, rather than to him, but luckily something stopped me just in time. "They were filled with joy," I said.

"I know that. They have some notions that we Romans could well learn from. Monotheism, for example." He made me sit on a couch beside his throne and stared into my face with those wolf's eyes of his. "Think of it. One god, not many. God, in fact. Just God."

"That is indeed their belief, Caesar."

"Just the one, eh? No other divine beings?"

"None. Apart from angels."

"Why are you smiling?"

"I'm sorry, Caesar. I smiled at the beauty of the concept of angels."

"You may only smile if I smile, but for a shorter duration. You may laugh if I laugh, but with less noise and only after a pause."

An armed detachment of the Praetorian Guard stood four square behind him, each man wearing the same grim veteran's face, matching as exactly as did their weapons and armour. These were the ruffians who had made this young lunatic emperor. They glared at me. The marble walls were stark but for a row of standards, bronze and silver Roman eagles frowning down at their prey. "I understand, Caesar. I apologize."

His frown eased. "Now, as to this temple of theirs. Tell me all about it."

He listened, rapt, as I described the magnificence of Herod's temple, its huge size and the endless sacrifices that were conducted in it. He was very thick with Herod Agrippa, Herodias's brother, who had evidently inspired him with tales of its grandeur, and he was hungry for every detail I could furnish him. I was careful not to smile or show any signs of emotion at all. When I came to the Holy of Holies, he grew intensely excited and jumped up from his throne. "It's quite empty, is it not?" he said, pacing up and down.

"Nobody is allowed to enter it but the High Priest. However, it's said to be completely dark and empty. It once contained the Ark of the Covenant, but—"

"Empty and dark!" He raised one lean arm to the heavens, his eyes bright. "Don't you understand what that means?"

"What does it mean?" I asked cautiously.

"Emptiness is a state of expectation, Marcellus. Darkness calls for light. They're waiting for their god to be revealed to them. I am going to send them a statue."

"A statue, Caesar?"

"A statue of myself. In gold. I'll have it done in accordance with their sacred images and inscribed in their language. They'll erect it in the Holy of Holies." He was ecstatic. I listened, stunned, as he planned this extraordinary insult to the Jewish faith, which would certainly plunge the whole region into the bloodiest of wars. "I shall have myself represented as Moses, with rays of light emerging from my brow, giving them the Law. What do you think?"

"It needs extremely careful research," I said.

"You're right, you're right. I entrust you with the task of advising me, Marcellus. See to it." Then, as abruptly as it had taken hold of him, the mania seemed to drop away from him. "We will discuss it greater detail when there's more time," he said, seating himself once more. "Do you need money?" Without waiting for me to answer, he turned to the secretary. "Take ten thousand sesterces in gold from the Treasury for Marcellus. He is now my councillor on Eastern affairs."

"Caesar, you are most generous," I said. I was, indeed, glad of the money. As Pilate had once said to me, the salary of a provincial governor is not very great, unless one steals, as most of them did; and I had lost almost all my regular income.

He beamed at me. "I'm very glad we had this talk, Marcellus. You understand me. That is a rare thing in mortals."

I was careful to smile back at him, less widely than he, and only after a measured pause. "Thank you, Caesar."

As he was dismissing me, something came to his mind. "Oh, by the way. Your predecessor appeared before me a few weeks ago."

"Pilate?"

"Yes. He arrived in Rome after the death of the god Tiberius. I examined the evidence and pronounced sentence. He's banished to Gaul for life. All his possessions are confiscated."

"And his wife?" I couldn't help asking.

"She's banished, too, of course." He waved me away.

And so, at a stroke, they were no more.

As far as I could learn later on, Pilate had delayed returning to Rome as long as possible, fearing that Tiberius would identify him with the disgraced Sejanus. With Tiberius dead, he had hoped for a more lenient judgment from Caligula. It was an error. Had Pilate gone before Tiberius, he might have had some slight chance of escaping justice. Caligula did not know the meaning of mercy.

I returned to Sextilia's house in a somewhat dazed state. "How did you find the emperor?" she asked.

"I need a drink," I replied. She merely lifted one eyebrow in response. None of us ever said aloud that we thought he was mad. It was too dangerous a thought to entrust to anyone. As we sat in her garden with a jug of wine, I told her about my interview and my new appointment. She was delighted.

"Dear Marcellus, I'm so proud of you. Ten thousand sesterces in gold!"

"Nevertheless, the post is a precarious one. I must get back to my work as soon as possible."

"I suppose Caligula told you about your friend, Pilate?"

"Yes."

"The wife wasn't spared. They left Rome some weeks ago, reduced to abject poverty. I'm sorry, Marcellus. I know you had hoped for a different conclusion."

It was too painful to discuss. "There's nothing to be done."

"You're right. The chapter is closed." She poured me some more wine. "I wrote to you about Daphne. You didn't reply, so I assume you thought I was being intrusive. I will not repeat what I said in that letter, but I do urge you to find a nice young virgin bride now. You're thirty-three, my dear boy, and you need companionship in life. You're one of the most eligible bachelors in Rome. You can command anything you want in a wife – beauty, wealth, family. Doesn't your mouth water at the prospect?"

I kissed her hand. She was as much a mother to me as Vitellius was a father. Vitellius had entrusted me with many gifts and letters for her and the boys and I spent the day yarning to them of the glories of Antioch and of the successes which Vitellius was enjoying in Syria and Judaea. They shone with pride. From that time, however, my life began to be separated from theirs. The boys were now adult and somewhat resented my closeness to their mother and father; I think they were anxious about their inheritance. Anyway, my political career had separated itself from Vitellius', although we continued to serve the same emperors. He gave them everything, whereas I always held something back for myself. My path was a quieter one, a less public one. He, for example was able to stomach Claudius's succession of dreadful wives, which I was not; he reaped rich rewards by worshipping at their shrines.

The next day I went back to my own little house in the city. Agata and her son had returned from the country and were opening the shutters and taking the covers off the furniture. The rooms smelled of time having passed in silence. The house felt singularly empty. I did not realize what it was until the evening fell, and then I understood. Livia's ghost had finally departed.

Having lived in, and grown accustomed to, surroundings of some splendour, my townhouse now seemed small and noisy to me. I also had Caligula's ten thousand sesterces jingling in my pocket. Property prices were rising fast in Rome. I decided that I would look for a new home.

When the place was habitable again, I finally went to get Daphne.

They were gathering the last apples and grapes, which glowed purple and gold among the sere leaves. The air was crisp like their flesh, and smelled sweet, of their skin. In those days, that area was still rural, and had not yet been built up to give housing for the masses. It was all farms and fields still, providing the tables of Rome with fruit and cereals and its armies with strong young men.

I reached Octavia's farmhouse to find the yard deep in fallen leaves, the whole place silent. I locked the wheels of the carriage and got off. There was no sign of life. I looked up at the house. It seemed desolate. The shutters were closed fast, some of them overgrown with the creeper which clung to the facade, its leaves now blotched red and black. The house seemed to have sunk into a profound sleep, like the palaces we heard of in our childhood fairy-tales. My skin crawled. A cold terror overtook me. What if sickness or criminals had swept the house in my absence? What if she was no more?

I hammered on the door, my heart racing. There seemed to be no sound from within. I walked around the house, shouting their names. Then Octavia opened the door, looking as usual like a farm-er's wife, in country clothes. She had aged in these past years, her face lined and shrunken. We embraced one another. She stepped back to look at me, holding me at arm's length. "You have left your youth in Palestine, Marcellus. You've become a man. You have come for your woman."

There was something tragic in her face and I felt my knees turn to water. "Where is she?" I asked.

Octavia turned away. "She's waiting for you by the fire."

Daphne had risen from her chair in the next room, a book in one hand. I cannot describe the expression on her face; it was as though she were listening for some sound that couldn't be heard by the ears. She had made herself a gown of the silk I had sent from Antioch. It shimmered green and gold in the firelight. Her black hair had grown long, and though it was tied with ribbons, it reached to her shoulders.

If I had become a man, she had become a woman. I had left behind a shy girl of twenty three. I returned to a woman whose dignity and beauty stunned me. She dropped the book and held out her hands to me.

"Oh, my dear," she said.

I caught her up in my arms and held her tight against me. "I have missed you so terribly," I said.

"I thought you wouldn't come back to me."

"Daphne, my Daphne." I kissed her face a hundred times, until she laughed and begged for a respite. Then I kissed her properly.

"We mustn't forget Octavia," she whispered, trembling.

We found her in the kitchen, seated by the stove, staring into space, a bunch of celery forgotten in her lap. "I don't know what I'll do without her," she said absently. Her tears were falling fast.

Daphne knelt at her side and kissed her hands. "I've promised you that I'll come back often," she said. But I could see that Octavia was truly grief-stricken. She didn't want us to linger. Daphne's things were already packed. I loaded them onto the carriage. I tried to thank Octavia as best I could. It was hard to find words, especially in the face of her pain. She had grown to love Daphne. I echoed Daphne's promises that we would see one another again soon, but I knew how forlorn the house would be without her presence in it, and what a desolate winter Octavia had to look forward to.

It was too soon for me to see what she had done for Daphne, but over the next days, I understood. She had opened her heart to the younger woman and had shared its treasures with her. Under Octavia's tutelage, Daphne had grown and blossomed. She had acquired polish, grace and dignity. She had absorbed lessons which I could only guess at, developing her natural intelligence and feeling into the most refined sensibility. No society could have been better for her than that of this quiet, elderly patrician with her gravitas and her culture.

Octavia stood in the yard of her house, watching us leave. They both wept bitterly.

That night we lay together in our old bed, staring into each other's faces.

"Why did you write me that strange letter?" I asked.

"I wanted you to know that you were free to stay with her."

"There was no question of that."

"I didn't think you would come back," she said again. "I thought you would leave me for that woman."

"She's gone."

"I know that." She touched my cheek. "I am sorry, Marcellus, truly. You could have saved her."

"I don't think so. She has some sickness of the soul that I can't understand. She has found her own salvation – also in a way that I can't understand."

"You mean this new religion of hers?"

"Yes. Her life is despair, but that keeps her alive."

"Did you tell her about me?"

"I couldn't. She had heard something. I don't know what she thought. I couldn't explain. What matters is that I love you."

Her fingers traced the line of my nose. "You look like a pirate now. You've been so very far while I watched the seasons pass. There's so much you have to tell me, and I have no news for you, except what you see in your arms. That house was so silent, Marcellus. There were days in which we didn't speak more than ten words to each other." She paused. "Yet we talked without stopping. She had a great effect on me."

"I can see that. You're different in every way, Daphne. In your speech, even in the way you walk."

"Does it disturb you?"

"It makes you lovelier than ever."

"You're not disappointed in me?"

"I am lost in you and found in you."

A few weeks after my return I sold the little townhouse for a good price and with the assistance of Caligula's money, bought a villa on the Capitoline Hill, which had a sprawling garden, clean air and spacious views over Rome. We built a swimming bath there and planted cypresses which are now tall enough to be seen from all parts of Rome.

At the end of the year, when the winter cold had descended, I went to Caligula and requested permission to marry Daphne. He was very pleased with me at that stage, and mad enough to consider my request quite normal. He gave me his blessing.

I freed Daphne and married her on the same day. Her freedom lasted no more than a few hours, as she somewhat ironically remarked. We had never felt such happiness.

We went to the temple of Venus and made a sacrifice – a white kid, which was what Daphne wanted. It was a beautiful moment. She braided violets around its horns. Those violets have never stopped blooming and their smell is always sweet.

My marriage to Daphne could hardly have come as a surprise to those who knew me. Yet many of those I considered friends now publicly expressed their repugnance or disapproval. Marrying a slave was not for aristocrats, irrespective of the personality of the slave. By this misalliance, they said I had sentenced myself to a life of obscurity and ostracism. There's no doubt that it had an effect on my life and career. Sextilia was never the same with me, though Vitellius took it in his stride.

My clientele changed. The upper classes no longer brought their distinguished problems to me. Wealthy freedmen, however, did. And so did those whose legal problems involved questions of civil liberty or changes of status. My income shrank for a few months and then returned to its former level, leaving me financially unaffected. None of it mattered to me. I had found the treasure of my life.

Shortly after our marriage, Caligula grew gravely ill. People whispered that he had brought the crisis upon himself by a long bout of drinking and sexual abandon, taking advantage of his new power to indulge his basest passions, as Tiberius had done before him. If that is true, then the shock to his system would have been great, since he'd had a soldier's life up to that point, marked by discipline and physical fitness. I am inclined to disbelieve it, however, since he always struck me as a man more of the spirit than the flesh, even if the spirit was a mad one. To me, it seemed rather to be some dire disturbance of the brain. I went to see him at the height of his sickness. He lay on a couch, his body arched as though in agony, his fingers clenched in his own hair as though he wished to tear his head off his shoulders. His face was frightening, with bared fangs and foaming lips. But the strange, pale eyes were fixed on the parade of well-wishers who passed before him, wailing and supplicating the gods to spare his life.

It has to be remembered that at this stage, Caligula was adored throughout the empire. He was regarded as a saviour. He had not yet become the King Stork who was to succeed the King Log of Tiberius. The world trembled lest its beautiful young emperor be snatched away. If only we had known.

My turn came to pass before him. I knelt beside his couch.

"Mighty Caesar, I have made sacrifices each day to the gods. We pray for your speedy recovery."

He seemed to recognize me and spoke through clenched teeth. "The gods – the gods—"

"The gods will watch over you."

He nodded and made a gesture for me to go, his eyes already rolling to find the next well-wisher. There was, I noticed, a group of his friends and relations in another part of the audience hall who prayed constantly and loudly, asking the gods to take their lives instead of his. Luckily I did not join these. When he unexpectedly recovered, he promptly had them all executed, to make sure there was no possibility of the gods going back on the deal. Caligula did not like loose ends.

The illness left him odder than ever. He began to display that morbid suspicion of everyone around him which marked the lives of so many emperors and made their friendship so perilous. He committed the first of his murders, which was also the most dismal of all his crimes. Tiberius had left a grandson (Caligula was only an adopted grandson) as a co-regent with Caligula. Caligula suspected him of having designs on the throne, even though he was no more than a child. He adopted the boy in order to separate him from his protectors and then compelled him to commit suicide. The boy was so young that he had not yet had instruction in arms and had no notion of killing himself or anyone else. He begged the Captain of the Guard to cut his throat, but the officer was reluctant to spill royal blood. They had to show him how to hold the blade and where to drive it in, and so the wretched child made away with himself.

Caligula had a particular taste for this form of murder – obliging his enemies (and very often his friends and relations) to kill them-selves. Rather than face the disgrace of execution, most obeyed.

Like other Roman women, Daphne wept over this pathetic event. "Poor little boy! I'm so afraid for you, Marcellus," she said, clinging to me. "Please be careful of that monster."

"Don't worry, my beloved. I know how to handle him."

Despite my assurances, I was afraid. To be in Caligula's presence was to be confronted with a volcanic madness. Even if one had
survived a meeting with him, he might later remember that you had
smiled – or not smiled – at an inopportune moment, and order you
destroyed. He was perilously sensitive to any hint that he was being
mocked.

I recall another episode which illustrates the effect he had on
those around him. The Jews of Alexandria had sent a delegation to
Caligula to protest against the atrocities that were taking place in
that city. As his counsellor on Eastern affairs, I was commanded by
Caligula to attend the meeting. The Alexandrians were led by Philo,
a great philosopher and statesman, with whom I was privileged to
correspond for some years until his death. Philo was an orator, and
made a very affecting and persuasive speech to the emperor, itemiz-
ing the injuries inflicted on the Jews, which had truly been terrible.

"Men, women and children have been burned alive, my lord, in
the middle of the city. Wood was piled on them and set alight, their
screams were mocked as they died in agony. Others were bound
and dragged into the market place, where they were trampled and
beaten to death, their bodies torn into so many pieces that there was
not even a fragment left for our rites of burial. Our holy synagogues
have been burned down and the sacred objects in them destroyed."
Philo stretched his arms out to the emperor in a grand gesture. "My
lord, you will ask me how such atrocities could be committed within
your empire, you will demand to know whether the perpetrators
had no fear of punishment or shame at their own misdeeds? The
answer will astonish you. They believed that what they did was a
compliment to you. They have convinced themselves that you have
an inveterate hatred for the Jews, and would approve of these horrible crimes. My lord, we beseech you—"

Caligula had appeared to listen carefully, his chin cupped in his
hand. Now he raised his hand to interrupt Philo. "Tell me – why is
it that you Jews will not eat pork?"

"My lord?"

"Pork. The flesh of the pig. What is the difficulty?"

"Pork? My lord I—" Philo was quite dismasted by the question, so little germane to his tragic theme, and could not frame an answer. In the silence, one of the Alexandrian Jews emitted a high-pitched giggle. Caligula bent his terrifying brows on the wretched man, who buried his face in his hands. To no avail. His shoulders continued to shake. Soon all the others had dissolved into fits of hysterical laughter.

Of course, it was nerves that unmanned them so. The persecution they had suffered, the importance of the mission, the deadly reputation of the emperor, all had combined to produce panic. In the same way, one sees a class of schoolboys surrender to a madness of giggles in the presence of a particularly severe master.

Certainly, the deeper the emperor's frown became, the more they laughed. They laughed with white faces and sweating brows, their eyes rolling in fright.

"What the devil are you laughing at?" he demanded suspiciously. He thought they were mocking him.

"Oh, my lord," one of them gasped, "you are so very witty."

"I was not trying to be witty."

The more they tried to suppress their fatal mirth, the more it erupted from them in snorts and shrieks. Even Philo was affected. I could see – as we all could – that they were within moments of death. I stepped forward.

"Caesar, if I may? Philo has proposed, very properly in my opinion, the erection of a golden statue of your divine self in the Grove of Augustus in his city."

Philo looked at me in astonishment, but Caligula's brow cleared at once. "A golden statue? Yes, very proper."

It was a great good fortune that I was able to distract him, and he began eagerly to discuss the size and design of the supposed statue until his good humour was restored. He dismissed the exhausted Alexandrians some time later unharmed, but the embassy had collapsed and the persecution of Jews in Egypt continued with his tacit approval. After this fiasco, Philo put his hand on my shoulder.

"I thought I was a dead man."

"He believes he is a god. It's best to humour him. Come and drink wine."

And so, despite the absurd and melancholy circumstances, began a friendship which has given me much pleasure over the years. We corresponded diligently and I have in mind to publish Philo's letters, for he was a great mind and a great author.

At around this time, two familiar faces appeared in Rome – Herod and Herodias, summoned by Caligula to appear before him.

They were very frightened, as well they might be, and the night before their audience with the emperor, they begged to see me, hoping that I would be able to intercede for them with Caligula, despite our past differences. I told them I would do what I could.

"But I should warn you," I went on, "that the emperor takes little advice from anyone these days. The only people who seemed to have any influence with him were Macro and his wife, and he got sick of their nagging and made them kill themselves."

Herod's face fell. "If he killed Macro, he will kill anyone."

"It is true, then," Herodias said. "He is mad."

"He is very single-minded," I replied diplomatically. The two of them had changed a great deal. While she was still a beautiful woman, Herodias looked harder and colder and had developed nervous mannerisms of many kinds – beating her palm incessantly on the arm of her chair, tapping rapidly with her foot or frowning in a way that made deep clefts in her brow. Herod had put on weight and was no longer athletic-looking. His hair was quite white now, his handsome features spoiled by a sagging jowl.

"He has lost confidence in me," Herod said in despair. "It has all been most unfortunate. If only you had helped me when I asked, Marcellus."

The war with Aretas had produced disastrous sequels, as we all knew. Herod's army was destroyed, in part because many soldiers defected from the army of Herod's brother, Philip, to fight against Herod, and in part because Herod's own men fought with such little valour. Both circumstances were a measure of how much he was hated by the Jews. The rabbis said that Herod's defeat was a divine punishment for the killing of John the Baptist, just as many said that Pilate's dismissal was a punishment for the execution of Jesus.

His army broken by Aretas, Herod appealed to Tiberius, whom he had flattered diligently all his life, even naming his new city on Lake Galilee after the emperor. Tiberius commanded Vitellius to march against Aretas and send him to Rome in chains. With considerable reluctance, for he intensely disliked Herod, my uncle took two legions and set off against Aretas. However, Tiberius died (or was murdered) before Vitellius reached Nabatea. When Vitellius received the news, he promptly turned around, leaving Aretas with the land he had taken from Herod, and went back to Antioch. It was effectively the end of Herod's power. With his kingdom, his reputation and his army in tatters, he was much diminished. He was seen to be no fit king of the Jews.

"It is unfortunate, yes." I said. "But you are unjust to blame me. If you had not married Herodias, and sent Aretas's daughter back to him, he would have remained your ally."

"You are the last person to give advice about the perils of love, Marcellus," he replied.

"That is true."

Herod gave a heavy sigh. "And then there is the present difficulty."

"The present difficulty" was an unwise squabble over money with his influential nephew, Agrippa. One of them had made a loan to the other, and the other had not paid it back, though I forget now who lent and who borrowed. The fact was that Antipas was disgraced and had no influence with Caligula, while Agrippa was one of the emperor's closest friends. Agrippa, moreover, had his eye on Herod's kingdom. The outlook was bleak.

"You've done well for yourself, Marcellus," Herod said, looking around my villa. "I wish I had a nice little place like this in Rome. This would suit me down to the ground. Eh, Herodias? Palaces are all very well, but one never knows when the roof is going to fall in. And one grows so sick of living in barbarian lands. A cosy nook like this is just what one wants."

Of course, he had been brought up in Rome as a protégé of Augustus, and to him the territories he was given to rule over were alien and barbarous. They were a strange tribe, these children and grandchildren of Herod the Great. Their father had left them the whole of Palestine to be governed between them and they lost everything, many ending in disgrace or premature death. They squandered their huge fortunes in luxurious living, borrowed from everybody, married one another's wives and entered disastrous wars with their neighbours. By the time of the Jewish-Roman War, almost all their lands had reverted to direct rule from Rome. Yet there was something likeable about them all, a certain exotic glamour.

"Do you hear anything of Pilate?" Herod asked me as we parted.

"Nothing. I believe he has been sent to Gaul. He was stripped of everything."

"He is another whom you could have saved, Marcellus," Herodias said grimly. "If not him, then at least her. She loved you. But it seems you have no heart."

"I have a heart, but I cannot be expected to save those who destroy their own lives."

"You'll do what you can for us?" Herod pressed.

"I will speak for you tomorrow," I promised.

But it was the last time I was to see either of them. The audience the next day did not go well. I was not asked to attend, and so could not plead for Herod, even if I'd found anything to say in his defense. The emperor deposed him and sent him into exile with immediate effect. To Herodias's credit it should be said that she declined when Caligula offered to exempt her from the banishment. She was beautiful, and Caligula would have liked to keep her as a toy. She elected to stay at her husband's side. I think she and Herod truly loved one another. And she was well-advised to go, because when Caligula tired of his toys, he tore them apart like a spoiled child. Herod and his wife left Rome under a heavy guard and never returned. Herod's death was announced a few years later. As I've said, Caligula was not a man who liked to leave loose ends.

Caligula didn't last very long as emperor, but the effect he had on Rome over three or four years was disastrous. From the start, he seemed to regard his emperorship as a license to fulfil his most vicious fantasies and inflict the greatest cruelties he could invent on his fellow-Romans. He had been thrust onto the throne to replace an emperor seen as corrupt and a bad influence; but we frogs soon learned we had replaced King Log with a murderous King Stork whose beak was sharp and tireless.

The Augustan era was well and truly over. We had entered a reign of blood. Blood was what Caligula's appetite principally demanded. Though he took any woman he wanted, his pleasure seemed derived from the pain and humiliation he inflicted on them, their husbands and families – for he loved mental cruelty as much as physical cruelty. The only women whom he took to his bed with any kind of romantic impulse were his own sisters; and he soon murdered or exiled these.

As the Senate tried to restrain him – and then became the object of his implacable hatred – he came to rely more and more on his private imperial councillors, of whom I was one. It was a remunerative but perilous business which strained the nerves terribly. I never knew when the summons might come, brought by stern-faced Praetorian Guardsmen at any hour of the night or day, to "discuss" issues with him, which meant listening to his endless monologues. These summons became nocturnal, since he slept most of the day, and soon took on a very sinister dimension.

Long after midnight, we were awoken by the Guards pounding on the door. I answered in my dressing gown. "He wants you," their captain said grimly.

"Of course. Let me dress."

"No." The captain, a scarred veteran named Cassius, laid his hand on my shoulder. "He wants you *now*, Marcellus. Come."

My heart sank. As they hustled me in my nightclothes through the empty streets, I racked my brains for any inattention, any hint of a yawn that I might have let slip. Or had some careless word of criticism, spoken to some spy, reached the emperor's ears? They hadn't even given me time to say farewell to Daphne or my son.

"I hope the emperor is well?" I asked Cassius cautiously.

He grunted. "The emperor is not well. Rome is not well."

I did not pursue the conversation. This Cassius had served with Caligula's father in the German wars, but was unfortunate in being the butt of the emperor's jokes, because he had lost his genitals to a German spear-thrust, a mutilation which Caligula found highly amusing.

Caligula's screams were echoing through the palace as we approached his chambers. He was clearly in a rage. He was revealed in full armour, despite the lateness of the hour, with a drawn sword in his hand. His face was terrible. My bowels turned to water as he strode towards me. He levelled the point of his sword at my throat.

"You, Marcellus!"

In that moment I believed I would never return home alive to Daphne. Somehow, I did not flinch, and my voice came out strong and clear. "My lord? What is the matter?"

"Treason!" he screamed, the froth of his lips spattering my face. "I am surrounded by traitors! Do you not know that?"

I saw that his sword was stained with blood. And when he turned away, I saw the three bodies on floor. All were naked and weltered with blood but I saw that all three were still alive. They had been bound hand and foot. Caligula marched to them and plunged his sword into the belly of one of the men. I recognized him suddenly as a man I knew, a magistrate in whose court I had appeared several times as counsel. As the wretched man writhed and shrieked, the emperor sawed opened his abdomen completely.

"You see?" he demanded, turning to me. "You see what they send me? Assassins! Filth!"

The sights and sounds of that room had shocked me into a kind of icy trance. Perhaps it was that disbelief which allowed me to appear normal. "Who has sent assassins, my lord?"

"The Senate. Who else?" He knelt by his victim and pulled out a fistful of entrails. "It is written here!"

I had to turn away. The Praetorian guard were watching with stony faces. They were no strangers to the battlefield. Nor was I. But the sight of a Roman emperor disembowelling a Roman magistrate with his own hands was beyond our experience. "My lord," I said, "that—that is the magistrate, Gabinius."

He turned from his bloody work to glare at me with his wolf's eyes. "What are you saying, Marcellus?"

"That the man is known to all—"

"Known to all! Am I in error?" Caligula rose to his feet and walked back to me with his smeared arms outstretched. "Have I made a mistake?" He was smiling, his voice suddenly soft. "Are you telling me that I am wrong?"

I knew that in an instant I would be joining Gabinius and the others in that lake of blood. "No, my lord."

He cocked his head. "I am not in error?"

"It is not possible for you to be in error."

"Why not?"

"Because you are divine. Gods cannot err."

He nodded slowly, satisfied. "That is the correct answer."

The fatuous lie I spoke then was repeated countless times over the succeeding years. How will the generations to come forgive us? Our lives hung from that thread, that lie. If I hadn't spoken it, I would never have left the palace that night. It was all I needed to say. I stood rooted to the spot as Caligula paced up and down the chamber, ranting against his enemies, screaming imprecations against the Senate and the magistracy, declaring again and again that he was a god.

When he pulled off his helmet, sweating with exertion, it was revealed that he had bleached his hair golden. He continued in his harangue for hours, pausing only to inflict further wounds on his three victims, hacking off noses and ears, digging out eyes, severing fingers joint by joint. Mad as he seemed, he was careful that his prey did not die too quickly. The pleasure that he took in this dismemberment was all too evident. I have seen soldiers torment the captives of war in a similar way, but that was after a long and savage campaign, after the loss of comrades and the hardening of emotions that comes from months of war. This had come from the blue, manifesting itself in the person of a young emperor who had never seen battle and who was to be the guiding star of a new empire based on justice and reason.

It was necessary only to agree instantly with whatever words he threw at us. The rest was his show. Only when all three of his victims were beyond any further suffering did he throw down his sword and stretch to face the rising sun. He seemed to have purged himself of his rage and was now in jovial mood.

"Take these fine gentlemen back to their homes and show them to their wives," he ordered the guards. He insisted that all the severed organs pertaining to each man be gathered in a sack, along with the lifeless torso, and exhibited to the families. I was compelled to drink a cup of wine with him while the results of his butchery were gathered up. I cannot recall any drink which I have desired less or which has sat worse on my stomach. But I was alive, and the sun was warm on my face.

When at last he allowed me to return home, I found Daphne in a pitiful state of anxiety. I was so spattered with blood that she almost fainted when she saw me. I could not tell her what I had seen that night, and could only shake my head in answer to her questions.

Was he mad? Or did he represent the baseness to which absolute power reduces a morally weak man? Certainly, there was never anything truly irrational in what he did. No; everything was directed towards the gratification of his own desires. The slaughter of Gabinius and the two others, who turned out to be Gabinius's brother and brother-in-law, was no arbitrary act of lunacy. All three were wealthy, and married to beautiful wives. Immediately after their deaths, Caligula confiscated their wealth and debauched their widows. Perhaps most importantly, he had sent a clear and brutal message to the Senate – for Gabinius had served his second term as a magistrate, and would soon have been appointed a Senator, along with his brother.

Later, of course, this carnage was dwarfed by greater cruelties and even more savage attacks on the Senate, which he would have destroyed if he could, being the only thing standing between him and absolute rulership of the world. The stories are well-known to all: how he made his horse a Senator and had the beast led into the Senate, snorting and kicking; how he dragged venerable Senators behind his chariot through the public streets; how he trumped up charges against those Senators foolish enough to argue with him, and made them fight one another to the death like common criminals in the Circus Maximus; how he commanded dozens of eminent men and women to kill themselves – and was obeyed. Some of these tales are exaggerations. But not all.

What I recall is that Caligula gave Romans a taste for gruesome spectacle. He was addicted to the Circus and its cruelties towards beasts and men, and he turned his craving for blood into a national sport. By the time of his death, vast amusements in which hundreds were slaughtered had become fixed events several times a week. The plebeians would cheer even when there was no bread to eat, even when the emperor, for want of criminals, turned the spectators in the stands themselves over to the lions. And emperor after emperor was happy to gratify this appetite after him. It became, in the end, the beat of Roman life.

I was to attend many more such interludes in Caligula's palace and accustomed myself to seeing some of the noblest individuals in Rome brought to a cruel and ignominious end – the men hacked to pieces, the wives raped and degraded. I, like everyone else, stood by in craven silence as these things were done, thinking of my own wife, my own children – and myself.

The only period during which there was some relief from the terror was the year during which Caligula was away from Rome, conquering Britain. However, upon his return, with a single British chieftain as captive and a pile of seashells that he displayed as "the spoils of war," he seemed to have lost his wits altogether.

His obsession with his own divinity began to provoke ridicule. He took to appearing in public, dressed as Mars (or Venus), and demanding to be worshipped. We had accepted the concept that dead emperors could be regarded as gods, or that some barbarous foreigners might worship living emperors in their own barbarous temples. But Caligula wanted the Romans to venerate him as a living god in Rome. We were growing decadent, but we were still Romans, after all was said and done.

There was also turbulence throughout the Empire, some of it provoked by his interference. He certainly never took my advice on any issue which regarded the eastern regions. I've mentioned the ill-treatment of the Jews in Alexandria, the exile and murder of Herod and the attempt to install his own image in the Temple of Jerusalem. All of these interventions worsened the situation and tended towards the war which eventually broke out. There were other troubles which I won't go into here.

Over the time that he was emperor, he questioned me about such things as monotheism, the architectural design of the temple in Jerusalem, the meaning of the Messiah. He showed some interest in Jesus and John the Baptist, but decided they were minor figures compared with himself. In fact, he grew disillusioned with the Jews as whole in the end. He was bitterly angry at their disinclination to accept him as their god. He could not forgive it.

Finally he had the golden statue of himself made and commanded Petronius, Vitellius' successor in Syria, to install it in the temple of Jerusalem, taking with him several legions to enforce his will. Petronius hesitated over this unenviable task, whereupon Caligula grew furious and sent Petronius a letter ordering him to commit suicide. Luckily for Petronius, the letter arrived together with another announcing the death of Caligula, so he was able to go back to Antioch alive. I don't know what happened to the golden statue. I helped to design the thing and know that it was a bizarre object. I presume it was melted down and used for coinage. I believe Petronius had the distinction of being the last person ordered to kill himself by Caligula.

The strange trajectory of Caligula had come to an end. The Senate had had enough. Fatal words were whispered in secret places. The same Praetorian Guard who had ushered in Little Boots now ushered him out. Fittingly, he was killed while returning from the games, trapped in an underground passageway like a rat.

Among his assassins was the captain, Cassius. Caligula had never missed an opportunity to mock him for the loss of his manhood; he now returned the joke by hacking off the dying emperor's genitals.

# CHAPTER SIXTEEN

# TWO JOURNEYS IN THE REIGN OF CLAUDIUS

Amid the turbulence caused by the assassination of Caligula (Cassius the ringleader was himself executed by some of the Praetorians who had rather enjoyed Caligula's style of government) Claudius was now proclaimed emperor. They say he was found cowering behind a curtain, anticipating his own demise. It was a source of some surprise to himself and others that he had reached the age of fifty without being poisoned or stabbed in the back, the fate of most of his family. He had achieved this by burying himself in his library for most of his life, engaged in the study of such unmentionable subjects as farting and Etruscan history.

Neither farting nor the history of the Etruscans was considered a decent subject at that time. However, through the latter I had made some acquaintance with Claudius over the past few years. He had consulted me on some matters of Etruscan religion from time to time and we had developed a respect for each other. Moreover, he was keenly interested in the law, so we had much in common. Behind his back, the clever people of Rome called him "The Pumpkin," but the simple ones liked and trusted him. Early on in his reign, while the terror of Caligula was yet fading, Claudius took me over as an advisor and maintained my retainer. Vitellius became censor, with authority over the membership of the Senate, so our position was even more secure.

At this point, people began to whisper against Vitellius. They said that he had conspired with Claudius in the murder of Caligula.

I do not know the truth of this, since I kept well clear of the business of making and unmaking kings. But if it is true, Vitellius did Rome a great service by removing a madman and replacing him with one eminently sane.

People also began to say that Vitellius was a timeserver, pandering to the whims of one emperor after another. They said he was a puppet who had connived at the excesses of Tiberius and Caligula, and flattered Claudius shamelessly. Perhaps that is true, but who did not do these things? To oppose any of these men was certain death. There were very few open critics of the emperors in those times, and the few that arose all met bad ends. This created an atmosphere of endless conspiracy and intrigue. The unwavering loyalty of Vitellius was of great importance to the stability of Rome.

By then our second child had been born, also a son. We had named the first Lucius, after Vitellius. To our surprise, Claudius himself offered to be godfather and namesake to the second. It came out quite suddenly during one of our weekly meetings.

"If you can't find a better one, I suppose you could use my name," he said, without looking up from the documents I had brought him.

I spoke sincerely. "That would be a great honour, Caesar."

He arched his eyebrows, still without raising his eyes. "Yes, it would, wouldn't it? I wouldn't wish any child to look like me. The gods forbid. But the name's all right. Very patrician."

"I will name him Claudius, Caesar."

He nodded. "You can bring the child to see me when he's a little older. I'll try not to frighten him into fits."

He habitually spoke in this self-deprecating way, though he would be enraged if anyone else referred to his disabilities. Oddly, as he sat reading, he was a fine figure of a man, scholarly-looking and quite robust. It was when he was active that his ailments leaped to one's attention. His knees crossed clumsily and gave way beneath him as he walked, as though he were a badly managed marionette; when he exerted himself, his upper limbs would also sometimes spasm and cease to be of use to him. His speech was hard to follow at the best of times. When he was excited, his saliva would spray in all directions and he became unintelligible. The contortions of his face during these efforts could be frightening.

I liked Claudius very much. We thrived under him. He was a gentle and humane man for the most part, though he dispensed his share of terror when he was irritable. In an age of cruelty and violence, he was little understood by his contemporaries, who mocked his disabilities and his scholarship. But he favoured me because I was Etruscan, first of all, a lawyer in second place, and in third place, married to a former slave. Claudius was sympathetic to the lot of slaves. He appointed many freedmen to high positions, a controversial policy but one which brought much new talent into the administration.

The right of men to enslave others was said to be enshrined in the *jus gentium*, under the principle that if everybody did it, we could do it too. Yet we knew that to be enslaved was not a natural state. In our law, a slave was a thing. Any cruelty could be inflicted on a slave without penalty – and the owners of slaves could be extraordinarily cruel at the time of which I am writing. Slaves could own nothing and whatever was accrued through them, even their children, belonged to their owners. This conflicted with the most fundamental of our laws of persons. Slavery was only justifiable through the demonstrably absurd declaration that a slave was not a human being.

The laws which existed at that time were, for the most part, designed to curtail the freedom of slaves even further. I was one of the few jurists to have proposed laws which improved the lot of slaves. It was my good fortune to attract the patronage of Claudius. It was he who enacted the first of my laws, that dealing with the abandonment of sick slaves. As one who suffered from illness all his life and had lived in the margins of his world, he had a special understanding of the subject. At that time there was the custom of abandoning sick and worn slaves at the temple of Aesculapius, built on an island in the Tiber, which had as a result become a stinking charnel house. Those slaves who managed to recover were promptly

snatched up and put back into service by their owners. I proposed
a law by which any slave abandoned in this manner automatically
acquired his or her freedom and that any master who killed a sick
slave rather than free him could be charged with murder.

"You'll be proposing a revolution next," Claudius said dryly. He
thought it over for a few days and then issued the decree with a few
amendments. It wasn't a popular law but it added to the security of
slaves and meant that some owners, at least, took the trouble to seek
treatment for their sick slaves.

Other laws followed later on, such as that removing the owner's
power to kill slaves at will, that imposing restrictions on the harsh-
ness of punishments, that preventing the sale of children away from
their parents, that curtailing the owner's right to re-enslave those
whom he had freed and so forth.

This work brought in no fees, of course, and it has taken the best
part of three decades of persuasion and argument for these principles to be enshrined in law. However, I regard this as my legacy and
the best part of what I leave to posterity. However, these are topics
which can hold little interest for my reader, unless he or she is also
a slave of one sort or another, and I must continue with my story.

At about this time, a project to which I had devoted much time,
money and attention began to bear some fruit. Though it had
engrossed me a great deal, I had said nothing of it to Daphne.

Daphne was growing into her maturity. Motherhood had completed the work that love had begun. When I asked her why she
no longer wrote any poetry, she would point to our sons and say,
"These are my poems. I need no others." I took that as an expression of happiness.

After the birth of Claudius, she was a goddess, full-hipped, full-
breasted and smiling. She was the centre of our household and the
centre of my existence. I hastened back to her from any absence,
even a few hours, impatient to hold her in my arms again.

The summer was scorching that year. During the dog days, our house on the Capitoline received the sun's rays in full. Daphne and I delighted in our pool, which was paved in a mosaic of sea-creatures and fed by cool spring water, with cypresses growing along the edge. After our swim one afternoon, we retired to our bedroom and there made love to the evening song of nightingales.

After we had done, she lay on her back, smiling up at me, while I, raised on one elbow, planted kisses on her damp skin. "I have been engaged on a rather difficult commission," I told her.

"Is now the time to talk of work?" she asked.

I kissed her dark nipples, which were relaxing after the tautness of climax, their texture becoming as smooth as the skin of ripe plums. "I hope you will forgive me. The commission concerns you."

Her fingers twined lazily in my hair. "Then you may bore me with it."

"I've paid agents to do some work for me. It has taken some years, and many false turnings and blind alleys. Which is why I haven't bothered you with it until now."

"You're talking in riddles, my beloved."

"There are two women living in Pompeii."

"And there is a man in the Moon."

"The man in the Moon is unrelated to you, insofar as I know."

She laughed. "And the ladies in Pompeii?"

"That we must ascertain."

Slowly, her fingers stopped playing with my hair. "What are you saying to me?" she asked in a quiet voice.

"They are sisters. It's said they are called Aglaia and Thalia."

I looked at her. She had become very pale. "What else?" she asked.

"One is older than you, the other younger." She laid her hand on her heart and appeared so shaken that I rose and brought her a cup of wine. "Drink. Forgive me for springing this on you. Are you unwell?"

She drank sparingly of the wine. "No. But my heart trembles. Are they slaves?"

I held her to me, for her warmth had fled and her skin had turned cold. "My dearest one, you must know that nothing is certain. I've debated with myself whether to tell you, even now. My agents have been searching Italy for these women, with nothing more than their names. Most of the threads they followed came to nothing. Even this information may be false, or an empty coincidence. The younger of these women, Thalia, is a slave, working in the household of a merchant. The elder, Aglaia, is a prostitute in one of the city's brothels. I haven't been able to ascertain whether she is a slave or a freedwoman." Daphne began to cry. I caressed her hair tenderly. "They are said to be Thracians, enslaved as children and brought to Rome by pirates. The summer recess is almost upon us. I had thought to travel down to Pompeii and visit these two women myself—"

"I will come with you," she cut in swiftly.

"The boys?"

"The women will take care of the boys," she replied, wiping the tears from her cheeks. "I must see for myself."

I could tell by her face that there could be no arguing with her. I kissed her. "Very well. We'll travel together. But Daphne—"

She laid her fingers on my lips to silence me. "You don't need to say it. I will not cherish too much hope."

I kissed her fingers. "Sometimes in life it is best to be prepared for disappointment."

"I am prepared for anything," she replied.

This search for Daphne's sisters had been a long and slow business. Daphne herself knew almost nothing of their fate. The influx of slaves into Italy had now grown enormously. Every battle, every siege, every conquest, yielded a tide of men, women and children for the slave markets. Some of the more wretched of our conquests – for example Britain, which was conquered by Claudius around this time – yielded almost nothing but slaves. Their abundance and cheapness meant that owning a slave or two became possible even for the lower classes, while a rich man might own many hundreds. To find two women among so many was almost impossible.

I had undertaken it nevertheless, and for many years had sent scouts to all the cities, enquiring among those who bought and sold slaves. Of course, there had been a mass of rumours and false reports which had led only to pointless expense. Indeed, I believe the task would have been impossible, but for the imperial census which Claudius, that great archivist, ordered. Vast lists were compiled and brought to the censor's offices in Rome. This meant that I could have them thoroughly combed by my agents, and in doing so, they had come across the names of these two women. They were not uncommon names, but the instance of their being sisters was less common.

Daphne was put into a state of intense agitation by the news. In some ways, I regretted having told her without having investigated myself first, because any consequent disappointment would be shattering – and the results of such a search were far more likely to bring disillusionment, in one form or another, than anything else.

Nevertheless, we prepared for the journey south; and when the summer recess began, we set off for Pompeii.

Pompeii, as those who remember it will attest, was in those days a handsome, thriving city, dominated by the mountain Vesuvius, to whose fertile flanks it clung. It was a holiday town. The climate was mild in winter and in the summer its sea breezes provided a welcome change from the stinks of the capital. There was, besides, an air of easy sex in the city that was very different from the tense atmosphere of Rome. The city was full of brothels, and the main worship of the city (apart from money) was the phallus. And anyone who had a phallus could have it very satisfactorily worshipped for a price. Indeed, the mountain which loomed over the Pompeians, though they did not know it, was the greatest of all the phalluses, straining to heaven and about to spout.

The market was bustling, though nothing had really been the same since the earthquake, the scars of which were still everywhere to be seen. Some of the great houses of the city had been restored, or were still in the process of restoration. Some remained in ruins, their owners having fled and never returned. Most Pompeians, reckless or brave, had remained and continued to flourish in a kind of feverish way, despite the tremors that shook the city almost daily. And the town was always thronged with visitors on business. For my part, I would not have spent a day in the place if I'd had the choice; I felt uneasy there.

I stopped a man in the lane that ran down the side of the Temple of Aphrodite and asked for directions. Daphne had been compelled to remain at the inn, despite her great apprehension, since no decent Roman woman could be seen in this quarter. She was waiting anxiously for my return. The man pointed me to a house which stood on the corner, painted red, with heavy green shutters.

I went inside and was greeted by the usual thug who guards such places, with a mixture of threat and sly good-fellowship. When I asked for Aglaia by name, he stared at me with his small, cruel eyes. "Who gave you that name?" he demanded suspiciously.

I replied diplomatically, since I had no intention of revealing my true mission. "A friend who knows the city's pleasures well."

He laughed and tapped his fleshy nose significantly. "Aha! A stranger in the city, but a discerning customer. You have already found out the best. I hope your balls are full, my friend, because she will suck them dry as raisins."

This Pandarus made me pay heavily in silver to gain entry to the place, and guided me up the narrow staircase. The music of a bagpipe, which is believed by the Pompeians to inflame lust, was skirling in some part of the house, together with the suggestive thump of a tambourine. There was a reek of hashish and sex in the crooked corridors. Pandarus pushed me through a little door-way into a room which was almost completely dark. He slammed the door behind me. I stood like a fool in the blackness for a few moments, until there was a stirring in the bed, and the spark of a flint being struck. A wick caught alight in a little pool of oil and a face materialized from the darkness.

It was an angular face with hollow cheeks and narrow lips. My first feeling was that this could not be Daphne's sister. There was no resemblance at all. Disappointment washed over me.

"Have you lost your tongue?" she asked in a husky voice. "Take courage."

I saw she was holding out a cup of wine. I took it from her. I could smell the defrutum, which they boil in lead pots, making it thick and sweet, but also poisonous. "I have come from Rome to see you," I said.

She arched her thin eyebrows. "My fame has truly spread far and wide." She patted the bed. "Sit beside me and tell me what it is you desire."

I sat where she indicated, catching the rank smell of her bed, overlaid with the sharp perfume of musk. The walls were covered with erotic paintings, flickering as though alive, but the room was little bigger than a cupboard. "I want to talk to you."

"You may talk." She drank from her own cup. "Aglaia is listening."

"Aglaia has a sister, I am told."

"Many sisters. As many as you can pay for."

"I mean a blood sister. In this town. Named Thalia."

She looked at me sharply. "You are wrong."

"I hope not. I've been told that Thalia—"

Her lean arm flashed out, tipped with bronze. The dagger was small but needle-pointed. "Don't take her name in your mouth again, or I will cut it out, along with your tongue."

"You mistake me." I pushed the blade carefully away from my throat. "I mean nothing gross."

"I don't want to hear name spoken in this place."

"I understand."

The blade vanished as swiftly as it had appeared. But her eyes were watchful now. "If you want two, I will call another from this house. It will cost you double."

"I don't want sex."

"Then what do you want?"

"I will pay well for any information you can give me."

"Information? About what?"

"About yourself." I was still trying to see any lineaments of Daphne's face in hers, but the light was dim, and her hair hung over one half of her face in the loose style that these women affect. And there was something hard about her expression, an immobility or deadness, that made it seem she was one of those speaking masks in the temples. "Forgive me – I mean nothing unseemly – do you have any other sisters?"

"No," she said shortly.

"You are sure?"

She finished her wine and flicked the lees into the chamber-pot. "I had another sister once. But she died."

"Are you sure that she died?"

"I hope that she did. She had too much capacity for suffering."

"What was her name?"

Instead of answering, Aglaia opened a little box which stood at her bedside and took out some scraps of things which I could not make out well in the faint light. She held something over the lamp-flame, which glowed in the twin black pools of her eyes. Suddenly, I could see Daphne in her face – the Daphne I had met first at Felix's house, degraded and worn. She and that Daphne were sisters, though now there was little resemblance between this wraithlike creature and my glowing wife. A mixture of emotions filled my heart – pity for her, conviction that I had found her. A fume of white smoke came up from the thing she held. She sucked it deep into her lungs and closed her eyes. I waited in silence. At last, she exhaled, slowly, as though reluctant to let the smoke go from her body. An acrid cloud filled the room. "What's her name to you?" she asked, her voice papery from drinking the smoke.

"It may be a great deal. I've told you, I will pay."

She held out her hand. I placed a silver sestercius in her palm. Her mouth turned down at the corners. "Like all men, you promise much and deliver little."

"I have more."

"Yes. I can see you're a rich man." She looked me up and down, her eyes now heavy with the drug. "My sister was named after that tree which is sacred to Apollo."

"Then I think I know her."

She showed no surprise, but sucked in the smoke from her flame again, holding it in her lungs like something precious. She exhaled. The air in the little room was becoming thick. "Do you bring me news of her?"

"Daphne isn't dead. She's alive. A freedwoman. She is well." I paused. "She is my wife."

Aglaia nodded slowly. "Then Apollo watched over his little tree."

"We have two children. Sons." She made the sign of averting the evil eye but gave no other answer. "She is in this city, Aglaia."

At last she seemed to rouse herself. "Why did you bring her here?" she demanded angrily.

"Why? She longs to see you!"

"I will not see her."

"Aglaia—"

"The living cannot see the dead."

"I tell you, she is alive."

"But I am not."

I was taken aback. "As you said, I am a rich man. I can afford to make my wife happy. I can buy your freedom and take you back to Rome—"

"You're a fool if you think that."

"Why?"

"I will never leave this room."

I tried patiently to explain. "I will pay what they ask, whatever it is. You need not be afraid. I am a friend of the emperor. I can obtain your freedom. Do you understand? You can leave this life behind."

"I have left all life behind a long time past." She sucked at the last fumes and dusted the white ash away. "What is your name?"

"Marcellus."

"And what is Marcellus, that he is so great?"

"I have been Governor of Judaea. I am a lawyer and an advisor to the emperor Claudius."

"And so young. And so handsome. My little sister has done well for herself."

"I love your sister. It is my greatest wish to see her happy."

"Then make her happy."

"She wants to see you."

"I cannot see her, Marcellus. Even if the door were open, I wouldn't go through it. I have not seen Thalia for years and I have asked her to forget me. I cannot see Daphne, or be with her children, or appear in the light of day. I cannot see myself in a mirror. I cannot be in her life and she cannot be in mine. I will remain in this darkness until one day some client cuts my throat. That is all I wait for."

"These are terrible words," I exclaimed.

"Your opinion is not needed. I will live until my throat is cut. I have decided on that. I will wait. They will not make me less than I am. But if I leave this house, I will be much less than I am now. I will be an object of loathing to myself and to all others."

"That is not true."

"It is true. I would kill myself at once in the street. Do you think I want my sisters to know me?" She spoke in a voice that I find hard to describe; it was emotionless, and yet it held a great suffering. It was like those ancient streets one sees whose blunted and all-but-obliterated stones speak of the countless feet that have worn them down. It filled me with horror to think that this could also have been the fate of Daphne. "I have been in this house for fifteen years, Marcellus. I cannot count the thousands who have used me here – or the children they tore from my womb. I do not want Daphne to see me. Or to see her."

"And if I tell you that her heart is full of love for you? And that by refusing to see her you will wound her deeply?

"I don't want her love and I have none to give her."

"Aglaia," I pressed gently, "Daphne and I both made great changes to our lives when we married. And the gods have given us great happiness."

"Marrying your housekeeper is not the same as taking a Pompeian whore for a sister-in-law," she said. Her voice did not rise or fall, but her tone was not one that brooked any argument. "Tell Daphne that I greet her. That I am glad she is well. That we will not meet again in this world. That she must forget me. Now go."

I took out my purse and offered it to her. "There is gold in here."

"Keep your gold."

"At least let me give you money!"

"I don't want your money."

"Is there nothing I can do for you?"

"Yes. You can leave me." She turned away from me and huddled against the wall. I reached out to lay my hand on her shoulder. Then I withdrew my hand without touching her. What touch could she possibly desire?

It was cruel to remain. All she had was her endurance, her refusal to be less than she was. I could only hope that she might change her mind in the months or years to come, and ask us for help. I would have paid a great deal to have redeemed her from that life and restored her to Daphne. I would have given much to have been able to bring better tidings back to my wife.

I rose from the couch and left Aglaia there in the red-painted, windowless room. My last sight of her was of her hollow-cheeked face as she blew out the oil-lamp, the erotic frescos around her plunging into darkness. She seemed to prefer the darkness.

Pandarus was waiting for me outside, his meaty face suspicious. "I heard a lot of talking, my fine gentleman, but no fucking," he said aggressively.

"I am satisfied," I replied, pushing past him. He grasped at my arm, perhaps hoping to extort more money from me, but I shook him off. The daylight was dazzling. The mountain towered over me, seeming to oppress me. As I walked home, I was debating with myself how to tell Daphne. I knew it would be terrible to her to know that her sister lived such a life and would not hear of being freed from it.

That red house is gone now, together with all who suffered or joyed in it, and all who dwelled in that great city. Nothing remains but a black sea of stone.

I think that Daphne understood Aglaia's feelings better than I could. Certainly, the news that I brought back was dreadful to her and I don't think that she ever quite recovered from it. There has always been a shadow, since that day. There are moments, in the happiest of our hours, when I see her eyes gaze beyond what we have before us, and I know she is thinking of Aglaia. I, too, have felt that shadow. I think of her from time to time, in that dark compartment, compelled to suffer degradation daily and hourly, and refusing to be destroyed – or rescued.

Daphne, too, was conscious that her own fate might have been similar. The capture of women to fill the brothels of the empire was an immense trade, and in many ways, reason enough for a war. I never met a Roman woman who was not disgusted by it; it was a stain upon us all; and yet those who spoke out against it were very few.

But Daphne accepted the message her sister had sent without question. She did not ask me to return to Aglaia – which in any case would have been futile – and she sent no message of her own. She has not referred to Aglaia since then. We do not speak of her. Yet she is with us.

It took Daphne a day and a night to compose herself after my return from the brothel. We then went to the harbour to find Apicius, the owner of Thalia.

He was a prosperous merchant in the dried fruit business, who imported many of his products from the Levant and owned a large warehouse at the port of Pompeii, where his ships docked. The quantity of bees at his premises was impressive; they buzzed around us in clouds, driven mad by the sacks of dried figs, plums and nuts that reached almost to the ceiling. He had barrels of honey from

Smyrna, pistachios from Syria, raisins from Corinth, dates from Arabia, walnuts from Dacia, almonds from Sicily, all kinds of dried apricots, medlars, chestnuts—I forget what else, a treasure-house of delicacies for the gourmets of Rome.

He greeted us courteously, a portly man, his face resembling one of his own walnuts, since it was tanned brown, plentifully furrowed, and habitually wore the widest possible smile. His eyes, however, were shrewd.

"An honour, a great honour," he said when we had presented ourselves. "This calls for a libation." He took us into his office, where he gave us a cup of heavy, amber Marsala wine and heard us out, nodding vigorously but showing little surprise at anything we said. He looked from one of us to the other as we spoke, his assessing gaze suggesting to me that we would be asked a high price at the conclusion of negotiations.

His reply was lengthy. He began by explaining to us that he had purchased Thalia as a small child, on the quay at Ostia, because she was "so dainty" and he had wanted a pretty little handmaiden for his daughter.

"I like to spoil my daughter," he told us. "I am a sentimental man. It's my profession, you might say. My trade is sweet things. May I ask you to try this?" He produced a silver casket, which he opened reverently. It was filled with crystals which at first appeared to be large diamonds. He gave us one each. "I import these from India. Taste."

We tasted the crystals hesitantly. They were shockingly sweet. "What is this?" Daphne asked.

He smiled with satisfaction at our expressions. "Xenophanes said, 'If the gods had not made yellow honey, men would think figs far sweeter.' Now we can say, 'Apicius has surpassed yellow honey.'"

"Is it a mineral, like salt?"

"No. It is made from a large, green reed, which is boiled in vats."

"Without honey?"

"Without the need for bees. Or figs. What do you think of that? Lay but one of these crystals on your tongue, and you have transcended honey. You have tasted paradise."

"It is extraordinary," I said. "But forgive me, we came to you because—"

"It can be used to cure melancholy in women. The most intractable cases yield to it. Give the afflicted person but a spoon of these crystals when sorrow is most heavy, and her heart is lightened at once."

"Extraordinary. However—"

He cut in again. "It can be dissolved in drinks as easily as dew dissolves in the sun. It turns the juice of lemons into a delicious draught. It turns water itself into honey. It counteracts the effects of poisons and makes the bitterest medicines palatable to a feverish child."

"I see. But Apicius, the purpose of our visit—"

"If Xenophanes could have tasted this! For each sweet, another sweeter can be found. You see? One thing surpasses another as we approach to the Platonic Absolute."

"You are a philosopher, indeed. But the purpose of our visit—"

"In short, the purpose of your visit is to buy your good lady's sister from me."

"Yes," I said with some relief.

He sat back. "I will not sell her," he said, his cunning eyes moving from my face to Daphne's.

"You will not sell?" I exclaimed, my heart sinking. Had we come to Pompeii to face a double disappointment?

"Your tale is very touching," he said. "Like these crystals – we call them *khanda*, by the way – it surpasses the ordinary and conquers the bitterness of life. As I listened to you, I was transported out of my routine morning into a fairy-tale." He made a flourish with his hands. "Your sister belongs to you, good lady. I give her to you freely."

Daphne stiffened. "Do you mean that?"

"Thalia has been my daughter's lifelong companion. She's been treated as a pet or playmate, with only light duties, since childhood. She has even been allowed to study alongside her mistress, and she can both read and write. Her hands have no calluses and her teeth are like pearls. And—" He raised a fat finger, lowering his voice. "She is a virgin. You have my word. Nobody has touched her. I ask you to imagine to yourselves what such a girl is worth. But let us say no more of that. She shall be yours and she shall be free." He laid his plump hand on the silver casket. "I ask, in return, only this: that you will take some of my crystals to the emperor in Rome. With my humblest good wishes. In my profession, a recommendation is worth more than a purse of silver. There are many who sell figs, but I am the only one who has *khanda*. I am hoping for great things from it. I believe that one day it will be found on the table of every wealthy man in Rome. It will replace honey. You see? To have the attention of the emperor—you understand me?"

"I understand. And if I can achieve it," I promised him, "these crystals of yours will become diamonds."

"Then each of us has a treasure and we will say no more. Come and taste that which surpasses khanda."

Daphne was trembling as he led us into his warehouse, through a droning haze of bees, between mazes of sacks and barrels and baskets. At the back of the store was a little room. Apicius indicated the door to Daphne. "She is in here." Daphne looked at me quickly, her face white, then pushed open the door.

Revealed within, like the queen bee in a hive, was an enormously fat young matron. She beamed at us, the eyes in her pretty face becoming mere slits as her cheeks spread. I was somewhat taken aback. Daphne herself stopped in surprise. Then the woman came forward towards Apicius. "Papa!" she said, reaching out her plump hands. And behind her was revealed a diminutive young woman with chestnut hair and Daphne's dark eyes.

She and Daphne faced at one another in silence. I can see Thalia's face before me now as I write, at first merely curious, then slowly changing as long-obliterated memories began to surface, until her mouth trembled and suddenly two streams spilled from her eyes, splashing on her breasts and onto the dusty floor at her feet.

Daphne took Thalia in her arms. "*Boubouka mou,*" she said. "You have come back to me."

Thalia was now, as we reckoned, about nineteen years old. She had not suffered to the same degree as Aglaia – or Daphne herself, for that matter, though her life had been by no means so easy as Apicius would have had us believe. Apicius's corpulent daughter, Drusilla, had treated her as any child will treat a doll, sometimes crushing it with affection, other times casting it aside, not infrequently administering cruel punishments for no other reason than that she was out of sorts. Drusilla was about to be married to a wealthy young fellow of the city, and so her parting with Thalia – though accompanied by fat tears and wailings – was not an overwhelming sorrow to her. Like so many who claimed to love their slaves, the love was skin-deep. That which was of such overwhelming importance to Thalia and Daphne was of little importance to Drusilla or her father.

But to us – to us! Daphne and Thalia had lived in shattered worlds for so long. Their reunion was a gift from the gods, from the divine hands that sometimes smash to smithereens the frieze of our life and sometimes glue it together again. Two figures from the three that once belonged together, from the family that was once whole, had been united. After the bitterness of the meeting with Aglaia, the meeting with Thalia was sweet beyond honey.

There was no cause to delay in Pompeii, and we set off within a few days for Rome, leaving the place behind us, along with its mountain which – as we have all heard with astonishment and horror – was eventually to destroy it.

I kept my promise to Apicius and took his crystals to Claudius, who was interested in them, though he disproved Apicius's claim that they were an antidote to poison by experimenting on criminals, to the disadvantage of the criminals, all of whom died. *Khanda* did not come to replace honey, which was judged far cheaper and healthier. However, by this means, Apicius gained an entrée to the wealthiest households in Rome, where his name has become a byword for delicate eating, himself eventually entering the equestrian class by sweetening dishes in the right kitchens. Of greater importance to Apicius and his household, by moving to Rome they escaped the holocaust of Pompeii.

In the final year of Claudius's reign, I received a letter from the Roman magistrate of Lugdunum, in Gaul. His name was Fabianus. He opened with a formal salutation and then moved directly to his topic:

*As you may know, the former Prefect of Judaea, Pontius Pilate, together with his wife Claudia, were exiled to this place seven years ago by the Emperor Gaius Caligula. They have lived here in poverty, quietly serving out their sentence.*

*I must inform you that Pilate is now dead. She survives, with her child. They live in conditions which I believe would bring pity to the hardest heart. To say that she is destitute is not an exaggeration.*

*I write to you to ask if you will use your influence with the emperor to intercede for this woman and request that she may be pardoned and allowed to return to her home, sick and exhausted as she is.*

This letter affected me deeply. I showed it to Daphne, who said at once, "You must do something, Marcellus."

I went with the letter to Claudius. He was interested in the case and issued the requisite pardon without demur. Not all emperors would have done as much; the natural kindness of the man and his affection for me combined to make it possible. He also felt connected in some strange way because Lugdunum was his birthplace.

When I returned home with the pardon, Daphne and I sat in the garden to talk.

"She had another child, after all," she said.

"So it seems."

"It's pitiful, Marcellus." She laid her hand on mine. "You must go to her and bring her home yourself."

It had been my own thought; but my thoughts and hers were by then indistinguishable at times. "You don't mind?"

"I'll be afraid for your safety, but not for any other reason."

I smiled and kissed her on the lips. I bought extra horses and hired a strong servant that week; and leaving Daphne with the children, I set off for Gaul.

# Chapter Seventeen

# The Island Of The Exiles

The distance from Rome to Lugdunum is some five or six hundred miles. My last journey had been to the warm south; now I was once again entering the cold north, where as a young man I had first experienced war and the death of comrades.

We made a large detour to avoid the worst of the Alps, since it was now winter; but we were still compelled to climb high up into the ice and the bad weather. We were hard on our horses. They died or grew lame and were replaced several times in various places. I hadn't moved from Rome in seven years and I was unaccustomed to the rigors of travel. I was forty years old, no longer a young man. Nevertheless, my strength and endurance returned during the long journey.

We were not always lucky enough to find lodgings on the route and spent many nights huddled beside our beasts, with nothing more than a few smouldering twigs to warm us. At one point we were trapped in a narrow valley by a snowstorm for some days and I began to fear that our bones would remain there. Had I had time to plan and mount a larger expedition we could have travelled in far greater comfort, though at a slower pace; but I was concerned that time was running out.

I don't remember how long it took – perhaps two months in all. We came out of the snow and descended from the Alps to a dull and rainy plain where two rivers, the Rhodanus and the Souconna, flow together. On the marshy land around this confluence, the town of Lugdunum had been founded. It was an important place, not so much because it was very large – it was still only an overgrown village – but because it was the starting point of all the principal Roman roads through Gaul.

My chief recollection of the place is of mud – mud and rain. The sky was heavy and dark, swelling downwards with the weight of water in it. The mere act of walking was a burden. Each foot would soon be weighted down with several pounds of Gaulish clay, producing a nightmarish sensation of effort and slowness.

Before even looking for lodgings in the place, I went to the magistracy to find Fabianus, the official who had written to me. As ill luck would have it, he was away on some errand to a neighbouring settlement. His staff, for the most part Gauls, seemed to know little about the people I had travelled so far to find. They were awed by my presence but apparently unable to find the address I wanted. At last someone was produced who gave me directions to the Island Of The Exiles, where he said Procula lived.

The Island Of The Exiles! What an image of despair that name evokes, of abandonment and shame! Lugdunum was the terminus to which many fallen grandees had been consigned including, as I later learned, Herod and Herodias; so that Pilate and Herod would have been neighbours and would have been able to enjoy many a dinner together, contemplating former greatness and present ignominy.

The convergence of the two rivers had created a long and winding peninsula between them, which dwindled eventually to a narrow, soggy spit of land bounded on either side by the rushing brown waters. This prison created by nature and the elements was the Island Of The Exiles.

There was no escape on either side, since the rivers were fast and wide. Anyone leaving the zone had to pass through the town and would be observed. Conversely, all visitors to the Island were noted by the legionaries who glowered under their tents at every crossroad.

The place was infested with spies and informers, as well as assassins. Every move was watched and reported on, every incautious word could be relayed to Rome. Those whose sentence of banishment was a euphemism for execution – like Herod – had their throats quietly cut here, or died writhing in agony from poison.

Upon this spit of land stood a collection of dreary dwellings, some no more than hovels. They were linked by a miry road that led to a refuse tip on the final point of land, where detritus could be pushed into the water and carried to oblivion, a piece of symbolism that could have escaped few. It struck me to the heart that Procula had spent seven long years in such a godforsaken place. In my own happiness and success, I had not thought of her suffering, keeping her in my mind as a golden dream. The dark reality shocked me.

I left my servant with the horses. But I seemed unable to find her house. Those on whose doors I pounded did not open to me – or were perhaps dead within. The road was tramped by a few Gauls dragging stinking sacks to the dump but none of these understood my questions. I speak no Gaulish and their Latin was very fragmented. I began to grow desperate, my heart weighed down with forebodings.

It was raining hard. I was drenched and shuddering with the cold. Everywhere around were large, black crows, complaining in harsh voices against the weather. At last an old woman seemed to grasp what I wanted, and repeated the name, "Procula."

"Yes, Procula!" When I nodded, she smiled at me, toothless and wrinkled, and beckoned me to follow. She took me to a rocky field where some women were working in the rain, gathering thorny brushwood for fires. I searched among their huddled shapes for the slender figure I knew so well while the old Gaul gurgled at me in her own tongue, tugging on my coat. It was some time before I realized that she was indicating the ground, and that I was standing at a grave.

The soil was too muddy for inhumation, as I understood it. Corpses floated to the surface. Accordingly, unknown hands had piled stones on her body, covering it from carrion beasts. That was all there was. I stood in the rain with the pardon in my pocket, staring at the end of the golden dream, too exhausted for tears.

Others had been buried here under nameless cairns that were dotted among the thorns. One, I presume, marked the resting place of Pilate. Others showed where Herod, Herodias, Archelaus and other children of sunnier climes had been laid to rest under the lowering sky. Such were the monuments of those who crossed the will of Roman emperors.

When I emerged from the darkness of my thoughts, I saw that the crone was still standing beside me, waiting for her compensation. I pointed to the grave of Procula and mimicked the action of rocking a baby in my arms. The old woman nodded, seeming to understand. She led me back down the track to the town.

She knocked on the door of a house in a back street. Faces peered through the grille at us. At first they wouldn't open, seeing a stranger. The old woman argued fiercely with them until finally they admitted me.

I walked into a gathering of some thirty or forty men and women in the midst of a communal meal. They watched every movement I made. Some of them spoke Latin and I was able to explain who I was and why I had come. I showed them the pardon I had obtained from Claudius. Many of them began to cry.

Their leader, a middle aged woman with apple red cheeks and bright blue eyes, invited me to join them. I sat and ate with them while they talked to me about Procula.

It had been Procula, they told me, who had founded the little community. They were all townspeople, of various classes. They told me their congregation was larger, but that some had travelled to neighbouring settlements to carry the word.

Although they had been broken by her death, they believed she was in Heaven and assured me that they would continue in the faith she had taught them. After the meal they took me to the rear of the house. They had made a pitiful little synagogue whose stark interior was decorated only with a wooden cross, the symbol of sacrifice. It was the first time I saw this instrument of torture held up as the emblem of God. I asked them what they knew of the man who had died on it. They told me what she had told them – that he was a god, killed by the Romans, who had come back to life and who shed light on the darkness of others.

I recalled the night she and I had spent together in the house of Peter in Jerusalem, and my own inability – or refusal – to feel what she felt.

"She saw him with her own eyes," their leader told me in awe. "He arose from the dead and promised that all who believed in him would also arise and have eternal life."

It was the first time I understood something: that Christianity is the sense we try to make of the Crucifixion.

They didn't want to give up the child. They regarded it as holy, since they had regarded Procula as holy. They were also distraught that I was a pagan, and were extremely anxious that the child would not be brought up in its mother's faith. Afraid as they were of me, I think they would all have risked crucifixion in defense of the child. It was not until I swore to them that I would bring the child up to know its mother and her God that they finally produced her.

She was about six months old, with hair of a rich, reddish gold. Her eyes were brown. Procula had named her Mariam – the Hebrew name of the mother of Jesus. We never Latinized the name to Maria. She remained Mariam, as Procula had wanted.

"You could see that she had been a beautiful woman," Fabianus told me. When he arrived back at Lugdunum, he gave me lodging in his house. We fed for a number of days on a side of venison that seemed too tough and rank to decay. "I'm glad you found the child. They insisted it had died with the mother, though I knew they were lying to me. What do you intend to do with her?"

"If my wife agrees, we'll adopt her."

"You have no children of your own?"

"We have two sons."

He sniffed. His long nose dripped constantly with the cold and his eyes were inflamed. "Good luck to you. Mine all died of fevers."

"I'm sorry to hear that." I tried to warm my hands by his meagre fire. "What made you write to me?"

"Pilate would mention your name quite often." He glanced at me from his red rimmed eyes. "And I know you have influence with the emperor." He hesitated. "I pitied her. But to tell the truth, I wanted rid of her. I'm not sorry she's gone. She was a good woman, but this cult of theirs was troublesome."

"In what way?"

"All cults are troublesome, of course. This one more than most. They venerate a certain Christos who dies and is reborn. I don't know who Christos is. Some Jew. But once they're infected, they stop making regular sacrifices. They won't pay temple taxes. They won't worship the emperor. They recognize no authority but Christos. Worse than that, they try to convert everyone else to their beliefs. I've executed several of them, but it doesn't help. The more you crucify them, the more it spreads." He glanced at me. "I hear there has been a lot trouble with these same people in Rome?"

"Yes. A lot of trouble."

"The emperor has expelled them all, hasn't he?"

"Yes."

"You can do anything you want to them. It doesn't help. They welcome torture. I liked her, but I wanted her out of Lugdunum. If I can't suppress these Christians, I'll be in serious trouble with the governor. It's been quieter since she died, I have to say."

"And Pilate?"

"Drank himself to death," Fabianus said. "He was no trouble at all. Quite a decent fellow, except when he couldn't afford wine. He did some clerical work and that supported them, after a fashion. Our exiles are mostly very well behaved. They know that the little they have can be taken away from them."

"I understand."

"To tell you the truth, I don't enjoy being a jailer. I can't even bear to see a bird in a cage. But that's the job I have and I do it to the best of my abilities." He leaned forward confidentially. "Tell me. Is it true Claudius is an idiot who drools and can't control his bladder?"

"He's very far from an idiot and he appears to control his bladder perfectly – though I can relay your question to him if you wish it."

He smiled weakly. "Just asking."

His hospitality gave me a chance to rest before the homeward journey. The addition of the child to our party obliged me to buy a covered cart. I also bought a Gaulish slave, a young woman who had lost her infant but had milk. She was a savage little animal but seemed to know how to care for children. They huddled in the back for warmth on the long journey back to Rome while my servant and I took turns at the reins. Mariam cried seldom, bearing the journey with remarkable stamina.

The buds were on the trees by the time we reached Italy. The Gaulish slave escaped and ran away as we were crossing the Alps. I don't know what became of her. My servant had caught a fever in Gaul and grew very sick. I left him in Lucca to recover.

Mariam and I travelled alone through Tuscany, along the roads cut by my vanished ancestors. I had to stop frequently to find women with children at the breast, a very tedious business. If I had not been able to speak to them in Etruscan, I doubt whether they would have helped me. And I still had to pay for every drop of sustenance in silver.

Though many of the women assured me the child could live for days without suck, I was very anxious. As a result of all this, Mariam has drunk from the breasts of half Europe. I am sure it has marked her. She carries a great deal with her.

I put her inside my shirt to keep her warm, and bound her tightly to me with my traveling cape as we rode, and there she slept most of the time, hardly stirring. Perhaps she found the rocking of the cart soothing. Sometimes she would stare up at me with her big, dark eyes. The journey seemed to mark her in some other ways too, for this stepchild of ours has been a great traveller in her life, full of courage and good humour, and always close to my heart.

I reached Rome rather haggard and with a grizzled beard and Claudius screamed with fright when he first caught sight of me coming into the house. They hadn't known whether I was alive or dead. We all sat on the floor, clinging to each other. Mariam lay between us, looking up at us in silent wonder.

"Who is this?" Lucius asked.

"If you like, she could be your little sister." I looked into Daphne's eyes.

She picked up the child and examined her very carefully all over. "I've no milk. But it's time she was weaned, anyway."

"Are we going to keep her?" Lucius demanded.

"Yes," Daphne said, cradling the child in her arms. "We're going to keep her."

# EPILOGUE

The sea is filled with magical beings, as the land is. One day dolphins appeared suddenly, leaping in and out of the bow waves, keeping pace with our galley. Mariam joined me at the rail to watch them. She was entranced. "They're smiling!"

"Do you know that they have breasts and suckle their young?"

She leaned over the rail and called out to them. They kept pace with us for a while and then darted away to other games, leaving the translucent water quivering with their absence. Later, I found her drawing the creatures in the travel journal I had given her. She told me she had asked the sailors and they had confirmed my tale of the breasts of dolphins. "You can hardly see them, but they give milk. They also told me dolphins mate face-to-face," she added, "and sing like women. I'll never eat dolphin again."

We landed at Caesarea after three weeks to find the harbour almost too busy to enter. A huge plunder of gold, silver, ivory and precious wood was being loaded onto the spoil ships. Objects precious or sacred, torn from temples, were jumbled in heaps in the quayside.

There was also human plunder. Their screams were anguished, men calling to their wives, women to their children as they were separated. The youngest and strongest, as well as those who would make picturesque ends – patriarchs with white beards, the most beautiful of the women – had been bought by the impresarios for the arenas of Rome. The less distinguished in appearance were relegated to the provincial amphitheatres of the Empire, from Antioch to the Atlantic. They were driven onto the ships, condemned to meet their end at the fangs of beasts or the blades of gladiators while an alien crowd roared.

The tents of the army stretched up the beaches as far as the eye could see. We found that Glabulus had six young infantry officers, billeted with him, taking up most of his villa. They were weary and cynical after four years of war. We ate with them on the night of our arrival, we two older men at each end of the table, the women interspersed with the officers, listening to their stories.

"I suppose it's something to have fought in the greatest war of history," one of the officers remarked laconically. He had lost a hand in the fighting. The stump of his wrist was covered with a leather pad on which was embossed the name Jerusalem. He seemed to be trying to become drunk, without success. "A million dead. We crucified fifty thousand at the fall of Jerusalem alone. The rest exiled. It's the end of the Jews." He helped himself to wine, using his stump to steady the cup. "They have gone."

The soldiers began to talk about the fanaticism of the Jews and the ineffectiveness of even the cruellest punishments. After a while, Mariam pushed her chair back from the table. "I think I'll go to bed early," she said. "I'm tired."

When she had left the table, the young officers also excused themselves and went off to drink in taverns. I sat in the garden with Glabulus and Portia.

"She looks like her mother," he said to me.

"I know."

"Why have you brought her?"

"She wants to see where it all happened."

"You should have come earlier."

"Her children were still too young to do without her. I hoped we would not be too late."

"I'm afraid that you are. However, you'll see what you'll see." He produced a bottle of plum spirit. "Let's drink to older and better days."

⚜ ⚜ ⚜

We set off to the interior two days later. My Senatorial rank had pro-
cured an escort of a dozen cavalrymen, baggage and extra horses.
This, together with the huge military presence in Judaea, made the
going slow. The roads and towns were congested with soldiers and
laden wagons. There were check points at every crossroad and ham-
let. Our safe conduct, signed by Titus himself, cleared away most
obstacles. But Judaea had been devastated. Everywhere we passed
ruins, some still smoking. The land was empty. There did not seem
to be one building that still had its roof and walls intact. The olive
groves had been hacked down. The fields had been burned and
were now high with weeds that straggled out of the blackened soil.

At a small village we came across long rows of stockades where
enslaved Jews were being driven together, waiting to be exported
and sold. We could hear them weeping behind the slave dealers'
palisades. In the distance were lines of crucifixes, stark against the
colorless sky.

The war had been in preparation for decades. The co-rulers
of Jerusalem, the Roman governors and the Jewish high priests,
seemed to have conspired to madden the populace with a series of
outrages.

One of these had been the killing of James, the brother of
Jesus, who was stoned at the order of Annas, the high priest. The
Roman governor, Festus, had worked himself to death trying to
solve their quarrels. A new governor was sent from Rome, but while
the Praetorium was vacant, Annas seized James. He was carried up
to the summit of the temple, old as he was, and thrown down to the
ground. When this did not kill him, they stoned him. He prayed
for them to be forgiven as they knocked his brains out. It was in
many ways an echo of the death of Jesus. Herod Agrippa dismissed
Annas, as Caiaphas had been dismissed after the death of Jesus. But
the damage had been done – another popular holy man had been
destroyed.

Things went from bad to worse. Festus was succeeded by
Albinus and then Florus, both corrupt men who ransacked Judaea
for their personal gain. Albinus unleashed convicted criminals on

the populace if they paid high enough bribes. Florus attempted to sequestrate the Temple treasure. When the Jews resisted, he butchered upwards of four thousand men, women and children, many of them Roman citizens of high rank. It was the final straw. Judaea had risen up in revolt. Four years later, the results were all around us.

In the military camps where we spent the nights, we saw soldiers being treated for arrow and slingshot wounds, evidence that some sporadic fighting was still going on; but the war was effectively over.

We approached Jerusalem on the third day and entered an area of darkness. Dust, smoke and ash floated in the air, dimming the sun. Creaking wagons rumbled out of the clouds, dragging blocks of white marble away from the city. I recalled Herod, sprawled at his banquet table, boasting of how those stones had been hewn with such pains. One after another the wagons groaned by us, pulled by straining teams of oxen. We were pushed to the side of the road. We had to cover our faces against the dust and wait for several hours.

In the afternoon we made a little progress and then encountered one of the legions on the move. Huge colossi loomed out of the dust: catapults, ballistae and towering siege engines, rolled by teams of engineers. The carpentry of the Roman army is a fearsome thing. I had never seen artillery of this size; these engines could launch heavy boulders hundreds of yards. Their size and strength meant that they could be fired only a few times each day, but the cumulative effect was devastating. They had dealt with Jerusalem and were now being steered towards other fortresses in other places. The impression of the inexorable might of Rome was overwhelming.

Soldiers followed, the men staring wearily at us as they passed, their shields on their backs, the plumes of their helmets waving. They carried the impedimenta of a prolonged battle, a portable town. A man with a lame mule, seeing we were Roman, pulled the cover off his cart, grinning. It was piled with severed Jewish heads, which he was selling as souvenirs. The eyes and mouths had been sewn shut, the flesh had been smoked. Mariam turned away, covering her eyes.

We climbed to the Mount of Olives in the evening. I had hoped that there might be something left, but the city no longer existed. Its walls had been breached by the siege engines, the dwelling places of gods and men emptied and razed. Its ravines were filled with bones. Its palm trees had been cut down, its gardens seared. In their place, a forest of crucifixes stood, where the captives had died in agony. The palace where I had lived was utterly destroyed. Of the temple precinct, nothing remained. There was only a flat plain where it had been, staring up sightlessly at the sky. A bright and proud light had been extinguished.

The last marble blocks were being dragged away as we watched. The beams and pulleys were being managed by teams of prisoners. Jews were being made to dismantle the house of their God, under pain of scourges. The temple itself had burned down to the rock on which it had stood, which was blackened by fire and strewn with ash. The Holy of Holies, which had so fascinated Caligula, was open to the sky. A team was ploughing slowly across the precinct, as Carthage was once ploughed. The action was a symbolic one. A couple of soldiers followed behind the plough, their heads down, looking for scraps of gold or silver which the blade might turn up.

The Temple was no more, just as Jerusalem was no more. It had been made by hands and unmade by hands. That which remained was a city invisible, and a memory.

# Note

Of the Marcellus who replaced Pilate, almost nothing is known except his name. Josephus Flavius tells us he was a friend of Vitellius who oversaw the province until the appointment of Marullus.

Following Josephus, the main dates appear to be as follows:

Pilate was the prefect of Judaea from 26 to 36. The year and date of the crucifixion of Jesus are unknown but must have fallen on a Passover between these two dates. I have set my story in the year 33.

Lucius Vitellius was a consul during 34 and was appointed to govern Syria in 36. Marcellus was made governor of Judaea at the same time, being replaced by Marullus in 37.

Pilate was recalled and sent into exile by Caligula in 36 or 37.

Paul came to Jerusalem around 36 and experienced his conversion on the road to Damascus around 37.

Herod Antipas was exiled to Lugdunum (the modern Lyon) in 39. He died there.

Caligula was murdered in 41 and was succeeded by Claudius, who died in 54 and was succeeded by Nero.

James the brother of Jesus was executed by the high priest Annas in 62, shortly after the death of the Roman governor Festus. Albinus and then Florus governed Judaea until the First Jewish Revolt broke out around 66.

Jerusalem fell to the Romans in 70. It was almost completely destroyed and its populace driven into exile.

Printed in Great Britain
by Amazon.co.uk, Ltd.,
Marston Gate.